Praise for *New York Times* bestselling author Lindsay McKenna

"McKenna provides heartbreakingly tender romantic development that will move readers to tears. Her military background lends authenticity to this outstanding tale, and readers will fall in love with the upstanding hero and his fierce determination to save the woman he loves." —*Publishers Weekly* on *Never Surrender*

"Talented Lindsay McKenna delivers excitement and romance in equal measure." —*RT Book Reviews* on *Protecting His Own*

"Lindsay McKenna will have you flying with the daring and deadly women pilots who risk their lives…. Buckle in for the ride of your life." —*Writers Unlimited* on *Heart of Stone*

Praise for *USA TODAY* bestselling author Delores Fossen

"Clear off space on your keeper shelf, Fossen has arrived." —*New York Times* bestselling author Lori Wilde

"[*Savior in the Saddle*] takes off at full speed from the first page and doesn't surrender an iota of the chills until the end." —*RT Book Reviews*

BR

NEW YORK TIMES BESTSELLING AUTHOR

LINDSAY McKENNA

WILD MUSTANG WOMAN

If you purchased this book without a cover you should be aware that this book is stolen property. It was reported as "unsold and destroyed" to the publisher, and neither the author nor the publisher has received any payment for this "stripped book."

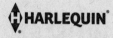

ISBN-13: 978-1-335-66252-1

Wild Mustang Woman
First published in 1998.
This edition published in 2023.
Copyright © 1998 by Lindsay McKenna

Targeting the Deputy
First published in 2021.
This edition published in 2023.
Copyright © 2021 by Delores Fossen

Recycling programs
for this product may
not exist in your area.

All rights reserved. No part of this book may be used or reproduced in any manner whatsoever without written permission except in the case of brief quotations embodied in critical articles and reviews.

This is a work of fiction. Names, characters, places and incidents are either the product of the author's imagination or are used fictitiously. Any resemblance to actual persons, living or dead, businesses, companies, events or locales is entirely coincidental.

For questions and comments about the quality of this book, please contact us at CustomerService@Harlequin.com.

Harlequin Enterprises ULC
22 Adelaide St. West, 41st Floor
Toronto, Ontario M5H 4E3, Canada
www.Harlequin.com

Printed in U.S.A.

CONTENTS

Lindsay McKenna is proud to have served her country in the US Navy as an aerographer's mate third class—also known as a weather forecaster. She was a pioneer in the military romance subgenre and loves to combine heart-pounding action with soulful and poignant romance. True to her military roots, she is the originator of the long-running and reader-favorite Morgan's Mercenaries series. She does extensive hands-on research, including flying in aircraft such as a P3-B Orion sub-hunter and a B-52 bomber. She was the first romance writer to sign her books in the Pentagon bookstore. Visit her online at lindsaymckenna.com.

Books by Lindsay McKenna

Shadow Warriors

The Wyoming Series

Visit the Author Profile page
at Harlequin.com for more titles.

WILD MUSTANG WOMAN

Lindsay McKenna

To all my faithful readers. A big hug back to you!

Chapter 1

Kate Donovan wanted to run and hide—again. In a few moments, the only man she'd ever loved would be picking her up at the halfway house in Phoenix, Arizona, to take her home. Home to the Donovan Ranch just north of Sedona. Her stomach roiled and the butterflies fought with one another as she stood on the porch of the rambling ranch house. Shame ate at her, as it always did.

She had just been released from an eighteen-month prison term when Sam's shattering phone call came, ripping open every other festering wound within her. When she'd been put into prison, only her two younger sisters, Rachel and Jessica, had been there to support her through the embarrassing trial. Kelly Donovan, her drunkard father, hadn't come near her or the courtroom. He had been too ashamed of her. And now that she was coming home, he wouldn't be there for her, either.

Tears burned in Kate's eyes and she forced them back, as she'd learned to force everything else in the last eighteen months. Sam had called her last night to tell her that her father was dead. He'd died in a head-on collision with a drunk driver the morning of her release. Suddenly the irony of the situation struck her: Kelly had hit the bottle when his only son, Peter, had died in the closing days of the Vietnam War. Kate's brother had been Kelly's whole world. All his love, what there was of it, had been pinned on Peter—not Kate or her sisters. Why should she expect him to be there for her now?

Lips parting, Kate stared down at her plain oxford shoes, long past due for the trash bin. She felt just like that leather—beat-up, stretched beyond the point of usefulness. She felt *old.* Oh, how old she felt! And Kelly's death lay like a numb, heavy blanket over her already deadened senses. Going to a federal pen on trumped-up charges of ecoterrorism had stolen her life from her.

She still knew she was innocent. The FBI, frightened by the extreme views of the environmental group she belonged to, had planted an agent in their midst. And the agent had used her and developed a plan to blow up the nuclear plant outside of Phoenix. The worst part was it had been the FBI agent's idea! Kate had argued against it, but the more militant members thought it was a plan worth considering.

Now she was going home again. And now Kelly was dead. Her father was dead. Hell, he'd never been a father! He'd been a ghost in their lives after Peter died.

Rubbing her wrinkled brow, Kate drew in a deep, ragged breath. When Sam had called last night—out of the blue—she had been stunned into silence by the sound of his deep, healing voice. She'd never forgotten that first, trembling kiss he'd given her when she was barely a women. And now, at thirty-seven years of age, she still filled with warmth at the memory.

She moved woodenly along the porch, feeling the remnants of the late November heat. The halfway house was designed to give women coming out of prison a few days to adjust to being on the outside once again. Kate was grateful for the space—a room of her own, no clanking and clanging of bars, or the endless noise of women talking…. She shook her head, feeling a little crazy.

Placing a hand on a wooden post that needed to be sanded and given a new coat of paint, Kate stared sightlessly past the brown lawn and the bare cottonwood trees that stood at the end of the property. The house was not in a good neighborhood, and though it was almost noon, the sidewalks and street were empty. Suddenly she felt frightened. Was it her father's unexpected passing that scared her? Or was it that she would be seeing Sam today when she thought she'd never see him again? Both? Probably. She dug her fingers briefly into the wood of the post and felt its dried, splintered texture. Arizona heat sapped the life out of everything. Kelly Donovan had sapped the life out of her.

Kate wanted to feel something at her father's death, but she felt nothing. The numbness that inhabited her had begun with her capture by the FBI agents; it had protected her as she faced the accusations made during the trial, and as she was locked away behind bars. For almost two years, she'd felt nothing. Kate laughed— a short, explosive sound. Well, she was feeling plenty now, but it had to do with Sam McGuire.

Gripping the post, she hung her head and felt tears

crowd into her tightly closed eyes. Sam... The memory
of their youth, their beautiful innocence as they'd fallen
in love was one of the few unsullied things in Kate's
life. Another was her mother, Odula, who had died ten
years ago of a sudden heart attack. Kate was lucky her
mother had loved her and her two sisters with a fierce-
ness that defied description, that Odula had tried to
make up for Kelly's behavior as a father, a negative role
model in their lives.

Sam is coming....

Opening her eyes, Kate groaned, her gaze pinned on
the end of the street, where she knew he would turn to
come down to the halfway house. What must he think
of her? He'd probably swallowed the FBI's lies, blasted
out in the newspaper headlines. He hadn't come to the
trial, as Rachel and Laurel had—but why would she
expect him to? She'd had no direct contact with him
since she'd left the ranch at eighteen years old. Absolutely none. Back then Kelly had been drunk most of
the time and Kate was just glad to grab her high school
diploma and get the hell off the ranch. After graduation, Sam had married his high school sweetheart, instead. And Kate had eventually left the state entirely
to start her own life.

Some life... Once more humiliation flowed through
her. She was the oldest of three daughters and she was
the one who had managed to screw up her life the most.
Rachel had become a world-class homeopathic doctor
who taught in London, England, and Jessica ran her own
healing-arts business in Vancouver, Canada. Kate had
nothing to show for herself—just endless low-paying
jobs that she usually got fired from because she was
smarter than the guy who owned the business—and she

made the mistake of telling him so. Kate the hothead. She'd been that way ever since Peter died. How much she had loved her older brother! They had all grieved deeply for his loss. Only Kelly had never gotten over his son's death like they had.

None of her sisters had stayed at the Donovan Ranch after age eighteen. They had fled just as she had. And why not? Kelly had made it clear he didn't love them or need them or want them around to run *his* ranch. Peter had been the heir apparent, chosen to take over the Donovan Ranch and give it another glorious generation, replete with grandchildren for Kelly. Yep, Kelly had had all his dreams in place—and none of them had ever included his three daughters. Well, his dreams had died with Peter. And now he, too, was gone.

Kate heard a low growl, the unmistakable sound of a heavy truck. Her heart raced as she lifted her head and turned to look down the street. There was a dusty Dodge Ram pickup turning the corner. The truck had obviously seen a lot of hard use and more than likely earned its keep in the ranching world—just like the man in the black Stetson behind the wheel. *Sam McGuire.*

Suddenly Kate felt anxious, more frightened than the day they had pronounced her sentence to the maximum-security prison. Her eyes widened as the truck pulled to a halt along the curb and she saw Sam McGuire for the first time in eighteen years. Her hand slipped from the post and she moved to the front steps. *Sam.* Oh, how she still ached for him! How many dreams during how many nights had she had of Sam kissing her, loving her, holding her? *Too many,* her wounded heart screamed. *Too many.*

Somehow she was going to have to hold herself to-

gether. Somehow she'd have to keep from revealing to
Sam how she really felt. Too many of life's events stood
between them. He was married. He had a son named
Christopher, the last she'd heard. That's what Jessica,
her youngest sister, had told her in one of the few letters they'd exchanged over the years.

As Sam eased out of the truck and shut the door,
Kate couldn't stop her gaze from moving hungrily over
him. At thirty-seven years old, Sam looked wonderful. He'd always been tall, almost six foot three inches,
his shoulders broad and square. Kate remembered his
proud bearing in high school. Even then, he'd had natural leadership ability. He had always walked with a kind
of boneless grace, very male, very in charge.

But the years hadn't been kind to him, Kate realized.
His square face was deeply lined at the corners of his
gray eyes, telling her of the endless hours he'd spent
out in the hot Arizona sun. The deep grooves bracketing his mouth told her he'd held a lot of what he felt inside. His skin was deeply tanned, his dark brown hair
cut military short.

She noticed he was wearing a clean, long-sleeved,
blue denim shirt, the sleeves rolled carelessly up, and
a fresh pair of jeans. Kate knew how dirty and dusty
ranching work was. Obviously Sam had taken some
pains to shave, shower and put on clean clothes before
seeing her. Even his boots, tobacco brown, were not the
normal scuffed and scarred pair he would wear while
working, but were polished and free of dust.

Raising her eyes, she saw that his black Stetson was
set low so that she could barely see those piercing gray
eyes of his as they met hers. For an instant, Kate felt
a thrill of joy, deep and shattering, as their eyes made

contact. And then, just as quickly, she crushed those wild, euphoric feelings.

Unable to hold his searching gaze, Kate broke eye contact. She stood there, her head hung, waiting. Would he judge her? Call her a criminal? Kate knew that word had spread throughout Sedona about her prison term. She knew her name was dirt. Inwardly, she tried to steel herself against Sam's accusations, spoken or not. How badly she wanted to look into his eyes again. At the first contact she'd felt only joy. Joy! How long had it been since she'd felt anything? *Too long,* her heart whispered. *Far too long.*

Sam tried to hide his surprise at the woman before him. Kate Donovan, the girl he'd known in high school, had been a winsome creature, wild like the wind. She had been the spitting image of Odula, her Eastern Cherokee mother, with that thick, black mane of waist-length hair that reminded him of a horse's flowing mane. She had Odula's startling blue eyes, so large and innocent with awe over life itself. Taller than most of the girls in high school, she stood at five foot eleven inches by the time she was a senior. For Kate, who had always tried to hide like a shadow, her height was one more thing that kept her from feeling like other girls her age. Now he saw that it still set her apart.

As Sam slowed his steps, he held Kate's intense blue gaze and felt a stunning force wrap around his heart and squeeze it hard.

Never had he forgotten kissing those full lips that were now compressed with holding back so much emotion. His body went hot with the memory—the memory of holding her, loving her, making her his. As a sophomore in high school, she'd given him her heart and virginity willingly. Passionately. And how he'd loved her—he still did. Shaken by the avalanche of emotion that had somehow, over the years, managed to survive, despite all his bad mistakes, Sam felt a keen, crying ache in his heart—for Kate.

It was her eyes that showed him the extent of her suffering. They had always been special, with golden flecks of sunlight dancing in their depths. As Sam searched her gaze now, he found only dullness and darkness. Could he blame her? She'd just been released from prison. A place like that was enough to kill any-one's spirit. He didn't believe Kate was an ecoterrorist. Yes, she was outspoken, brash, and didn't always think things through before acting. But she wasn't a killer as the media and FBI painted her. Kate wouldn't hurt a fly. She was a warm, loving girl who'd embraced life. And he'd loved her for years.

Now, as he slowed to take the steps up to the porch where she stood waiting for him, he felt naked with pain. Her pain. And he tasted bitter remorse in his mouth for what he'd done to her.

She looked so different from the young girl he re-membered. No longer did she have that thick, black mane that swirled endlessly around her proud shoul-ders. Instead her hair was cut very short and clung to her well-shaped skull. She'd had a thin, model's body in high school. Now, as she stood before him in a pair of Levi's and a pink, short-sleeved shirt, he saw she had filled out in the right places, had some meat on her bones.

Sam could feel the internal strength in Kate; he al-ways had. Her body was firm, and he guessed that she'd exercised a lot in the prison just to keep from going insane. How else could she have stood being locked up for a year and a half? Of the three sisters, Kate was the wild mustang among them. Sam had seen mustangs die, literally, of grief when imprisoned in a corral or box stall. Such was their need for freedom, for the wide-open spaces where they could run at will.

Kate was like that—wild, free and untamable. That was why he'd fallen in love with her so long ago. That's why he'd never gotten her out of his mind or heart. And he'd tried.

Studying her oval features, her high cheekbones set off by beautiful, wide-set, sky blue eyes, Sam saw the years of suffering in her face. He saw lines at the corners of her eyes, slight but present. And more than anything, he saw how the corners of her mouth were pulled in, a sign of the emotions she held at bay. He laughed to himself. Didn't he do the same thing?

When he saw the sudden panic in Kate's eyes, her uncertainty, he automatically took off his hat and halted at the base of the steps. He recognized that look of fear. He'd seen it in mustangs when he approached them too quickly. They were wary and distrustful, just as Kate was now. Could he blame her? He'd had so many dreams for them—hell, he'd managed to kill all his dreams and destroy Kate in the process. His heart ached as he saw that deep, ingrained fear in her eyes. What had prison done to her to make her react like that to him? When she was a wild, young filly, she'd been fearless. Bitterly, he remembered how life could make one scared and cautious. He had been stung a couple of times over the years. He no longer felt reckless or fearless himself.

He wanted to say so much, and yet it all jammed up in his throat. Suddenly the red bandanna he wore around his neck felt tight, and trickles of sweat slid down his temples as he played nervously with the edge of his Stetson.

"It's good to see you again, Kate," he said, meaning it. He saw a glimmer of tears in her eyes and felt her desire to move closer. At that instant, all he really wanted to do was open his arms, whisper for her to come forward so he could hold her. Just hold her. He knew that was what she needed, then as well as now. Of all the Donovan girls, Kate had taken the most abuse from Kelly because she'd fought back like the rebellious teenager she was. And she was the most injured by her father's ways. Sam saw that now as never before. So instead of reaching for her, he slowly lifted his hand in welcome. He had to move slowly in order not to scare her into running—again.

Without warning, the past came tunneling back at him, sharp and serrating as a knife blade stuck in his chest, hot and passionate as her breath had been when he'd found her crying outside her locker in the hallway of the deserted high school one evening. Oh, Sam had known Kate was an outsider at school. He'd been the star running back of the football team, while she was a quiet, mouselike sophomore who hid out in the library between classes.

He'd just come in from a very late football practice. Weary, his helmet dangling from his long, bruised fingers, he'd seen a darkened figure crouched beside a locker at the end of the highly waxed hallway. It was almost nine p.m., and there were only a few lights on. Sam frowned, shoved his damp hair off his furrowed brow as he walked softly toward the hunched, sobbing girl.

As he drew closer, he saw that it was Katie Donovan.

His heart lurched and his steps slowed. She was wearing jeans and a white tank top, her thick, black hair like a cascade around her shaking shoulders. The sobs coming from her twisted his heart. For so long, Sam had wanted to meet her, but she evaded him every time he tried. Yes, he'd heard the stories about Old Man Donovan. No one in Sedona had missed hearing about his infamous drunks. Sam could understand why the three Donovan girls were like shadows around school. If he had a father like Kelly Donovan, he'd be ashamed, too, and probably hide out like they did.

Sam halted beside Kate, who sat on the floor next to her open locker, her knees drawn up tightly against her, her face buried in her arms. As he leaned down, the light casting long, gray shadows around them, his eyes narrowed. *What the hell?* He saw blood drying on her arm. His gaze traveled to her tank top, where a rusty stain appeared. Shocked, he realized that Kate was hurt.

Without thinking, he took the white towel from around his neck, crouched down and reached out.

"Kate?"

Her head snapped up. Sam heard her gasp. She jerked her head to the right, toward his low, concerned voice. Her red-rimmed, tear-filled eyes widened.

Sam heard himself gasp. His hand froze midair, the towel in his fingertips. Kate's left eye was blackened and swollen. Blood was leaking out of her nose. Her lip was split. Gulping hard, Sam realized someone had beat her up. Who?

"You're hurt...." he rasped, before getting down on one knee and pressing the towel gently into her hand. "Hold on, let me get you some water...."

Still in a state of shock, Sam went to the lavatory

down the hall. He found a cup and brought it back, filled to the brim with cool water. Kate refused to look at him as he knelt back down beside her.

"What happened?" he demanded, dipping the edge of the towel in the water. He saw her fighting valiantly not to begin crying again as he slid his hand beneath her trembling jaw. As gently as he could, he wiped the congealing blood away from her soft, full lips, nose and chin. She was so scared. Her eyes were wide with shock and fright. Never had Sam felt more protective— or more angry at whoever had done this to her.

"I—I got thrown off a horse," she rasped.

He grinned a little, one corner of his mouth lifting. "Try me again. No horse is going to give you a black eye and a split lip. You trying to tell me you caught a horse-shoe in the face? I don't think so. 'Cause then you'd be dead."

Choking, Kate closed her eyes. "N-no...."

"Here," he said soothingly, dipping the towel again and carefully folding it up. "Put this on your eye."

She did as he instructed.

Sam put his hand on her shoulder. He felt her tremble. She wouldn't look at him. "Heck of way to encounter a girl I've always wanted to meet," he weakly joked.

When Kate hid her face in the towel and leaned heavily against the locker, Sam realized that something was terribly wrong.

"Kate?"

She didn't answer.

Grimly, Sam maneuvered around and placed his hands on her shoulders. She was quivering like a frightened animal. "Kate, what happened?"

She sobbed and refused to look up at him.

Smoothing the curtain of black hair away from her damp, flushed face, he muttered, "Come on, we're getting out of here. Can you walk?"

Sam helped Kate to her feet. He was a lot taller than her, but she was tall for a girl. Slipping his arm around her waist, he allowed her to lean against him, her legs none too steady.

Later, out at the quiet football field, sitting in the bleachers—his arm around her shoulders, her face pressed against his neck—Sam had finally pried the truth out of her. Kelly had beaten her up. Her own father had struck her repeatedly.

Sam sat there till late that night, chilled by the wind off the Mogollon Rim. Kate's words and sobs tore huge chunks out of his heart, and he felt her pain.

In the next two years, Sam would come to know Kate intimately. Would see for himself the trouble between her and Kelly. And he would love her. Wildly. With abandon. Together they would weave dreams. Dreams that he would later smash by his own foolish actions.

Sam's face wavered in front of her. Kate swallowed abruptly and blinked rapidly to make her tears disappear. She stared at his proffered hand, a hand scarred and callused from years of laboring on a ranch. His voice, low and deep, moved through her like a healing salve. The shame that consumed her lessened momentarily, too. He was holding out his hand to her. Was it a gesture of peace? Of welcome? Or was he just performing a necessary social grace? She wasn't sure.

Kate wanted to believe that Sam was welcoming her. But she knew better. He'd never showed up for her trial, never wrote her a letter or tried to call her. Why should he? There was nothing between them now. He was married and had a son. He had a life of his own. He owed her nothing. Absolutely nothing. A two-year high school crush did not make him responsible for her after they'd broke up. As her gaze moved from his strong, square hand up to his barrel chest and the dark hair that peeked out at the top of his shirt collar, she swallowed convulsively. If Sam knew how many torrid dreams she'd had of him over the years, even he would blush. And not much made him blush, as she recalled.

Her gaze ranged upward to his mouth, and she began to feel heat pool in her lower body. It was a warm, wonderful sensation. She remembered that well-shaped mouth as no other; it was wide and quite capable of a wicked, boyish grin. Kate had always loved Sam's rolling laugh and she hotly recalled his mouth closing commandingly over her lips, to fuse them to his own. Now that strong mouth was compressed and Kate grew frightened. She'd seen that kind of response to her before: she was bad news, tainted, an awful person. Yet as she met his gaze, that curious warmth still flowed through her. The sensation caught her off guard.

Kate knew Sam could be a hard-nosed son of a bitch when he chose to be, and usually with reason. But that side of him wasn't present now. His eyes, usually gray and glacial looking, were a warm slate color at the moment, and she could feel her response to him building. She hadn't expected warmth from him. Without thinking, Kate lifted her slender hand and slid it into his waiting one. Sam was just being civil to her because Kelly had died the night before, that was all.

The strength of Sam's hand enclosed hers. Her flesh was damp with fear as she felt the monitored strength of his callused fingers. Heat jolted up her arm at the contact, and almost as quickly, Kate pulled her hand away. If she allowed Sam to touch her for one more second, she'd burst into tears and take that dangerous step forward, falling into his arms.

"Sam..." She choked and broke off for a second. "Thanks for coming to pick me up. You didn't have to."

Shaken, Sam settled the well-worn Stetson back on his head. Kate's handshake had been weak, clammy and unsure. How unlike the Kate he used to know. Anger stirred in him as he wondered how much prison had beaten the life and spirit out of her. There was so much to ask, so little time. Other things had to take priority right now.

"I wanted to, Kate. It was the least I could do. I'm sorry about Kelly's passing. At least he went fast and didn't feel a thing."

Sam's deep murmur fell over her like a warm, nurturing blanket. Kate absorbed his care like a love-starved child. Standing uncertainly before him, she felt his gaze ranging over her from her head to her toes, and it made her feel painfully vulnerable. Her fingers tingled where he had held hers briefly. Did Sam realize that even now his gentle strength fed her spirit? When he'd touched her, she felt the first spark of hope in many years.

As she risked a quick glance up at him, she wondered if he knew the power and sway he held over her. Probably not. It was her neediness, her love for him that was making her feel this way. If nothing else, Sam always did what was proper. He could be counted on to do the right thing—just as she could be counted on to do the wrong thing.

Grimacing, Kate took a step back. "You've got a

life of your own to run," she said. "You didn't have to come and get me, too. I appreciated your phone call last night about Kelly."

Sam moved up the stairs and worriedly assessed Kate. She was pale. Although she had Odula's dark, golden coloring, her skin seemed bleached out. He guessed it was from too many hours spent in the prison and not enough in sunlight. Kate had always been a sun lover. She hated being indoors, and had spent most of her time outside working on the ranch, laying wire for fencing, helping with the cattle or the horses—any excuse not to have a roof over her head. The three sisters had built a huge tree house in the white-barked arms of the Arizona sycamore out in their front yard. Kate had spent many nights sleeping out there under the sky, rather than in her bedroom where such starry beauty couldn't be seen.

"Listen," Sam told her heavily, "I called Rachel in London and Jessica in Vancouver. I told them Kelly was dead. Rachel will be here tomorrow evening. Jessica will come in the next morning. I..." He shrugged. "I took it upon myself to set the funeral for the third morning."

Kate's mouth thinned. "That's fine, Sam. Thank you. I don't imagine there was anyone else there that cared about Kelly's passing."

"No, not too many at this point."

She pinned him with a dark look. "You didn't have to do this, either."

"I worked for Kelly for five years, Kate. I owe the man something."

She shrugged. Sam was that way. He had loyalty to others regardless. Kelly had destroyed any loyalty Kate had to the Donovan Ranch—or to him. Her father had killed his daughters' love, their dreams of being a part of the ranch's growing history. He'd driven them all off. According to Kelly, only Peter had been capable of carrying on the legacy. He was a man. They were women. Women couldn't possibly do a man's job, Kelly had told them repeatedly.

"Who's the ranch manager now?"

Sam shook his head. "No one, Kate."

She glanced at him quickly. How strong and stalwart Sam seemed. She ached to take those few steps and move into his arms. Every cell in her body cried out for his touch. He was so big and tall and solid, as if he could weather any of life's storms and live to tell about it. Well, she'd suffered through one too many storm and had been beaten down once and for all. She felt weak. At this point she was incapable of finding any strength left in her battered soul to dredge up and call her own.

"But... I thought Kelly had a ranch crew—"

"He fired them over time. The last foreman, Tom Weathers, quit two years ago. Kelly was running the entire ranch by himself when he wasn't hitting the bottle."

Grimly, Kate took in a ragged breath. "Yeah, Kelly had a way of firing people, scaring everyone off with his drunken rages. Nothing changed, did it?" She looked at Sam and saw tenderness burning in his eyes. And though Kate hadn't expected that from him after all that had happened, she reveled in it.

Rubbing his mouth, Sam said, "After your mom died, Kelly hit the bottle pretty continuously. Over the years, he did chase off everyone."

"He fired you?"

Sam smiled slightly. "Yeah."

"That was stupid. But then, Kelly was known for

doing stupid things." She laughed sharply. "Of course, I'm his daughter and I'm well-known for doing stupid things, making lousy choices, too…."

Sam hurt for her and had to stop himself from reaching out to touch her sagging shoulder. Kate had once walked so proudly. Now he could see she how broken she was. Broken, hurting and badly scarred. "Look," he rumbled, "you're nothing like Kelly, believe me…." Sam caught himself before he said too much. He saw the suffering on Kate's angular features. How badly he wanted to reach out and stroke her short hair, a touch to tell her everything would be all right. But it wasn't the right thing to do at the moment.

"Kate, I know you just got out of prison, and I know you have plans for your life, but right now, one of you Donovan women has to come home. You've got a thirty-thousand-acre ranch to run and no one is there to do it. There's beef to care for, roughly fifty Arabian horses that need tending. You need to come home and decide what you're going to do with the ranch now that Kelly's gone."

She stared at him. "There are no cowhands or wranglers at all?"

He shook his head. "None."

Stunned, Kate stared at him. "But the cattle and horses—"

"I know. I was over there early this morning doing the watering and feeding. I did a little vetting on a couple of Herefords. Probably the last place you want to be right now is on that ranch, but without one of you there, the place is going to turn into a disaster. The animals will suffer and die… I know you don't want that. I can come and help you out a bit, but I've got a job at the Cunningham ranch next door."

"I didn't know…." she whispered. "Oh, Lord, Sam, Kelly never wanted any of us running the ranch…especially me…."

His fingers ached to reach out and touch her. Comfort her.

Kate rested her brow against the post, her eyes closed. She felt the bite of the warm wood pressing into her flesh.

"It's a hell of a time, Kate. You deserve better than this. You have what it takes to run that ranch. I know you do. But if you don't come home, the ranch is going to die. It's in rough shape, anyway. Maybe, when you and your sisters get together after Kelly's funeral, you'll make a plan and decide what to do with it."

Lifting her head, Kate nodded. "Kelly has probably destroyed the ranch like he has everything and everyone else," she said woodenly.

Sam stood there, feeling every nuance of the rejection and pain her father had caused her. There were times when he hated Kelly for chasing off his children. The sisters had loved the ranch with a loyalty unlike any other he'd seen.

"The ranch is gutted, Kate. You might as well know it now, so there're no surprises when I pull in the driveway. Are you ready? I've got to take you over to the funeral home in Cottonwood first, where Kelly's being laid out, and you have to fill out some papers."

Pain crawled into her heart. For a moment, Kate felt grief over Kelly's passing, despite the fact that she hadn't spoken to him since she'd walked out at age eighteen. All he'd ever told her anyway was that she was no good. A loser. That she'd never amount to anything.

Kate looked over at Sam and found his face deeply shadowed, his mouth a hard, set line, his gray eyes burning with that same tenderness that fed her. "Okay, take me home, Sam. But I'm not staying long. Kelly killed my desire to stay on that ranch one more day than I have to. It was all his and Peter's, and he never wanted us around."

Chapter 2

Sam wondered what was going on inside Kate's head as she sat, seat belt on, looking straight ahead as they drove toward Sedona. For the past hour she'd been silent. How mature and beautiful she looked, yet so different from the teenage girl he'd once loved. Life had a way of changing everyone, he decided.

"You need to know something about the ranch, unless you've been in close contact with someone about it."

Kate slanted him a glance. "I usually got in touch with my sisters once a year and that was it. Since Mom died, none of us had a clue as to what was going on at the ranch." And then, more softly, she added, "And we didn't care, either."

"Kelly made sure of that," Sam agreed sadly. He frowned.

"Do you really hate the ranch?"

She shrugged. "How can you hate the place where you were born and grew up?" Kate waved her hand helplessly as she drank in the sight of the desert surrounding them. They were on I-17, heading toward Black Canyon. From there, they would climb from near sea level to five thousand feet, to the high desert plateau. The tall saguaro cactus that dotted the landscape here would disappear, replaced by shorter prickly pear cactus, which could stand the colder temperatures of winter better than the sensitive saguaro.

"I recall you seemed to love the ranch back then."

"Yes," Kate whispered, "I loved the ranch. I guess in my heart of hearts I still do. In a way…"

"The past has a funny way of looking better than it did at the time?" he teased gently, glancing at her and then focusing on his driving.

"Doesn't it always?"

"Sometimes. Sometimes it gives you hope for making the future turn out the way you want it." Sam shrugged. "I used to have dreams a long time ago. I don't anymore. Maybe you still have dreams.…"

His enigmatic answer was too deep for her to delve into. Instead, Kate absorbed Sam's proximity. In the cab of the Dodge Ram, Sam McGuire seemed even larger— and as solid as the truck he drove. He had about as many scars as this vehicle did, too. She noticed them not only on his hands, but on his arms and face as well. Ranching life was hard. Brutal sometimes. It demanded your blood upon occasion. Such as now. They had already talked about the funeral arrangements, having stopped at the funeral home and gotten them mercifully out of the way. Kate still didn't feel anything about Kelly's passing. Maybe it would hit her later.

Her heart was expanding, though, with euphoria. She knew it was because of Sam—his guiding, steadying presence. She stole a peek at his rugged profile. He was not a drop-dead-handsome man. His face was wind worn, sun beaten, his flesh tough and dark. His dark brown eyebrows were thick and straight above those gray, frosty eyes that had always reminded Kate of an eagle's. Those eyes never missed anything and she doubted Sam missed anything now. Inwardly, Kate waited for him to bring up her prison term or in some way use it against her.

Sam hadn't been that kind of man in the past, but things changed, she reminded herself. She wasn't the wild, rebellious fighter of her youth, either, anymore. Questions about him begged to roll off her lips, and finally, she broke the pleasant silence between them.

"You said you work for Old Man Cunningham?"

His mouth twisted. "I'm their ranch foreman. Have been for the past five years."

Raising her brow, Kate laughed a little. "Old Man Cunningham. Who could forget that bristly old peccary?" she said, comparing her ornery old neighbor to the wild pig that ranged across the Southwestern deserts. The analogy was a good one. The boars, which weighed well over a hundred pounds, had savage, curved tusks on either side of their mouth. They had poor eyesight and, if frightened, were known to charge the unlucky person and shred him to pieces. Cunningham was like that. Not only did he wear thick glasses that made his watery blue eyes look huge, he had an explosive temper. He abused everyone verbally, beat up his three sons with his fists and generally made everyone who had to deal with him miserable. Cunningham had the largest spread in central Arizona, over seventy thousand acres, which unfortunately ran alongside the Donovan ranch. Kate couldn't count the times Cunningham and Kelly had gotten into range fights over infractions. It had been ridiculous.

"I'm surprised you traded the Hatfields for the McCoys," Kate murmured wryly.

Sam turned and caught her slight smile. It wasn't much of a grin, but it was a start. He could feel Kate beginning to relax by degrees. How badly he wanted to tell her how much he missed her presence in his life, but now was not the time for such a revelation. "Yeah, well, Old Man Cunningham's last foreman quit on him just as Kelly fired me. I got wind of it and went over and asked for a job."

"Talk about going from the frying pan into the fire."

He chuckled and saw her smile deepen. Kate had a soft inner core to her she rarely let show. But now he was seeing her softness. "At the time, I was saving a lot of my paycheck for my son's college tuition," he admitted. "Cunningham made me an offer I couldn't refuse."

"Oh, I see...." Pain stabbed at Kate. How could she have forgotten that he was married and had a son? Her blind heart still wanted to see Sam as that fifteen-year-old football star she'd fallen so madly in love with—and was still in love with, she reminded herself. How did one erase love from one's heart? Kate had tried in many ways. She'd run from the ranch and from Kelly. And soon afterward Sam had married, at age seventeen, when he'd gotten Carol O'Gentry pregnant. Kate, right or wrong, couldn't stand knowing that her two-year relationship with Sam had been built upon sand. He'd loved Carol all along, she figured. He'd taken the love she herself had willingly shared with him, but his heart had never been hers. Well, that was the past. They were older now and life moved on.

Sam saw the flash of pain in Kate's darkening blue eyes. He felt it. But then, he'd always been in close psychic touch with her. It was as if he sensed more than heard her words, or maybe he read her thoughts from her expression. But Kate wasn't one to give much away in her voice or face or body language. Kelly had probably driven all those normal reactions out of her early on. So Sam had always relied on his feelings and sensitivity where Kate was concerned. He could always pick up nuances in her low voice. Or he would see the gold flecks in her eyes blotted out by some thunderstorm within her, and he knew that she was upset. She was a hard woman to read by most standards, and he was glad he'd gotten to know the soft, gentle, womanly Kate in his youth. That was the woman he'd fallen helplessly in love with until...

Sam frowned, shutting the door on his own bitter, stupid errors. He'd made a lot of mistakes, but the worst was what he'd done to Kate. Maybe now, in some way, he could make up for his transgressions.

"Cunningham is still meaner than a frightened peccary," he told her. "He's in his seventies now, partially blind because of his diabetes, and he still drives his sons into the ground."

"Nothing's changed." Kate shook her head. "He and Kelly deserved one another."

"They were a lot alike," Sam agreed.

"So, how do you tough it out with the old bastard at the Bar C?"

"A day at a time."

Kate laughed for the first time. It felt so good to laugh again. Sam joined her, and she marveled at how that tough, hardened mask on his face dropped away temporarily. It was a precious moment she grabbed and held in her heart. His eyes grew warm, his strong mouth curved, and she reveled in that thunderous, rolling laughter that she'd always loved to hear.

"He's meaner than a green rattler," Kate muttered. "He always beat his boys. I remember going to school and seeing Chet and Bo with strap-mark bruises on their arms. I don't see how they took it."

Sobering, Sam said, "Unfortunately, abuse begets abuse. Chet and Bo are still at the ranch. The youngest son, Jim, is an EMT and firefighter in Sedona. He got out at age eighteen, like you did."

"He was smart."

"Yes," Sam agreed slowly, weaving around some slower traffic on the freeway. "Jim was. He's stationed at Sedona Fire Station #1. He lives in town now. I know he's tried to heal the rifts in his family, with very little luck so far."

"Bet he doesn't go home to visit much, does he?" Kate knew Jim was smart enough to stay out of such a dysfunctional, abusive household, as she had.

"When he was a hotshot with the forestry service up at the Grand Canyon, Jim used to come home once a year, for Christmas, and that was it. Usually things erupted in a fight and he always left sooner rather than later. But he'd always come home again the next year to try and heal the family. He had a girlfriend, Linda Sorenson, who lived in Sedona. He was going to marry her, but that soured, too. Now that he's an emergency medical technician in town, I see him pretty regularly."

"Cunningham is angry at the world and takes it out on everyone. Nothing changes, does it?"

With a shrug, Sam said, "Some things do and some things don't." He glanced at her. "I hope you're prepared to see the ranch. It's pretty much a class A disaster area."

"I'm more worried about getting the livestock water and food."

"I know. When we reach home, I'll give you a hand."

She warmed to his care. "You ought to get a medal, Sam. You don't have to help us."

"A long time ago a certain pretty girl taught me a lot of things. Good things." He slanted a glance at her and saw color rising to her wan cheeks. "I don't think you ever knew how much influence you had on me back then, Kate." Sam wanted to say, *You taught me about loyalty, for one thing. And being responsible.* But he didn't, because he'd been disloyal and irresponsible toward her. His brows dipped as he focused his attention on his driving once more. "Maybe I can return the favor a little now."

Kate drew up one knee and clasped her hands around it. She felt the heat of a blush working its way up from her neck into her face. How long had it been since she'd blushed? She couldn't remember. Sam had that effect on her. He always had. Muttering, she continued, "I'm surprised. All we did was fight during those two years we were going together back in high school."

Chuckling, Sam said, "I'd call them constructive discussions, not arguments. Kelly and you got into hot fights with a lot of yelling. We never did that. And a lot of your anger was because of him, not between us. You had to let off steam somewhere." He shrugged. "I understood you, Kate, and I didn't mind if you got cranky and temperamental every once in a while. I knew what it was like living with Kelly and I saw what he did to you and your sisters…." Sam stopped. The past hurt too much for him to go on. He replayed again that first poignant meeting with Kate at her locker. Although Kelly had fought with Kate a lot, he'd beaten her up only once—that night. Sam had found out later that Odula had given her husband an ultimatum: that if he ever laid a hand on one of her daughters again, she'd divorce him. Kelly had backed down. To Sam's knowledge the rancher never *had* laid a hand on Kate or her sisters again, but he'd mercilessly badgered Kate mentally and emotionally, instead. Sam figured those beatings were no less injurious.

"I guess you and I really didn't fight," Kate replied, studying his harsh profile, his hawklike nose and that chin that jutted out proudly, daring anyone to take a swing. She remembered touching that face, running eager fingers across it, feeling his lips kissing her palm, her arm, her… With a broken sigh, she said tiredly, "That was a long time ago, Sam. Water under the bridge. We've both changed. A lot."

"In some ways, yes, but in others—" one corner of his mouth crooked a little as he met and held her fearful glance for a second "—you haven't. You're just as pretty as I recall. Your hair is shorter, but your eyes still remind me of the wide, blue sky we live under." Sam stopped himself. He hadn't meant to get intimate with her. Cursing himself for lapsing into how he felt, he added, "But you're right. We all change."

The abruptness of his last comment hurt her. How often during the last eighteen months had Kate remembered all those affectionate words Sam had used with her during their relationship? If he knew, he'd be embarrassed. "I've changed all right."

"The question is," he murmured, "once you see the ranch, will you stay or go?"

"Knowing Kelly, the ranch is probably pretty much destroyed. That's what he did after Peter's death. Then he killed Mom with his drinking. She didn't die of a heart attack. Her heart was broken. There's a difference. Mom had such dreams for the Donovan Ranch."

"And not one of them came true," Sam agreed. Broken dreams. Yeah, he knew a lot about those, too. And he had no one to blame but himself.

"She envisioned a place where all things lived and grew. She hated to see the cattle raised and then slaughtered." Kate shrugged. "So do I."

"You're a lot like Odula," Sam said. "You not only look like her, you have her big heart, as well."

Kate held out her hands, studying her long fingers, the bluntly cut nails. "As a kid growing up, I always had dirty hands. But it was the dirt of Mother Earth under my nails. I loved it. I loved being with Mom out in our huge garden. I even liked weeding." Kate smiled fondly at those memories and clasped her hands around her knee again. "And all Kelly wanted to do was cut down more of the forest on our property, use it for more fencing for more cattle." She shook her head. "I remember times, Sam, that my mom would go for a walk away from the ranch house. I'd find her sitting on her favorite rock behind a juniper tree, crying."

Sam heard the pain in Kate's voice. "Why was she crying?"

"Because, as I found out when I was older and could

understand it all, Mom had agreed with Kelly to start a farm, not a ranch. She came from the Quallah Reservation in North Carolina. Her people, the Eastern Cherokee, were farmers, not ranchers. It grieved her to see the cattle slaughtered. One day she told me about her dreams for all of us. When she got done, I cried with her, because our lives had taken another direction instead."

"Kelly's direction?"

"How'd you guess?"

"He was known to be a hardhead."

"You're being kind, Sam. But then, you always were. I was the one who called him what he was."

"Kelly came from this spread. He was a dyed-in-the-wool Arizona rancher, Kate. He didn't know anything else."

"But that didn't mean he couldn't have given in and let Mom realize some of her dreams, too." Angry now, Kate muttered, "He could have given her that apple orchard she wanted. What would it have hurt that selfish bastard to buy five hundred apple saplings and plant them for her? What he did instead was give her for a garden an acre of land that she had to till with the tractor. Trained in traditional healing arts, she wanted an herb garden to make medicines for her family, but he said no. She wanted to take the fruit of the earth and make this place an Eden. Kelly turned it into a perpetual slaughterhouse with the cattle. Everything hinged on those cattle." Grimacing, Kate glared at Sam. "It still does."

"He could have given Odula some of her dreams," Sam agreed quietly. "One person doesn't have the right to destroy the dreams of another." Like he did. He was no better than Kelly.

Kate winced and stared out her window at the dry desert, the prickly cholla, the saguaros that stood like sentinels, their huge arms raised toward the endless, bright blue sky. "Kelly destroyed four women's dreams," she said finally. "It was his dream or no dream at all."

"Maybe if Peter had lived things would have been different."

Shrugging tiredly, Kate said, "Maybe you're right, Sam. But it's too late for all of us. Peter died in a war without reason. Rachel, Jessica and I grew up in a war zone afterward. The war in our house killed my mother. It drove us all away—until now."

Without thinking, Sam reached out briefly and settled his hand on her shoulder. He felt her internal tension through his fingers.

"You're coming home, Kate. The ranch is in bad shape, and I don't know what your dreams are anymore. Maybe you'll sell it off before it goes into bankruptcy. Maybe you'll decide to stay and fight for your mother's dreams and make them come true after all."

Kate shut her eyes, her heart pounding, at Sam's brief touch. His fingers had a strong and steadying effect on her reeling emotions. Somehow, in his presence, her numbed senses were coming alive. She was shocked but grateful. Kate thought prison had destroyed a vital part of her. Apparently it hadn't. Sam was able to bring that part of her out from hiding deep within herself. For the first time, she felt a glimmer of hope.

Lifting her head, she looked into his warm gray eyes.

"Sam, in some ways, you haven't changed at all. Hope for the hopeless—that's you. I'm going to let the ranch go bankrupt. I don't have any money—not a cent. Let Kelly's dream die. It doesn't deserve to live any longer, as far as I'm concerned."

Nothing could have prepared Kate for what she saw as Sam drove through the huge entrance gate of the Donovan Ranch. It was a ranch with a hundred-year history behind it. A colorful history. A tragic one. The gate itself had been made by Kelly's grandfather out of large, flat chunks of red sandstone, white limestone boulders and black lava that had been mortared together. The twin towers rose ten feet in the air, joined by a huge black piece curving across the top on which was written Donovan Ranch.

Kate looked hungrily down the rutted dirt road. She knew it led back off the highway for five miles, to the main ranch headquarters. On both sides, she saw cattle ambling about, looking for sparse bits of grass to eat. The cattle looked thin. Almost starved. It angered her.

"The cattle seem in bad shape."

Sam drove gingerly down the road, avoiding the worst of the ruts. "We've had drought for two years, Kate. There isn't the normal forage available."

"I suppose Kelly didn't supplement with hay?"

"He couldn't. He was out of money. The local feed store refused to loan him any more money. He never paid his bills."

"Do you know how much in debt he was?"

Sam pointed to the glove box. "Kelly kept all his important papers in the rolltop desk in his office. I got them and put them in there. His will is in there, too."

"Kelly never believed in banks or safety deposit

boxes, did he?" Kate asked as she opened the glove box. She glanced at Sam.

"Have you looked through his stuff?"

He shook his head. "No. That's not my business, Kate. Maybe when I was ranch foreman it was. But not now."

"So," she murmured, unfolding the will, "how much in debt was he?" Kate knew that all the local ranchers knew a lot about each other's business. There were only one or two feed stores to get grain and hay from, so information was concentrated and gossip was normal.

"I heard a hundred thousand dollars in debt," Sam said almost apologetically. He saw Kate wince. Her lovely, full mouth thinned as she read over the two-page will that Kelly had written some time ago. "The local bank is foreclosing on the mortgage," he warned her. "And unless you or your sisters can come up with a hefty chunk to salve the bank's continuing loss with Kelly, they will foreclose."

Kate skimmed the handwritten document, made out in her father's scrawly, almost unreadable writing. Her heart squeezed in pain. He had made her executor, leaving everything to Kate to dispense with as she wanted. The discovery was shattering. Unexpected.

"I don't believe this," she whispered, gripping the papers with both hands.

Sam slowed as the road began to snake back and forth.

"What's wrong?"

"This is crazy!" Kate held up the will to him. "Kelly's leaving everything to me! Me, of all people. I thought he hated me. We fought so much. He disowned me...."

"I don't think he hated you, Kate. You were a lot

like him in some ways. You two had a lot of fights, but I find it hard to believe that a father could hate his own daughter."

"How could he love a daughter who is hardheaded? Stubborn? A daughter with a hair-trigger temper?"

"You are all of those things." Sam glanced at her. "You have your mother's heart, though. And that's where you two parted company. A lot of your arguments with Kelly were over rights for your mother and two sisters."

Kate tried to think despite the shock and pain. "Kelly wrote this a year ago. I was in prison. And he left me everything. How…why?" Tears burned unexpectedly in her eyes, and for once, Kate let them come. Distractedly she wiped at them with trembling fingers, barely able to breathe. "He never came to my trial, Sam. I thought he hated me. That he was ashamed of me. I thought that was why he didn't come. So if he was ashamed, why did he write his will this way? I don't understand it. I just don't…"

As gently as he could, Sam said, "Listen to me, Kate. You're in shock over Kelly's passing. You're probably pretty numbed out from being in prison, which had to be a hell in itself. You haven't had time to come up for air and adjust. Your father just died. You've inherited a ranch that's got a broken back. You're a hundred thousand dollars in debt in a blink of an eye. That's a lot to handle, Gal."

Gal. He'd often called her that as a term of affection when they had gone together so long ago. Kate felt the tenderly spoken word sink into her shaken senses and take the edge off her pain for a moment. Her fingers tightened around the will and the print blurred before her eyes. The jostling of the truck on the endless ruts brought her back to reality.

"Prepare yourself," Sam warned, as they climbed a small hill.

Almost eagerly, Kate looked up. She knew this knoll; just past it the land dropped a thousand feet into Echo Canyon, where there were black walls of lava created millions of years ago when volcanic activity was high. Oak Creek meandered along the bottom. A moment later she saw the layers of red sandstone beneath the white limestone cap of the canyon.

The last mile of the road wound like an angry snake downward.

There was only enough room for a single vehicle. To her right was Deer Mountain, a huge rounded hill covered with prickly pear cactus, junipers and large, smooth black boulders. The mountain got its name because the small deer of the area laid under the junipers and slept during the noontime heat, only to come down the mountains at dusk to drink from the creek near the ranch house before they began foraging.

Down below, Kate caught glimpses of the Donovan homestead. Over the years, many cottonwoods had been planted—her mother's wish, because cottonwoods were sacred to Native Americans. Now the darkly polished leaves of those tall, spreading trees were in fall color and hid the ranch from prying eyes. Odula had loved privacy. Kate recalled the bitter fights her mother had gotten into with Kelly. She'd fought for every tree she'd planted around the main buildings of the ranch. Kelly had refused to help, saying it was a waste, but Odula had wanted the shade and coolness, not to mention the privacy.

Kate recalled helping her mother plant those magnificent cottonwoods that now graced a good ten acres of the ranch's central core. The red, yellow and orange leaves, combined with the red, black and white of the canyon walls, made a kaleidoscope of colors.

"It looks so beautiful," Kate murmured, her voice wobbly as she strained to drink in the familiarity of the place where she had grown up. "I've been gone so long...." And how could she have stayed away? This was such a magnificent place. Her mother had called this canyon Rainbow Canyon, not Echo Canyon as Kelly's forebears had named it. Yes, it was a rainbow of living, vibrant colors. Kate's gaze darted here and there. She saw the many caves up on the wall of the canyon, some of which she and her sisters had played in as youngsters. They'd found many Indian relics, some quite old, but had left them undisturbed.

The memories came flooding back...hundreds of them, good and bad. Kate found herself drowning in her feelings from the past. As the truck took the last curve onto the flat canyon floor, Kate gripped her hands in her lap, afraid to breathe. Sam had said the ranch's back was broken. What did he mean?

She didn't have long to find out. The cooling screen of cottonwoods gave way, revealing the main ranch house for the first time. Built of a creamy adobe brick, it was a sprawling place, the roof angled just enough so that the little rain they got would run off. Kate remembered the flowers that her mother had once planted around the fence surrounding the main house. Now that fence pitched forward, in dire need of paint and repair, with yellowed weeds growing around it.

Kate's heart beat hard as Sam braked the truck in

front of the house. She saw that the windows were grimy and dirty and cobwebs were everywhere. The front door was hanging open, the wood split from a kick or two. Several windows were cracked and some had panes knocked out of them. Kelly's drunken rages, Kate thought, as she climbed out of the truck. She felt as if she were in a nightmare.

To the left of the house was a huge barn. Sam hadn't been wrong about a "broken back"—the ridge line of the roof was sagging badly and several shingles were missing. The barn doors hung askew. The wood was gray and weathered, in dire need of a protective coat of paint. Beside the barn were many corrals filled with Arabian horses—too many for the size of the enclosures. Several of the posts were leaning at an angle and barbed wire, which shouldn't have been used to restrain horses anyway, was rusted and poorly strung.

She felt Sam come and stand at her side. He placed his hands on his hips as she surveyed the horse area.

"Kelly did his own trimming and shoeing on the Arabs," he told her in a low voice. "Most of those animals are down on their heels. That's how long it's been since they've been trimmed."

Kate grimaced. "They have water?"

"Yes, plenty." Sam motioned toward them. "What you're running low on is hay. I'm bringing a truckload over for you tonight. There's no sense in letting these animals starve from neglect."

Kate hung her head. "Sam, you're a real guardian angel. Somehow I'll pay you back. I promise...."

He gazed down at her. "You owe me nothing, Kate. Consider this a gift."

"If Old Man Cunningham found out you were shipping a load of hay over here, he'd hit the ceiling."

Grinning a little, Sam said, "He doesn't know where it's going. And he won't, either. I'll pay him for it. The check will go into his bank account and he'll never know the difference."

Kate turned, unable to deal with his generosity. To the right of the ranch house were five other houses, as well as the outbuildings that housed an aging grader, a bulldozer, a backhoe, two tractors and other farm equipment. She could see all the work that needed to be done. Kelly was a master mechanic, but he'd often left parts lying around, dirty bowls of oil here and there, not to mention greasy rags. Some things never changed.

"You got wheels," Sam said, pointing to a green-and-white Ford pickup that had seen better days. "I checked it before I left to come and get you. It runs, but if I were you, I'd keep an eye on the oil gauge. This thing had blue smoke rolling out of it."

"That truck looks like it's twenty years old," Kate said.

"Kelly never threw anything away. He always repaired it himself. And if he couldn't, it sat."

"The place looks like a dump," Kate said grimly. Gone was the pristine house, the sparkling windows, the white picket fence with bright wildflowers adorning it like a colorful necklace. When her mother was alive, things had been kept clean. The place looked like a garbage pit in comparison.

"I know," Sam said sadly. He cupped her elbow and led her through the gateless picket fence. "The inside of the house is filthy. Kelly lived pretty sparsely."

Kate tried to steel herself but it didn't help. Her

mother had kept this old, rambling ranch house neat as a pin, with no dust, no sand on the floor. As Kate entered the broken front door, which hung to one side, she gave a little cry of distress.

The interior was dark. Cobwebs laden with layers of dust hung everywhere, like grayish white chandeliers. The grit of sand crunched under their feet. The oak floor had once been a pale golden yellow; now she couldn't see it for the dust. Odula's frilly white curtains had been traded for dark maroon ones that were drawn shut across each window. The odor of whiskey assailed her nostrils. The smell of garbage sickened her.

When she got to the large kitchen, Kate gagged. Kelly had left food out on all the counters. Sacks of garbage were everywhere. She saw cockroaches scurry away as they entered the room.

"This is horrible," she whispered, gripping the doorjamb and staring into the dark depths. "Horrible...."

Chapter 3

The screeching crow of a rooster very close to the bedroom window awakened Kate from a deep, healing sleep. Wrinkling her nose, she pushed the covers away from her upper body. Burying her head in the pillow, she lay there for a moment without moving. Every bone in her body ached as she felt the fingers of reality tugging at her. The bed was soft. There were no clanking bars, no chatter of women and guards. Just the blessed sound of a damn rooster crowing its fool head off. Her mouth twitched and she slowly rolled over, luxuriating in the bed and the sense of serenity she'd felt ever since opening her eyes.

The ceiling of her old bedroom met her gaze. The paint was chipped and peeling. The brass bed she slept in had been hers since she was a child. It felt good to be back in it—it reminded Kate briefly of being in her mother's arms. The goose-down quilt was warm and comforting across her tall, lanky form. The window was open to the cool November morning and she could hear the soft snort of horses, the whinny of a foal, the lowing of cattle in the distance.

All those animals were her responsibility now. That made Kate sit up. She rubbed her puffy eyes with the backs of her hands. Wearing only a clean T-shirt given to her by the rehab house, Kate pushed herself out of bed and headed down the hall to the bathroom. She'd managed to make the house more livable yesterday. The last thing she'd done before hitting the bed at one a.m. was to clean the kitchen. She couldn't stand filth. And that was what Kelly had lived in. The place was a pigsty. Although the house still seemed gloomy, she felt strangely buoyant.

As she took a quick, hot shower and scrubbed her hair, Kate's thoughts returned to Sam. He'd remained with her all day yesterday, helping her, working his tail off to feed, water and vet as much as he could. He'd also brought enough hay for the next three days to feed the Arabian horse herd.

After her shower, Kate dressed in a pink tank top and a pair of Levi's, then hunted up her old cowboy boots. Someone—probably her mother—had put them in a box. They were ancient, the leather hard and cracked, but they would have to do until she could buy a new pair. One didn't live on a ranch and not wear protective boots. Running her fingers through her damp hair to put it into place, Kate hurried to the kitchen. To her surprise, she inhaled the odor of fresh coffee perking. Who…?

Warily, she slowed down as she approached the

kitchen. A radio was playing softly, nice instrumental FM music, the kind she'd missed in prison. All she'd heard there was hard rock, until she'd thought she'd go insane from the raucous sounds. The odor of bacon frying tempted her. Someone was in the kitchen. Mystified, Kate halted at the door.

"Sam!"

He was at the electric stove, a skillet full of potatoes and eggs in hand. "You look a lot better than I feel," he muttered, and turned back to his duties at the stove.

"But—how? I mean, I didn't hear you come in." Kate moved to the coffeemaker and poured herself a cup of coffee. Her heart was beating strongly in her breast, and she tried not to stare at Sam like the love-struck teenager she'd once been. He wore a white cotton shirt, the sleeves rolled up his arms, a faded pair of Levi's, a belt and cowboy boots. The red bandanna around his throat emphasized the thick, corded muscles of his neck. The way his shirt stretched revealed the power of his chest and the breadth of his shoulders. There was nothing weak about Sam. There never had been.

He was clean shaven. She saw where he'd nicked himself on the side of his hard, uncompromising jaw. A piece of paper was still stuck on the wound.

"Dress you up, but can't take you anywhere," she murmured, moving over to where he stood. Gently, she eased the tiny piece of paper from the cut on his jaw.

Sam stood very still. He felt Kate's warm presence so very, very close to him. As her fingers brushed his jaw, his heart thudded hard in his chest to underscore how badly he ached for her touch, no matter how brief. When she lifted the paper away, he cut her a sidelong glance. Kate's cheeks were a bright pink color. It re-

minded him of the few struggling pink flowers outside the picket fence. Her eyes… Lord, her eyes were
clear, and for the first time, he saw glints of gold in
them. Groaning inwardly, he fought the urge to turn
and place his arms around her, crush her against him,
find that soft, parted mouth and take her. Take her all
the way to heaven. He knew he could. He knew that in
his heart and soul.

"Thanks," he rumbled.

Kate dropped the paper into the cleaned trash can at
the corner of the kitchen sink. "You must have gotten
up awful early to get over here."

"A little," he hedged, pouring the concoction onto
two awaiting plates. "Come on, let's eat. We've got a
lot to do this morning before I show up at the Bar C at
eight a.m."

Grateful beyond words, Kate sat down. "This is almost like breakfast in bed."

Sam lifted a forkful of potatoes and eggs and looked
at her over them. "That was kind of the plan. I was going
to have a 'Welcome home, Kate' breakfast waiting for
you down here when you got up. You beat me to it."

Touched, Kate ate hungrily. She was starved, in fact.
Ranch food had a taste all its own. Prison food was like
cardboard. "The rooster woke me up."

"You might take the woman off the ranch, but you
won't take the ranch out of the woman."

Kate watched him eating his meal. Sam's plate was
heaped with food, but then, he would be working a good
twelve hours today and he needed that kind of fuel.
There wasn't a scrap of fat on his hard, well-muscled
body, either. Ranching didn't encourage excess weight.
She had none herself, but for different reasons.

Looking around the clean kitchen, Kate marveled at the difference. "This place looks almost livable now."

Sam nodded. "It reminds me of the place when Odula was alive."

"Yes," Kate whispered, suddenly choked up with memories of her mother. "Over the years I've come to realize just how lucky I was to have her as a mother."

"She was special," Sam agreed. He stopped eating and studied Kate's features. He saw the pain and loss in her eyes and heard it in her low voice. "You're so much like her." Kate was the spitting image of her, but Sam didn't say that. She had Odula's dark, good looks, those blue eyes that were so thoughtful and filled with intelligence. Although Kate's black hair was still damp and clung to her shapely skull, she was beautiful, in his eyes. He still saw some of that wild, rebellious mustang in her, although it was deeply hidden.

"I got over here at four-thirty this morning," he said, breaking the silence. "The horses are fed and watered. I let the cattle out of the pens and they can graze for what they can find. This first pasture goes for a hundred acres, so they'll find enough for the next couple of days, until you can get some help here."

"It seems so overwhelming, Sam." She put the fork down and shook her head. "The last thing I remember thinking last night before I fell asleep was that I need money to get this place on its feet. I don't have any. I didn't earn very much while being in…prison."

Being careful not to respond to the word *prison,* Sam kept on eating. His jaw was still warm where Kate had touched him. She had the touch of a hesitant, wary butterfly, he decided. "Then you're going to keep the ranch?"

Shrugging, Kate continued to eat. "I don't know. I'm waiting to see what Rachel and Jessica say. If we don't have two pennies to rub together among us, the ranch will go into bankruptcy."

"Do you have any idea of their finances?"

Rubbing her brow, Kate said, "No." She saw him frown. "I haven't been very good about staying in touch with them the last two years...."

"But at least you're talking?"

She nodded. "Rachel and I have had our fights, and Jessica, bless her spacy little self, stayed in touch, too. I'm on good terms with them, Sam."

"Good, because right now, if you're going to save your home, it's going to take the three of you, all the money you own and a hell of a lot of elbow grease, time and miracles."

Wouldn't it though? Kate remained silent. She knew so little about her sisters. A letter or phone call once a year had maintained the ties, but she knew hardly anything about how life had treated them. She focused her attention back on Sam.

"Why are you doing this?"

He raised his head and held her soft blue gaze. "Why?"

"Is there an echo in here?"

He grinned a little, wiped his mouth on the paper napkin and put the plate aside. "Why wouldn't I?"

"Don't answer a question with a question, Sam McGuire. So what if you worked for Kelly for five years? What did he ever do to make you this loyal and helpful to us?"

Sam withheld the real answer to her question. Instead, his mouth curved into a lopsided grin. "Cowboy's code. You help your neighbor when things go to hell in a handbasket."

She studied him ruthlessly, combing his innocent features with her eyes. "I know you better than that, Sam. How about the truth?"

"That *is* the truth," he said gently, slowly getting out of the chair. The wooden legs scraped against the linoleum floor.

"Humph," Kate said, rising in turn. "No one from the Bar C came over here in the last ten years except you." She took her plate to the sink, rinsed it and put it in the newly cleaned dishwasher. Leaning against the counter, she took the mug that Sam handed her. There was such a wonderful familiarity with him. Things had always been so easy between them—until the breakup of their relationship. Kate had had a terrible fight with Kelly one day and, in desperation, she had run way from home, but not before leaving Sam a note saying that she couldn't take it anymore. She'd planned on leaving not because she didn't love Sam, but because at home she was trapped in a bad situation that had no end. She'd left the note at Sam's house, saying goodbye—forever—and then had hitched a ride to Phoenix, truly intent on leaving.

For two weeks, Kate had walked the streets of Phoenix aimlessly, alone, hurting and confused. A policewoman, sympathetic and helpful, had finally picked her up, and Kate went back home. Kelly had tried to be apologetic. Her mother, who had been crazed with grief and worry, welcomed her back with open arms, as did Rachel and Jessica.

It was when she went back to school the next day, her nerves in knots about trying to find some way to apologize to Sam, that Kate had heard the news. In her absence, Carol had walked into Sam's life. Carol had stolen him from her. Maybe that wasn't entirely true, Kate acknowledged. Her own decisions played a key role in all of this. Sam had thought she was gone forever. Carol was pretty, a cheerleader, and Sam was the star of the local football team. It was a natural pairing. And Kate? She was a ranch brat who worked several hours before going to high school and afterward until dark, taking care of the cattle and horses, with her family. She didn't have time for clubs or after-school activities— certainly not cheerleading. But then, Kate reminded herself, she'd never have made it as a cheerleader. She just wasn't the outgoing, bubbly type. She had too much Indian in her; she was too deeply introverted.

"Does Old Man Cunningham know you're over here?" Kate wondered, sipping the fragrant coffee.

Sam leaned back against the counter, leaving about a foot of space between them. "No."

"Do you live at the foreman's house at the Bar C?"

"Yes."

"I don't imagine your wife appreciates you being over here."

He raised his brows and studied her briefly. "She doesn't care."

"Why?"

"Because Carol and I got a divorce last year."

Kate felt the blood drain from her face as she stared up into his dark gray eyes. "Divorce?"

He shrugged and looked away. "You don't need my tales of woe on top of your own right now. After our son, Chris, went off to college in California-Stanford— Carol and I decided that it just wasn't working."

Kate swallowed hard, wanting to know more. But it wasn't the time or place to ask questions. Stunned by his admission, she felt her head reel and her heart pound. Sam was as loyal as they came. What had caused him to consent to a divorce? Looking away, Kate muttered, "At least you stayed together until your son was raised. That's something a lot of couples don't even consider nowadays."

"Yes," Sam said, pushing away from the counter, "and they should. At least, Carol and I did. We agreed that Chris needed that kind of stability."

"So you made the best of it."

Sam's mouth quirked. "We did what we had to do." He paused thoughtfully, then said, "Listen, we need to move about thirty of the Arabs into a new pasture area. Let's saddle up and get it done. That way, it will give you about a week's grace on feed for them."

The familiar, soothing sound of creaking saddle leather, the jangle of a horse's bit, was like music to Kate. She and Sam rode on two of the ranch's Arabian horses as they moved the herd to an upper pasture, much closer to the Mogollon Rim area. The Rim, as they called it, was a huge jutting masterpiece of black lava, red sandstone and white limestone. It rose two thousand feet straight up from the desert floor of the ranch. The north pasture hugged the foot of the Rim and Oak Creek flowed through it, a natural source of water for the horses.

As Kate and Sam rode, their legs briefly touched every once in a while. Kate thrilled to the unexpected contact with Sam. He sat so straight and proud in the saddle, born to the rocking motion of the bay gelding beneath him. The November chill made her feel alive, though she was glad for the denim jacket she wore over her tank top. The air was sweet with the odor of the pine trees that topped the Rim ahead of them.

The huge, carved canyon was over twenty miles long, ending at Flagstaff, and the Donovan spread included four miles of it, so that the canyon mouth actually occurred on the ranch.

Kate loved the canyon area of the ranch. It was a startling contrast to the prickly pear and juniper of the hot desert. The tall Ponderosa pines stood like proud sentinels on the Rim, reminding her of Sam's proud stance when he walked.

The horse she rode was a bay mare named Cinnamon, a long, rangy Arabian looking more like a Thoroughbred at fifteen hands high. She sighed as Cinnamon danced. How good it felt to have the movement of a horse beneath her! How much she had missed this!

"You're looking awful pensive," Sam observed. He saw the joy in Kate's eyes as she turned her attention to him. For the first time, he saw the soft corners of her mouth turned upward, not in. The flush on her cheeks only made her more desirable in his eyes.

"I was just thinking how much I missed all of this," she said, gesturing toward the mouth of the canyon directly in front of them. "How could I have left this place? It's heaven. It really is."

"Sometimes when a caged animal is freed, the taste of freedom is pretty heady."

Kate understood the analogy. Her gaze dug into his, though the rim of his black Stetson was tipped so that she could barely see his eyes. "You're right," she admitted. "I hated prison. I hated everything about it." She inhaled the pine-scented air, the dampness that flowed out of the canyon to the dryer reaches of the desert. And then she regretted her words because she saw Sam's face close. No longer was there that wonderful openness they'd just shared. Internally, she tried to prepare herself for his judgment.

"You're no killer," Sam told her in a low voice, holding her startled glance. "I never believed what I read in the papers about you...about that group you got tangled up with."

Relief sheeted through her and Kate could no longer hold his dark, burning stare. Then she forced herself to look at him again. He deserved her courage, not her cowardice. "You're right," she whispered, her voice raw with emotion. "I did get tangled up with the wrong bunch. They were hotheads, Sam. At least some of them were. Stupid. Just plain stupid. I was stupid, too. But I never was involved in the plans to blow up that nuclear power plant, I swear to you. It was the undercover FBI agent who suggested it and then whipped the men into planning it. I was against it from the beginning, but they just laughed at me."

"So the men who planned it skipped across the Mexican border and you took the fall for them?"

Grimacing, Kate nodded. "Yes, the three men who planned it are somewhere in South America." Free. Not imprisoned as she had been.

"Sounds like the FBI wanted a scapegoat, Kate. You were at the wrong place at the wrong time and they wanted to make an example out of an extremist environmental group. You got left holding the bag."

Nodding, Kate compressed her lips. "I didn't think you'd understand, Sam. I guess I was figuring you would swallow the FBI and newspaper stories."

Chuckling, he reached over and gently touched her shoulder. How badly he wanted to slide his leather-gloved hand around her tense body and hold her. Kiss her senseless. Forcing himself to break contact, he said, "You and I have a long history, Kate. You're like a wild mustang. You want your freedom and you want to have your say. Nothing wrong with that. Maybe you made some poor choices about who to hang out with, but that's all. I remember when a calf or foal would die, you'd cry. I recall a time when the horse you were riding hit a gopher hole and broke its leg. I was with you when that happened. You couldn't shoot the horse, even to put it out of its misery. So why would I think you were capable of blowing up a damn nuclear power plant that might kills thousands of human beings?"

Tears swam in her eyes and she looked away, trying to get hold of her unraveling emotions. A lump formed in her throat. She was so close to sobbing. Her fingers tightened around the reins as she continued to avoid Sam's probing gaze.

"I—I just made some very stupid choices with people," she agreed. "I can't kill. I never could. But they wouldn't believe me, Sam." She turned to him, tears burning her eyes. "Do you know how angry and frustrated I was? I was so ashamed. I could barely look Rachel and Jessica in the eye when they came to my trial. I didn't blame Kelly for not coming. I knew I was the worst disappointment in his life…."

Pulling his horse to a halt, Sam turned the animal around so he was facing Kate. Their legs touched, his dark leather chaps against her slim jeans-clad leg. "Listen to me," he growled, reaching out and cupping her jaw. He felt her tremble. "Not everyone is ashamed of you. I'm not—I never was. Yes, there are going to be people in Sedona who have judged you, Kate. But folks who know you will know you are innocent." He brushed his thumb against her cheek where the tears had fallen. The suffering on her face nearly cracked his massive control. As her lips parted and trembled, all he wanted to do was kiss her and take that pain she was suffering into himself. Right now he was stronger emotionally than she was. He knew he could do that for her, but would she let him? Sam was very unsure. The old Kate he'd known well. This was a new Kate—a woman damaged badly by prison, by being unfairly branded as a terrorist. He had no idea what those wounds had done to her—yet. And until he did, he could do little but be supportive and try to nurture her in small ways.

A breath escaped Kate as she closed her eyes and laid her cheek into his gloved palm. How strong Sam felt. She wanted desperately to be in his arms, to once more feel those iron bands closing around her and holding her safe. "I feel like raw meat inside," she continued, unable to look at him. The hot tears beaded on her thick lashes and then fell down her cheeks. "I'm so afraid to go into town, into the feed store, and sense their eyes on me, to feel them judging me, Sam."

"I know," he rasped. "I know."

Pulling away from his touch, Kate blinked her eyes rapidly and then wiped the tears away. "But I've got to do it. I can't keep running and hiding. I started that habit at seventeen. And when I was eighteen, I ran away from this ranch—and Kelly—for good. I've been running ever since. I've made a mess of my life, Sam. I feel bad inside. I'm ashamed. My sisters are successful. They made something worthwhile of their lives. I haven't. I'm the oldest and I've screwed up everything I ever touched."

Sam forced his hand down on his leather chaps. Kate's voice tore at him. She had no idea how much he still loved her—had always loved her. And she wouldn't know, either. He was a failure, too—at his relationship with her in high school, and later with his loveless marriage. Kate would never love him after all the lousy mistakes he'd made. He was the real loser here, but she didn't realize it. All the dreams they'd shared during those two years together were shattered. Gone.

But Sam had to put aside the past for the time being. There was enough going on right now. He knew Kate was suffering over Kelly's death. As much as she hated Kelly, he was still her father, and she had much grieving to do. After eighteen months in prison, she was suddenly free and that had to be causing her a hell of a lot of readjusting, as well. And then to have the ranch going into bankruptcy, to have her roots, her heritage taken away from her—something he knew was so intrinsic to her—made him wonder how she could handle it all.

One thing Sam had discovered early about Kate was that her hellish years growing up with an alcoholic father had made her strong. She had a backbone of steel. Sam knew some steel was flexible and could be tempered by heat and fire, while other steel was brittle and couldn't stand stress at all. What kind was Kate made of? What had life done to her? Had it tempered her strength and courage so that she could bend and weather all of this? Or would she crack under the strain, broken like this ranch was? Sam had no answers. And as much as he wanted to help Kate, he knew the outcome depended solely on her own grit, her spirit to fight back, to reclaim her rightful heritage—no matter what odds were staring her in the face.

"Well," he told her heavily, "I'm no prize either, if you want to look at it that way."

Sniffing, Kate wiped the last of the tears from her face.

"What are you talking about?"

"I made the worst decision of my life by marrying Carol. It was eighteen years of hell. A prison. So, if you made a mistake and spent only eighteen months in a prison, who's the stupid one here?" He grinned a little, trying to lift her spirits.

Kate stared at him, openmouthed. "But—I thought you *loved* Carol."

Grimacing, he took off his hat and rubbed his furrowed brow with the back of his arm. "You talk about mistakes. Kate, when I got your note that you were running away for good, I believed you. I knew how bad it was for you at home, and you'd often told me you thought that running away, leaving Sedona, was the only thing that would help." He stared down at his leather-clad fist. Forcing himself, he looked up into Kate's eyes.

"I got roaring drunk three days later. I'd been in touch with your mother. The police were looking for you. I knew you'd really left this time. Not that I blamed you...." He shook his head sadly, his voice dropping with regret. "A couple of my friends saw how down I was by your leaving. They talked me into going to a party. Carol was there and she was drunk, too. I remember passing out. The next thing I knew, I was on her parents' bed, buck naked, and so was she. I should have had a condom. I should have said no, but things got pretty hot and I had sex with her. Talk about stupid mistakes." He rubbed his jaw. "It was my fault as much as hers. Grieving for you being gone, I was drunker than hell, with hormones raging and no condom. Well—" he glanced at her grimly "—Carol ended up pregnant from that one time. My parents were heartbroken. They had college in mind for me. Instead, I married Carol out of responsibility to our baby."

Kate's heart ripped with pain. Sam's pain. "I'm so sorry, Sam! I never knew.... When I left that time, I thought I was running away for good." She tried to take a deep breath, but her heart hurt so much, it was impossible. Her voice was barely above a whisper. "What a mess I made by doing that. I felt horrible leaving you, but I had nowhere to turn. As much as you tried to protect me, Sam, you couldn't. I knew that. Kelly had threatened to come after you, too. He knew we loved each other. I was afraid if I ran to your house, he'd follow me and hurt you, so after leaving that note, I hitched a ride to Phoenix." Shrugging painfully, Kate held his saddened gaze. "I spent two weeks just wandering around. I was so hungry.... I didn't have any money, so I begged for food at the back of restaurants." She sighed. "I'd always thought you'd fallen in love with her and out of love with me because I left you. Not that I blamed you...."

"No, Kate." Sam cleared his throat and looked up at the sky, now alive with high clouds turned a dark pink and lavender as the sun approached the horizon. "I was so damned ashamed of what I'd done—how I'd fouled up my life, college plans, and hurt my parents—that I let you think that. I was just too damned cowardly to really tell you the truth. Until now."

Joy and shock suffused her. Kate stared at his grim features. "And the past eighteen years was to—"

"To give Chris, our son, some stability. I owed him that much. It wasn't his fault we screwed up. As it stands, he's going to college and he'll get a good start in life. I made my bed and I laid in it, Kate. I never was angry at you for leaving me that note. If anybody understood, I did. At least you didn't make the kinds of mistakes I made. You made others, that's all. But nothing worse, in my eyes, than the one I made with you."

He'd been in a loveless marriage for eighteen years. Kate sat in the saddle, her feelings in turmoil, her head spinning with realizations and guilt over her own adolescent rebellion, over running away. By doing that, she'd set both herself and Sam on a course with disaster. "I guess," she murmured, "there's all kinds of prisons, aren't there?"

"Yes," he answered. "The key is to survive them, Kate. That's what you've got to do now. Somehow you have to find the internal strength, the guts, to get through this—Kelly's passing, your responsibilities for the ranch. There's a great burden sitting on your shoulders, a hell of a lot of decisions in front of you. But you're Odula's daughter. You've not only got her blood, and her love of the land, you have her spirit." He swept his arm toward the canyon walls. "I couldn't have survived my time in prison without being on this land. There's something special here, Kate. I don't know what it is, but it has me by the throat and I don't ever want it to let go.

"This land fed me, nurtured me through those years with Carol. I love my son deeply, and I was able to impart my love of this land to him. It's a part of him now,

Chapter 4

Late in the afternoon, after vetting several young Arabians, Kate sat near a long wooden water trough. She dipped her hands into it and splashed her face, finding the water cool and refreshing. Murmuring over the luxury of it all, she straightened and wiped her eyes. This was a far cry from being in prison!

In the corral where she stood, there were twenty young foals, all black for the most part. It was amazing that the broodmares were bay, chestnut, white and gray, but the foals turned out black. Her gaze moved to a barbed wire enclosure away from the mothers and babies.

A black stallion, his coat gleaming in the November sun, paced back and forth endlessly. Gan, which was Apache for devil, didn't deserve such a name, Kate thought. Sam had told her that Kelly had won the black like it's a part of you and me." He sighed, looking down at his hand on the saddle horn. "I hope that you stay here. Stay and try to root yourself here—for a lot of reasons. Some of them are purely selfish on my part. Others are not." He glanced at her through slitted eyes. "You're like a tree torn up, roots and all. Now you're getting a chance to come back, dig a hole and replant yourself. It won't be easy. It'll take back-breaking work. A commitment like I gave to my marriage, really. I don't know where the money will come from. I hope one of your sisters has it."

Shrugging, Sam reined his horse away from hers. "Come on," he said gruffly, "we've got to get the herd moving. I have to be at the Bar C soon or Old Man Cunningham will fire me for sure."

Arabian stud in a poker game in Sedona with some of his old cowboy buddies ten years earlier—shortly after Odula's death.

Her father had gotten drunk one night and gone to the Red Rock Inn, a famous landmark where cowboys frequently gathered to drink whiskey, smoke and play cutthroat poker. It was on that night that Kelly had bet his entire herd of prized, registered Arabian mares against Ben Turner's black stud. Luckily, Kelly won. But he hadn't won much, according to Sam. The horse, a hellion, was unmanageable. No one could ride Gan. No one could get near him except with a crop or some other protection in hand. The only reason the stud had been kept alive was the fact he could throw black foals a high percentage of the time. And in the world of Arabian horses, the color black was rare, so people paid more money to have one.

Kate's heart went out to the black animal. She decided that the stallion had probably met with heavy abuse in his younger days and had turned on humans as a result. Sam had told her that Kelly, in his drunken rages, would go out and throw rocks and jeer, tease the animal unmercifully. When Sam found him doing it, he'd haul Kelly away from the nervous stallion, which would be shaken and enraged. More than once Kelly had been bitten by the stud. Kate shook her head as she stood there watching the beautiful horse. Kelly had had it coming, there was no doubt.

Sam had left hours ago and she felt the emptiness inside her. Kate already missed his larger-than-life presence. She missed *him,* but was afraid to admit it to herself. Picking up the plastic toolbox containing vetting supplies, she leaned down and slipped between the slats of the fence. The work was endless, but she loved it. Being outdoors again, breathing fresh, pine-scented air and experiencing the dryness of the desert, was far preferable to being incarcerated in a prison.

Her muscles ached here and there; the long horseback ride with Sam had been heaven, but she hadn't put a leg over a horse since she'd left the ranch years ago. Now the muscles in her legs were tightening up. Her arms and shoulders were sore from helping Sam move fifty bales of alfalfa hay from his truck into the barn. But it felt good to be physical again. More and more Kate realized how much she'd missed this ranch, her roots.

When she thought of Rachel arriving tonight, her heart squeezed in fear. Her sister was two years younger than she. In high school, Rachel had been the popular one, voted school president her final year. And despite all her ranch chores, she'd managed to be a member of the debate club, too. Everyone knew and liked Rachel. She was beautiful, Kate acknowledged, with thick, long, brunette hair, dancing green eyes, a willowy figure. And she was smart as a whip.

Making sun tea later, Kate placed a gallon jar of cold water with four tea bags out in the sunlight, then sat down on the porch. It, too, needed a coat of paint. Everything did around the ranch. As she sat there, her arms resting on her knees, Kate wondered how she could revive the place. Hourly, she found herself wanting to save it more and more. Sam was right—her roots, her history, were here. Everything she was and was not came from this old ranch. Now it looked like her—battered and nearly destroyed from years of neglect. She'd nearly destroyed herself with a lot of bad choices, Kate acknowledged. But the circumstances of her life weren't anyone's fault but her own.

The fact that Kelly had left her as executor of the will and owner of the ranch bothered Kate more than she was willing to admit. How many times had he said she'd never be able to run a ranch of this size? That she and her sisters didn't have what it took to do so? So why had he left it to her? Why?

Near sundown, around six p.m., Kate heard a truck pull into the driveway. She wiped her hands on a towel and hung it on a peg. The odor of a pot of chili cooking on the stove permeated the kitchen as she moved through the room. Was it Rachel? Her heart sped up in anticipation.

The knock at the door, which she'd repaired earlier, echoed through the living room.

"Come on in," Kate called from the kitchen entrance.

Sam poked his head in the doorway.

Blinking, Kate halted midway through the living room. "Sam?" He'd said this morning that he wouldn't see her until the weekend.

"Howdy. Sorry to drop by unexpected," he said, standing uncertainly.

Frowning, Kate gestured for him to come in. "That's okay. What's wrong? You look worried."

With a grimace, he took off his hat and entered the room after wiping his dusty boots on the mat. "No more than usual. I just thought I'd drop by and see how you were getting on." If he'd been brazenly honest, Sam would have added, *I had to see you.* And he did. Almost every minute of his day, he'd rerun one of their conversations or visualized the precious smile that shad-

owed her so very serious mouth. He craved to see more
of that dancing light in her eyes. Sam knew he didn't
have the right to be here. At all. But he couldn't help
himself as he stood there, hungrily absorbing the sight
of Kate into his being.

"I was just going to eat some chili. Come on in,"
she invited. He looked tired, but then Sam had been up
since four this morning, put in half a day's work here
at the ranch and then gone over and put in eight solid
hours at the Bar C. She noticed his jeans were soiled
and his once-white shirt was dusty and had splotches
of sweat across it. How handsome he looked even now,
she decided, as she walked back to the kitchen with him.
Automatically, her fingers grazed that spot where he'd
cupped her face earlier that morning. The love she felt
for him welled up in her, and she was unable to stop it.
The feeling was good, strong and grounding. Another
part of her, the scared, frightened mustang, wanted to
run—again.

Automatically, Kate filled two bowls with chili and
took some freshly made cornbread out of the oven. She
cut several thick slices and gestured for Sam to sit down
at the kitchen table.

"Dinner?" Sam grinned, looking at the hefty bowl
of chili filled with onions and green Mexican chilies.
The smell was mouthwatering.

"Why not? You've earned it. Wash your hands at the
sink and then we can sit and eat. You can tell me over
the dinner table what my next problem is."

Once they both sat down to eat, Kate marveled at
how delicious the spicy chili tasted. Her mother's rec-
ipe. Mexican food was a main part of their fare, but so
was fry bread, cornmeal and a lot of vegetables from

her mother's background. By contrast, Kelly liked Irish stew, corned beef and cabbage and plenty of potatoes. All these things drifted back to Kate as she ate hungrily. Sam sat opposite her, eating just as much as she did. He went through half the cornbread, and she wasn't surprised. The sun tea made the meal complete. This was the first meal she'd made at home and it tasted marvelous.

"So," Kate murmured, placing her empty bowl in the sink after eating, "how did your day go? Like mine? Busier than a one-armed paper hanger?"

Sam took one more piece of cornbread, slathered it with butter and squeezed some honey from a plastic container over the top of it. "That sounds about right," he growled, giving her a slight grin. Kate was a damn fine cook, he'd discovered. But then, she was good at anything she set her mind to. As she stood at the kitchen counter, her back against it, sipping sun tea from a glass and studying him, he saw exhaustion around her eyes. Knowing her, she'd worked nonstop. Kate was a worker of the first order. She always had been.

"Listen," Sam said gently, as he wiped his hands on the napkin, stood up and walked over to her. "Why don't you rest a little, Kate? You're looking pretty worn out." Fighting himself, Sam cupped her shoulders. He ached to lean down and kiss her parting lips. He saw the surprise and then the molten longing in her blue eyes. And just as quickly, it was replaced with hurt. How badly he'd hurt both of them. Sam wished there was a way he could apologize enough to Kate on that account.

Kate held herself very stiffly, afraid to move, afraid to breathe. His hands felt stabilizing. Wonderful. How she wanted simply to surrender, lean against his powerful, strong form. Uncurling her fingers, she whispered unsteadily, "Please..."

Sam could smell her clean hair, and he longed to press his face against her head and inhale the sweet fragrance. He felt her tremble violently as he held her shoulders. Allowing his hands to drop back to his sides, he realized she didn't want him to touch her. He'd overstepped his bounds—damn his own selfish need and hunger for her! Moving away from her, he said gruffly, "Look, you have Kelly's funeral in a couple of days. Your sisters will be here. Right now you need them more than me."

Bitterly, Kate turned. She saw the dark, hooded look in Sam's eyes. Her body ached for his continued touch. "They may not want to save the ranch. They may not care anymore, Sam. Not that I could blame them. Kelly ran us off. He made it clear we weren't capable of running a ranch. As far as he was concerned, women were good for only one thing—having kids."

Sam raised his eyes toward the ceiling. "Kelly was old-fashioned."

"He was of caveman mentality," Kate retorted. "He *never* respected the three of us. Hell, he never respected our mother, and she was ten times smarter than he was. But he was too proud, too stiff-necked to listen to her counsel." Kate looked around the kitchen, her voice wobbling with sudden grief. "He didn't think women were worth a plugged nickel. Only a man could run this ranch." Her eyes hardened and she put her hands on her hips. "I swear, Sam, if I can, I'll save this ranch even if I have to kill myself doing it."

Sam knew there was no love lost between Kate and her father. Kelly had made sure of that. "Look," he soothed, "wait until Rachel gets here. You ladies have your mother's intelligence. My bet is that among the three of you, you'll come up with a plan to save the ranch."

When Kate saw Rachel climb out of her rented vehicle, all her fear left her. Whatever their past, it didn't matter at that moment. Her sister was home. Rachel's long, reddish-brown hair was still thick and curly, falling below her shoulders. At thirty-five, she was tall, proud looking and still just as thin and ballerinalike as she'd been as a girl. Slightly shorter than Kate, Rachel wore a long-sleeved, dark green sweater, a black skirt that fell to her ankles and sensible dark brown shoes.

Kate flew off the wooden porch, her arms wide. "Rachel!" she cried.

Rachel smiled tiredly and opened her own arms. "Hi, sis…."

Kate squeezed her hard, tears coming to her eyes as she stepped back to look at her sister. Behind her, the night was coming on, a dark cape over the twilight sky. "I'm so glad you're here."

"Me, too." Rachel smiled unsteadily, tears in her eyes. "How *are* you?"

Kate shrugged. "I'm free of prison, if that's what you mean," she said a little defensively.

Rachel picked up her leather traveling bag from the rear seat, then a black physician's bag. "Let's go inside, shall we? I'm beat from a nine-hour flight across the Atlantic and then a five-hour flight out of New York."

Warily, Kate took the rest of her luggage and led her into the house. "You'd better prepare yourself," she warned.

Somehow, Kate felt responsible for the bad condition of the house as Rachel walked through it to her old bedroom, down the hall and across from Kate's.

"Kelly really let the place go, didn't he?" Rachel said, dropping her luggage on the recently made bed.

"Yes. Everything around here is either broken or ready to fall apart. Are you hungry?"

Rachel pushed her dark hair away from her face. "No…thirsty though."

"Come to the kitchen. I've got fresh coffee made."

Rachel smiled. "No coffee for me. I'm on a homeopathic remedy for grief and coffee will antidote it."

Kate smiled a little, falling in step with her sister. Despite her fears she was glad to see Rachel and already felt the effects of her solid, soothing nature. "That's right, you're a homeopath. I tried to figure out what you did from those once-a-year letters we sent to one another. It's a type of alternative medicine?"

"Yes," Rachel said, "it's a natural medicine discovered over two hundred years ago in Germany, and it's practiced around the world."

"You said you're teaching at Sheffield College near London?" Kate poured her some iced tea and they sat down at the table.

"Thanks, Katie. Yes, I'm one of the instructors there." Rachel reached out and gripped her hand. "How are *you,* though?"

"I'm home," Kate said simply. "It feels good, Rachel. Really good. Better than I thought it would."

Sipping the tea, Rachel studied her as a comfortable silence fell between them. "I'm talking more about how you're handling Kelly's death. Where are you at with that?"

Rachel's hand was warm and dry as she folded it over Kate's. Kate had always marveled at her sister's beautiful hands. They were so long and artistic looking. Hers, in comparison, were large knuckled with blunt-cut nails and lots of old ranching scars covering them. Moving her gaze back up to her sister's face, Kate saw that Rachel's green eyes were filled with concern, and she tightened her grip.

"I heard it from Sam McGuire," Kate continued. "He called to tell me about Kelly at the halfway house I was staying in when I got out of prison a couple of days ago."

Gently, Rachel said, "How are you *feeling,* Kate?"

Frowning, Kate pulled her hand away. "I'm not feeling anything," she said flatly. "Not a damn thing, and I don't care if it's right or wrong."

"There's nothing wrong with that response," Rachel said. "Grief has many faces."

"I'm not grieving," Kate said, her eyes flashing.

"I am." Her sister sighed. "I took *ignatia amara,* a homeopathic remedy for grief. When Sam called me, I started to cry."

"Why? All Kelly ever did was make *us* cry. I'm not shedding one tear for that bastard after what he did to all of us."

"He was a very injured human being," Rachel said slowly.

"He injured all of *us!*" Kate lowered her voice. "I'm sorry. I'm just upset. So much has happened since I got home."

"Tell me about it?"

How like Rachel, Kate thought, to be the listener. She always had been. Having her here was good. Kate felt less threatened now. Almost relieved. Rachel was the cool-headed one in the family, more like their mother, who had always listened in silence and then chewed over everything internally before speaking her thoughts. Kate, on the other hand, had inherited Kelly's hair-trigger temper, his brusqueness and lack of diplomacy.

"It's almost eight. You have to be dead on your feet," Kate protested.

Shrugging, Rachel smiled warmly. "Hey, I haven't seen you in so long. So what if I'm tired? I'll sleep in tomorrow morning. We have a lot to catch up on, Katie." Looking around, Rachel's voice lowered with emotion. "And I want to know about our home, and what is going on with it."

Kate snorted. "Our 'home' is a hundred thousand dollars in debt and a week away from being foreclosed on by the bank unless we declare bankruptcy. Either way, we're going to lose it."

Chapter 5

The next morning Kate, with Rachel's help, fed the cattle and horses. It was nearly eight a.m. when a small red compact car came zooming down the dirt road of the canyon. The two sisters stood on the porch and watched the vehicle's progress and the huge cloud of dust it kicked up in its wake.

"That's Jessica," Kate said with a laugh.

Rachel laughed in turn and dusted off her hands. "Yep. Jessica's never slowed down." She looked over at Kate. "She's how old, now?"

"Thirty, I think." Kate shook her head, then studied her sister, who had traded her professional clothes for a long-sleeved white blouse, jeans and boots, and braided her hair into two long, thick plaits. They reminded Kate of their mother, who'd always worn her hair in braids prettily decorated with pieces of colorful yarn and feathers. Absently, Kate touched her own short hair. She wanted to grow it long once more to try and reclaim her Native American heritage. "Last night when we stayed up late talking, I got to thinking that we three haven't stayed in touch like we should have. We just sorta scattered like a flock of startled quail and went three different directions."

Rachel nodded. "And to three different countries. I live in England. Jessica lives in Canada."

"Kelly did it." Kate knew she sounded bitter and didn't care.

Rachel reached out and squeezed her hand. "Katie, some day you'll be able to let go of your anger over what Kelly did to us. He did the best he could. He was just a very wounded human being."

"Aren't we all wounded?" Kate demanded, her anger rising. "Just because we are doesn't mean we go around beating the hell out of our kids or pushing them away and telling them they're no good because they happen to be female and not male." Her voice shook and Kate forced herself to take a deep breath. "You're right. I've got a lot of anger."

"I can give you a homeopathic remedy to help you start processing it," Rachel said.

"Maybe," Kate muttered as she watched the red car pull into the driveway. "I'll let you know." She didn't know that much about homeopathy, and thankfully, Rachel didn't push it on her. Right now, they had a ranch to try and salvage. Kate would use her anger constructively this time around. Maybe she would do something right, for once.

She couldn't help but grin as Jessica, who at five foot six inches was the shortest of the three, came leaping out of the car like a colorful whirlwind in a bright red cotton skirt, a purple-and-pink blouse with long puffy sleeves, and a violet scarf around her neck. The youngest of the sisters had Odula's long, black hair, sparkling gray eyes and Kelly's thin, wiry build.

"Katie! Rachel!" Jessica shrieked, running toward them with her arms outstretched.

Kate laughed and stepped off the porch. Jessica looked so fresh and unscarred by life. Her small, fine features, like delicate porcelain, showed no sign of stress or aging. She was the same little elfin sprite Kate had grown up with. As Jessica threw her arms around her, Kate could smell the perfumed fragrance of some flower.

Rachel joined them, and more laughter, tears and embraces followed. How good it felt to have the arms of her younger sisters around her! Kate felt Jessica squirming like a wildly happy puppy—she was never able to be still for more than a heartbeat. As Rachel's husky laughter fell over them like a warm, welcoming blanket, Kate felt her anger dissolve, replaced by an unparalleled joy surging upward. How much she loved her sisters! And how much she had missed them—their counsel and shining personalities—in her life. As they stood in a small circle, hugging one another, she realized for the first time just how much she'd lost by running away from the ranch. She should have stayed to watch them grow and mature. Would she ever learn not to run?

Finally, when they all separated, Kate looked at them. Rachel had tears in their eyes and Jessica was crying unabashedly. Pulling out some tissues she had in her pocket, Kate said, "Come on, you crybabies, we've got a lot to talk about." She gestured for them to come into the ranch house. "Blot your eyes and let's get down to business or we'll have a lot more to cry about."

Jessica sat with a cup of tea between small, delicate hands, each slender finger of which was ringed in silver or gold. Kate served Rachel a cup of hot tea also, and after pouring herself a cup of strong coffee, she told them the bad news about the ranch, not sparing her sisters the bottom line.

"Kelly left the ranch to me in his will," she told them in a low voice.

Jessica brightened. "Oh, that's wonderful, Katie! You're the firstborn. It should go to you."

"Kelly wanted it to go to Peter," Kate growled.

Rachel reached out and touched Kate's hand. "No matter how much you dislike Kelly, he loved you, Kate, the best he could. I think he showed that by giving you the ranch."

She wasn't willing to agree with Rachel's assumption. "I haven't got two cents to rub together. I'm flat busted." She looked at them, her voice earnest and low with passion. "I love this place. When I first came here, I was ready to let it go, but… I can't now. I can't explain why."

Jessica sighed. "Oh, Katie, this is our home. Our *roots*. How could any of us let it be taken from us?"

"Are you saying you want to save the ranch?" She prayed that they did.

"Why not?" Rachel said, sipping the tea. "This ranch has a hundred-year history. It has Donovan blood, sweat and tears in the sand. I feel it's worth trying to save."

Jessica removed a wispy lock from her brow with a graceful motion of her hand. "Katie, you may not have any money, but you have heart. I have some money saved from my business. It's not much, but…"

Kate looked at Rachel, who was by far the most successful moneywise of the three of them. "What about you, Rachel? We need money. Do you have any you want to pour into this broken ranch we call a home?"

"I lay awake half the night thinking about that," Rachel admitted slowly, turning the white, chipped mug around in her hand. Her broad brow wrinkled and she slanted a glance toward Kate. "All my life, since I can remember, I've wanted a healing place, a clinic to take care of the poor, the elderly and the babies. When I discovered homeopathy, I knew it was the vehicle for my dream." She shrugged and tried to smile. "That's why I went to England, to get the very best training in the world. That's why I've worked over there, teaching as well as running my private practice. I didn't want to leave the U.S., but I had to in order to get the education."

"So, this clinic," Kate prompted. "Are you building it over in England?"

"No…" Rachel laughed softly. "The other part of my dream was to have it here, on the ranch. Remember how Mom used to tell us she had a dream of a medicine house? A place where she could use her herbs, flowers and poultices on people who needed healing?"

Jessica nodded and smiled tenderly. "Mama *was* a healer. Look at you and me, Rachel—we're in the healing arts. I've got my own natural essence company and you're a homeopath. Both are alternative medicines. Both of us got our training from Mama's herb garden. She taught us everything she knew and we just carried it forward, that's all."

Kate felt like a failure—again. Odula had shown the

three of them her healing skills, taught them her tremendous herbal and floral knowledge, and Kate had stupidly walked away from all of it. All because of Kelly. She saw now the mistake she'd made. In getting rid of Kelly, she'd also cut out and run from the good things she'd been given and taught. Thankfully, Rachel and Jessica had not done what she had. But that made her feel even worse. Fighting her own feelings of inadequacy, she looked at Rachel.

"What is your bottom line on this, Rachel?"

Opening her hands, Rachel said, "I can't leave in the middle of a school year at Sheffield. My contract is up December of next year. I could leave at that time, come back here and work with you to try and save the ranch. I have fifty thousand dollars saved."

Kate gawked at her sister. "You're kidding me! That's a lot of money!"

Rachel grimaced. "Katie, that money was squirreled away over a fifteen-year period for my dream of having a homeopathic clinic."

"I've got it!" Jessica cried, pushing her chair away from the table. "I know what we can do!" She whirled around on her tiptoes and clapped her hands. "It's so simple! Rachel, you come back home a year from December. I can make it home by May at the earliest. My company can't be picked up and moved just like that—I have to do some serious planning." Eagerly, she placed her hands on the table and looked at them. "I've got twenty thousand dollars in assets I can give, Katie. Why can't we all come home as soon as possible? Rachel, you can still have your clinic. Build it here, on the property! And I can build my greenhouses and the other buildings I need for the natural essences I make.

We could do our work here, at home. Oh, wouldn't that be a wonderful dream come true? Mama always wanted us to stay on the ranch!"

Kate sat there, feeling Jessica's boundless hope. It all sounded so good and so easy. "I guess the only thing I can bring to this deal is my elbow grease," she joked weakly.

Rachel grinned. "You're the one who's going to be working herself to the bone, with us unable to be here to help at first. Besides, Katie, it's your *heart* that's really invested in saving our home. We have money, but so what? You'll be here, working dawn to dusk." Worriedly, she added, "And you can't do this alone, Katie. We're going to need a foreman. Someone who can help you out daily."

"We don't have *that* kind of money," Kate protested. "I've been running some figures in my head. We could sell off half the cattle herd. That would cut down on the needed hay for the coming winter and stop some of the financial hemorrhaging. We could also sell off about fifteen head of the black Arabians for the same reason. They'll fetch a decent price because black is rare and in great demand."

"If we did that," Rachel said, "would it pay off the hundred thousand owed on the ranch?"

Kate grimaced. "No. We can probably get twenty thousand out of the cattle and horses we sell off. If you put in your fifty thousand, and Jessica her twenty, that's getting us up there." She clenched her fist. "But the bank may want the whole hundred thousand dollars no matter what we try and do."

Rachel nodded. "The funeral is tomorrow morning. How about if I call up the banker for an appointment with him tomorrow afternoon? I can only stay three days and then I've got to get back to England. Let me handle this part of it, okay?"

Kate was relieved. "No kidding. Your diplomacy is a hell of a lot better than mine! Hoof-in-mouth disease, you know?"

Jessica giggled. "Katie, you have other strengths that we don't. Let's all of us use our skills to the best we can. The three of us can do this! I'm so excited!" Her eyes shone with hope.

"Still," Rachel warned, "as soon as I can get the banker to give us some breathing room and refinance the ranch, we need a foreman."

"We don't have the kind of money it would take to get someone, Rachel." Kate sighed. "Foremen are special. They know everything from accounting to calving and then some. I can't just hire some wrangler looking for work."

"You mentioned Sam McGuire last night," Rachel said primly.

"What about him? Can you lure him back from the Bar C to take over here? You know, he worked here for five years. Maybe he wants to come back."

Instantly, Kate was on her feet. The chair she was sitting on tipped, but she caught it before it fell over. "Sam's got a job already."

Jessica frowned and tugged at a lock of her hair. "So what? Can we lure him away from it? I'll go see him, Kate—"

"You will not!"

Rachel frowned. "Kate, don't get stubborn about this. You need help. Sam McGuire is a known quantity. You're right—we can't just hire some tumbleweed wrangler that drifts from ranch to ranch looking for work. Sam's a hard worker. He's loyal and he's smart."

Panic set in and Kate began pacing the floor of the kitchen. Rachel's argument was on target, she acknowledged as her heart pounded hard in her breast. "But he's already got a good-paying job."

Rachel laughed. "Oh, yes, at the Bar C. Come on, Katie! Old Man Cunningham is a mean old peccary. His wranglers work for a season and then quit on him. He can't keep anyone for long. He's got high turnover because he's grumpy." She grinned mischievously. "I'd like to give him *Bryonia* to sweeten his disposition up a little."

They all chortled.

Rachel shrugged eloquently. "I'm sure Sam would consider coming back now that Kelly's gone. He *loved* this ranch. I talked to Kelly one time on the phone about Sam and he told me that Sam was like a son to him."

Kate halted and stared at Rachel. "He said *that?*"

"Yes, and a lot more, but I'm not going into that now." She eyed Kate. "Do you want me to ask Sam or do you want to do it?"

Swallowing hard, her throat dry, Kate rasped, "No... I'll approach him."

"He's been helping you out ever since you came back," Rachel said gently. "I've got to think he cares about our ranch or he wouldn't have done it."

Standing very still, Kate realized Rachel's wisdom. "You're right," she whispered, "I've got to get out of the way and let the ranch be helped, not hurt by me. Okay, I'll ask Sam sometime after the funeral. He'll be coming to it."

Rising to her feet, Rachel smiled. "Good. Don't look

so glum, Katie. It's not the end of the world, it's the beginning. Come on, I'm going to give you some *natrum muriaticum.* I think you need it."

At that moment, Kate felt too enmeshed in the violence of her own feelings about Sam to care about a homeopathic remedy. A huge part of her hoped he would say no to their request. Another part had never stopped loving him, or wanting his daily presence in her life. How could she keep her feelings toward him separated from the hard, demanding ranch activities? He didn't love her. Too much time and hurt and life responsibilities stood in the way, Kate knew. But that didn't stop her from loving him. Even now.

Sam would live in the foreman's house, not in the main ranch house, but that was still too close for comfort. Kate was scared—more than she ever had been before. She'd known fear when the sentence for an eighteen-month prison term was announced by the judge, but this was different—and far more personal. She was afraid that she couldn't keep her feelings private from Sam.

Tasting the fear, she watched Rachel walk over to her homeopathic kit, which sat on the kitchen counter. Her sisters were so solid and normal compared to her. They were successful, had saved money, had dreams and goals, and worked hard toward them, while she'd made a mess of her life.

"Here," Rachel murmured, patting several small white pellets in Kate's hand. "Take these. It's potentized table salt. It's for people who bury all their feelings, Katie."

Wryly, she looked at Rachel. "Me?"

Laughing, Rachel slid her arm around her shoulders.

"Yes, you, Miss Toughie. Go on, put them in your mouth and let them melt away. And then take a shower and go to bed. You'll feel better tomorrow morning." Rachel lost her smile. "Tomorrow, we bury Kelly."

"Bless him," Jessica whispered, her eyes filling with tears. "He was such a tortured soul. He's in a far better place now, with Mama."

Kate didn't know what had happened to her emotions, but the funeral for Kelly hadn't been as arduous as she thought it might be. Kelly Donovan was buried on the family plot on the ranch, surrounded by heavy wrought-iron posts that needed painting. Ten other graves were in that rectangular enclosure on a hillside covered with Ponderosa pine. Mercifully, the ceremony was short. The minister said all the right things and then shook their hands and left. Jessica paid him the 120 fee for his services.

Sam McGuire had come and stood next to Kate during the funeral. Afterward, he settled his dark brown Stetson on his head. Today he wore a dark brown blazer and a white shirt with a big bolo tie sporting a turquoise stone in the center. His Levi's were clean, and he wore his go-to-town cowboy boots, the same ones he'd worn when he'd picked her up at the halfway house down in Phoenix. Kate had watched the warmth of Rachel's and Jessica's welcome for Sam. Her's had been a curt and short greeting in comparison. She chided herself relentlessly. Why couldn't she be just as warm and outgoing as her two sisters? She was a crab compared to them. She always had been. It was her anger against Kelly, Kate decided. Damn him, he'd always ruined her life. Always. And now, as she stood alone under the pines near his fresh grave, she was the one on whose shoulders the responsibility fell to try and save the ranch. Could she do it? They had enough money to probably give them breathing room, but to make a ranch profitable was another thing all together.

Hands damp, she saw Sam excuse himself from her sisters and purposefully walk toward her. She felt heat leap to her face as his dark gray gaze settled on her. He looked grim—she could see sadness in the set of his mouth and in the darkness of his eyes. Sam wasn't the kind to pretend something he didn't feel, Kate thought.

"Want to go for a walk?" he asked, tipping his hat to her.

Kate wished the heat in her face would subside. She'd blushed like this in high school every time Sam looked at her that way. "I guess…." she murmured. Kate knew her sisters didn't need her right now. Rachel was meeting with the banker at two p.m. today and she'd fill them in on whether or not the bank was going to foreclose on them. And Jessica had some of her own business to attend to back at the ranch.

Sam gently placed his hand on her elbow and led her down a well-worn deer path, moving more deeply into the woods. "You look mighty pretty in that dress."

Kate tried to steady her reeling senses. Sam's hand was firm yet careful. He was so strong and tall—like the mountains. But she felt like a raging river without banks right now. "It's not my dress. It belongs to Rachel. She loaned it to me because I didn't have any…."

Sam smiled down at her. The dark blue, long-sleeved dress was conservative and fit Kate well. Small pearl buttons down the front stopped at a white belt around her waist, setting off the white collar. The material was soft and flowing and fell around her slender ankles. Sam noted that she was wearing different shoes, too. Knowing Kate had little money, he suspected Rachel had loaned her them, as well, but he wasn't going to inquire and embarrass her further. He saw the wariness in her eyes. Always the wild, untamable mustang, he reminded himself.

He smiled inwardly. A mustang could be tamed, but doing so took patience and time. He had both. But what gave him the right to try and tame Kate? To try and win her heart again? He was a miserable failure at so much in his life.

"Well," he murmured huskily, "the dress brings out the sky blue color of your eyes."

His compliment went straight to her heart and Kate absorbed it greedily. She tried to think through the haze of feelings and desires that Sam automatically stirred up in her. "Thank you…."

"You ladies talk about the fate of your ranch?" Sam asked, halting beneath a huge pine. He didn't want to drop his hand, but he did anyway. He stood before her, taking her in more fully. Kate's hair had been coiffed, he was sure, by Jessica, who had those feminine skills. A pair of gold earrings with small pearls adorned her delicate earlobes. Even a touch of lipstick graced her lips. But her real beauty was completely natural, Sam thought. Kate was a living, breathing part of this harsh, extreme land that either tore a person apart or built character. Kate had character.

"Yes," she said in a strained voice. She twisted her hands and looked down at them. "Sam, they had an idea. It was this… I mean, no, it's a good idea, I think." Kate took a huge breath and forced herself to look up at his craggy, sun-darkened features. She was so scared. "Rachel thought it would be a good idea to hire a ranch foreman—I mean, to help me—us—because they can't come home for six months to a year from now due to their other commitments. It would be just me. And I don't want to hire just any old person to help me. They felt I should ask you to come to work for us...." She looked away, her voice strained. "We can't pay you what you're worth, but as soon as we got the ranch back on its feet, we could pay you more and more over time."

In that moment, Kate had never wanted anything more than to have Sam say yes to her proposal. The fear that he'd reject her lingered. She still loved him, even if he didn't love her.

Sam took off his hat and ran his fingers slowly across the rim of it. "I see...."

Opening her hands in frustration, Kate blurted, "You worked here before but it'll be different this time, Sam, I promise. I'm not Kelly. I need someone who's got business savvy about ranching. I've forgotten so much over the years. I need help. It's true that Rachel and Jessica are giving the money, but I can't run this place single-handedly." She earnestly searched his face for some kind of a sign. Right now, Sam's face looked like the craggy cliffs of Oak Creek Canyon—completely unreadable. More panic set in, and she began to talk very fast, stumbling over her words.

"Look, I know I'm an ex-con. I know I have a bad history with people around here. I'm sure you're concerned about your reputation, but I'll try and be good. I'll try to make good decisions and I'll listen. I really will. I know I'm stiff-necked and pop off at the wrong time. But I'm older and I've learned. Please, could you consider it? I'll stay out from underfoot. I'll handle the accounting, the money part of it, and you just tell me what to do and I'll do it—"

Sam gripped her arms. "Kate," he rasped, "stop it. Stop it and listen to me. You don't need to cut yourself down like this."

Helplessly, she stared up at him. "I'm no prize," she said in a choked voice. "I know that. And I'm a hothead. I know that, too. But Sam, this ranch is my *heart*. My *soul*. I'll do *anything* to save it, I'm discovering. But I need someone like you. You're as straight and true as an arrow. You don't lie. You don't play games. I need that kind of man to help me save our ranch…our home…."

His nostrils flared as he stared at Kate's upturned face.

Her cheeks were flushed and he saw the pain and pleading in her huge, wide eyes—the eyes of a hurt child in some ways, he thought. His fingers tightened slightly on her arms. He had a tough time believing she was asking him to come back to the ranch to help her. For an instant he saw longing in her gaze. For him? How was that possible, after all he'd done to her?

"Rachel said Kelly thought of you as a son. Is that true?"

Sam nodded, still looking into her wide, beautiful eyes.

"Did he mean that? He was so hung up on his grief for our brother…."

Gently, Sam allowed his hands to slide downward. Kate felt good beneath his fingers, though he felt her tense a little. "I think," he admitted, "at some point Kelly realized his grief for Peter had torn the family apart. But by the time he realized that everyone was

gone. He told everyone in Sedona I was like a second
son to him, and for a couple of years, he was a fairly
decent man who didn't hit the bottle too often."

Kate stared up at him. "But the three of us weren't
good enough, were we?"

His fingers stilled on her hands. They felt damp and
cool in his. "If that was so, why did he make you the
owner of the ranch, Kate?"

She avoided his burning look.

"Kelly might not have been one for a lot of truth or
honesty, but when it came down to it, I think he was
apologizing to you. Maybe letting you know he loved
you in his own way by making you executor."

Though pain crawled through her gut, Sam's hands
felt comforting on hers. She compressed her lips, her
voice low and trembling. "But you said he treated you
like a son."

"For a while," Sam reminded her wryly. "He got
over that, too."

"How? By hitting the bottle again?"

"'Fraid so, Kate."

"I feel so confused," she whispered unsteadily, and
then looked up at him. Kate felt the tenderness of his
gray gaze enveloping her like a warm, embracing blanket. She felt his fingers tighten momentarily around
hers. "I'm sorry, Sam, I didn't mean to lay all this on
you. I know how badly Kelly wanted a son. It's not
your fault."

"No insult taken, Kate." He tried to smile, but failed.
"I'll give my two-weeks notice today. All right? Stop
talking about yourself this way. So you made some mistakes. So what? What's more important is that you've
learned from them. I can see that better than anyone

else can." He lifted one hand and grazed her flushed cheek with his index finger. The startled look in her eyes caught him off guard. Kate pulled away from him, her hand on her cheek where he'd just touched her. In that moment, Sam realized that she didn't like it—or him. Whatever had been brought to life between them so long ago was really dead and gone.

The pang in his heart felt like a stake had just been driven through it. Settling his hat on his head, he looked up beyond her to the mountain cloaked in pine. Kate and her sisters needed his help. Kate didn't want him back on a personal level—that was obvious. All right; somehow, he'd rein in his feelings for her. He'd work damned hard to keep how he felt about her to himself. She wanted a foreman, not a lover or possible partner in her life. His mouth compressed. Lowering his gaze, he met her wide, pleading eyes.

"I'll do it, Kate. Did you hear me?"

Still disbelieving, she nodded. "You really will?"

"Yes," he said heavily, turning to go back down the slope, "for you and your sisters."

Kate reached out, wrapping her fingers around his lower arm. "Sam…wait…."

He stood perfectly still. Kate's fingers were warm and soft against his hard flesh. "What is it?"

"If Kelly saw you as a son," she began, searching his somber features, "I don't understand why he didn't leave you the ranch, instead."

Sam pulled out of her grip, because if he didn't, he was going to haul Kate into his arms, crush her against him and take that ripe, soft mouth with his. His lower body ached with need—need of her and only her. More harshly than he intended, he rasped, "Kelly saw me as

Peter's replacement, that's all. Don't make anything out of it. I think he loved you, Kate, and leaving you the ranch was the only way he could show you he did."

Kate stood there, still dizzy with realization as Sam walked in long, steady strides down the slope to where the vehicles were parked near the grave site. In her wildest imagination, she couldn't envision Kelly calling any man his son except Peter. Rubbing her brow, she slowly started back down the hill. Her mind spun with more questions than answers. If Kelly had adopted Sam like a son, he'd obviously wanted him to marry one of them, hadn't he? That was silly. They had all left the ranch. What kind of harebrained scheme had Kelly thought up? Sam had worked for Kelly after Odula had died, and Kelly had been hitting the bottle pretty regularly around that time, grieving, she suspected. That was it. Kelly was probably roaring drunk when he'd said those words, that was all.

Still, as Kate stepped carefully around the black rocks sticking up through the carpet of brown pine needles, she was shocked by the implications of her father's words. Who had Kelly seen as Sam's wife? It couldn't have been her, that's for sure. Jessica? Rachel? With a shake of her head, she jammed her thoughts on the matter deep inside her. Right now she had to focus entirely, along with her sisters, on saving the ranch—if the bank would allow it to be saved.

Chapter 6

Kate felt loneliness eating at her. It was exactly one week after Kelly's funeral and her sisters were gone. Already she missed them terribly. Their support as far as the ranch was concerned was enormous. But more than anything, they had helped ease the shame she felt over her recent past. They had listened to her story of what had happened. Jessica had cried. Rachel had told her that something good always comes of bad experience. Kate wasn't so sure. Standing on the porch of her home, watching the sky turn lavender before the sunrise, she wondered how she had remained sane in prison.

This morning, now that the feeding and vetting were done, she wanted to ride out to a particular pasture that needed repairs on the fence. Chet Cunningham had nastily called over and demanded they fix their rotting fence posts and string some new barbed wire to keep their cattle off the Cunningham property. In her leather saddlebags were pliers, wire cutters and heavy leather gloves. Plus a new homeopathic first-aid kit that Rachel had absolutely insisted she take with her. Rachel had even made one for Kate to carry in her truck! Kate had laughed, but she was grateful for Rachel's care.

There were five houses on the ranch property and new guests had arrived two days before Rachel and Jessica had left. Morgan Trayhern, the man who had commanded her brother's company, had been written about glowingly by Peter in a number of his letters to Kelly and Odula before that tragic day he'd died on a hill in Vietnam. Many years later, Morgan had flown in to talk to Kelly about his son's death, and apologize. Now Morgan and his wife, Laura, had asked to come and stay at the guest cabin for a couple of weeks.

Apparently, Morgan and Laura had been involved in a very traumatic kidnapping. Kate was uneasy about the South American drug connection, but had some of her fears eased when she was told a crack Army officer, Major Mike Houston, would be guarding the ranch during their stay. Morgan was recovering from his recent imprisonment and coma. Dr. Ann Parsons from Perseus, Morgan's mercenary outfit, was also on call at the ranch during their stay.

Kate had approved their visit because Rachel had urged her to fulfill the old family obligation. Kate had no reason not to. There were houses available down in the canyon for Morgan and his wife, as well as the major and the doctor. Kate had met Dr. Parsons earlier in the week, and a part of her wanted to mingle more directly because she liked the tall, thin doctor. Maybe it was Ann's large, compassionate blue eyes that drew Kate.

Or maybe it was simply because Ann was around Kate's age. Kate had found out via Rachel, who was inquisitive when she met new people, that Ann had been an Air Force flight surgeon and a psychiatrist until Morgan had snatched her from the military and asked her to head up their medical trauma section. Ann was, according to Rachel's whispers, more like a sister to Morgan, which explained in part why she was here at the ranch to take care of him.

Kate walked a long circle around Morgan's other friend, Army Special Forces Major Mike Houston. Part Quechua Indian, with his mother from Mexico, Mike was a big, barrel-chested, square-faced man in his thirties with frosty, dark blue eyes that reminded Kate of a cougar she'd once met up on the Rim. Though Mike's intelligent eyes were not yellow like the cougar's, his huge black pupils seemed to drill right through her, just as the cougar's had on that fateful day. And there was an air of danger as well as mystery around Mike.

Jessica, sensitive as she was, was mesmerized by Mike Houston from the moment she met him. More than once she had drawn Kate aside and whispered that he reminded her a lot of her friend Moyra, who worked at Jessica's company up in Vancouver. Moyra, who was from South America, was a member of the highly secret and mysterious Jaguar Clan, and according to Jessica, Mike had the very same lethal energy around him that Moyra did. The fact that he'd been down in Peru for nearly ten years, working as an American advisor to halt shipments of drugs into the U.S., told Kate a lot about the man.

Kate pooh-poohed a lot of Jessica's psychic information, while Jessica was dying to ask him if he was a member of the Jaguar Clan, but was afraid to. Kate just laughed and shook her head over her little sister's curiosity about the soldier. Though Houston was laid-back, Kate could feel an air of tension around him. It was nothing he broadcast directly, because his mouth would often curve into a casual Texan smile of welcome that would make most folks feel at ease.

As Kate walked to the barn, she saw her two ranch guests out at one of the Arabian broodmare corrals looking at some of the growing foals. Ann and Mike each stood with one foot propped up on the lowest rung of the corral, their arms draped lazily over the uppermost one. Even though they wore jeans and short-sleeved cotton shirts, there was no hiding their military background. As Kate drew nearer, she could see that Mike often stole a swift glance at Ann when she wasn't paying attention. Kate saw the familiar look of longing on his face. She'd seen that expression on Sam's face when he looked at her.

A slight smile tugged at her lips. The major seemed very interested in Ann—man to woman—if she was reading the situation correctly. And why not? Ann was an attractive woman, with shoulder-length hair that fell in a soft pageboy about her oval features. Though the color seemed almost black, Kate saw the reddish gold cast as a slight breeze lifted a few strands in the early morning sunlight. If Ann was aware of Houston's keen appraisal, she didn't show it. Maybe it was a one-way street, Kate thought as she drew close enough to speak to them. Just as her love for Sam had turned out to be. Suddenly, she felt very sorry for Mike Houston. It was hell to fall in love when the other person didn't return the feeling.

"Good morning," Ann exclaimed, turning and smiling at Kate.

"Hi, Ann." Kate nodded in Mike's direction as he turned. That easy Texan smile came to his square face, while those frosty blue eyes warned Kate that this man was a warrior in every sense of the word. "Watching the babies?" she asked, slowing her pace and pointing to the corral, where several foals three to six months old frolicked at their mothers' side.

With a soft laugh, Ann nodded. "I love babies."

"That's good to hear," Mike said enigmatically, turning and watching the foals kicking up their heels.

Ann raised one eyebrow, but said nothing. Her blue eyes sparkled as she met and held Kate's gaze. "How are you doing today?"

Knowing Ann was a psychotherapist as well as a medical doctor, Kate really didn't want to reveal too much. "Okay," she murmured, standing near them, her gaze on the horses in the corral.

"Mmm," Ann said, "one day at a time. I understand."

Opening her mouth, then closing it, Kate realized that Ann *did* understand. If Mike hadn't been nearby, Kate would have been tempted to confide in Ann. But of course, Ann was a guest here. The doctor was here for Morgan and Laura, not her. Changing the subject, Kate said, "Will you go for a ride later?"

Mike twisted his head and grinned. "Us Texas boys just can't stand not throwing a leg over a good horse." His gaze settled warmly on Ann, who had her back to him. "What about you, Ann? I know you're from Oregon, and you've probably never been around horses much. Would you go riding with me?"

Kate saw the merriment in Ann's eyes as she turned

and held the major's teasing stare. She sensed a warmth between them. Maybe Mike's ardor wasn't one-sided after all.

"Just because I'm from Oregon doesn't mean I never saw a horse before."

Mike held up his hands in surrender. "Now, Ann," he drawled good-naturedly, "I didn't say there weren't any horses in Oregon."

Kate grinned. She liked the parry-riposte between them. They made a handsome-looking couple. Mike was like Sam in the looks department, with a rugged, weathered face that had been shaped and molded—sometimes brutally—by life's circumstances. Ann was beautiful in Kate's opinion—even if she was skinny as a rail. That woman could stand some meat on her bones, Kate thought, studying her thin hands—a surgeon's hands. Often Kate had seen her embroidering or knitting out on the front porch of the house where she was staying.

"I think," Ann said seriously, "us folks from Oregon ought to teach you Texas men a lesson in horseback riding." She glanced over at Kate. "Don't you think?"

Laughing, Kate nodded and pointed a finger in Mike's direction. "I think you just stepped into a bear trap, Major Houston."

"Ouch," he jested with a widening smile. "Okay, the gauntlet has been thrown. I'm just dumb enough to pick it up."

Ann smiled. "You'd pick up any gauntlet that was thrown, Mike, and you know it. And dumb? No, I don't think so. I might accuse you of many things, but that's not one of them."

"Oops, guilty twice over." With a sigh, Houston said,

"I guess I'll just have to go saddle up two horses and find out."

"How about if I saddle my own?" Ann said pointedly.

"That's three," Mike said, deflated. "I think I'm getting the message. Not only do women from Oregon know about horses, they know how to saddle them."

Ann winked at Kate. "Not only that, we can ride like the wind, Major."

Kate lifted her hand. "Okay, you two go riding. I'm sure you'll enjoy it. There're two geldings, a chestnut and a bay, on the left side of the barn aisle. They're good, gentle trail horses. I've got some work to do, so I'll see you later."

As Kate walked on past them into the barn, where Cinnamon greeted her from the box stall at the end of the aisle, she heard Mike's deep, husky laughter as he continued to tease Ann. Somehow, Kate knew that Ann would handle that Texas know-it-all cowboy just fine. Mike was intelligent, but Ann had a street smarts that would get him every time.

Kate chuckled, eager to saddle her mare and get to work. Earlier, she'd heard that as soon as Mike was done with his assignment to guard Morgan and Laura for the next two weeks, he was going back down to Peru to continue interdiction activities. She wondered if Ann figured into his future plans.

As Kate reached Cinnamon's stall, the bay mare nickered again and thrust her muzzle over the top, looking for the carrot Kate always carried with her. Feeding the mare, Kate found her thoughts moving back to Ann. Ann had turned her resignation into Perseus before coming to the ranch. Now Kate wondered what a woman like her was going to do after quitting such a high-powered, well-paying job? She'd heard Rachel confide that Ann wanted to work with the poor and underprivileged in Washington, D.C., but Kate wasn't certain that was what the doctor would do.

Patting Cinnamon affectionately, Kate led her out of the box stall, tied her in the aisle and began to brush her down before saddling her. Yes, the day was turning out to be pretty good so far, even if Kate had fence mending staring her in the face for most of it—one of the most dreaded jobs a rancher had to undertake. Still, the day held hope, and this was the first time Kate had actually felt that particular feeling for a long, long time. What would make her day complete would be to see Sam—but that was impossible.

Absorbing the bright blue sky, the dry desert air, the soft scent of scrub juniper that dotted the rocky, red clay and sand, Kate felt peace settling around her. The rhythmic movement of her surefooted horse, the chirping of birds hiding in the dark green arms of the junipers, conspired to make her feel a momentary trickle of happiness. Of late, she'd been slightly less numb inside, which was amazing to Kate. She'd thought her feelings, pulverized by the trial and prison, were dead and gone. Rachel had told her the remedy *natrum muriaticum* would help bring them back. But whether it was the natural remedy or her time on the ranch that had brought her senses alive again, Kate hung on to each fleeting feeling as it arose in her.

The fence line curved up a slope covered with yellowed chaparral, prickly pear and slender stalks of dead grass. The black lava rocks scattered throughout the region poked up through the red clay ground, which was almost as hard as they were. Kate frowned as she noticed some broken strands of wire. Fence mending was hard, dirty work and she was glad the morning was cool. Doing this kind of work in hundred-degree summer heat was blistering and sapping. It wasn't her favorite duty, anyway.

Today Kate wore a red flannel, long-sleeved shirt over a white tank top and a pair of Levi's that were finally getting broken in. Jessica had gone into Sedona one day last week and bought Kate seven new pairs of Levi's, seven flannel shirts in a rainbow of colors, heavy socks to wear with the new pair of cowboy boots Rachel had bought her, and a brand-new black Stetson cowboy hat with a wide brim to protect her face and neck from the powerful sunlight. They'd also purchased several skirts and two dresses, though Kate didn't know when she'd wear them. Her sisters had always been good to her, but now she felt as if she was truly being taken care of by them. Maybe that's why she missed them so much—they were nurturing like their mother had been. How come she wasn't that way? Or maybe she had been at one time, but life had beaten it out of her? Kate was unsure.

Cresting the hill, Kate pulled her horse to a stop and dismounted. The Arabian had been taught to ground tie, which meant that when Kate dropped the reins to the ground, the horse wouldn't move. Pulling on thick, protective gloves, she set to work on the twisted, broken barbed wire. Off in the distance, perhaps half a mile away, she saw another fence crew working—from the Cunningham side of the property.

Kate slowed her step and narrowed her eyes. Her heart sped up. It was Sam and three other wranglers out fixing their fence line. For an instant, she stood very still, transfixed by Sam's seemingly larger-than-life form. He was sitting astride a big, rangy chestnut gelding with four white socks and a white blaze on its face. The blue-and-black checked shirt Sam wore emphasized the breadth of his shoulders and power-ful chest. A red bandanna was around his neck, and he wore a denim jacket that matched the color of his Levi's.

Swallowing convulsively, Kate forced herself to get to work. Picking up one end of the barbed wire, she took a twelve-inch strand and twisted it around the bro-ken part. Leaning down, she retrieved the other rusty end and connected them. Though the whole fence line needed to be replaced, as Chet had nastily informed her on the phone, this would have to do for now. At least, until she had more help. Since Sam had given his no-tice to Old Man Cunningham, he hadn't been over to the Donovan ranch. She couldn't blame him for being cautious. That old bear Cunningham would probably fire him on the spot for disloyalty.

How she missed Sam! How many times had she awakened in the morning, thought of him working with her at the ranch again, and gone into an absolute panic? Often during her twelve-hour workdays the thought of spending more time with him sent her into a spasm of euphoria mixed with fear.

As she connected a second strand of barbed wire, her sensitive ears picked up the sound of a galloping horse. Kneeling on the ground, she finished the con-nection and then looked up.

It was Sam. Her hands froze on the wire as she watched him riding up the slope toward her like a man born to the saddle. He rode with such ease and grace, his upper body absolutely still, his hips moving with the rhythmic motion of the horse, his long, powerful legs wrapped strongly around the animal. Slowly, Kate forced herself to stand up. She saw the hardness on Sam's face and in those cool gray eyes barely visible below the brim of his black Stetson.

Just getting to see him was wonderfully healing for Kate. She moved to her mare and took off her gloves, stuffing them back in the saddlebag. As Sam drew his horse to a halt, she managed a lopsided smile of greeting.

"Great minds think alike?" she asked, pulling out a thermos of hot coffee.

Sam tipped his hat to Kate. Her cheeks were flushed from work, from the chill of the November air, and her black hair curled around her face, slightly damp at the temples. Did Kate know how beautiful and wild she looked? Sam wondered as he dismounted.

"I think so," he said with a brief smile. Searching her large, blue eyes, Sam saw some of the darkness he'd noticed at the funeral was gone. That was good. He watched as she poured some steaming hot coffee into the thermos cup. Her hand shook a little. "Chet told me he'd called you up a couple of days ago, griping about this fence line." Sam looked back at his hardworking crew down below. "Thought I'd get this done before I left. I've got two other crews laying new wire and post about a mile down the line."

"He wasn't exactly nice about it," she agreed. "I'm glad your men are fixing the rest of it. I wasn't looking forward to doing this all day." Kate offered him the cup of coffee. He shook his head, but thanked her. Nervously, she sipped the hot liquid, almost burning her mouth. It never failed to amaze her how ruggedly handsome Sam was. Sweat stood out on his furrowed brow and his gray eyes were fathomless, as always. Kate wished she could tell how Sam felt by looking into his eyes, but he was like that rock canyon wall—unreadable. As she stared at his mouth, her lower body tingled in memory of his kisses so long ago. Kate had never forgotten his touch, his strength, or his tenderness with her. For a man of his size and power, Sam had always been exceedingly gentle. She had given her virginity to him and he had cherished that moment with her as something not only special, but sacred. Kate had felt like the most loved woman in the world.

Coloring, she looked away and pretended to be watching the crew below. It was a good thing Sam couldn't read her mind! What would he think of her, a foolish young girl in high school who still had a heartbreaking crush on him when she was old enough to know better? The coffee burned her tongue. She frowned.

Cinnamon's soft snort made her glance toward Sam. He was gazing at her. Instantly, her heart slammed against her ribs. His gray eyes were narrowed, thoughtful and burning with that look—the look she'd never forgotten from her youthful days with him. It was a smoldering look, of banked coals ready to explode into life. It was a look that had come into his eyes when he wanted her, wanted to make hot, passionate, unbridled love with her.

She had to be crazy. Kate chided herself and dipped her head, focusing her attention on drinking her coffee. Sam didn't desire her. That was the past. She'd misread the intent in his eyes, that's all.

"How are you getting along without your sisters?"

Sam asked, stroking Cinnamon's mane as he stood beside the mare. He'd seen high color come to Kate's cheeks as she'd dodged his look. Damn, he hadn't meant to give away his real feelings for her. Did she notice just a little how much influence she still held over him? Even though she was dressed in work clothes, they could not hide her femininity, the graceful way she moved her hands or quirked her full lips. No, beneath that wide hat brim was a mature woman's face. A face he wanted to touch with his fingers and retrace to see if he remembered it as well as he thought he had.

Kate shrugged and kept a safe distance from Sam. "I miss them terribly."

"I was hoping the three of you would get along." Sam used his thumb to push his own hat higher on his head. "Any word from the bank on what they've decided to do with the foreclosure?"

With a slight smile, Kate turned to him. "Thanks to Rachel's diplomatic skills, she managed to talk the bank president into not foreclosing. My sisters have pitched in seventy thousand dollars against the hundred thousand that's owed. I've got a buyer for half the beef herd and I'm sending twenty Arabian yearlings to an auction that will be held down in Phoenix in a couple of weeks. I'm hoping we'll get another twenty thousand."

"Smart move," Sam said. He watched her toss away the last few drops in the plastic thermos lid. "That's good news."

"The best," Kate agreed, realizing she had to put the cap back on the thermos in the saddlebag that Sam was standing next to. She moved slowly toward him. It was then that she noticed the left side of his jaw looked a little swollen and bruised.

"What happened?" she asked, pointing at his hard jawline. "Did you tell Old Man Cunningham you were giving your two weeks' notice and he nailed you with a right cross?" It would be just like him to do that, Kate thought.

Sam saw the wariness in Kate's eyes as she hesitantly approached him and her horse. He stepped back to give her some breathing room and instantly saw relief in her gaze. That hurt him and he wrestled with the pain. "It was Chet," he admitted. "The kid's a hothead of the first order. Cunningham and I got into an argument after I told him I was giving my notice, and Chet walked in on it. The kid took a swing at me and connected."

Kate saw merriment in Sam's gray eyes as she quickly twisted the cap back on the thermos and tucked it down into the saddlebag. "Somehow, knowing you, Chet got the worst of it in the long run." She pulled her leather gloves back on.

Chuckling, Sam moved around the head of the mare, his hands resting on his hips as he surveyed his line crew. "He's nursing a broken nose."

Laughing, Kate went back to work on the third strand of barbed wire. "Well deserved, I'm sure. He's the youngest?"

"Yeah," Sam rumbled, kneeling down beside her and picking up the broken end of a strand of barbed wire. "Mean as a green rattler." Green rattlesnakes were the most poisonous of all the rattlesnake species in Arizona.

"He was always that way," Kate murmured as they worked together. Their fingers met briefly. Kate inhaled sharply and dropped the wire. How silly of her! Scooping it back up, she took the other end Sam proffered.

He was so dizzyingly close, she had to force herself to remain calm as she twisted the ends together.

"Chet was the youngest and the most spoiled," Sam continued. He watched her work with quick, smooth efficiency. "For someone who hasn't been doing ranch work for a long time, you haven't forgotten much, have you?"

Laughing a little, Kate shook her head. "Listen, so much has come back to me since I got home, Sam, it isn't even funny. I thought when I ran away at eighteen that I'd forget all of this." She slanted a glance at him, amazed at how open and readable his face was right now. The flecks of silver in his gray eyes warmed her and so did the careless grin shadowing that strong, wonderful mouth of his.

"You never really left, Gal." Damn! He hadn't meant to call her again by the affectionate name he'd given her so long ago. Sam saw his words have an immediate effect on Kate. Her hands froze in midair for a second. And then she ducked her head and quickly finished connecting the barbed wire. Scrambling to cover his error, he added huskily, "Your heart and soul are here, like you said before. I don't know too many people who can cut those parts out of themselves and survive very long." He eased to his feet and stepped back a little to give her the breathing room she obviously needed.

Shaken with longing, Kate stood up and brushed off her dusty, red-clay-covered knees. "I guess part of me didn't leave the ranch. Not really." She removed a glove and pushed several curls away from her temple. Sam had called her his pet name, Gal. The word had rolled off his tongue like hot honey across her screaming, sensitized nerves.

Moving over to his gelding and picking up the reins, he said, "I'd better get back. Is there anything you'll need in the next week before I come over?"

Touched by his concern, Kate shook her head. "I just need to clone myself and be two people, is all," she said, laughing softly. Sam moved with the ease of a man born to the saddle as he mounted his chestnut gelding. He sat tall and proud in the saddle, his shoulders back, his posture like that of a military officer. Yet there was such ease and grace about him even then.

"Look," Sam said more seriously, "if you run into trouble or need help, Kate, call me? You've got my phone number."

"Yes, I do. I'll be fine, Sam." She put the pliers back into the saddlebag.

He liked to watch Kate move. Nothing was wasted in her motions. She was always thinking, and he liked that about her, too. Ranch life was hard and ranchers learned to conserve their energy, finding the shortest routes, watching where they put their feet because rattlers abounded in the area. Even in November, which was hotter than usual this year, some rattlers were still out and about instead of crawling in their holes to hibernate the winter away.

Sam paused before turning his horse toward the Bar C. "I may be out of line," he said, catching her gaze, "but I'd like to take you to dinner, Kate." He saw her eyes grow huge with shock. Girding himself for her answer, he pushed on. "I can't take time out from my normal ranching duties right now or Old Man Cunningham will pitch a fit. I'm free after eight. How about dinner down at the Muse Restaurant in Sedona? They've got the best New Orleans lamb in Coconino County.

We could talk business strategy. I've got some ideas, some plans I'd like to discuss with you before I come over as foreman."

Her heart skittered. Her mouth went dry. Resting her hand on the horn of the saddle, Kate gazed up at Sam's tall form silhouetted against the sky, and felt warmth sheet through her. "Well…" she murmured, "I don't know…. I haven't been to Sedona since I got out of… since I got home."

Sam understood Kate's hesitancy. Her prison experience was so fresh and she was afraid people would look at her, whisper hurtful things. "Kate, I don't dare come over to your ranch right now. I need a neutral place. I don't need another dogfight with Chet, which will happen if he finds out I was over at the Donovan Ranch."

"I see…." She had to say yes, she realized. This was for the good of the ranch. "Okay," she said a little breathlessly. "I'll meet you there for dinner at eight tonight?" The thought of going out with Sam made her giddy. The prospect was scary. And wonderful.

He tipped his hat, the corner of his mouth moving into a slight smile. "It's a date, Gal. I'll see you then."

Pressing her hand against her pounding heart, Kate watched Sam turn the horse around and trot back down the hill toward his crew. What had she just done? It was for the ranch, she chided sternly. It wasn't a date. But Sam had just called it that. And he'd called her by that endearment, Gal. Her hands shook as she picked up the reins and mounted Cinnamon.

There was no sense riding down the slope to repair the rest of the wire, because Sam's crew was coming to fix it. She turned her mare around and went in the opposite direction. There was plenty of wire to be fixed at the other end. As she rode that way, her mind spun. She had refused to leave the ranch last week when Rachel and Jessica wanted to take her shopping in Sedona. Kate just didn't want prying eyes on her. She was too well-known, her past too fresh and herself too raw to handle those accusing stares she knew she'd get.

Now she was glad her sisters had purchased several skirts and two dresses for her during their shopping spree. At the time, she'd told them the new clothes would probably gather dust in her closet, that she really didn't want to go to town or dress up. Well, now she did. Less than a week later! Kate shook her head. Which outfit would she wear tonight?

Sam couldn't stop staring at Kate as she walked into the Muse Restaurant promptly at eight p.m. She looked stunning in a dark brown corduroy skirt that hung to her ankles and a dark blue denim jacket with deerskin fringe hanging from each shoulder. The jacket was tailored so that it emphasized Kate's slim waist, and there was ivory-colored hairbone pipe, four inches long, on each side of the elk buttons. Around her throat was a five-strand hairbone-pipe choker, and on her ears, she wore long elk-bone earrings decorated with red, blue, yellow and black beads, the Eastern Cherokee colors. The dangling earrings only emphasized Kate's long, slender neck. As she walked proudly, the fringe on her gold deerskin shoulder bag swung gently. Sam smiled. She still looked like an Indian, even with her short hair.

If Kate was worried about other people, it didn't show.

Her shoulders were back, her chin lifted with pride, and her sky blue eyes glistened with gold flecks. He took off his hat as she approached the lobby where he'd waited. As she stepped up to him, he caught a faint whiff of a flowery fragrance. Even though Kate wore no makeup, she was the prettiest woman in the very popular restaurant.

He grinned. "Are you the same Kate Donovan I saw this morning stringing barbed wire?" he teased.

Breathlessly, Kate gazed up at him. "I clean up pretty good—is that what you're saying?" She gripped the deerskin handbag hard, her knuckles white, she was sure. Caught between worrying what the Sedona townspeople thought of her and Sam's glittering appraisal of her, she felt nothing but panic. Stepping closer to him, however, she felt protected in some ways. In other ways, she did not.

Hat in his left hand, he placed his right hand on the small of her back as the hostess hurried over to seat them. "Gal, you're decked out like a show filly for a class A horse show and you just took grand prize."

She laughed softly at his drawled comment. "Only another rancher would know that was a compliment, Sam McGuire." How feminine she felt!

The look he gave her, that smoldering gray gaze, made her feel deliciously sensual in her new clothes. As they followed the hostess through the restaurant, part of Kate's worry about prying eyes melted away beneath Sam's steadying hand. His touch was healing. Provocative. Necessary to her. Miraculously, as they were seated in a black leather booth in a dimly lit corner, Kate felt her fears of going out in public abate to a large degree.

Sam ordered hot coffee and so did she as they looked over the extensive menu of food reputed to be the best New Orleans cooking in the Southwest. Glancing at him over the edge of the menu, Kate studied Sam. He wore a tobacco brown suede blazer, a crisp white cotton shirt, a bolo tie with a dark green, crystalline stone Kate recognized to be diopside, a mineral found in copper mines. His dark hair gleamed in the light, and his face was clean shaven. He'd obviously taken pains to be at his best. Even his nails were blunt cut and scrupulously clean though a cowboy's hands were usually rough and callused, with the red clay of the Arizona desert under his nails. When he'd guided her to the table earlier, she'd inhaled the odor of soap and that special scent of him as a man.

The low lighting in the quiet but busy restaurant made Kate feel as if she and Sam were the only two people in the world. As she circumspectly looked around, she realized that she didn't recognize anyone. That made her feel relief. No prying eyes. No accusations. Just Sam and her. Together. Alone.

Setting the menu aside, she laughed a little nervously. "I feel like déjà vu."

Sam looked up from his menu. "Oh?"

Shrugging delicately, Kate whispered, "Like we were teenagers again. Kids. Like so many years hadn't gone by."

He put the menu down and held her warm blue gaze. He saw such life in Kate's eyes. And, just as he had in the past, he reached out, his fingers capturing hers. "Some things time can't destroy," he told her in a low voice laced with feeling. "What we had, Kate, was good. The best. I never forgot it. I never forgot you."

Chapter 7

As inconspicuously as possible, Kate pressed her palms flat against the linen napkin in her lap to get rid of the nervous dampness. Sam was too close, too virile, and too many memories of what had been—and would never be in the future—were flowing unchecked. Every time she looked at his scarred hands as they played with his coffee cup, she recalled his hands upon her, loving her; she recalled soaring with him in the beauty of their untrammeled passion. Somehow she had to put a stop to this flood of memories and feelings.

"Is Old Man Cunningham making your last two weeks miserable?" she asked.

Sam smiled a little, enjoying the way the shadows lovingly caressed Kate's oval face. "Chet's the one acting out for his daddy. He's got a busted nose, so I think he'll back off now, but with him, I'm never sure."

"A hothead is a hothead," Kate said wryly, managing a one-cornered smile.

"You're not a hothead, Kate. You're a passionate woman who lives her beliefs and isn't afraid to put her money where her mouth is. Chet, on the other hand, is a spoiled kid gone sour. His daddy has contributed to his continuing ways."

She sighed. "That was one of the things I was worried about when I came back here—what people would think of me. When I realized you were going to pick me up, I was so frightened." Kate met and held his warm gray gaze. "That was silly of me, looking back on it now. You've always given people a lot of rope to hang themselves with. Even back in high school, you never bad-mouthed anyone. You never said they were useless or bad or—"

"You thought I'd think you were bad, Kate, because you went to prison?"

Avoiding his gaze, she nodded. She placed her hands around the coffee cup, her voice low. "I thought the worst. Kelly always said I had a bad streak in me. He blamed my rebellious nature on my mother's side of the family."

Reaching out, Sam laid his hand over hers. "Kate, life makes people misbehave. They aren't born 'bad.' Take a look at that black stallion of yours. Over the years, when Kelly was drunk, he beat that poor animal. When I was there, I put a stop to it, but the stud is mean now, and he doesn't trust humans. That horse is seen as 'bad' by an outsider, maybe, but knowing that Gan got the tar beat out of him, we know he isn't really." Sam smiled and caught her wary gaze.

"Same can be said of you. Kelly had a lot of failings

and he usually blamed them on other people when he could. You were firstborn, and you got it in the neck. Don't let him calling you bad keep rubbing you raw."

She pulled her hand from beneath his, the need for him overpowering and heady. "I went to prison, Sam. That will be with me until the day I die. There's plenty of folks around here that won't let me forget it."

"So? Are you going to live your life for them or live life for yourself?"

He was right. She took a nervous sip of the coffee. "I'm running scared. I'm jumpier than I ought to be. What I need to do is forget about what other people think and put that energy into saving the ranch."

Leaning back in the chair, Sam nodded. "That's the spirit. You have time now, Kate. And I'm sure there will be folks who say things about you, or look at you funny, but just keep your back straight, your shoulders squared and walk proud. If you don't, this will destroy you."

"I know...."

Sam leaned forward and placed his hands on the table. The waitress came and they gave their orders. He was privately pleased Kate ordered the same meal he did—lamb, mashed sweet potatoes and a salad. After the salads arrived, he moved to another topic that interested him.

"You know, I don't know much about your sisters' businesses. You said they're coming back to the ranch six months and a year from now, but what will they do?"

Kate played with her salad, her appetite gone. She nibbled on the romaine lettuce half-heartedly. "Rachel is a homeopath. That's an alternative medicine that's practiced around the world and gaining popularity here in the U.S.—again. Rachel said that one out of every five doctors here by the turn of the century was a homeopath. And then the AMA came in and things got more political. There was squabbling in the ranks of homeopaths, and they lost out. By 1940, there were very few left. Now," Kate said more brightly, "there's a goodly number of them in the U.S."

"She's coming back to hang out her shingle in Sedona?" Sam ventured. He enjoyed Kate's company. She was relaxing now and he saw the eagerness and excitement dancing in her eyes.

"Not exactly," Kate hedged, placing the half-eaten salad aside. "Rachel's had this dream of founding a clinic for the poor and the elderly. She wants to practice from the ranch. We've got one building, a real old one, that needs a lot of work, but it could, over time, be turned into a clinic."

"And that's how she'll make money?"

"Kind of… She has had a thriving practice over in London and gets paid well for teaching at Sheffield College. The clinic is going to be on a donation basis, so Rachel won't earn a whole lot."

Sam frowned. "Is her idealism getting in the way of reality? If you three ladies don't pool your resources and add to a common till, you won't be able to keep that place afloat. There're too many maintenance costs involved. The cattle—"

Holding up her hand, she said, "I know, I know…." Kate looked up at the ceiling briefly. "This is Rachel's dream. She's worked a long time to make it a reality. I can't just tell her no." Looking at his scowling features, she added, "I was hoping that when you got over here, you and I could sit down and create a long-range business plan on how to continue making the monthly mortgage payments on that land Kelly bought when we were kids. That acreage is what is hurting us financially. The ranch is paid for in full, but that land isn't."

"Running a ranch daily takes a lot of cash flow," Sam said. "Vet bills alone will eat you alive if something goes through a cattle or horse herd."

"Or drought, like we have right now," Kate agreed. "If we didn't have water rights to Oak Creek, I don't know how the cattle would fare."

"You'd have to sell them off or have them die of thirst," Sam told her.

Kate nodded. "It's funny how all this knowledge of ranching is coming back to me, Sam. I thought I'd forgotten it." She held up her hands. "Look, blisters. My hands have grown soft over time."

He captured one hand. Her fingers were long and he saw red blisters here and there on her palms. "You've been digging post holes?" Many of the main corrals at the ranch were in dire need of being replaced.

With a laugh, she nodded. "Sure shows, doesn't it?"

Grinning, he reluctantly released her hand. "Ranching isn't for wimps," he agreed. Looking up, he saw the waitress coming with their main course. "I don't know about you, Gal, but I'm starved. Let's dig in."

Kate hadn't realized how much fun she would have with Sam tonight. It was as if they were teenagers in love again. He spun story after story over their delicious meal of lamb chops. Sometimes she laughed so hard her stomach hurt.

Sam waved his fork in the air. "Have you seen a black cat hanging around your barn yet?"

Wiping her eyes, Kate said, "Yes, he's like a shadow."

"That's One Ear. I don't know how old he is, but

he's been the ranch mascot since the time I was there. I saw him the other day and was surprised he was still alive. One Ear hunts pack rats, exclusively. I don't see many cats living too long doing that, but he's made it an art form."

Kate knew that Arizona had some of the largest rats in the nation—pack rats. They could get to be the size of a cottontail rabbit, and cats often lost the battle to them as a result. Pack rats were a real problem, especially when they found an entrance beneath a house or up into an attic. They would chew through wiring, setting a house on fire while electrocuting themselves, or eat through a wooden frame and drywall. They were highly destructive, not to mention disease carriers of the first order.

"I'm glad One Ear is around."

"You should be. That cat is ornery, but then, hunting pack rats has made him that way. I remember one time Kelly was drunker than a skunk and he weaved his way out to the barn to feed the horses. I guess One Ear was up in the rafters of the barn, going hell-bent-for-leather after a pack rat. Well, the rat lost its balance going across a beam that Kelly was under, and it landed on him. About a split second later, One Ear landed on Kelly's back to get to the pack rat. I heard Kelly shouting and cursing a blue streak and went running out to the barn to find out what was going on."

Sam chuckled. "Kelly was lying in the aisle of the stable area, twisting, squirming and shouting. One Ear was leaping and hissing. What had happened, as near as I can put together, was the pack rat landed on Kelly's shoulder and made a dive down the collar of his shirt. That black cat was biting, swiping and clawing at Kelly's backside, where the pack rat was trying to hide. Kelly was shrieking and hitting at his back with his hand, and rolling around on the floor, trying to get the cat to quit attacking him."

Kate put her hands to her mouth to stop from laughing too loudly. She loved Sam's face as he told a story; he lost that usual hardness, that implacable look. His gray eyes danced with humor; his mouth hitched into a grin.

"What happened?"

"Well," Sam drawled, wiping his mouth with a napkin and putting his plate aside, "I saw the pack rat zoom out the bottom of Kelly's shirt, which was in shreds at this point from One Ear's clawing attacks. It took off under a box stall and so did the cat. Kelly was lying there in a daze, swearing. His shirt was in shreds. He was a little bloodied, so I took him to the water trough outside and I threw him in it."

"You threw Kelly in it?" Kate's eyes grew round at the picture that presented. Few people ever stood up to Kelly. Obviously, Sam had.

"Better believe it. I got some soap, took off what was left of that rag of a shirt and scrubbed the hell out of his back while he cursed and swore some more."

"Kelly wasn't known to be grateful to anyone," Kate said. "Did he get any diseases from that pack rat?"

"No, just a tread-marked backside was all. After that, he hated One Ear. He wanted to shoot the cat, but I wouldn't let him. When I got fired, I thought about trying to find One Ear and take him with me, but he's wild and won't go up to a man. It was nice to see him still at the ranch."

"Yes," Kate said with a chuckle, "he survived Kelly, too."

A deep voice interrupted their banter. "Well, well, what's this? The ex-con out on the town?"

Kate's heart squeezed in sudden terror. She looked up toward the source of the male voice. Chet Cunningham stood there leaning against the booth, his nose bandaged, both his eyes blackened. He held a beer in one hand, his dark gaze stripping her.

Sam lifted his head and looked up at Cunningham. "Chet," he said in a low, warning growl, "I'd suggest you amble back to the bar where you came from and leave us alone."

Smirking, Chet raised the bottle to his lips and took a good long gulp from it. Wiping his mouth with the back of his hand, he grinned wickedly. "Now, McGuire, you might be boss on the ranch, but here you're nothing. I don't have to do what you want." He straightened up, lightly touching the bandage on his nose. "You broke it."

"I'll break it again if you don't leave."

Kate's heart pounded in her chest. She felt shaky. Darting a look around, she realized that most of the people in the restaurant were staring at them. Her worst fear had just come true.

Chet took another swig of the beer. "Big, tough bastard, aren't you, McGuire?" His lips lifted in a sneer as he leaned over the booth. "Well, I'm not afraid of you, mister. I never was." He glared at Kate. "You two rattlers deserve one another. Katie Donovan," he crowed in a loud voice. "Man, she's gonna blow up Sedona now that she's home." He weaved backward, caught himself and leaned over the booth again. "Blowin' up a nuke plant, huh? Man alive, you're a terrorist of the first order. Who you gonna take care of next? The bank that owns your broken-down ranch? The hay-and-feed company Kelly owes thousands of dollars to? Hell, you're just like your old man—no good...."

At that instant, Kate felt rather than saw Sam get to his feet. He reached out and grabbed Chet by the collar of his shirt.

"That's enough," Sam snarled, spinning the younger cowboy around.

Kate saw Chet lift the beer bottle in reaction. She opened her mouth to scream a warning. Too late! She saw the bottle smash against Sam's upraised hand as he protected himself from the coming blow. Glass shattered everywhere. Within moments, Sam had dragged Cunningham to the side door and pushed him out.

Hurrying, Kate left the booth and followed them.

"You son of a bitch!" Chet roared, sprawled out on the concrete sidewalk. "I'll kill you!"

McGuire leaned over him and poked him in the shoulder with his index finger. "You get up and I'll break the rest of your face, Chet. Lie there and get a hold of yourself." Breathing hard, he saw Kate approaching. Damn!

Chet glared up at him. "You're a dead man, McGuire. Deader than hell. You just don't know it yet."

Pain began to drift up Sam's left hand where the beer bottle had struck him full force. Chet had been aiming at the side of his head, and the cowboy could have taken out Sam's left eye if he hadn't reacted when he did. He saw that Chet's round face was red and flushed. Cunningham was so damned drunk he couldn't get up if he tried. More important, Sam worried about Kate, who stood slightly apart, her hand pressed against her mouth, her eyes huge with terror—and pain. A lot of pain. Damn Chet and his big mouth.

Turning, Sam took Kate by the arm and gently steered her toward the parking lot at the rear of the restaurant. He'd get her to the truck, then go back, pick up his Stetson and pay the bill. "Come on," he said, "let's go."

Kate hurried to keep up with his long stride. "I'm sorry, Sam. This was my fault."

"Like hell," he muttered, opening the truck door for her. "Chet's been moody all his life. Me leaving the ranch has made him meaner than usual." He searched her pale features, her broken spirit obvious in her darkened eyes. "I'm sorry this happened, Kate. I really am. Consider the source. Chet's drunk. He's stupid."

"I saw the other people. I saw their faces...."

Angrily, Sam whispered, "Kate, let it go! Stop giving your power away to Chet or anyone else who might think less of who you really are." His adrenaline was making him shaky. He was furious at Chet for hurting Kate. "I'll be back in a minute. Just sit here." He opened the door to his pickup.

Kate nodded and climbed in. She clutched the deerskin purse in her lap. With the door closed, the silence inside the truck was suffocating. Closing her eyes, she tried to deal with the pain that Chet's attack had brought up. In a few minutes, she opened her eyes and saw Sam's large, dark figure emerging from the restaurant. Chet was still lying on the sidewalk, probably passed out. Sam moved around him, heading for the truck, and Kate tried to pull herself together. She didn't want Sam to know just how shaken she really was. He climbed in the driver's seat, and in the gloomy light, she saw his left hand. Dark blood was streaming down his fingers.

"You're hurt," she said in a choked voice, taking several tissues from her purse.

Sam shut the truck door. "Yeah, he got me with that bottle," he grumbled, holding his hand up and looking at it more closely. The blood dripped onto his Levi's. When Kate's hands captured his and she pressed the tissue to the cut, all the anger went out of him. She was leaning against him, close and warm, and her care and attention pulled the plug on his fury toward Chet. Inhaling sharply, he could smell that light, flowery fragrance she wore on her skin. Her soft, thick hair brushed against his jaw as she peered closely at the wound. He felt her breast press against his right arm, her thigh against his. Biting back a groan, he sat very still as she worked to stop the bleeding. His body ached. For her. All of her. In the years since he'd seen her, Kate had matured physically. Now he was wildly aware of her firm flesh against his, the womanly strength, yet incredibly gentle touch of her hands on his.

He hungered for her. As she unbuttoned the cuff of his shirtsleeve and pushed it up his arm, he wanted to lean across those scant inches between them and kiss her exposed neck.

"Sam, this is bad," Kate said, wobbling. "That beer bottle sliced you open. We have to get you to the hospital to get this cleaned up and stitched."

Groaning, but not because of his cut, he muttered, "Let me wrap it in a handkerchief and you can clean it up once we get home."

Kate twisted her head toward him. How close Sam was! She stared, mesmerized for a second, her gaze on his strong, compressed mouth. She saw dots of perspiration on his upper lip. As his gaze lifted and she met his dark gray eyes, a bolt of heat surged through her. Her lips parted. How badly she wanted to kiss him, to feel his mouth once again on hers. And then, just as quickly, she pulled away. How selfish of her at a moment like this—when Sam was hurt—to be thinking of such things.

"Give me your hanky," she said, moving away from him. "And let me drive. You can make it up to me tomorrow by driving me back to pick up my car."

Sam didn't argue, the cut in his hand hurting like hell itself. He climbed out of the pickup, made a couple of tight wraps around his hand with the handkerchief and allowed Kate to climb into the driver's seat. He saw the worry on her face.

"This isn't anything, Kate," he protested as he climbed into the passenger seat.

"Yes, it is," she whispered fiercely. Backing the truck out of the parking lot and driving into the November darkness, Kate felt some of her trembling abate. With both hands on the wheel, she drove away from Sedona. Away from all the staring, prying eyes that had judged her. And Sam had defended her. Now gossip would spread about him. His reputation was unsullied up to now, she was sure. He didn't deserve to be dragged down in the mud because of her own bad name.

She wanted to get back home just as soon as possible. At least at the ranch, there was safety.

"This is going to hurt," Kate warned Sam as she sat down at the kitchen table. Stitching up animals was one thing. Doing the same for a human being unstrung her a little. Sam sat there, his coat off, the sleeve of his shirt rolled up haphazardly on his dark, hairy arm so that she could get a good look at the damage the beer bottle had done.

Sam watched Kate's face. Her brow puckered and her mouth thinned as she gently laid his hand on a clean white towel. Most of the bleeding had stopped by the time they'd gotten home, but a good two-inch gash was laid open on the outside edge of his left hand. He felt the soft coolness of her fingers against the throbbing heat of his hand.

"You know," he told her huskily as she prepared to stitch the wound closed, "every time you touch me, Kate, the pain in my hand goes away."

Taking a deep breath, Kate put on thin surgical gloves so that she wouldn't infect the just-cleaned wound. "I think this cut is making you loco, Sam Mc-Guire."

He grinned a little. "No, Gal, its you—your healing touch." *It's always been you,* he thought. When Kate lifted her head and looked at him, he saw tears in her eyes. She quickly forced them back and concentrated on the task at hand. Sam decided to remain quiet and watch her work. There was such gentle delicacy to Kate. He wished that she would realize that about herself. Kelly had really hurt her as a child growing up. One day, Sam hoped she'd let those tough, outer walls dissolve so that the old Kate, the real Kate he'd known and loved so fiercely, would emerge.

As she began to stitch up his wound, Sam said in a low voice, "You haven't lost your touch, Kate. Maybe you don't recall this, but I remember times you took care of sick and ailing animals and they always survived. Your two sisters are both in the healing arts. But you're like Odula—you heal with your touch. You don't need a homeopathic remedy or a natural essence." He smiled a little, enjoying her focused care. "A healer. That's you, Kate."

Grimacing, Kate kept her attention on the process. Sam's hand was so large, his flesh work-hardened. She felt each of the thick calluses that over time had built up on the palm of his hand and his fingers.

"Right now, I'd like to punch Chet Cunningham in the nose. What he did was wrong, Sam. You're going to be laid up with this hand a good three weeks. He really hamstrung you."

"Not too much work for one-handed cowboys, is there?"

She glanced up and caught his boyish grin. Returning to her task, she muttered, "Not really. Old Man Cunningham will probably give you walking papers sooner rather than later."

"So?" he teased. "Just lets me come over here sooner and be a crippled cowboy helping you."

She laughed and felt the tension draining away from her. "No kidding! No post hole digging for you."

"But I can use the time and work out a solid business plan for you."

Kate shook her head. "Sam McGuire, I swear if the good Lord gave you mud to work with, you'd find a way to market and sell mud pies and make a profit doing it!"

Chuckling, he leaned back and closed his eyes. Kate's touch was more than healing, it was opening up his heart and letting him hope for a future with her. Not that he deserved a second chance. Sam knew he didn't, but his heart cried out for her still. "Now, Gal, there's always a silver lining to every cloud. You know that."

Glumly, Kate shook her head as she finished. Taking the white roll of gauze, she carefully wrapped the wound. "Hope? I lost that a long time ago, Sam." Soon his hand was swathed in a protective dressing. Pleased with her efforts, Kate sat up and took the plastic gloves off and dropped them in the waste basket. In the bright light of the kitchen, Sam looked a little washed out. She suspected he was in a lot more pain than he let on.

"Rachel gave me this homeopathic first-aid kit," she said, opening it up on the kitchen counter. Pulling out a small booklet, she opened it to read. "She said there's information on remedies that I could use around the ranch, both on people and animals. Let me see if there's one here for you."

Sam sat there, his long legs sprawled out. "My hand feels pretty good now."

"Hmm, here's something." Kate brought the kit over to the table and sat down. "It says for cuts to use calendula. Interesting," she said looking up at him. "That's a flower something like a marigold. Anyway, calendula is for open cuts and lacerations. It helps them heal up faster. The only time it can't be used is in a puncture wound."

"Well, give me some," Sam urged. "I don't want to be crippled for three weeks with this thing."

Opening one of the small amber bottles, Kate poured six or seven small white pellets into his hand. "You're supposed to put these in your mouth and let them melt away."

Dutifully, Sam did as he was told. He didn't care if the homeopathic remedy worked or not. For him, just getting to spend time with Kate was all that mattered. She sat watching him expectedly.

"There. I feel better already."

She laughed and it was a sound without strain. "What a fibber you are."

He joined her laughter. In that moment, he felt that familiar closeness he and Kate had shared with one another so long ago. Some of the color had come back to the high slope of her cheeks. Her large blue eyes were no longer shadowed. Sam thought he saw flecks of happiness dancing in their depths. Because of him? Because they were together? He wasn't sure.

The last thing he wanted to do was leave. But he had to. Rising slowly, he smiled down at her. "I *do* feel better." Reaching out, he grazed the soft, warm skin of her cheek. "But it's because of you, Kate. It always has been…."

He saw her eyes widen—beautifully—and he saw desire in her gaze. For him? It was the first time he'd seen that look since they were in high school. When she placed her hand lightly and tentatively against his chest, his flesh tightened instantly. With a groan, he leaned down.

Kate felt his hand still against her cheek, rough, stimulating and making her want him with every cell in her screaming, hungry body. Without thinking, she flexed her fingers against his chest. How badly she wanted to kiss Sam! Looking up through her lashes, she saw his gray eyes burning with raw need of her. Instantly, her breath caught. She read the intent in his narrowed eyes. He was going to kiss her! Why, after all these years, would he want to do that? Her past was so shameful— how could he want her now? The thoughts dissolved the moment his mouth made hot contact with her parting lips.

Suddenly, Kate didn't care any longer. She lost herself in the masterful power of his searching mouth. His breath was warm and moist as it flowed across her cheek. His hand guided her and tilted her head just enough so that he could fully enjoy her. The taste of him was wonderful, his mouth strong without hurting her. Oh, how Kate had needed his touch! With a soft moan, she found herself a willow leaning against the hard planes of his body. His fingers moved through her hair and she felt his other arm encircling her waist and bringing her against him.

All she'd ever wanted, Kate discovered as she returned his searching, tender kiss, was Sam. The years stood between them and yet, miraculously, they melted away. His mouth curved and followed the line of her lips as they yielded to his sweet, molten assault. Her senses reeled and then exploded outward like the heat flowing through her, making her shaky, making her want him in every possible way. His hands felt strong and steadying against her head, against her bottom as he cupped her body to his. She absorbed his strength and felt his harsh control at the same time. There was no mistaking the fact that he was fully aroused. As she eagerly returned his kiss, lost in the light of explosions moving like a golden haze throughout her, all she wanted was to consume him as he wanted to consume her.

And then reality hit Kate. All the old memories, the shame, the fact that she'd led such a bad life, avalanched upon her. As she pulled away, she realized that Sam's kiss had been born out of the excitement of the night's activities—of Chet's attack upon him. That was all.

Nothing more. People often did crazy things after a trauma. Hurt flowed through Kate as she stepped away, her fingers touching her wet, throbbing lips. Her heart was thudding hard in her breast. Her flesh prickled everywhere he had touched her.

As she looked up, she saw the molten look in Sam's eyes. At the same time, she saw a question in his gaze and then disappointment. It was obvious to her that he was sorry he'd kissed her. She wasn't. But that didn't matter, she realized as she took another step away from him.

Sam reached over for his cowboy hat, which rested on the table. His body ached like fire itself. He saw the pain in Kate's eyes, the way she was looking at him. How could he blame her? He'd overstepped his bounds completely with her. There was no way she could want him back in her life on a personal basis.

"I'd better go," he said roughly.

As he moved through the darkened living room, heading for the front door, Sam cursed himself. Why had he kissed Kate? Why? All it had done was hurt her. What a selfish bastard he was.

Chapter 8

Sam knocked several times at the door to the main ranch house but there was no answer. The light was on in the study, where Kate spent a lot of time when she wasn't at his side working hard from dawn to dusk. By this time, she was usually in bed. When he'd left the barn after tending to a number of calves that had recently been born, he saw the lights at the house were still burning. Concerned, he'd decided to drop by.

Looking up to the sky, he saw white flakes start to come down on the gusts of wind. It was late December now, nearly midnight, and the sky was spitting ice crystals that he knew would turn to snow any minute now. After a two-year drought, all of a sudden rain and now snow were being dumped on them.

After a moment's hesitation, he quietly entered the house and shut the door, taking off his damp hat and hanging it on a peg next to the entry. After he shook the accumulated ice crystals off his sheepskin jacket, he carefully wiped his boots on the rug in front of the door.

"Kate?" His voice rang oddly through the house. Sam waited a moment, sensitive about giving Kate her space, but didn't hear her reply. Ever since that kiss, things had been tentative between them. Sometimes he saw sadness in Kate's eyes. Other times desire—for him. He wasn't sure what was going on, and he was too scared to confront her about it. His gut told him to back off, wait and be patient. Despite his regrets about ruining what might have been for them, Sam found himself hoping for some kind of future that included Kate. He had no business thinking such a thing. His head was clear on why. His heart, however, had a mind of its own. Scowling, he walked toward the office, which was situated on the north side of the house.

The door was open, as always, and the light spilled out into the gloom of the darkened hallway. He placed his hand on the doorjamb and halted at the entrance. His face softened. With the accounting books opened before her Kate was fast asleep. His mouth compressed with concern. Sam knew she was worried about the money. He could see a lot of paper wadded up and littered around the chair where she sat sleeping. Money. Wasn't it always money? The ranch teetered on a thin line between disaster and survival, thanks to mounting feed prices, a drought that had wiped out normal food supplies, a heavy bank debt and constant need for materials for fences and the like.

Kate had her Pendleton jacket hung over the back of the chair. She wore a light pink flannel shirt and a pair of jeans, muddied from helping him calve hours

earlier. Her feet were encased in thick, pink socks and
her muddy cowboy boots sat on some newspaper next
to the antique oak desk. An ache built inside Sam's
lower body as he absorbed her soft features. Kate was
allowing her hair to grow, and it was slightly curled and
ruffled around her face. Beneath the light, he saw the
reddish highlights. Her lips… Inwardly, he groaned. Her
mouth was one of her finest attributes, in his opinion.
So soft and kissable. He ached to kiss her again. If it
ever happened—and his heart certainly hoped for that
opportunity—it had to be Kate who initiated the kiss,
not him. Sam was damned if he was going to be like a
thief in the night, stealing from Kate once again. He'd
hurt her once and he swore he would never do it again.

Worried about the flush he saw blooming on her
cheeks just below her thick lashes, Sam thought about
how Kate had been using every bit of her physical
strength to keep this ranch going. She was up at four
a.m. every day. By ten p.m., she was usually so exhausted she weaved when she walked. On most nights
she was in bed shortly thereafter. Yes, he had her pattern of living down pat. The foreman's house sat three
hundred feet away from the main house, so he couldn't
help but notice such things. His hours were the same as
hers, but he was used to the brutal demands of ranching. Kate had just jumped in and was still adjusting.

Sam wanted time with her—quality time. But there
had been no opportunities. A series of disasters had occurred as soon as he'd quit the Cunningham Ranch and
come over to her ranch. A late thunderstorm had blown
up a day after he'd arrived, and lightning had struck
nearby, starting a small fire. Fire was always a worry
here and the sudden blaze had destroyed three hundred

acres before the borate bombers flown in from Phoenix had gotten it under control. All the fence posts had to be removed and replaced with new posts and wire, to keep the cattle from wandering onto Cunningham property.

And then prices on feed shot out of sight, and supplies took a much larger chunk of money. It was as if the bleeding at the ranch changed to a hemorrhage. The effect of the drought in the Midwest, where the wheat, oats and corn were grown, had finally reached Sedona and managing the ranch finances became a juggling act for Kate. She had to rob Peter to pay Paul, as she put it.

The cattle could go without grain, but the young Arabian horses could not if they were to get the nutrition they needed for strong bones in such a desert environment.

How peaceful Kate looked sleeping, Sam thought as he quietly moved closer. He remembered her sleeping in his arms so very long ago. At that time, her hair had been long, halfway to her waist, and he recalled how thick and silky it lay against his chest as she nestled her head in the crook of his shoulder to sleep. An ache spread throughout him at the memory and Sam laughed at himself, stopping inches from where Kate was sleeping. The last six weeks had been a living hell for him. *Hell.* They were so busy trying to keep things going, that they rarely saw one another except while vetting and caring for the animals which wasn't often enough for him.

Sam leaned over and lightly touched the curls near her unmarred brow. His fingers itched to graze the slope of her cheek. *No.* He couldn't. That wouldn't be fair to Kate. He pulled his hand back and allowed it to drop to his side.

When he'd moved into the foreman's house, Kate had helped him unpack some of the boxes. In one, she found the framed photo of Chris, his son. In another, a photo of Carol. He'd seen the look on her face, the pain and sadness as she put the pictures aside. Frustration moved through him. How could he get Kate to understand that he was interested in her? She had shown no overt signs of interest in him, that was for sure. Yet she'd returned his kiss just as eagerly and passionately as he'd explored her delicious mouth.

Releasing a long breath of air, Sam got an idea. He saw the white snowflakes striking the window just beyond the desk. Yes, maybe it would work. Maybe he could devise a way to get Kate to rest, even for part of a day. She desperately needed a small vacation of sorts. Christmas was only two days away and he'd seen two presents sitting on the coffee table in the living room, but no tree was up. Maybe his idea would work.

Gently, he closed his hand over Kate's shoulder and squeezed slightly.

"Kate?" Sam realized just how deeply she was sleeping when she didn't respond to his call. He saw the beginnings of shadows beneath her eyes. She was working herself, literally, to the bone. Matter of fact, she'd lost a good fifteen pounds in the process, from what he could see. The hollow of her cheeks was more pronounced, the flesh tighter against her sloping bones. They were working so hard that they ate on the run or grabbed whatever was easily available. In reality, they needed four wranglers plus themselves to keep this ranch at operating level. Could the two of them continue this murderous pace until next June, when Jessica arrived home?

Sam leaned over, extending his large hand across the

soft smoothness of her shoulders. He could feel how firm and physically fit the ranch work had made her. "Gal? It's time to go to bed." He gave her a small shake. Her lashes fluttered and she moaned softly. The beginnings of a tender smile pulled at Sam's mouth as he watched her start to surface from her deep sleep. "Come on, Kate. You can't sleep over the accounting books. You need to get a bath and go to bed...."

Kate felt more than heard Sam's low, vibrating voice. She loved the deep tone of his voice because it always made her feel safe and nurtured. His hand was on her shoulder, gently moving in a slow, provocative circle. Was she dreaming again? Dreaming of his loving her? How wonderful his strong fingers felt against her sore, tired back. Forcing her eyes open, she raised her head. Sam's shadowy features made her blink. Sitting upright suddenly, she felt him remove his hand.

"What's wrong? Does one of the new calves have a problem?" she asked in a muffled tone.

"Whoa, there's no crisis," Sam said, holding up his hand.

He forced himself to take a step back as she sat up and rubbed her eyes. "Everything's fine. I saw the light on in here. It's not like you to be up this late, so I knocked on the door." He smiled a little and rested his long fingers across his hips. "I found you asleep on the books there. It's midnight, Gal. You need to be in bed."

Her skin felt like it was glowing everywhere he'd touched her. Kate was barely functioning. Her heart, all her sleepy senses, were hanging on Sam's husky voice and his nearness. He rarely came into her house. Blinking to drive her exhaustion away, Kate rubbed her face.

"Oh...thanks, Sam.... I was just trying to find some

extra money. I was thinking that maybe I didn't add or subtract right...."

Kate looked utterly vulnerable in that moment as she sat there, her hands curved across her thighs. He wanted to sweep her into his arms, carry her to the bedroom, lay down with her and simply hold her against him until she dropped off to sleep. She needed some holding, some attention, and he knew it. This ranch was extruding every emotion she had out of her. He knew Kate was taking the success or failure of the ranch on her shoulders. It wasn't right, but that's what she was doing. She still felt such guilt over her past that she was probably using the ranch as a way to right old wrongs.

Grimly, Sam said, "I want you to sleep in tomorrow, Kate. I'll get up and do the feeding. Then, when I'm done, you and I are going to saddle up a couple of horses and we're going up into the canyon."

She stared at him. "What?"

He gestured to the ledger books spread out on the desk. "This ranch is bleeding you dry, Kate. I want you to take a day off. Sleep in tomorrow morning, have a nice, leisurely breakfast. I'll drop by when I get the chores done."

She smiled and rubbed her brow. "Sounds like heaven to me, Sam McGuire." And then she studied his harsh, unreadable features. "Why are you doing this? You're working twice as hard as I am."

He matched her smile. "Because you need a down day, Gal, that's why. Aren't you a little curious about what we'll be doing up in the canyon?"

Sam's teasing warmed her and she laughed a little as she stood up. "Well, yes...."

Nodding, Sam walked to the door. "Good. I'll see you tomorrow around ten a.m., then."

"This is beautiful!" Kate told Sam with a sigh. They rode together through the dark green Ponderosa pines, which were covered with a cape of fresh white snow. The storm that had raged throughout the night was the first big snowfall of the season. Bundled in her sheepskin coat and gloves, her black Stetson keeping her head warm, Kate smiled over at him. "Prison took so much out of me," she confided, absorbing the majesty of the pines as they rode up the snowy slope.

Sam silently congratulated himself on his idea. Behind his black gelding was a packhorse carrying a surprise picnic lunch, hot chocolate in two large thermoses, an ax and enough rope to bring a spruce tree home for Christmas. The weather was cloudy, the sky roiling with dark and light gray shapes. Every now and again a patch of blue could be seen, and even a surprising glint of yellow sunlight briefly shone before the swift-moving clouds swallowed it up.

"Out here," he told her, "you can not only feel your freedom, you can taste it." The rushing and bubbling of Oak Creek was to their right as they followed it higher up the hill. The heavy scent of pine filled their lungs and Sam drew the fragrance deep into his chest.

Kate reached out, resting her gloved hand on the arm of his sheepskin jacket. "This is heaven, Sam. Heaven," she said. How much she wanted to kiss him again! She was afraid to ask. Afraid to explore the possibilities of why it had happened in the first place. More than likely, the kiss had been a knee-jerk reaction after the fight with Chet. If only it had been for other, more important reasons…

Sam's heart expanded powerfully at her touch. Right now, Kate looked like the eager young girl he'd known before life had tripped her up so badly. Her sky blue eyes shone like those of a child. Her soft lips were parted and expectant. The high color in her cheeks simply made her eyes that much more startling and lovely to look at. Despite the fact that he was losing his heart all over again, he grinned at her.

"Start looking for just the right tree to bring home so we can put it in your living room. Christmas shouldn't be celebrated without one."

Sobering, Kate allowed her hand to rest on her thigh. The steady movement of the horse beneath her was soothing and something she loved. She was afraid to ask, but she was going to anyway. Kate had made every attempt to stay on a business footing with Sam, keeping things from getting personal. She was afraid if she dropped that decorum she might make a fool out of herself. She'd seen those photos of Chris, his son, and Carol, his ex-wife, on top of his television set.

"Sam…do you have plans for Christmas Day?"

Surprised, he looked at her. "Why?"

"W-well…" Kate stumbled over her words. "I just thought that—that Chris might be coming home. You said he was on Christmas break from college and I thought he might be—be visiting you for a while."

He shook his head, noting the wariness in Kate's eyes. "No. He's going to visit Carol in New York City."

"Oh, I see.…"

"You thought he was coming out for the holiday?" Sam had wondered why Kate hadn't mentioned Christmas to him. It was as if she was avoiding the holiday completely, which wasn't like her. He recalled how much she'd loved Christmas in her younger years. Odula had always had a party, inviting many elderly neighbors who could not afford a holiday meal. The Donovan Ranch at one time had been known for its charity work with the poor and elderly, thanks to Odula. When she died, the gift of charity died with her.

"Yes, I thought you might want to spend time with your family," Kate admitted.

Sam shook his head and watched a huge chunk of snow slide off a nearby pine. The wind was still gusty, and the pines ladened with their white covering, began to lose their adornment. "When Carol and I got our divorce, she moved back East. Back to where she was born—New York. I didn't want Chris torn between choosing one or the other of us for holidays. He decided that every other year he could be with me on Christmas. This year, he'll be with Carol and her family."

"I see…." Kate saw a blue jay flit between the pines, its call loud with warning. The horses were beginning to climb steadily, their breath white like steam, shooting from their nostrils.

"How about you?" Sam asked. With the banks of Oak Creek on one side and a heavy brush barrier on the other, they had to ride close together, their legs touching now and then. He didn't mind the closeness and Kate seemed to like it, too.

"Me? Oh… I just arranged for a beef to be sent to the mission in Cottonwood so they would have food to serve to the homeless over Christmas. That steer you took to the packinghouse in Sedona last week is the gift

I'm giving them. They're trucking it down this morning to the mission."

He smiled warmly. "Just like your mother."

Blushing, Kate avoided his hooded gray eyes. She heard the emotion in Sam's deep voice and his approval of her charity. "I want to try and bring back some of the traditions we had when Mom was alive. There's no way we can open the ranch up this year to the elderly. But maybe next year... I always loved being able to help the old ones. They don't all have relations nearby to celebrate with them this time of year. We always had a great time. I know the three of us always looked forward to Christmas Day and all."

Sam remembered very clearly about those times. He'd been part of that special celebration himself when he was going steady with Kate. Odula and her three daughters had worked endlessly in the big kitchen, roasting turkeys, making pot roasts with all the fixin's for the thirty or forty elderly people who would be bussed out to the ranch to enjoy a real family dinner with them. Even Kelly would straighten up his act, get cleaned up and behave.

In that moment, Sam felt the sharpness of his love for Kate. It had never died. It had just hibernated all these years.

Waiting. Just waiting. The joy he heard in her voice as she spoke about helping the elderly, and the golden light dancing in her eyes, made him realize how much he'd missed out on because of his own stupid moment of drunken need. Disgusted with himself, Sam wished he could change the past. He wanted a second chance with Kate.

"Odula's spirit lives on in you, Kate. She'd be proud of you," he murmured.

"Thanks, Sam. I'm beginning to realize how much of my mother is in me and how much I never let grow outside of me." She gestured to the snow-laden pines that surrounded them. "We *always* came up here for a Christmas tree as a family every year. I loved it! All of us on horseback, with a couple of packhorses. We made a picnic and day of it." Her voice grew heavy with feeling. "And you remembered this, didn't you? I'd forgotten. I've forgotten so much that's important...."

He pulled his gelding to a halt and dismounted. Without speaking, Sam placed his hands around her waist and lifted her off her horse. Bracketed by the animals as they were, the movement brought them together. Sam took off his heavy gloves and framed Kate's upturned face. The hope of the world lay in her widening eyes. Wordlessly, her lips parted, just begging to be kissed by him. A fire raged, barely in check, within his aching lower body. He felt the smooth warmth of her skin beneath his hands as he looked deeply into her eyes.

"Maybe a lot of things have changed, Kate," he rasped, feeling the movement of the horse pushing her fully against him. "But people's hearts hold memories. Lots of 'em." He managed a wry, one-sided smile. "My reasons for doing this are plenty. You've been working yourself to the bone. You've lost a lot of weight and I'm worried about that. And your family's traditions are important." Looking deeply into her glistening eyes, he continued, "I feel that in some small way I can help you get back in touch with some of those parts of yourself. Let me help you when I can. I've hurt you once. And God help me, I've never been so sorry. This time around, Kate, I'm going to try and be a positive influence in your life, not one that rips you apart like I did before. If you could just trust me a little, Gal—just a little…" He grimaced and scowled. "I know I'm asking for the moon. You have every right to tell me to go to hell and never look back. I can't change the past, but I can make sure the present is different—better—for you.…"

His rough, callused hands felt so steadying, so right to Kate. Completely off guard because Sam had only been this intimate with her once since she'd come home, Kate pressed against him, feeling the heat and vibrating strength of his powerful body. She heard his words, understood them too well, and allowed his raw emotions to blanket her in those moments out of time. Without thinking, she lifted her hands and enclosed his as they lay against her face. Hot tears spilled from her eyes, trailed down her cool skin and laced through his fingers.

"Don't you realize how good you've already been to me?" she said in a wobbly voice. "You didn't judge me when I came out of prison. Without you, Sam, this ranch would have fallen flat on its face. Look how much you've done." Sniffing, she gave him a trembling smile, becoming lost in his dark, stormy gaze. "The past is done, Sam." She saw a flare of some unknown emotion in his eyes and his fingers tightened briefly against her flesh. "I don't bear any grudges, believe me. We both made mistakes."

Taking a deep, shaky breath, Sam nodded. "What I did to you, Kate, is unforgivable.…"

"You thought I had run away for good," she whispered, allowing her hands to move to his upper arms. "I can understand why you got drunk that night. We loved one another and what I did to you wasn't right. I know that now—hindsight's always twenty-twenty, isn't it?" Her mouth stretched into a sad line. "You made love to Carol out of grief, Sam. That's something else I know and can understand now that I'm older, more mature. I'm sure you weren't expecting her to get pregnant. It probably came as as big a surprise as any you've ever had." She sighed, looking up at him. "At least, you did the right thing. You were responsible to her—and your son. I really admire that, Sam. It says a lot of good things about you. Even though you made a mistake, you rectified it."

Standing here, protected from the chill of the winter air by the warmth of the horses, Kate absorbed the heady scent of the pine and Sam's hands upon her face, and felt as if all her dreams had come true. She reveled in his attention and the care that radiated from him as it began to heal another old wound in her heart, whether he knew it or not.

Using his thumbs, Sam wiped the remnants of tears from Kate's cheeks. Allowing his hands to fall across her proud shoulders, he sighed. "You're right—I didn't fall in love with her," he rasped, holding her gaze. He saw her eyes widened with surprise. "I was shocked by the note you left, but I knew this had been building for a while. Mustangs run when they're threatened, and Kelly had pushed you as far as you could go. Something had to give. And like you said, hindsight is always twenty-twenty." He grimaced. "You ran. You had no choice. I felt so damned helpless. I couldn't protect you from Kelly, or from the hell in that house you had to live in. When I got the note, I knew you meant it. I loved you and I understood, but it made me reel. I got drunk. I did some stupid things. Things I've paid part of my life to try and correct." His hands tightened on her shoulders.

Digesting his admission, Kate studied him in the soft silence of the forest, letting the bubbling sounds of Oak Creek sooth some of her wounded feelings. "You're letting me off too easily, Sam. If I hadn't run away in the first place, none of this would have happened."

Harshly, he whispered, "You saw no other choice at the time, Gal. I never blamed you for what you did. I understood why you did it. I might have been stupid, Kate, but I wasn't going to do what some guys did if they got a girl pregnant. I wasn't going to walk away and pretend it didn't happen." Anger tinged his words. "I really screwed up. I had the best thing in the world, and in one night, I threw it away." His fingers dug into her jacket. "I threw what we had away, Kate, and I've been the sorriest bastard ever since. I take responsibility for my choices. Being drunk was no excuse. Having had a lot of time to look back on it, I realize I was an egotistical fool. I was the star running back of the football team. I liked all the attention Carol gave me. She'd been following me around all year and I liked her attention a little too much."

Standing there against Sam, Kate felt his anguish. "Teenage hormones and a swelled head to boot?"

He nodded and held her wounded gaze. "Yes. A bad combination. Hell, Kate, at that age, what did we know? I didn't realize I already had the woman I wanted to spend a lifetime with. I was careless, and I thought I knew everything. I played with fire and it burned me. Worse, it burned you, too. If I could do it all over again—but hell, it's too late."

"Did you *ever* love Carol?" Kate asked faintly. Her

head swam with the question. How could anyone live for eighteen years with someone they didn't love? That seemed like a horrible prison sentence to her—far worse than the one she'd endured for eighteen months. In one way, Kate was aware of Sam's loyalty and responsibility. Maybe it was his ranch upbringing, where kids were taught from the time they were born that their actions and words carry weight, that their decisions have consequences, and that if they start something, they have to finish it. Maybe it was the code of the Old West, where a man was his word. Where any decision was accepted with the full weight of responsibility to go with it.

Sam allowed his hand to skim the sleeve of her coat. "No. Not real love…" Not like the love for Kate he'd continued to carry in his heart like a torch that refused to go out.

"What a horrible sentence," she whispered.

"Don't feel sorry for me, Gal. I brought it on myself. Carol and I learned to be friends, instead. We had a lot of rough times and we worked on them together. I admire her, too, for what she did for Chris. It says a lot about her commitment and responsibility to the situation." Sam captured Kate's gloved fingers. "What I feel bad about, what I want to repair between us, is what it did to *you*. Somehow I want to make up for all the pain I've caused you, Kate." His mouth became a slash of pain because of all he felt over his stupid actions and decisions. "You were the innocent one in all of this. I saw what life did to you. You ran away from home once and for all soon after graduation. Right after my wedding. You see, I knew your *real* reason for leaving. You left because I'd married Carol."

Feelings surged up through Kate, and she felt a lump

growing in her throat. She wrapped her fingers tightly around his, her other hand resting on his massive chest. "No, Sam," she whispered brokenly, "I didn't leave because you married Carol."

He raised head and studied her intently. "You didn't?" They had been two months away from graduation when everyone in school found out that Carol was pregnant and he was going to marry her. It took only a day for the gossip to fly around the school. Then Sam never saw Kate again. She became like a shadow at school and avoided him completely. They had never gotten to talk after that.

"Only my family knows the real reason why I left, Sam. Kelly was drunk all the time. He and I got into the worst argument we ever had when the police brought me home from Phoenix." Kate moved away from Sam, to her horse, and picked up the reins from the snow-covered ground. Her hands shook. "You never knew what happened, Sam. No one did." She couldn't look at him. Instead, she looked at the tall pines behind his massive frame. "Kelly was afraid all along that you and I were going to run off and get married someday. He said I needed to go to college first and get the education that he never got. This happened the day before I found out you were going to marry Carol. Anyway, Kelly and I got into a yelling match. I told him I didn't want to go to college, that I wanted to stay on the ranch and keep learning how to run it. He got angry. Angrier than I'd ever seen him in a long time. He accused me of going to bed with you—which I had. Before, I'd always avoided telling him and Mother the truth. But that time I did."

Sam stood very still. He saw the anguish in Kate's

face as she held the reins tightly in her fingers and stared down at them.

"What did Kelly do to you?" he asked hoarsely.

"It wasn't pretty," Kate admitted hollowly. "He slapped me across the face and sent me flying."

"That son of a bitch."

"My mother came running in, saw what happened, and she flew into Kelly like a hornet." Kate touched her nose. "That's why it's crooked. He broke it when he hit me."

Sam's hands clenched into fists. "That's why I never saw you again at school? You never showed up for the graduation ceremony, either. I was looking for you... but when I called your house, I got Kelly. He told me to never call again or try to come out to the ranch to see you. He said if I did, he'd shoot me on sight. I took him at his word."

With a strained laugh, Kate nodded and turned to him. "Yes, Kelly was good for his word, wasn't he?" The rage banked in Sam's eyes surprised her. His mouth was set and his hands were clenched in fists at his side. "Rachel, bless her, said nothing at school. We were all too ashamed of it, anyway. She got my assignments, my books, and I finished out the last two months of school at home, on the ranch. Kelly never told me you tried to call me." Kate opened her hands. "What a mess, huh? I got my diploma and left the next day. I took a job in Santa Fe, New Mexico, as a waitress. There, no one knew me. By that time, my nose was healed up. I tried to start a life on my own...."

Wearily, Sam walked up to her. She stood alone, suffering, so proud and so distant from him. "I'm sorry, Kate. So damned sorry. I didn't know any of this...."

She twisted to look up at him and saw the agony clearly written on his features. "After I left home I learned a lot of things over the years, Sam. Especially about having an alcoholic parent. All of us, in our own way, supported Kelly's drinking. We enabled him to carry on and hid from the world the best we could what his drinking did to us."

"It wasn't a secret around Sedona," he muttered.

"Yes, and over time, it just got worse and worse."

A shudder worked through him. "Kate, I'm sorry. For everything."

Her mouth curved faintly as she held his saddened gaze. "I know you are, Sam. You are a good man. You married Carol out of responsibility, not love, in order to give Chris a home and two parents. You yourself were raised by your dad when your mother died giving you birth, so I can understand how important it was to you that your son got the things you didn't."

He nodded. "That's how I felt, Kate. I never knew my mother. I didn't want Chris to grow up without two parents. I knew what it was like and I can't forget the hole that's still in me because of it."

"So you walked into a prison where there was no love, to give him that gift." She shook her head. "I don't think I would've had the guts or the heart to do that, Sam. I admire you for it. I really do."

"I don't regret my choice," Sam said. "Chris is a great boy and I love him as much as life. Carol was and is a good mother to him. We made an agreement early on to do the best we could for his sake." Looking up, Sam saw a bald eagle skimming the tops of the pines along Oak Creek, looking for a noon meal of trout. "She was never happy out West. We agreed a long time ago to divorce once Chris left for college. Our duties to him were over at that point, and he's old enough to understand why we got a divorce. Carol's always wanted a career in photography and now she's got one back in New York City. All's well that ends well."

Kate studied him, aching to reach out and touch his clenched jaw. "What about you, Sam? Are you happy? Are you living your life the way you dreamed about doing? Or maybe you don't have dreams like Carol did?"

He raised his head, a sad smile lifting one corner of his mouth. "My dreams died when you left, Kate." He saw her return his smile, hers soft and edged with shyness.

"Surely you must have at least one left?" she asked.

He shrugged painfully. "None, Kate. I had one hell of a great life when I was a kid in high school. You and I dreamed together of getting married, having a ranch and kids.... Well, that was a long time ago."

Kate nodded, the silence falling gently between them. "If you could dream," she whispered, "what would it be about now?" She held her breath as she watched him wrestle with her question.

"I don't deserve to dream, Kate."

Reaching out, she touched his arm, her fingers curling across the sheepskin coat. "Yes, you do."

Her touch was galvanizing. In that moment, Sam was ready to risk it all. The words came out choked and low. "Then I'd dream of having you back in my life again."

The emotion behind his admission embraced her. Kate saw hope burning in the depths of his gray eyes. "You—would dream of me back in your life?" She found that impossible to believe.

With his thumb, Sam pushed the brim of his hat upward an inch or two on his brow. The startled look on Kate's face said it all. "Am I a nightmare to you, instead?" He held his breath even though he'd asked the question teasingly. What if she said yes? Then the rest of his hope would be destroyed—forever.

Tears burned in Kate's eyes. Wordlessly, she leaned upward and placed her hands flat against his chest. She saw surprise, then joy followed quickly by desire, in his widening gray eyes. Her heart cried out for him, despite all the pain, the past mistakes they'd made that had convoluted and stained their individual lives. Parting her lips, she pressed them against the hard line of his.

Instantly, she felt Sam's returning hunger, his mouth shamelessly taking hers, molding, melding her tightly against him. This time the kiss was not tender or gentle. It was taking, giving, sharing a desire whose flame had never died out over time. Her breath became short as he took her, his hands sliding behind her, pressing her solidly against his hard, trembling body.

The coldness of the air, the moisture of their breath, the moan that came up from her throat, all combined in a whirlwind of sensation. She slid her fingers along his freshly shaved cheeks, felt the warmth and sandpapery texture that was Sam. He smelled of pine and snow and that very special scent of him, only him.

This time there was no holding back with Kate. She had her answer. Whatever was left of their old love was still alive. Her arms slid around his thickly corded neck and she ached to feel his skin against her own. As his hand moved and caressed the side of her breast, she trembled violently. Oh, how long had she gone without his touch? His exploring, searching hands slid down her body, eliciting fire she longed to share with him.

The soft snort of the horses moving restlessly nearby brought Kate back to her senses. In a daze, she felt Sam's mouth leave her own wet, throbbing lips. As she lifted her lashes, she saw the burning, molten desire in his eyes, his face inches from her own. His breath was warm against her face. Weakly, she curled her fingers into the sheepskin collar of his coat to keep from swaying. Her senses reeled, awakened from some deep slumber. An ache between her legs told her how badly she wanted Sam.

"I..." she began unsteadily. "Sam..."

"I know," he rasped, drawing her against him again. His heart thundered like a freight train in his chest. He felt tied in a burning, painful knot of need for Kate. His mouth tingled with her softness, her womanliness. She was as eager and starved for him as he was for her, he discovered. That was heady knowledge. Sam had never expected such a gift from Kate, and he was stunned. He didn't deserve it—at all. Yet the generosity of her heart was overwhelming, and this time, there was no mistaking her intent. She had kissed him. It had been mutual. Sizzling. Needed.

Wryly, he looked down at her, one corner of his mouth lifted. With his fingers, he smoothed some strands of hair from Kate's flushed cheek. "I think we're upsetting our horses, don't you?"

Laughing self-consciously, Kate felt a fierce welling of love tunnel up through her. In that moment, Sam look twenty years younger, like the football star she'd fallen hopelessly in love with so long ago. His gray eyes were lighter and the joy in them thrilled her. Giddy, she said in a softened voice, "I think we've embarrassed them by our unexpected behavior."

Chuckling, Sam was delighted to see Kate return his touch as she grazed his hard jaw with her fingertips. The intimacy was nearly his undoing. He wanted to love her so damn badly he could taste it. He wanted to make up for all the years of pain he'd given her. Yet he was older and wiser now, and he also knew that waiting was not their enemy, but their friend. If Kate loved him anyway near as much as he did her, they had all the time in the world to discover and then explore it—together. To blindly rush in, driven by guilt or hormones, wasn't what he needed right now—he'd done that once and paid dearly and he wasn't about to do it again. That knowledge and experience gave him the ability to smile warmly down at Kate.

"The horses might be embarrassed, but I don't think we are. Are we?" He said it lightly, teasingly. There was no way Sam wanted to burden Kate or make her feel angst over their unexpected kiss.

Heat stung Kate's cheeks as she absorbed Sam's warm, caring look. It passed right on through her to her wildly beating heart, thrumming with untrammeled joy. Just getting to touch Sam was such a gift to her.

"No," she whispered, meeting his smile with one of her own. "I don't think we are."

Sam tore his gaze from her upturned features. Kate's eyes were alive with happiness. No longer was there wariness in them, or that darkness he'd seen so often since she'd gotten out of jail. Still holding her, he moved out from between the horses. "Look up there," he said, pointing to a good-looking spruce about two hundred feet up the snow-covered hill. "What do you think about that one as a Christmas tree?"

Kate was grateful for his return to less significant things. She needed time to feel her way through what had just occurred between them. Right now, her knees still felt a little like jelly. It was wonderful to just lean against Sam, to have his arm protectively wrapped around her shoulders.

"Yes, that looks like a good tree," she agreed a bit breathlessly.

"Good," he said, slowly releasing her and moving to the packhorse to retrieve the ax. "Let's get on with this Christmas celebration, shall we?"

Chapter 9

Kate couldn't still her excitement as the five-foot-tall blue spruce was set upright in the living room of the ranch house. They had gotten home by two in the afternoon, and by three the tree was up in the corner. A fire burned brightly in the red sandstone fireplace on the other side of the room.

"This is just like in the past," Kate said breathlessly as she brought out the Christmas ornaments from a closet in the hall. How familiar it felt to go to that closet and find the decorations there. Odula had taught them all organization, and everything in the house had a nook or cranny of its own. Placing the boxes on the davenport, she smiled up at Sam who was brushing off his hands.

Her body tingled in memory of his hands, his form, pressed against hers up on the mountain. Something magical had happened in those moments. Something that had set her heart singing.

"There are traditions that ought to be faithfully kept," Sam agreed. He peered into one of the boxes, where colorful ornaments sparkled back at him. "I wonder how many years these bulbs have been unused? The five years I was here at the ranch, Kelly never celebrated Christmas once."

Surprised, Kate began to string the lights on the tree, after trying them out and finding they still worked. "He didn't?" Sam came over to help her, picking up the other end of the lights.

"No, he'd get roaring drunk, sit on this couch and stare moodily into the fire." Sam wound the lights around the tree while Kate attached them here and there. The two of them worked in close proximity, their hips or arms touching occasionally. He savored each grazing touch.

"Probably remembering," Kate said sadly.

"If I were in his shoes, I'd be doing that," Sam murmured. He stood back while Kate plugged in the lights, illuminating the tree with colors. Nodding, he said, "Perfect."

Kate handed him a box of ornaments. Everything was perfect because she and Sam were spending time together once again. Over the past six weeks, they'd rarely seen one another except at work. "Did Kelly ever talk about us?" she ventured softly.

Sam set the box on a nearby chair. His hands were so large, the ornaments so small and fragile in comparison. Carefully, he began to hang them, one by one. "After Odula died, he went into a deep depression that lasted a year, from what I heard. He lost most of his wranglers in that time, staying drunk and firing them for no good reason. I was still working up at the Maitland Ranch near Flag, so I heard this stuff secondhand."

Sam picked up the silver star. "Kelly kept hiring and firing wranglers. He got a real reputation for drinking, exploding like an angry old peccary and firing the next poor cowboy that happened to have the bad luck of crossing his path." Sam frowned and placed the star carefully on top of the tree. When it slipped, he caught it and gently affixed it so that it remained upright.

"When he hired me about four years later, the ranch was a disaster site. I made a deal with Kelly—I would handle hiring and firing wranglers and he would stay out of my territory and keep the books." Sam grimaced. "That was a big mistake, but there was nothing I could do about that. He owned this place, I didn't."

"And so, at Christmastime, he'd just drink?"

"He'd never put up a tree and yes, he'd hit the bottle. He was lonely, though. After the chores were done, he'd invite me over for a drink."

Kate watched as Sam carefully placed another ornament on the spruce. "Did he—did he ever talk about any of us? My sisters?" she asked again.

Sam met and held her gaze. He saw the pain in Kate's eyes. "Plenty. Kelly was a storyteller. You know that. I'd sit here with him drinking my beer in front of the fireplace while he bragged on about you three girls."

Gawking, Kate whispered, "Bragged on us?"

"Yes." Sam stood back, appraising the tree. Slanting a glance at Kate, who looked stunned, he murmured, "Especially you. He loved you in his own way, Kate. I know you don't believe that, but he did."

She bridled. "A twisted love," she muttered, retrieving the boxes of bright silver icicles to hang on the branches. Handing Sam a package and taking one herself, she sat down to open it.

"He loved you the best he knew how," Sam said, sitting on the couch next to her. When Kate's mouth became fixed in a hard line, he added, "I'm not defending him. He had no right to strike you like he did, Kate. If I'd been around, I'd have decked him, drunk or not."

"It was the last time he ever touched me."

"Well, he'd done enough damage by badgering, manipulating and taunting you girls as you grew up."

"He thought we were boys, not girls. He didn't want little girls running around. He'd wanted four strapping sons instead."

"That was Kelly's loss," Sam growled. "The three of you are pretty special in my book."

"Rachel and Jessica are. I've managed to screw up my life every step of the way."

"Kelly rode you the hardest," Sam countered quietly. "He used to sit here and talk about how hard he'd been on you. How he had to be hard on you to make you into a strong woman so you could run this ranch someday after he died."

Kate's hands stilled on the icicles. "I was Peter's replacement?"

"Yes. I think Kelly thought he had to be brutal and tough toward you all the time in order to teach you how to run this place." Sam sighed. "He was wrong. You don't train children by beating them. All that does is scare the living daylights out of them and they do one of two things—rebel or run."

Kate stood up and began placing the icicles on the

tree. Her gut was tight with nausea and grief. "I did both."

"You could have done worse," Sam chided, slowly easing to his feet. He held her angry gaze as he walked over to the tree in turn.

"Like what? I rebelled against him from the time I was old enough to know that how he was treating me was wrong. And when I could, I ran as fast and hard as I could away from him." She looked around the room, her voice softening. "Away from here."

"What happens when you continuously beat a horse, Kate?"

"It'll either cave in, its spirit broken, or it'll fight back."

Sam hung some tinsel near the top of the tree. "I've always seen you as a wild, free mustang." His mouth pulled into a slight smile and he slanted a glance in her direction. "Right or wrong, I still do. Kelly beat you verbally and whipped you emotionally all your young life. You had those two choices staring you in the face. Somewhere in your heart, you knew Kelly wasn't going to ease up on you and treat you like an adult when you were eighteen. Maybe you sensed it. After he broke your nose in that fight, you knew you had to run. If you'd have stayed, it would have gotten worse."

"That I did know," Kate confided, slowly hanging the last of her tinsel on the tree. "I knew if he could hit me once or twice, he'd hit me again. I got tired of feeling like a target."

"He didn't see what he was doing to you. He thought he was grooming you to take over the ranch someday."

"He never told me that, Sam." She stood in the center of the room, feeling frustration and anger.

"Kelly didn't know how." Sam walked up to her. Kate's cheeks were flushed from the warmth of the fire. Several errant locks of hair dipped across her worried brow. "He sat here telling me how good a rider you were. How smart you were with the accounting books. He was proud of your straight A average in school, Kate. He dreamed of you going on to college and then coming back here after graduation, when he was going to hand over the daily running of the ranch to you."

Startled, she stared up at Sam's features. "If that's so, then why didn't he ever call me or write to me and tell me that? I kept in touch with Mom by phone and letter all those years. He knew where I was, what I was doing."

Reaching out, Sam tamed those unruly tendrils back into place. How badly he wanted to slide his fingers through her thick, silky hair. But he resisted. Barely.

"Pride, I think, stopped him. Stiff-necked pride," he told her, watching her eyes grow velvet with his touch.

"Damn him!" Kate whispered, tears flooding into her eyes. "It was his way of getting even with me for running away."

"No, I don't think so. In the later years, when Kelly had time to reflect on how he'd ridden you into the ground, I think he was feeling pretty guilty. And I don't think he knew how to tell you that or to say he was sorry." Sam reached out and placed a hand on her slumping shoulder. "If you had been here those five years like I was, you'd have seen photos of all you ladies on the television set. If anyone came to the ranch, Kelly bragged on about the three of you any chance he got. Some of the neighbors got tired of him saying the same things over and over again."

Sam smiled fondly in remembrance. "Believe me, Kelly was proud of you, Kate. He kept a shoe box in his bedroom that had all you girls' report cards in it. On some nights when I was in the office working on the books, he'd bring the box in, sit down and start pulling up different report cards, talking in amazement about all the subjects you three had taken and how smart you were."

Sam's hand felt steadying to Kate. She hung her head and ached to step into the circle of his arms once again. Somehow, she knew he'd hold her if she wanted. Her stomach hurt with pain and unrelieved grief and anger. "It was all so senseless," she whispered brokenly. "Damn him for not telling us these things."

Gently, Sam rubbed her shoulders, feeling the tension gathered in them. "Kate, give yourself some time. A lot's happened since you left. There's more to tell, but I don't think you're up to hearing it yet."

Sadly, Kate nodded. "Probably not, Sam. So Kelly loved us, but he didn't have the guts to tell us that to our faces. Wonderful. So the three of us have suffered half our lives because he was a coward and couldn't reach out to give us a hug or kiss us on the head." She pulled away, afraid that she was going to raise her arms and throw them around Sam's neck, seeking refuge with him. "You're right, Sam," she whispered bitterly, "I'm not ready to hear much more about Kelly and his drunken exploits." She turned and looked at the tree, her voice raw and unsteady. "All I want—need—is my family back. I can hardly wait for Rachel and Jessica to get home. I want things the way they used to be, only better this time. Much better."

Sam studied her profile and the anguished set of her

lips. "The past can't be changed, Kate. But you can change the present and plan for the future." He managed a slight smile. "You three ladies have a hard road ahead, but my money's on you to save this ranch and rediscover your roots."

Kate wasn't so sure of victory, but she didn't say so. Resting her hands on her hips, she looked over at him.

"I'm planning a turkey dinner with all the trimmings tomorrow evening, Sam McGuire. And then I'm going to open the gifts my sisters sent me. Just like we did every Christmas night. Would you like to join me? I'm not going to be like Kelly. I won't tell you I like being alone on holiday. And I'm sure as hell not going to hit the bottle to make up the difference. What do you say?"

He saw the defiance burning in her eyes. Here was the Kate he knew from long ago, the mustang, wild and free. Her spirit might be badly beaten, but Kelly had never broken her. He grinned. "I wouldn't miss it for the world, Ms. Donovan. What time is dinner?"

"Right after we get the animals bedded down and fed for the night."

"Six p.m. I'll be there," Sam said, picking up his hat and shrugging into his sheepskin coat. "With bells on," he promised huskily.

Sam followed Kate into the living room after the tasty homemade meal of turkey and trimmings. He wore his Sunday-go-to-meeting clothes—dark brown slacks, a dark suede blazer, a freshly pressed, white cotton shirt and a bolo tie. Having taken extra pains to shave closely before coming over for dinner, he'd nicked himself once or twice. But the extra care had been worth it. Especially now that he was alone with Kate once more.

He held a wineglass that she had just filled with sparkling grape juice. Unlike her father, she never touched alcohol. Odula had raised them to realize being Native American meant they would never be able to drink.

As he moved toward the tree, he noticed the dancing firelight reflected around the darkened living room. The lights on the tree were festive, and he felt happier than he could ever recall. The dinner had been intimate. And Kate looked beautiful in a dark pink corduroy skirt that fell to her ankles. A fancy white blouse with lace at the throat brought out her natural color, and the red velvet vest she wore over it heightened the bright color in her cheeks. He saw her frown and stop midway to the tree, where she was going to open the presents from her sisters.

"What's this?" Kate demanded, pointing beneath the tree. There was a third present there—one she did not recognize. And then she realized Sam must have put it there when she wasn't looking. She glanced over at him. He was smiling at her with his dark gray eyes.

"You're pretty sneaky, Sam," she accused, setting her wineglass on the mantel and moving to kneel on the red-and-green material that served as a colorful skirt beneath the tree.

"Now, I wouldn't say coyote sneaky," he remonstrated. "Clever, maybe?" In many Southwestern tales, the coyote was known as the ultimate trickster. Most ranchers saw them as sneaky. The Native Americans, however, saw the coyote as sacred and felt that tricks needed to be played on humans sometimes to teach them invaluable lessons.

Familiar with the tales, Kate chuckled, settling down and rearranging her skirt around her. Leaning toward the back of the tree, she pulled out another gift. "Maybe you're right. Here, come and join me. Santa Claus left something for you, too, I think...." She pretended to be studying the card on the long, rectangular gift.

Sam crouched down nearby, his body almost touching hers. He reached out and took the red foil package with a glittering gold ribbon. "Talk about sneaky," he exclaimed, his fingers touching hers in the exchange.

Chortling, Kate smiled up at him. "Once a coyote, always a coyote."

"Now you're a coyote," Sam drawled, studying the gift with obvious pleasure.

How close he was. And how incredibly handsome! Her gaze dropped, as it always did, to his strong, powerful mouth. Catching herself, Kate pretended to be interested in the gifts. She wanted to tear into Sam's gift first, but that wouldn't be right. So she picked up Rachel's large present and drew it into her lap. Not bothering with protocol, Kate eagerly tore into the gift, the lively green foil flying around her.

Sam watched Kate's animated features. She was like a kid again—exuberant, enthusiastic and completely spontaneous. This was the old Kate he knew and loved. He saw her smile blossom as she opened up the box to view the contents.

"I figured as much," Kate said, "a *big* homeopathic kit." She pulled out a huge white plastic container about the size of a bread box. Opening it carefully, she pulled out one of the five shelves. At least thirty small amber bottles, all with Latin names on them, stared back at her. "I think Rachel wants to make sure I have enough homeopathic remedies on hand to treat the whole world," she said with a laugh. Fingering some of the bottles, she added, "Rachel said we could use the remedies on animals, too. She said in a letter that we could save a lot on vetting bills if we switched to this type of medicine instead."

"Why not? If it's cheaper and it works, it's a good idea," Sam agreed. He leaned over and gave Kate the next gift. This one was from Jessica.

Opening it quickly, Kate smiled with pleasure. Inside the box were several colorful packages. One was a bath salt made from purple cone flower, another was bergamot bath oil. As well as a sponge, there were four bars of handmade soap that had the scent of jasmine. Kate read the card out loud. "You're going to need long, hot soaks in the bathtub at night after those hard days you're putting in. I make all these things by hand and sell them through my company. Enjoy them. Let them heal you after a tough day. Love, Jessica."

"How about that?" Sam said, looking through the many gifts. "Your sister is really creative."

"Yes, she is," Kate murmured, proud of her little sister. She picked up the bath salts and looked at the design on the front of it. "Mother Earth Flower Essences. That must be the name of her company." She laughed a little and fingered the blue turtle with a colorful array of wildflowers sprouting out of its back, a smile on its face. "This is just like Jessica. She *loves* turtles! Growing up, she always had one as a pet—an old desert tortoise that used to hang out near the watering trough in the north pasture. I remember she would take cut-up fruit and lettuce leaves to it every day or so without fail." Shaking her head, Kate whispered in a choked tone, "Isn't it funny how all the things we did as kids can later turn into something beautiful and meaningful like this? It's just amazing to me."

Reaching out, Sam picked up his gift for her. "I think you're right," he murmured. "Here, this isn't much, but I hope it brings a lot of the past back to the present, Gal."

Curious, Kate accepted the gift. It was a very small box. Sam had tried to wrap it the best he could, the ribbon slightly askew, the corners of the paper sticking out here and there, as if the gift was put together at the last minute. "You didn't have to do this, Sam."

He smiled enigmatically, his arms resting on his knees as he watched her face. "I've been wanting to give you this gift for a long time, Gal...."

Mystified, Kate opened the tiny box with trembling fingers. "What on earth could it be?" she wondered aloud.

He chuckled indulgently. "Open it and find out."

Tossing the paper aside, Kate slowly removed the lid. Her brows knitted. Inside was a piece of lined paper, cut lopsidedly and then folded. "What are you up to, Sam McGuire?" She picked up the paper and put the box aside. In the dim, dancing light, she could barely make out his scrawl. Holding the note closer, she read, "Go to the truck?"

"Yup."

Stymied, Kate tried to read the second line. "Sam, your handwriting is the pits. What on *earth* does this next line say?"

Placing his hand beneath hers, he helped her stand. "It says," he continued, as he steered her toward the door, "to go to my pickup, to the front seat. There's something waiting there for you."

The coldness of the night air hit Kate as she followed

Sam out onto the damp, dark porch. It had quit snowing hours ago and she could smell the pungent fragrance of the juniper wrapped in snow blankets as they stepped off the porch. Sam's big red Dodge Ram pickup sat a few feet away.

"You're being a coyote again, Sam." Her heart sped up as he kept his hand on her arm and led her to the door of the truck.

"Don't get all upset, Gal. Just open the door. Your Christmas gift is in there."

In the dim light from the ranch house window, Kate opened the door. She heard a little yap and her breath snagged. From the floor of the pickup, which was covered with newspapers, a little black-and-white form leaped right at her. She heard Sam's indulgent chuckle as the puppy, a New Zealand collie, jumped up on the front seat.

"Oh!" Kate breathed. The puppy wasn't more than eight weeks old, her black, shiny eyes like buttons, her mouth open and already gnawing on Kate's outstretched fingers. "A dog!"

"Not just any dog," Sam said, leaning over her shoulders as she scooped the puppy up into her arms and held it against her breast. "Remember how Zeke, your cattle-heeling dog, died when you were eighteen? He was New Zealand bred, and your mother had bought him fifteen years earlier. Zeke was the best cattle-heeling dog I'd ever seen." Sam smiled as Kate gazed up at him, tears in her eyes. "Right now, we can use every able body we've got, Kate. Having a collie will help a lot, especially moving those cattle from pasture to pasture. Of course, she's got to grow a little first."

Kate stroked the puppy's black-and-white-peppered fur. "She's cute, Sam."

He was so close. So wonderfully close. Kate felt comforted even as she recalled Zeke's death. At fifteen, the old dog had been a little too slow when one of the Hereford bulls got nasty. Zeke had been nipping at the animal's hind legs when one good kick had sent him to his death.

Kate closed her eyes, tears matting her lashes. She felt the warmth of the little puppy wriggling happily against her, felt her tiny pink tongue licking her fingers. "Oh, Sam," she whispered. Blindly, she turned and threw her free arm around his broad shoulder. Being careful not to crush the puppy, she leaned up to kiss his cheek.

In that instant, she felt Sam tremble. Without warning, his arms came around her, pulling her even closer, though he, too, was careful not to hurt the puppy. Leaning down, he intercepted Kate's kiss. Instead of finding his cheek, she found his mouth instead. Her world exploded. His mouth took hers, molded her to him. A soft moan came from her as she placed one hand against his chest. She felt his arms leave her, his hands settle on the sides of her face to angle her to better advantage and continue the breath-stealing kiss.

His mouth was cajoling, strong and consuming. A fire sparked and ignited hotly between them as he slid his lips along hers. Kate felt his warm, moist breath against her face. Her fingers curled against his chest as she returned the power of Sam's kiss. Instantly, she felt him tremble again. A groan, or maybe it was a growl, came from deep within him. She felt his fingers slide through her hair, cherishing her, stroking her as if she was some beautiful, fragile thing. Each stroke of his fingers against her scalp incited more heat within her. The beat of his heart felt sledgehammer hard beneath her palm. His breathing was erratic. So was hers. His mouth was commanding, her response hungry.

It felt as if a volcano, simmering deep inside her, had suddenly exploded. A hot, scalding heat flared upward through her, making her acutely aware of every inch of her skin beneath the clothes she wore. Her breasts tightened as his hands moved restlessly from her hair down her face, following the line of her neck and shoulders. She moaned as his hands brushed the sides of her taut breasts, which screamed out for his touch.

"Kate," he groaned. He couldn't get enough of her mouth, of her. She tasted sweet and tart to him. The eagerness of her response tore at his disintegrating control. Sam slid his hand around her hip, pinning her lower body to his. He let her feel the hardness there, the desire that raged within him. "I need you," he rasped against her mouth. Her lips were wet, soft and pliant beneath his, begging him to go deeper, to explore more of her. "I need you...." His words were lost as she returned his kiss, her tongue tangling with his.

The world closed in on them, the only sound their ragged breathing, the only sensation their hands touching, exploring one another. Kate was consumed by an inner fire Sam had ignited. His mouth was as she remembered from that morning up on the Rim—strong yet tender, directing without controlling. Each time he slid his lips against hers, a little more of her crumbled. Each trembling touch of his hands upon her face, her breasts, her hair, made her knees grow weaker and weaker beneath the onslaught. For that instant, Kate felt as she had when they were teenagers. She remembered that same hungry, exciting exploration of their bodies with their hands, their mouths....

The puppy whined and struggled, caught between them.

As if drugged, Kate pulled away from Sam, her other hand holding the puppy close. The tingle of her lips told her how powerfully Sam had taken her. Dazed, she stepped back, her knees wobbly. They were both breathing hard. His eyes were like glittering ice shards as he studied her in the intervening moments after their unexpected kiss.

"Time...." Kate whispered unsteadily, reaching up and touching his lips. "I need some time, Sam...."

Chapter 10

Kate sat on her bay mare, Cinnamon, overlooking a herd of Herefords recently moved to a new pasture that butted up against the Mogollon Rim. The towering ridge, a wedge of red sandstone topped with white limestone formed a watershed of sorts. Luckily, the high country on the rim got enough snow to fill the lakes and reservoirs there. However, rains that were supposed to come and feed the parched desert lands thousands of feet below it had never arrived that year.

Cinnamon snorted softly and switched her tail. The mid-March sun was bright and warm. Kate reveled in it. Down below, she saw Sam urging the stragglers into the pasture area. *Sam*. Her heart contracted as the memory of his branding kisses seared through her—just as it did every time the recollection came unbidden to her. Automatically, her fingers tightened around the leather reins.

She smiled a little, watching Pepper, the New Zealand collie that Sam had given her for Christmas, race around, nipping at the heels of cows that were lagging behind and calling for their wandering, errant calves. Not quite five months old, Pepper was already being faithful to her genetic background. In Australia and New Zealand, the dogs were prized for their ability to herd and keep sheep together. Here in the U.S., they were excellent at helping a cowboy move a herd of cattle.

Dismounting, Kate checked the cinch on her saddle. It felt looser than normal. Maybe because she'd tossed and turned so much last night, she hadn't been as careful or thorough as she should have been with her equipment this morning. Nudging aside the rope that hung from the leather-covered horn, she lifted the stirrup back over the saddle to take a better look. Sliding two gloved fingers under the soft cotton strands of the cinch, she decided it seemed tight enough. Oh, well, it must be her imagination.

Dropping the stirrup down against Cinnamon's barrel, Kate remounted. She heard an approaching horse and knew it was Sam on his big chestnut gelding, Bolt. Inevitably, her heart started skipping beats in anticipation of his nearness. Because the demands of the ranch were widespread, they rarely saw each other. This morning was especially wonderful because for a few hours they got to work together.

Sam pulled his Arabian gelding to a halt. Even though it was only ten a.m., he was sweating from the work. Taking off his hat, he wiped his brow with the back of his sleeve and studied Kate, who smiled at him in silent greeting. Her hair nearly touched her shoulders at the back now, soft and slightly curled. It didn't matter if she wore a Stetson, jeans and a long-sleeved shirt, she couldn't hide the fact that she was all-woman. Every now and again, the memory of their stolen kisses burned brightly within him. It had kept his hope alive these past three months. Did he really dare to dream the impossible—that someday Kate might love him as he had always loved her? Over the past few months, Sam had watched as Kate slowly began to shed her shell. She was not only opening up to him a little at a time, she was also much surer of her role on the ranch and more confident that she could save it. Yes, time was on their side, there was no doubt.

"We're done, Boss. Mamas and babies will be glad to munch on that green grass down below." He twisted around in the saddle and watched the herd of three hundred Herefords. Half the cows had already birthed their calves. The other half would be dropping their babies in the next month. It was a demanding time on the ranch right now. Usually, cows could calve without problems. But when there were problems, someone had to be nearby. The pasture was an hour north of the ranch, which meant one of them would have to drive out during the daylight hours at least two to three times a day to check the herd. Losing a calf meant losing a lot of money, and right now, Sam knew they were hitting bottom again financially.

Kate studied Sam's darkly tanned, glistening features as he settled his hat back on his head, his eyes glittering with some unknown emotion. She felt her body respond hotly to his gaze and she could practically taste her hunger for him. Only this time, she wanted to go all the way. To love him with all the fierce passion that clamored restlessly within her. Maybe that's why she wasn't sleeping well at night. How could she with the memory of the searing kisses they'd shared burning in her heart and mind?

Sam gestured to her horse. "Cinch problems?"

"It felt a little loose was all," Kate said. "Must have been my imagination." She gloried in the warmth of the sun on her back. With a sigh, she whispered, "Isn't this beautiful, Sam? A bright blue sky, temperature in the high sixties, green grass like a carpet under our feet and the smell of the pine nearby…" She closed her eyes and then laughed. "I sure wish I could bottle all of this up and wear it!"

Grinning, he moved his horse to parallel hers, their cowboy boots occasionally touching as the animals shifted. What he was looking at was beautiful: Kate Donovan on horseback. Since their stolen kisses, she'd been far more expressive with how she felt. Maybe she was beginning to trust him a little. He hoped so.

"Days like this ought to be bottled and sent east," he agreed, lifting his leg up and over the saddle horn. Leaning his elbow on that leg, he looked down to see Pepper panting happily between them. The dog was small, maybe all of twenty pounds, and Sam didn't know many creatures brave enough to plop down between huge horses with such trust.

"That dog of yours is turning into a good heeler," he told Kate, catching the dancing warmth in her blue eyes. He drank in the soft, upturned corners of her mouth. There was no question that Kate belonged out here, on the ranch. Somehow, being home was helping her to heal a lot of open wounds from her past, too. For that, Sam was grateful.

"Pepper's going to be great," Kate agreed. She leaned over the saddle, her hands outstretched. "Come on, Pepper," she called.

Instantly, the puppy leaped upward.

Kate caught her dog and hefted her up into her lap. She positioned the puppy carefully between her thighs so that she had a safe place to sit. Chuckling, Kate avoided Pepper's pink tongue and patted her head.

Kate and her dog and her horse. It was all so natural, Sam thought as he watched her laugh and play with Pepper. The dog adored her. Who wouldn't? He sure as hell did. As a matter of fact, he envied Pepper—at least Kate allowed the dog to get close to her. He turned away and momentarily scowled. Although his gaze was on the red-and-white Herefords that dotted the green pasture below, his mind and heart were elsewhere.

How many times had he awakened at night from torrid dreams of making love to Kate? He wasn't sorry at all for those rare moments when they could share an intimate kiss. Each was leading to more exploration, more trust and deepening intimacy between them. He *wanted* to taste her, feel her, share her breath, her caresses. In some ways, the kisses were softening Kate and making her more accessible. In other ways, she avoided him like the proverbial plague. Sometimes, without thinking, he'd get too close to her and she'd automatically step away from him. Sam didn't blame her. After all, he'd betrayed her once and he knew that the hurt was a tough wall to dissolve between them. Kate had to learn she could trust him not to leave her in the lurch again— that he would always be there for her.

Wiping the sweat collecting on his upper lip with his gloved hand, he furrowed his brow more heavily as he watched the cattle below. Sam released a long, ragged sigh, then he straightened in the saddle and lowered his leg. Picking up the reins, he looked over at Kate and Pepper. There was such life shining in Kate's sky blue eyes, in her smiling, parted lips as she stroked the puppy's head. "I've got to get back. Need to pick up sweet feed at the mill. Charley's got the order ready for us."

"Oh…" Kate quickly let Pepper slip gently back to the ground. "You're right. We can't take breaks like this too often." Picking up the reins, she clucked to Cinnamon, who headed back down the knoll at a brisk walk.

Sam joined her, keeping his horse a few feet from hers so that their boots or legs wouldn't accidentally touch. They headed for the big aluminum gate at the south end of the pasture. "Is there anything you want in Sedona while I'm there?"

Since Chet Cunningham had embarrassed her at the restaurant, Kate had not gone back to town. Sam understood why, but he also knew Kate couldn't keep herself locked up like a prisoner at the ranch for the rest of her life, either. If she wanted anything, she handed him a list and he picked up the items for her. Shopping for groceries wasn't one of his favorite things, but he did it anyway. He knew Kate was afraid to meet too many accusing looks if she ran into townsfolk in the aisles. Someday, that wound would scab over, too.

Stealing a glance at him, Kate said, "I thought I might ride into town with you. There're some things I'd like to pick up at the saddler in West Sedona."

Unable to hide his surprise, he stared at her.

"It's about time, don't you think?" Kate asked wryly.

"The time is right when you feel ready to tackle it, Gal." At least he was able to call her by this endearment. And every time he did, he saw Kate's tender re-action. That was all he could do right now. He couldn't touch her or kiss her anytime he wanted—at least, not yet. But the friendship and trust they were establishing was a good foundation.

"I'm such a coward at heart, Sam," Kate said with a sigh, waving her hand helplessly. "I know I've been hiding out here, using the ranch chores as a convenient excuse. Jessica read me the riot act on the phone the other night. She made me mad, but she was right."

"About what?"

"How I was letting Chet Cunningham, one person in ten thousand in Sedona, stop me from living my life fully."

Sam grinned sourly. "That little space-cadet sister of yours has her head screwed on straight."

With a laugh, Kate leaned down and patted Cinnamon's sleek neck. The horse automatically arched a little more in response. "Jessica *seems* to be spacy and ungrounded, but she's not."

"She reminds me of a leaf falling off a tree at the whimsy of the wind."

"Yes, but every leaf knows where it's going—to the ground." Kate grinned. "My little sister is flighty, but she's practical."

"Part of your mother's gift to all of you," Sam agreed congenially. The aluminum gate was double locked, so he dismounted and walked up to it. "You three ladies all have the genius of common sense," he told her, opening the gate and moving him and his horse through it.

"Mom could make a silk purse out of a sow's ear," Kate agreed with a laugh. She clucked to Cinnamon and moved through the open gate, with Pepper at the mare's heels. Kate watched as Sam carefully double-checked the gate to make sure it was secure. If the cows and calves got out, they could wander over nearly five thousand acres of desert unattended, and that wasn't such a good idea right now.

Kate enjoyed watching Sam as he mounted again, his actions graceful and confident. Giving her a significant look, he brought his horse into a walk next to hers. "So Jessica badgered you into coming to town with me today?" He would have wished Kate wanted to ride in the truck with him on her own accord, but that was pretty selfish of him. Wounds from the past took time to heal and he just had to dig down deeper in himself to find patience.

"Mmm, maybe not badgered. She sent me one of the natural essences she makes for her company. Matter of fact, it comes from broom snakeweed," Kate said, gesturing toward the desert. "It comes from right here. All that yellow-flowering brush."

Raising his brows, Sam said, "That's a pasture weed out here." Snakeweed was a prolific plant that during the spring rain would burst into life, with hundreds of tall, green arms and a cloud of little yellow flowers on top. The wind would pick up the fragrant scent, one of Mother Nature's perfumes. It smelled nice, but it also discouraged grass growth, so it wasn't a favorite of ranchers. But there was no stopping snakeweed, so one learned to live with it.

"I know," Kate said with a laugh. "Jessica said she made that essence several years ago when she was visiting a friend in Tucson. She told me it was a medicine that helped a person confront his or her fears. I've been taking four drops four times a day for the last couple of days and I have noticed I'm not as scared as I used to be when I thought about going into town."

"So, it helps with a person's fears, whatever they might be?"

"That's what Jessica said." Kate shrugged. "Seems to be working. My stomach doesn't clench into a knot when I think about going into town."

Impressed, Sam said, "She's really got something with that stuff of hers, doesn't she?"

"Listen, Jessica's natural essences are used around the world by people who don't want to use drugs. They're natural, and they work. At first, I was like you—unconvinced. But she's so enthusiastic about them and what they can do to help that I had to try them. She says she has another natural essence that cures depression."

"That's pretty heady stuff," Sam agreed. "Trade in your antidepressants for a little one-ounce bottle of a flower essence, instead. I'd do it, too."

"Besides, it's cheaper, safe and has no side effects," Kate added. "Drugs can't compete with that, and that's why her products are just flying off the shelf."

"And Jessica's money is helping to sustain the ranch," Sam noted. Faithfully, every month, the two sisters sent checks. Without those life-giving infusions, the Donovan Ranch would again fall behind in mortgage payments, and the bank, this time, wasn't going to be lenient. In Sam's opinion, the bank would foreclose without a bat of an eyelash. The banker, Fred Smith, was a good friend of Cunningham's, and over the years, the grizzled old rancher had made no bones about wanting to scoop up the Donovan ranch if the bank did foreclose. Then the Bar C would be the largest ranch in the State of Arizona.

"Yes," Kate said with a sigh, "thank goodness for their checks." And their weekly phone calls to her. How she looked forward to Sunday, when telephone rates were cheapest. She would spend at least half an hour talking with each of them, catching them up on ranch news, where they stood financially, and sharing how their personal lives were going. Next to being with Sam, Kate looked forward most to those life-giving phone calls from her sisters.

As the ranch house appeared in the distance, Sam gazed over at Kate, who had lapsed into deep thought, her face serene. "Why don't we take lunch in town?" He looked at the watch on his dark, hairy wrist. "It's nearly eleven a.m."

Startled by the suggestion, Kate felt heat rush to her face. "Where?"

"The Muse Restaurant?" he drawled good-naturedly.

Laughing, Kate said, "The way I feel right now, the Muse would be fine, too."

"The Muse has the best barbecued pork ribs in town...."

Matching his grin, she said, "Why not? I'm like a starvin' wolf." Then she patted her lean rib cage with her gloved hand.

"You got a deal. We'll pick up the feed and then stop at the Muse for lunch and go to the saddle maker afterward." Sam could barely keep the joy out of his voice. At last! Kate was moving forward again, growing and reaching out. This time he hoped like hell Chet Cunningham was nowhere to be seen. Usually the cowboy frequented Bailey's Bar in West Sedona. His appearance at the more posh establishment months ago had been a real fluke. Chet got into his share of brawls down at Bailey's, had seen the inside of Sedona's jail a number of times and had gotten out only because of Old Man Cunningham's power in the community. Well, it was noon, and Chet and his brother were probably riding the range, nowhere near Sedona, Sam hoped fervently.

Kate wiped her fingers on a linen napkin and grinned across the table at Sam. "This was a great idea. These ribs were good. I made a real pig out of myself." She looked at the scattered bones left on her plate. She'd eaten as if starved, but she knew that was because when Sam was with her, she relaxed. Since prison, her appetite wasn't consistent, but when Sam was around, she ate well. When he wasn't, she picked at food, not really hungry at all. And having lost twenty pounds in prison, she needed to gain them back in order to do the heavy, demanding ranch work.

Sam set their plates aside. The Muse was full of patrons, the waitresses hurriedly making trips between the tables and the kitchen. He and Kate had gotten a table for two against one wall, near a hat stand covered with cowboy hats. Earlier, when they'd arrived, Sam had cruised the bar area to make sure Chet Cunningham or his more obnoxious older brother, Bo, weren't in there drinking. Fortunately, they weren't.

"Let's head down to the leather shop," Sam said.

Scooping up the bones into a doggy bag for Pepper, Kate nodded and stood. "I'm ready." She was aware of several locals looking at her from time to time, but the broom snakeweed essence she was taking—and Sam's reassuring presence—took the edge off her normally nervous response to such curious stares. How proud Jessica would be of her progress. Coming into Sedona for the first time in nearly four months left Kate feeling really free. As she walked with Sam out the front door onto the patio filled with bright-colored flowers in terra-cotta pots, she realized how much she had been a prisoner of a different sort. And worst of all, she'd sentenced herself this time to hiding on the ranch.

Sunlight glanced down through the branches of the fernlike mimosa trees that bordered the patio outside the restaurant. She felt Sam's hand on her arm, and inwardly she tensed, but only for a moment. More than anything, she ached for his unexpected touches and those times when they could be together and share a warm, escalating kiss.

Kate wished she had the courage to tell Sam that she was dangerously close to surrendering completely to her emotions and letting go, that she was longing to love him completely. His kisses were like a teasing dessert, a promise of sweeter things to come. As he slipped his hand under her elbow, her skin tingled pleasantly, and she looked up at him. The dark gray of his eyes gave no hint of emotion, but his fingers tightened briefly around her elbow. How could she tell him she wanted more of his touches? That she wanted the kisses to move to a new, exploratory level? Sometimes she chastised herself for being such a coward. But at least this time she wasn't running. She was making a stand and a commitment to the ranch—and to herself. Kate knew that Sam's presence was very much a part of her being able to do that. He fed her strength and belief in herself.

Kate stepped off the red flagstone steps to the asphalt parking lot. Perhaps she needed to sit down and talk to him of her fears, her assumptions and her dreams. Maybe it was time. He deserved her honesty, not her cowardice.

Fay Seward was at a sewing machine when Sam and Kate entered the small leather store where everyone in town got their saddles, bridles and harnesses repaired.

"Howdy, Sam," she called as they entered. "Well, hello there, Kate. I'll be with you in just a sec…"

"Thanks, Fay," Sam murmured, tipping his hat toward her.

Kate smiled a greeting at the shop owner. Wearing wire-rimmed glasses that gave her a school-marm look, Fay was in her early fifties, her short, ginger-colored hair in tight curls around her oval face. Kate admired Fay's neat appearance despite the fact she worked at a man's job. As Kate wandered through the small shop, breathing in the wonderful smell of clean and rubbed leather, she gazed at all the new horse headstalls hanging on one wall, the new and used saddles sitting around on pine boxes with wheels. Fay's creativity could be seen everywhere. Some of the headstalls had brow bands of woven horsehair, black and white against the tobacco brown or chocolate color of the leather. She stroked several gently and relished the soft suppleness of the leather.

"Take a look at this," Sam called from the other side of the room. He pointed to a black saddle that had the center of it cut out.

Sauntering across the old, creaking wooden floor, Kate eyed the unusual saddle. "What kind is it?" she asked, running her fingers lightly across the polished black leather.

"It's a U.S. Army make—the McClellan cavalry saddle," Sam told her, examining the brass fittings mounted on the front of it. "And look at this—it was made in 1918. Fay must have sewn new leather straps on it."

"Who would ride such a thing?" Kate wondered. The saddle had a high pommel and cantle, but no horn. It would be useless to ranchers. There would be nothing to twist a rope around when they'd lassoed a steer.

Chuckling, Sam knelt down and closely examined the fine workmanship Fay had put into it. "Probably belongs to one of the Civil War reenactors from Camp Verde." He glanced up at her. "They've got an entire unit of men who wear Civil War outfits, go through the old cavalry drills. And," he continued, easing upward and patting the saddle affectionately, "they use equipment from that era on their horses. The McClellan was made during the Civil War and used up until the army traded tanks for horses after World War One."

Kate admired the saddle. "A lot of history here, isn't there?"

Sam was going to say yes when he heard the door open. Looking up, he instantly narrowed his eyes. In walked Chet and Bo Cunningham. Damn! Baby-faced Chet, his cheeks always red so that he looked like he was blushing, broke into a gleeful grin.

"Well, lookit what the cats dragged in, Bo...."

Kate froze. Her heart shattered. Chet Cunningham! She'd recognize that high nasal twang of his anywhere. Looking over at Sam, she saw his face become a thundercloud of anger, his gray eyes slitted and menacing. Slowly she turned to face her torturer. To her dismay, she saw Bo Cunningham standing beside the short, wiry Chet. Bo was around thirty-one, ruggedly handsome with dark hair like his father, and flashing black eyes he got from his Apache mother. Kate had never liked these two while growing up, though they all went to the same school together. The only Cunningham she liked was Jim, though she rarely saw the son who had gone on to work for the EMT. The other two brothers were nothing but trouble looking for a place to happen.

Kate felt Sam move closer to him. Much closer. She felt protected though she could feel the tension radiating around him. A chair scraped along the wooden floor and Kate's attention wavered. She saw Fay Seward frowning as she moved to the oak counter.

"You boys don't have anything in here to pick up, as I recall."

Chet grinned and swaggered over to the counter. "Miss Fay, how are you this fine day?" He tipped his hat to her in a dramatic motion.

Bo, who was built like his father at six foot three inches tall and more than two hundred pounds, kept his black gaze on Kate. "We're just passin' through, Miss Fay," he said in a low, soothing voice. His mouth twisted like barbed wire as he turned to Sam. "Saw your Ram pickup out front, McGuire. Thought we'd drop by and see how things were goin' at the Donovan Ranch." His smile hardened as his gaze pinned Kate viciously. "Looks like you got what you always wanted, Sam— the Donovan Ranch and that wild ex-con of a girl you were always moonin' over ever since she ran away in high school." He chuckled and moved over to the counter next to his brother.

Kate swallowed hard. From somewhere deep within her, she found her voice. It was low and husky when she spoke. "Bo, you and Chet are nothing but rattlers with nothing good to say about anyone. Time hasn't changed either of you in the least."

Bo spread his arms on the counter, staring at her from beneath the low brim of his dark brown, dusty Stetson. His mouth worked into a sneer. "Hey, Chet, listen to her crowin', will you? Now, neither of us have spent any time in a prison and yet here she is, chiding us." He chuckled.

Chet laughed, too. He raised his beat-up, sweat-stained straw hat off his head and scratched his black hair. "Katie Donovan always thought she was better than us. Always had her nose stickin' in the air at high school. Remember that?"

"Sure do," Bo drawled. "Miss Nose-in-the-Air. That's what we called her." His mouth twisted more. "Eighteen months in the pen didn't change her at all, did it?"

Kate was ready to take them on verbally, her anger soaring. Before she could, she felt Sam brush by her shoulder, his rage barely contained as he strode toward the two younger men. Worried that a fight might break out, Kate moved quickly in turn. Then she saw Fay pick up a baseball bat from beneath the counter.

"No," Fay growled at the Cunningham men, "if you two think you can come in here and bad-mouth payin' customers in *my* establishment, you got another think comin'. As if you two have any room to talk! Both of you boys have been in and out of Coconino County Jail more times than I've got fingers and toes. You quit pickin' on Kate. She served her time. It's done. It's the past, so you let it lie." She laid the baseball bat circumspectly on the counter between them, her hand over it, staring down the Cunningham men. "What'll it be, boys? A lump or two on your head if you keep shootin' off your mouths, or leavin' while your heads are still attached to your shoulders?"

Sam halted halfway to the counter. Automatically, he put his arm out to stop Kate from moving around him. His fingers bit deeply into her arm and he felt her trembling with rage, and he waited. This was Fay's establishment and her territory. She was tough but fair, and if she could handle the Cunninghams, he wouldn't step into the fray. But if they continued calling Kate names, he was going to settle the score with them outside—once and for all.

Bo eased into a standing position. He threw back his broad shoulders and chuckled. "Now, Miss Fay, we don't mean you no harm." He gestured toward Sam. "Nah, we're just droppin' by to say howdy-do, is all." He tipped his hat to the older woman. "We'll be leavin' now, nice and peaceful like. Chet?"

Chet grinned and followed his older brother out of the store. "Sure thing, big brother. We got some hay to pick up at the feed store." He tipped his hat respectfully in Fay's direction. "Ma'am? Have a nice day."

The door shut with a slam.

Kate released a broken sigh of relief.

"Those damned boys never grew up," Fay snarled, putting the baseball bat beneath the counter once again. "Old Man Cunningham spoilt those two varmints but good. Bad milk gone to sour if you ask me." She looked over at them. "I'm awful sorry, Kate and Sam. Try and consider the source and let it be like water runnin' off a duck's back, will you?"

Easing her fingers from Sam's upper arm, Kate felt his thick, hard muscles. He was as solid as the Mogollon Rim. Managing a weak smile, she said, "Thanks, Fay. This wasn't your fight. Chet has been gunning for me ever since I got out of…well, since I came home."

Snorting, Fay flashed an angry look toward the door. "Those two need their heads banged every once in a while to keep 'em in line. Chet hasn't a brain in that empty skull of his and Bo's more dangerous than a rattler." She walked briskly over to the wall of headstalls. "Come on, I've got those two bridles fixed for you, Sam. Here they are."

Relief washed through Kate as Fay went about the business at hand. Gratefully, she paid for the headstalls, glad that Fay didn't mention her prison past. The older woman treated her like she would anyone. And best of all, she had stood up and defended her. Kate hadn't known Fay well growing up, but she was coming to appreciate her forthright manner.

"Thank you," Kate murmured as she handed her the cash. "For everything.…"

Fay placed the headstalls in some brown wrapping paper and tied it up with string. "Teenagers in men's bodies if you ask me. Testosterone for brains. They don't think with their heads, they think with what's between their legs." She handed Kate the package. Squinting her blue eyes, she jabbed her brown, stained index finger at Kate. "Don't let a few snakes in the grass make you feel badly, young lady. Hell, no one has a clean past. I spent time in a local jail once for beating up my husband because he was beating up my daughter. And I've made a lot of decisions I ain't proud of, either. We've all got pasts. What you need to do is let it go. Walk proud, with no apologies." Her glance cut to the door. "Especially to the likes of those two troublemakers. Folks around here will judge you on what you do now, on a daily basis, if they've got any brains."

Barely able to stop from chuckling, Kate kept a respectful and somber look on her face. "Thank you, Fay. You're a wonderful teacher."

Taking off her glasses, Fay tenderly rubbed the bridge of her nose with her fingers. "Then take it to heart, missy." She put her glasses back on and looked over at Sam. "And you stop being so defensive about Kate, here."

Chastened, Sam had the good grace to blush under Fay's squinty-eyed look of censure. "I got a little tense," he admitted.

"I saw you cock your fist. That's why I went for the baseball bat. It makes for a real balance in a fight. I was countin' on you being smarter than those two rocks-for-brains, and holding your ground."

His mouth pulled into a sour grin. "Miss Fay, I would *never* think of starting a fight in your establishment." And he wouldn't. Fay Seward was known to be crusty, combative and downright cantankerous if she was unfairly disturbed. Every rancher in the territory knew that. And she was famous for her baseball bat. More than a couple of cowboys had tasted the bat's infamous reputation.

"Humph, you'd better now. Kate's got two legs and a brain in her head. She can speak up and defend herself." Fay's eyes flashed. "You're behavin' like a mongrel dog that's found his lifelong mate. Don't be like those two boys and let your brain turn to mush just 'cause you're emotionally in over your head."

Kate bit back laughter. She saw Sam's brow draw down in displeasure, but he didn't get defensive.

"Yes, Miss Fay," he murmured politely, and tipped his hat to her. "I'll come by for that saddle sometime next week?"

Fay twisted around, searching for the saddle that needed repair. "Yessir, you can come by next Friday. I'll have new straps and a cinch for it by that time. Good day to you both."

On the way home, Kate mulled over the entire sequence of what had happened in Fay's saddle shop. What had Fay meant when she said Sam was acting like a mongrel dog who had found his lifelong mate? She risked a glance at his harsh profile as he drove up 89A out of Sedona. Just as quickly, she moved her gaze out the window to drink in the juniper and desert pine that dotted the red sand earth. Wasn't his protective stance a normal, natural thing? Fay didn't think so. And what about Bo Cunningham's comment that Sam had what he'd always wanted—the ranch and her? That comment didn't make sense, either. Or did it?

Chapter 11

Early, unexpected April heat swept across the desert expanse, parching everything in its path. Kate felt a fine tremble of tension run through her as she sat on her Arabian mare, eyes squinted against the strong noon sunlight. She pressed her calves to the bay, and instantly, Cinnamon broke into a slow, controlled lope. Ahead of her, moving up a sandy slope littered with multicolored pebbles, Mormon tea plants that towered eight to ten feet tall and prickly pear cactus, was Sam. He, too, urged his rangy gelding, Bolt, into a lope.

Today they were gathering the three Hereford bulls from their collective pasture, to move them to three new pastures where they would each have a harem of cows to impregnate for the next year's calf crop. They'd decided to leave Pepper home for this job, as it was much too dangerous for a young puppy. Handling bulls was never easy work. It was hard, dirty and dangerous. Worse, neither Sam nor herself knew these bulls. Kelly had bought them after Sam had left the ranch. One of the things a rancher needed to pay attention to was the personality of a two-thousand-pound bull, which weighed twice as much as a horse. Sam and she had watched the bulls and gotten an idea of their temperament, so that when it came time to herd them, they could be prepared as much as possible for any exigency plans.

Even so, Kate had had a bad feeling when she woke up at four a.m. that morning. The moving of the bulls had been put off until it could no longer be ignored. Two people on horseback handling three bulls wasn't enough to get the job done safely. But they had no choice. These bulls were restless. They could smell the cows in season and were frustrated because they hadn't been able to breed. Bulls were not oriented by herd instinct. Once a bull smelled the scent of cows, he could break off at a moment's notice, hurtle his massive body right through a startled horse and rider and kill them in order to get to the cows.

Today, Kate wore leather chaps, as Sam did. The chaps were wide and flared at the bottom, covering part of her dusty, cracked cowboy boots. If a bull decided to take off, she or Sam could be brush popped through thickets of cutting chaparral, slammed into the long, crochet-needle-size spines of a Mormon tea bush or worse, be run into a five-to eight-foot patch of prickly pear cactus. The leather would be a good guard against abrasion, up to a point.

Flexing her gloved fingers on the reins, Kate felt Cinnamon move nervously beneath her, picking up on her tension. The sun beat directly down on them as they spotted the bulls just below the base of the hill, foraging for almost nonexistent grass. Spring was supposed to yield several inches of rain to feed the dry, arid land, but so far it hadn't. Now food was more sparse than ever and the bulls had ranged over a much larger area in order to survive. It would make herding them even longer and more difficult.

"There they are," Sam said, glancing at Kate as she pulled up beside him. He saw the grim set of her lips. She wore a red bandanna around her throat, protective chaps and gloves, plus a special long-sleeved, heavy twill shirt that would to a degree protect her flesh from brutal contact with Mormon tea and chaparral. Her face glistened; her sky blue eyes narrowed, intent upon the bulls.

He wasn't feeling too easy, either. Today they both wore pistols—Colts—around their waists. If a bull got mean and charged, it might have to be shot in order to save their lives. When blinded by the mating lust, a bull was a ton of raw testosterone and adrenaline on the hoof.

Sam rested his hand on the low-slung holster that held the Colt. Earlier, they'd put bullets in the chambers, locked and loaded them and put the safety on. Riding around with a bullet in the barrel of a pistol wasn't something he liked to do, but there wasn't much choice. If he knew the personalities of the bulls better, he might be feeling less tense. Therefore, out of a lifetime of experience, Sam treated the bulls like C-4 plastic explosives just waiting to go off at him. Or worse, at Kate. Worriedly, he assessed her. She seemed easy and relaxed in the saddle, but he saw tension in the line of her mouth.

"You sure you want to do this?"

She quirked her lips. "No, but I didn't see anybody else volunteering." Patting the bulging saddlebags behind her, she added, "I've brought two first-aid kits—one with dressing and bandages, the other that homeopathic kit Rachel sent—just in case."

Scratching away the sweat trickling down his cheek, Sam nodded. "Good." He sincerely hoped they wouldn't need either one of them. "We'll probably look like a couple of pin cushions before this little dance is over."

"Chaps will help."

"Help, but not stop all of those cactus spines." He motioned to the landscape stretching before them. Thousands of Mormon tea bushes stood with their arms full of greenish yellow needles. They reminded him of long crochet or knitting needles, sticking out all over the bush as if it were a giant pin cushion. "This is a bad area. Keep your face protected, Kate. I don't want you to lose an eye to one of those damn bushes." He hated Mormon tea. It was far more dangerous to a human and horse than the prickly pear patches that proliferated on the red, sandy desert.

Except for protective wrappings on their vulnerable lower legs, the horses had little way to defend themselves against hostile plants and bushes. The gelding Sam rode was long-legged, rangy and savvy. From years of experience, Bolt knew how to avoid these dangers. And the Arabian Kate rode was trail trained, also. These horses were smart and they knew how to read cattle. Sam knew his horse had plenty of experience with testy, dangerous bulls. He wasn't sure that Cinnamon had any such experience—and that put Kate at great risk. A horse not expecting to get charged by a bull could freeze—and leave it and its rider a handy target. If Cinnamon was used to docile Herefords and had no experience with the cantankerous behemoths, that was a high risk. But what else could Sam do?

He had known Donovan horses that had bull-herding experience, but when he returned to the ranch, they were all gone. And Cinnamon was new. He'd watched the mare and knew she had a good head on her shoulders. Her response in other situations had been steady and controlled. But bulls could scare even the most levelheaded of horses if they made a split-second charge. A horse could freeze or could leap to one side to avoid being struck. Worse, if Kate asked Cinnamon to make a swift countermove, and the mare, because of inexperience, didn't trust her mistress in the dangerous situation, they could be injured or killed.

It was very important that a ranch horse trust its rider completely. One wrong move, one misstep, could get them killed. There were places on the Donovan Ranch that could only be reached by taking the canyon walls. If a horse did not watch where it was placing its feet or heed the signals of the rider's legs or the reins, they could both slip to their death.

Scowling, Sam studied the three red-and-white Hereford bulls. Luckily, they'd found some pretty good patches of yellowing grass beneath a large stand of Mormon tea and they were closely grouped. That was unusual, but he hoped it was a sign of good things to come. He pointed his gloved finger at the bull nearest them, the largest one with the red ear tag hanging off his left ear. The bull lazily flicked at the flies buzzing around his massive head. "Let's call him One Horn. He's the biggest. I'll take him on. That next one, the middle-sized one, will be Red. The smallest over there we'll call Whitey."

Names would help them when they called out instructions or orders to one another. Red was a muscular powerhouse, his small eyes regarding them suspiciously even now. Sam didn't trust that son of a bitch, either. Whitey was the smallest of the three bulls, and looked the least interested in their approach. One Horn had one of his horns missing, and the other was deformed and thrust upward like a twisted dagger waiting to impale some unlucky soul. Sam didn't like horned Herefords. He'd argued against purchasing them, but Kelly had liked the old traditional Hereford breed with horns.

A Hereford's horns normally were small and curved inward toward the bull's face, which made them a lot less dangerous than other breeds of cattle to a cowboy who had to herd them. One Horn's straggly appendage was like a razor-sharp knife. A savage head toss by One Horn would be like experiencing the cut of a saber. The bull, if angered, could slice and gut open a horse chest to flank in one horrifying motion. It wasn't a very pleasant thought.

Kate's Arabian mare weighed only eight hundred pounds. Sam's gelding was a good four hundred pounds heavier—not to mention a lot taller. Herding bulls with heavier horses was smart because a bull could bump a horse and the horse could stand its ground and not get tossed around like a tumbleweed. Bolt was built like a proverbial tank, with a lot of width across his chest, heavy hindquarters for getting his rear legs solidly beneath him, enabling him to turn on a dime, and a long barrel that gave him the ability to reach a long, ground-eating stride very swiftly.

"None of them look very pleasant, do they?" Kate asked wryly, sitting up in the saddle and stretching her legs. In a few moments they'd be working hard. Once they got the bulls together and moving in the same direction, there could be no stopping or resting—or the bulls would scatter like leaves on the wind, and the herding process would have to begin all over.

"No," Sam growled. He gestured toward the bulls. "Watch One Horn. He's eyeing us. I looked at the breeding records in your office on these three bulls and he's the oldest. That means he's got more experience."

"Translated," Kate said grimly, "it means he knows how to down a horse and rider if he gets a mind to."

"Yes," Sam agreed unhappily. Reaching out, he gripped her upper arm momentarily. "If I yell an order to you, Kate, just do it. Don't wait, don't analyze, all right? You've got to trust me enough to know that I know what's right if these bulls get riled."

She smiled a little and reveled in the firmness of his hand on her arm. "I trust you with my life, Sam McGuire." The tenor of their relationship was continuing to evolve, their exchanges more open, filled with personal warmth. In the last month, Kate had initiated a touch now and then—not often, but it let him know that she was reaching out to him. He'd gotten the message. Now and then, in return, he would touch her. Usually in moments when he was worried for her safety. Like now.

Sam released Kate's arm, his gaze resting on her blue eyes flecked with gold. Yes, things were moving the right direction with her as far as he was concerned. The energy between them was one of friendship now and ripe with sexual tension. The next step would be a heady one to take, Sam thought as he pulled his hat down tightly so it wouldn't fly off once they got started herding these contrary bastards. In time, if everything went right, he knew Kate would let down her guard and trust him. In time, she might trust him enough to learn to love him once again—as he loved her.

"Let's move nice and easy toward them," he said from between tight lips.

Kate nodded tensely and rode at his side. Her heart skipped a beat as One Horn snapped his large head up toward them. He had small, beady eyes. Evil eyes, in Kate's opinion. There was an old horseman's saying that the smaller the eyes on a horse or steer, the less brains it had and the more dangerous it could be. The larger the eyes, the more intelligent it was and therefore easier to work with.

Upon Sam's command, they separated and quietly moved around the three bulls. Kate saw massive amounts of drool hanging in long, glistening strings from One Horn's white muzzle as he studied her. A chill crawled up her spine. Her hands automatically tightened on the reins and she gripped the barrel of her horse more securely with her long legs. Cinnamon sensed her tension and snorted, her own attention on One Horn.

To Kate's relief, One Horn grudgingly turned as Sam approached him, just like a docile steer or cow would. Cinnamon was trained for leg commands, and Kate pressed her right leg against the animal's side, turning left to cut off the other two bulls, which were beginning to go in different directions, away from One Horn.

Instantly, the bay responded and pebbles flew from beneath her rear hooves as she made the cut. Good. Red and Whitey stopped their escape plan and moved back toward Sam and One Horn. Releasing a breath of air,

Kate kept her horse reined in. If one of those bulls decided to charge, she knew it could turn its massive body and come hurtling at her in a split second. She needed to keep her distance in order to react in time and get the hell out of the way.

In her gloved right hand, she held her coiled rope. Not that they would ever try to lasso a bull—that would be foolhardy. With a bull's power and weight, he'd yank a cowboy straight out of the saddle. If the saddle cinch didn't break and shred under the bull's strength, the horse could be pulled off its feet and dragged along, too. No, the rope was for making occasional slapping sounds against her leather chaps, but that was about all.

For two hours they kept the bulls in a slow-moving, loose-knit herd. The rocky, cactus-strewn hills came and went. Kate was beginning to relax. Soon the breeding pastures would be coming up. She noticed that the bulls were lifting their noses more often to the air, testing it for the odor of cows in season and that they had picked up their pace to almost a trot. This was where it could get dangerous. No fence on earth could stop a bull if he chose to plow through it to get to the cows. The breeding pastures were smaller, the posts eight feet high with six strands of barbed wire, designed to detour a bull. But that's all the fence would do.

"Kate!"

Sam's voice thundered at her, interrupting her errant thoughts. Startled, she jerked her head and saw him pointing up to the right of him. A Hereford cow was loose. "Oh, damn," she whispered in a strained voice. Automatically, her hands tightened on the reins. Cinnamon tensed, waiting for a command.

The cow mooed plaintively toward the three approaching bulls. Kate knew without a doubt that the animal was in season. And she also knew that all three bulls had caught the hormonal scent on the air and were going to try and race one another to get to her first in order to breed with her. Double damn! Of all the things Kate imagined could happen, a loose cow wasn't one of them. She saw Sam swing Bolt abruptly. One Horn made a bid to veer off to the right toward the cow.

"Get to the cow!" Sam shouted. "Get her herded back to the pasture!"

It was a brilliant plan, Kate thought. Sam's experience over her own lack of it was obvious. Yes, get the cow herded up ahead of the bulls and they'd follow like mesmerized kids behind the Pied Piper. Sinking her heels into Cinnamon, she made the mare leap to the right. Dirt and stones flew as Kate galloped hard toward the cow half a mile away. Out of the corner of her eye, she saw One Horn toss his head ominously as Sam slapped his coiled rope against his chaps, warning the bull to go back and join the other two.

Kate had no time to watch. Hunching low, her hands against Cinnamon's sweaty neck, she rode at a dizzying pace toward the cow. The Arabian's small size allowed her to weave around the Mormon tea and cactus with finesse and ease. Cinnamon's ground-eating stride thundered beneath Kate. The wind whipped past her, the horse's black mane stinging her face as the mare ran. Up ahead, Kate saw the cow move toward the breeding pastures. Good! This was going to be easier than she'd thought. The cow could've turned contrary and headed straight to the bulls instead, causing all kinds of hell to break loose. If that had happened, the bulls would begin to fight one another, causing serious injury and maybe death to one or more of them. Tens of thousands of dollars spent on a good breeding bull could be lost in a moment like this. Kate didn't want that to happen.

Just as she crested the hill, she heard a bawling and bellowing behind her. The cow was trotting quickly toward the breeding pastures, no more than half a mile away at this point. Jerking her head to the left, Kate pulled her horse to a skidding stop.

"Sam!" Her cry careened down into the gully area between two hills, where he rode with the three restless bulls. *"Nooo!"* She saw One Horn toss his head and charge Sam. Without thinking, Kate sank her heels into Cinnamon. The mare hurtled back down the slope. Kate's heart slammed into her chest as One Horn bore down on Sam.

With a grunt, Sam jerked Bolt to the left as One Horn lifted his massive, drooling head and charged. Despite his heft and size, the bull moved like lightning. Bolt dug in his hind legs, throwing all his weight to the right. Sam stayed with the big gelding, his gaze pinned on the swiftly moving bull. Spittle flew up around One Horn's face and caught on the twisted horn, which glittered like a deadly knife.

Bolt knew what to do—he headed away from the bull at full speed. Sam felt his horse using every ounce of strength to create distance between them.

One Horn bawled angrily and made a sharp move to the right, to head them off.

Damn!

A small gully, cut deep and wide by thunderstorms and flash floods year after year, loomed before them. It lay at the bottom of two bracketing hills. Sam heard Kate's cry but he had no time to look up. A huge stand of Mormon tea appeared to the left of them, just before the gully. On the right was a five-foot-tall patch of prickly pear. The gulch walls were too steep for them to cross it at a dead run. If Bolt tried to leap across and scramble up the steep, rocky hill, he'd never make it.

The choices were few. Sam twisted his head. One Horn had read the situation correctly. Determined to cut them off, he was hurtling toward them, bawling, the spittle streaming out of his open mouth, his eyes red with rage. Sam began to pull back on the reins to signal Bolt not to try and make that deadly leap. The horse could break his neck, and so could Sam once Bolt, who was going too fast to negotiate the rocky hill properly, smashed into the other side.

Again Sam heard Kate's cry, this time closer. Where was she? No time to look. Where to go? The gulch and hill loomed before him.

Without warning, Sam hauled the reins against Bolt's thick, sweaty neck.

Instantly, the big gelding responded. The action threw them into the stand of Mormon tea. Sam tried to protect his face as the horse slammed full speed into the thick, tough greenery. The heavy branches scraped against him but that was the lesser of two evils. He heard Bolt grunt and stagger to the right as the horse lost his footing and they slid into the stand. One Horn bawled. The sound was right on top of them.

Bolt grunted, his hindquarters skidding across the sandy desert and sharp rocks. Sam hung on with his legs while trying to unstrap the Colt from his left hip. They had slid completely, like a baseball runner into home plate, into the thick stand of Mormon tea. The long, stabbing needles mercilessly gouged at horse and rider. Sam felt the jabs, but there wasn't time to focus on the pain. He heard the crash of One Horn following closely behind them.

Bolt, his hind legs beneath him now, was breathing hard. There were at least a dozen puncture wounds in the horse from the Mormon tea and the gelding's chest ran red with trickles of blood. As he directed Bolt to move swiftly out of the grove, Sam glanced behind them. One Horn was coming through the Mormon tea like it was a Sunday walk in the park, plowing the ten-foot bushes aside with his massive weight. Sam saw the killing rage in the bull's eyes, and in that second he knew that one of them was going to die very shortly.

Bolt also seemed to realized that this was a life-and-death confrontation. The horse spun to the left, the shortest way out of the grove. Dirt flew in all directions beneath the powerful, hammering strides of the animal. Once they cleared the bushes, Sam caught sight of Kate, her face white with terror. She was heading right toward One Horn, her coil of rope lifted toward him.

"No!" Sam shouted hoarsely. *No good! Damn!* Bolt weaved to the right in one smooth motion, his long legs eating up the distance between them. Kate couldn't take on that bull! But that's exactly what she was doing. She was trying to get One Horn's attention away from him and transferred to her. Damn her courage! Sam's lips lifted away from his teeth as he leaned forward, asking for every ounce of Bolt's power in order to close the distance. One Horn was torn between his moving targets. He slowed a little, looking first at Kate, then at Sam. But it was Kate's shrill scream that enraged the bull the most. In one lightning move, One Horn twisted to the right, bawling out his challenge and bearing down on Kate.

The ground was uneven—soft here, hard there. Bolt negotiated the terrain as he carried Sam closer. Cursing, Sam managed to get the Colt out of the holster. Trying to unsnap the safety while his horse was barreling down the side of the slope was nearly impossible. He kept missing the catch again and again. There was no way to stop One Horn now. They were trapped in a small area, the rocky hills acting like prison walls that refused them the room they needed to get away from the infuriated bull. The only way out of the situation was to kill One Horn before he killed one of them.

Kate sucked in a breath as One Horn suddenly spun around and bore directly down on her. Cinnamon reacted first, leaping to the right, her feet sliding down toward the narrow gulch. *No!* Instantly, Kate threw her weight to the left, and the horse steadied. Kate could hear the grunting, sucking sounds One Horn made with each galloping stride he took closer to them. Sam's voice thundered, but Kate couldn't make out what he was yelling. The bull was less than fifty feet away, his small, red eyes fixed on her. Drool streamed out of both sides of his mouth as he lowered his head to charge. The wicked horn glinted in the sunlight.

With a cry, Kate slapped her rope against the horse's rump. Cinnamon leaped forward, startled, and they galloped parallel to the gulch. Up ahead, a large patch of prickly pear loomed. She suddenly saw One Horn change course. He was trying to force her and the horse into the cactus patch or down into the narrow gully. The bastard! The bull was determined to kill them. And that realization startled Kate as nothing else.

Cinnamon realized the bull's intent, too. The mare was breathing hard, trying to outdistance the accelerating beast. Kate knew that the hill, covered with black lava and cactus, could be negotiated, but not at this speed or angle. She might take a horse up that steep face at a slow walk, but not at a wild, headlong gallop. Her choices were few. If she tried to go left, One Horn would intercept her.

For Kate, the only choice was the huge prickly pear patch looming before them. It was a good five feet high at the lowest point, and at least fifty feet deep. She knew now that One Horn was counting on the fact that she wasn't going to run her horse through that patch. But he was wrong. Gathering up the reins, Kate synchronized each movement of her body with Cinnamon's stride. In seconds, they were riding as if they were literally a part of one another. The mare steadied under Kate's hands and guidance.

Gripping her legs tight against the horse's barrel, Kate heard One Horn's breathing coming up fast behind her. She knew there was less than five feet separating them. She would have to jump the patch. Or try at least. Kate was hoping that the bull wouldn't plow through the cactus, being too old and wise to the pain the sharp spines caused. Would he stop? Would Cinnamon trust her and make the jump? The horse could refuse and skid to a halt, trying to escape to the right or left instead. If she did that, Kate knew, One Horn would kill them.

Everything slowed down for Kate. She felt each jolting, thundering movement of the horse, felt the hot sun beating down on her, tasted fear in her mouth and felt sweat stinging her eyes. Prickly pear branches grew at all heights, some five to six feet in the air. Would her small mare be able to jump not only far enough, but high enough? Kate didn't know. But she had to ask for a life-and-death effort from the mare. She placed her gloved hands on the sides of the animal's slick neck, the reins tight as she aimed for the narrowest point of the cactus patch. Applying pressure to the animal's sweaty, heaving sides, Kate signaled the horse to pick up speed in preparation to jump.

The wet mane stung Kate's face as she lifted her butt off the saddle, trying to give Cinnamon every chance to use her hindquarters to power them up and over the patch. Kate felt a moment's hesitation in the mare. Instantly, she pressed Cinnamon with her legs. The mare responded. If the Arabian didn't clear the patch, Kate knew it could badly injure them. Depending upon how the horse fell, Kate might be killed, too. In those slow-motion moments before she asked the Arabian to leap, Kate's heart centered on Sam. How she loved him! She swore that if she got through this alive, she'd tell him that.

Kate felt Cinnamon lifting her front legs as the horse began to leap. Everything began to swirl like a surreal picture in front of Kate's eyes and she pinned her gaze on the landing point. She heard Cinnamon grunt as she powered off the desert ground. They were airborne! Never had Kate sat so still. She felt her horse stretching, stretching forward. Then Cinnamon's legs and hooves tucked deep beneath her belly. Kate knew that if she moved in any way, she could throw the horse off and they could die. She saw the five-foot-tall cactus flash beneath them. The Arabian grunted as it grazed her, her tender belly scraped by the needles.

The bawling of One Horn shattered Kate's concentration. She had no way of knowing whether the bull was following them across the patch or not. Her eyes widened. Her lips parted in a cry. Cinnamon suddenly stretched her legs forward, her black hooves aimed toward that clear patch of ground. Were they going to make it? Her breath jammed in her throat.

Yes! Cinnamon cleared the patch by half a foot! The horse landed hard and Kate was thrown violently forward. Instantly, she threw the reins away to give the horse its head so that she might come out of the ungainly, off-balance landing. Too late! Kate knew Cinnamon had overstretched herself, giving all she had to save them. The mare's front knees buckled. Kate leaned way back, her spine touching the horse's rising hindquarters. Cinnamon was going to flip end over end! Fear engulfed Kate. With a cry of surprise, she allowed the forward momentum to rip her out of the saddle. Instead of hurtling over the horse's head, which would leave her in the path of Cinnamon's hooves, Kate pushed away with her legs. She tucked her head against her body as she flew through the air.

In seconds, Kate slammed into the hard, unforgiving ground. She heard Cinnamon grunt heavily off to her right and felt the ground shake as the horse landed in turn. Rolling to distribute the shock of the fall, Kate kept her arms tight around her knees. She heard several gunshots fired in rapid succession as she landed in a Mormon tea bush. Pain shot up into her back and she suddenly stopped rolling.

Straightening her arms and legs, Kate scrambled to her feet and anxiously looked toward the patch. Her eyes widened enormously when she saw One Horn staggering around in the middle of the cactus, his head bloodied. Sam was astride Bolt, his Colt aimed at the crazed bull. On wobbling legs, Kate watched the bull resist the bullets placed in his brain. Then One Horn's red-eyed gaze settled on her. Foam and spittle mixed with pink and red bubbles of blood running out of his mouth. He bawled in fury. Flailing, he fought to move toward her. Kate froze with shock. The bull was dying, but still trying to reach her!

She heard the Colt bark two more times in quick succession and saw One Horn's head jerk upward at the first shot. His forward progress stopped. The second shot felled him. He grunted, flung his head up in a twisting motion and crashed to the ground, only ten feet away from where Kate stood.

Chapter 12

Kate turned drunkenly to check on her horse. Cinnamon stood alertly, shaking off the excess sand after her fall. The mare seemed fine despite the almost deadly leap she'd made.

"Kate!"

Dazedly, Kate turned back toward Sam's voice. She watched him ride the gelding around the cactus patch, his face stony, his flesh glistening with sweat, his eyes dark and fathomless. Bolt's hindquarters lowered as the gelding slid to a stop, and sand flew up in sheets around them. Sam dismounted, his gaze pinned savagely upon her.

"I—I'm all right." Kate wobbled as he ran up to her, his hand outstretched. But she wasn't, and she knew it. She had nearly died. One Horn had plowed through the cactus patch after her. And Cinnamon had fallen. The bull would have gored her to death in the sand right where she stood if Sam hadn't shot him.

Sam reached out, his fingers closing over her shoulder. "Kate…you're white as a sheet," he muttered tightly. "Broken bones?"

"No…" Kate closed her eyes, a ragged sigh escaping her lips. "Oh, Sam…" She leaned forward, lifting her arms and sliding them around his neck. He was hot, sweaty and dirty, but she didn't care. At this moment, all she wanted was him and the sense of safety he'd always given her. She wanted to sob out her love for him, and the words were nearly torn from her as she collapsed into his arms.

"Come here," he rasped hoarsely, wrapping his arms around her. Crushing Kate against him, Sam steadied her against the hard angles of his body. She fit perfectly and he groaned as her head rested against his jaw. He felt Kate trembling, and it got worse the longer he held her.

"It's all right," he breathed huskily, turning his head and pressing his mouth against her damp, gritty hair. "Everything's going to be all right, Gal. I promise you…." He felt Kate moan as he pressed a not-so-innocent kiss to her temple. She shifted and lifted her face to him. He saw tears swimming in her dark blue eyes, saw the terror in them—and something else…. For those few seconds, Sam couldn't believe what he thought he was seeing. He remembered that look from so long ago. Did he dare hope? ·

"I almost died," Kate murmured, holding his stormy gray gaze. "I could've died and never told you, Sam…." She choked on a sob and moved her hands to his face.

"I love you… I never stopped loving you! I could have died just now and you'd never have known—"

Her words were caught by his descending mouth. He captured her lips fully, his mouth hot, hungry and seeking. Sinking fully against him and allowing Sam to take all her weight, Kate surrendered to him. Tears streaked down her cheeks, met and melted into the line of their mouths as they devoured one another. She'd almost died! Eagerly, she returned his powerful, molding kiss with equal need and fiery hunger. She could smell his masculine scent, taste his fear, feel the roughness of his beard scraping against her face. She suddenly remembered all those wonderful things about Sam that she could have never have experienced again if One Horn had gotten to her before Sam had killed him.

Knees wobbly, Kate tore her mouth from his, breathing hard. She gripped his arms to steady herself. Apologetically, she met his stormy, silvery eyes. She'd known this man before—the raw hunger in his eyes, the cajoling strength of his mouth upon hers, the roughened tenderness of his hands upon her body. "Sam," she whispered, "I—I think I'm going to faint…."

Kate awoke slowly. She felt the heat of the sun on her body, heard the soft snort of horses nearby. More than anything, she felt a damp cloth being gently dabbed across her brow where she lay. Lashes fluttering, she forced her eyes open. The cool cloth felt so good. She was hot, her skin sore and gritty. As her gaze focused, she realized belatedly that Sam was kneeling over her. And even more belatedly, Kate realized with embarrassment that she'd fainted.

"Just lie still," Sam urged quietly. He poured a little

more of the precious water from his canteen into his bandanna and wiped the sides of her face. Her eyes were half-open and filled with confusion. He saw her lips twist wryly.

"I don't believe it. I fainted. I've never done that, ever...and I've been in a few tight spots before. I must be getting old...."

Her voice was wispy and weak, completely unlike her. Sam placed the bandanna across her furrowed brow and unbuttoned the two top buttons on her shirt, pulling her collar wide. He'd removed her gloves and set them nearby, propping up her feet so that the blood flowed back into her head and upper body.

"Almost getting killed brings on a lot of reactions," he grunted.

Kate's lashes dropped shut as Sam carried her out of the sun and placed her beneath the spreading arms of a mesquite tree. Languishing there, grateful for his care, Kate slowly realized that she'd told Sam she loved him. Instantly, she opened her eyes and stared up at his hard, uncompromising face.

"The horses...are they okay?"

"Fine. It's you I'm worried about."

Pushing herself up on one elbow, Kate managed a broken smile. Sam helped her sit up and she leaned her elbows over her knees, hugging her head between her legs. Color was rushing back to her face now, and Sam knew she'd be all right. He tucked the damp bandanna into her hand.

"Keep wiping your face down and cooling off." He rose to his feet.

Kate looked up and did as she was instructed. Sam went over to Bolt, who stood no more than six feet away.

She wanted to cry as she saw about a dozen puncture wounds across his massive chest from his run through the Mormon tea. Trickles of drying blood made vertical stripes across his powerfully muscled body. Sam spoke gently to the gelding as he slowly ran his hand over the animal's chest in examination. Every once in a while Sam would jerk out a thin, needlelike spine causing Bolt to flinch.

Getting to her feet, her knees still a little weak, Kate moved over to Cinnamon, who had sought the shade of the mesquite tree as well.

"Let me check her over," Sam said from behind her, his hand settling on her arm. "Sit back down, Kate. Just rest a minute."

Ordinarily, Kate would have protested, but the sand and the shade looked awfully inviting. "Okay..."

She watched as Sam discovered at least thirty cactus spines in Cinnamon's belly, where she'd brushed the prickly pear in her lifesaving leap.

Sam crouched down, carefully picking the spines out one by one. Cinnamon never moved a muscle. "She did one hell of a job jumping that patch. I didn't think she would make it." He glanced over at Kate. She had gone pale again and he saw her lips compress at his statement. "Bolt *might* have made it, but I never thought this little bay Arabian could do it. When I saw you make the decision, I thought you were dead."

Kate wiped her brow with her trembling hand. She was still amazed at her reaction to the event. But then, she reminded herself, she'd never been the target of a two-thousand-pound bull intent on killing her, either. "I didn't have a choice. Cinnamon knew that."

Sam patted the mare affectionately after he'd removed all the spines from her belly. "She saved the woman I love," he told her huskily.

Kate swallowed hard as she watched Sam approach her. Her eyes filled with tears as he knelt down on one knee and touched her cheek, cupping it and making her look directly into his eyes.

"I'm going to tell you something, Kate. And maybe it's too soon and I'm out of line, but I just damn near lost you, so I'm saying it anyway." He held her glistening blue gaze as her tears trickled downward, meeting his palm as it lay against her cheek. "I never stopped loving you either, Gal. Not *ever*." Sam bowed his head, emotions overcoming him. When he got a hold on them, he looked up again, his voice oddly husky. "You've got more courage than brains in your head, you and that little horse you ride. My God, I thought you were crazy for coming back down that slope after us."

Surprised, Kate whispered, "Sam, One Horn had you trapped! What else could I do?"

His mouth twisted into a half grin. "Stayed up on the knoll and watched, you crazy woman."

Incensed, Kate sputtered, "Like hell, Sam McGuire!"

"You came down because you love me."

She stared into his stormy gray eyes and realized how upset he was. "Yes, I did. I didn't see any other options, Sam."

"When I saw you come riding hell-bent-for-leather down that slope, sand and gravel flying, my first thought was that you were crazy, until I realized why you were really doing it." With a heavy shake of his head, Sam rasped, "Kate, you're the bravest woman I've ever known. I think you knew One Horn would go after you. Didn't you?"

She shrugged helplessly and slid her hand against his roughened one. "If he didn't, *you* were going to be killed." Her voice cracked. "I—I couldn't stand the idea of that. I just couldn't...."

Pushing aside the damp strands of hair that clung to her cheek and temple, Sam whispered unsteadily, "I know... I know...."

Sniffing, Kate said, "All I could think about, Sam, was you—what we'd had a long time ago. When you came and picked me up at the halfway house, I felt so many things. I never stopped loving you even though you married Carol. It was probably just as well Kelly broke my nose and I missed those last six weeks of school. I couldn't have stood seeing you in the halls or the cafeteria...anywhere."

Sam eased back on his heel and watched Kate fighting her tears.

"And I never got to tell you back then the *real* reason why I married her," he rasped apologetically.

"You tried and Kelly stopped you," Kate whispered, wiping her tears away with her fingers. "It was just as well, Sam. You did the right thing. It's all in the past."

"Well," he murmured, his fingers grazing the slope of her dirty cheek, "what I'm interested in is you, me and our future, Gal." He lifted his head and watched the two bulls, which had found some dried grass in the gulch and were grazing peacefully. Turning his attention back to Kate, he smiled tenderly down at her. "We got some unfinished business to attend to first before we can really sit down and talk. You up to helping me herd these two thickheaded bulls to the pastures?"

Kate put out her hand as Sam rose to his full height, drawing her up with him. Warmth flowed through her fingers and up her arm as he held her hands, momentarily erasing all her aches and pains from the fall. "You know I am," she answered. "This isn't the first time I've been thrown off a horse, Sam McGuire. It won't be the last." Kate saw a one-cornered grin tug at his wonderful mouth. A mouth she wanted to kiss endlessly until the last breath left her body.

He led her over to Cinnamon, picked up the reins and placed them across the animal's neck for her. "Climb on," he told her, and helped her mount by cupping her elbow to steady her. Kate was quickly bouncing back from the incident. He saw the light shining in her eyes and the love there—for him alone. Sam felt like he was walking on air. Nothing else really mattered, but they had to keep their heads and get ranch work done first.

Giving Bolt a well-deserved pat of thanks, he remounted his rangy gelding, pulling the brim of his hat low on his brow to protect his eyes from the blistering sun overhead. He watched Kate rebutton her shirt, tug her leather gloves back on and settle her black Stetson firmly on her head. What a brave, gutsy woman she was. With a shake of his head, Sam moved his gelding over to where she sat.

"Let's go, Gal. After we get these bulls put away, I want to go home and get these horses cared for properly."

Kate nodded. The horses were their very next priority. She leaned over and gave Cinnamon an affectionate pat on the neck. "Let's go," she whispered. The animals' wounds would be cleaned, and then the horses would be washed down with a hose and carefully examined for any other cuts or cactus spine. Finally they'd be rubbed down, given a good ration of oats and released to the corral for a well-deserved rest.

As they moved the two remaining bulls out of the gully and up the steep slope of the hill, Kate's heart flew like an eagle soaring in that dark blue sky above them. Sam loved her. He'd said the words that she'd dreamed about so many lonely nights throughout her life. Barely able to deal with her wild flood of emotions, Kate forced herself to focus on the bulls. The danger wasn't over yet. Bulls were never to be trusted. Tonight, when the last of the demanding ranch activities were finished, she would have a long, searching talk with Sam—about their future. Never had anything been more tantalizing or hopeful in Kate's life.

The lights were low at the ranch house as Sam approached. It was dark now, nearly nine p.m. Ranch chores were not only demanding, but long. With only two people to do the work of six, it was a harsh way to exist, but he really didn't mind it. Freshly showered, shaved and wearing a clean set of clothes, he climbed the wooden porch steps two at a time. Taking off his hat at the door, he knocked against the screen. Soft, low music drifted from the front room as he walked. Kate come around the corner.

He couldn't help but smile in approval. She was dressed in a soft pink cotton skirt that fell to her ankles. The short-sleeved white blouse she wore had lace around the neck and exposed the delicious curve of her neck and collarbones. Her hair was washed and hung in soft curls just above her shoulders. She was beautiful.

"You clean up pretty good," Sam said in greeting as she opened the screen door to allow him entrance. He saw a flush creep into Kate's cheeks. She smiled shyly, a smile that tore at his heart and touched his soul. Here was the Kate he'd known as a teenager, but all grown up. Her sky blue eyes danced with warmth and welcome. When she reached out and slid her fingers into his, he gave her a tender look.

"I can say the same of you, cowboy. Come on in...." Kate felt a flutter of nervousness as she led Sam into the semidarkened living room. The music soothed her, as did Sam's long, easy stride beside her. She felt his fingers flex more strongly against hers. It was a small gesture, but an important one. His dark hair gleamed from a recent shower, and Kate was surprised to see he'd shaved. Generally, by this time of night, Sam's five o'clock shadow gave him a dangerous look. He wore a clean set of Levi's and a white, short-sleeved cotton shirt. Dark hairs peeked out at his throat, emphasizing his blatant, powerful maleness. She ached to love him, ached to become one with him.

As Sam settled on the couch next to Kate, she turned to him and tucked one leg beneath her, relaxing fully with him.

"Can I get you anything to drink?" she asked, realizing she was forgetting her manners.

Chuckling, Sam shook his head and gathered her hands into his. He liked having her leg tucked against his thigh, the pink of her cotton skirt outlining her firm, strong body beneath it. "No, Gal. Everything I've ever wanted I'm holding right now." He lost his smile and looked deeply into her eyes. Sam felt Kate's nervousness and the fine tension in her fingers. "We don't ever have much time around here," he began huskily, "and I don't want to waste it on preambles." Searching her shadowed features, he saw her lips part. Lips he wanted to capture and make his forever.

"I've got something I wanted to give to you for twenty-some years," he said, releasing her hand and digging into his jeans pocket. Producing a small, ivory-colored box, he slid it into Kate's hand. "Go ahead, Gal. Open it up."

Shocked, Kate stared down at the small cardboard box, which had yellowed from age. She stole a glance at Sam. His face was grim. She saw pain in his eyes and tension at the corners of his mouth. Stymied, she placed the box on her lap and carefully pried it open with her trembling fingers. Even in the dim light, she saw the beauty of a small, slender ring inside. Gasping, she removed the lid. There, nestled in the center of the box, was a sterling silver ring with blue turquoise set in a channel setting.

"Oh, Sam…." She touched the ring gently with her fingertips.

He turned and placed one arm on the couch behind her. "It was the wedding ring I was going to give you after we graduated, Kate. I had it made by one of our Navajo friends up on the Res. I told her I wanted a ring with no edges or anything that could catch on something. Around here, with ranch work, jewelry takes a beating." He smiled at her, at the tears glimmering in her eyes. Taking the ring out of the box, he picked up her left hand. He saw the bruises and cuts on her skin from today's near miss with death. Gently, he eased the ring on her fourth finger. It fit perfectly. That was a miracle to him, after all these years.

"I had planned to ask you to marry me the day after graduation, Gal," he told her in a low, off-key voice. "I had everything set. I had a part-time job up at the Maitland ranch waiting for me. I'd signed up to go to the university there. I'd planned on working during the day and going to school at night to earn my four-year degree. I'd talked to Steve Maitland, the owner, and he'd promised you a job if you wanted one. I'd even gone so far as to sign a lease on a little apartment up in Flagstaff. A place where we could settle in and make our first home."

"Oh, Sam...." Kate cried softly. She pressed her fingers to her mouth. Pain surged through her—the pain of a broken past. She saw him shake his head and felt him holding her hand gently with the ring around her finger. A wedding ring.

"I blew it," he rasped. "One night. One drunk. One mistake that cost me you. I know your running away wasn't the fault of my actions. But if I'd been more mature, less the egotistical football hero, I'd have waited for you and not fallen into Carol's arms because I felt sorry for myself."

Sam lifted his gaze and held Kate's. Her hand was damp and cool inside his warm, dry one. "Kate, I can't undo what happened. I was hoping when you came back that maybe, just maybe, there was a chance for us. It was a crazy wish that refused to die in me all these years. And since you came home, from time to time I thought I saw love for me in your eyes. Most of the time, I thought it was my imagination, because I wanted you so badly. But today—" he breathed raggedly "—today I knew. I knew without a doubt of your love for me. You proved it in a way that I never expected. There aren't too many women on a little bay horse that would take on a one-ton bull to save the man she loves, is there?" His mouth stretched into a tender smile.

Shaken, Kate sniffed. "I never thought of it that way, Sam. I knew you were in trouble. I couldn't stand the thought of you being killed by that bull. I had to do *something*."

Releasing her hands, Sam cupped her face and looked deeply into her teary eyes. "And you did. That was when I knew, Gal, that you loved me beyond your own need to protect yourself. The ring is yours, Kate. It's always been yours. I want you to keep it. I know we just got back together and I know we—you—need more time." He stroked her cheek with his roughened fingertips. "That's a wedding ring, Gal. It's my pledge to you. Someday, when it's right for you, I want to marry you. I want you to share my name. To share our future—together...."

Whispering his name brokenly, Kate leaned forward, sliding her arms around his strong neck. She felt Sam's arms lock around her, and the air rushed out of her as she buried her face against his. "I love you so much I ache," she whispered unsteadily. "Love me, Sam...just hold me and love me. It's been so long... I need you so badly—so badly...."

Within moments, Kate felt herself being lifted off the couch and into Sam's arms. Contentment thrummed through her as he walked down the hall to her bedroom, to that old brass bed with the colorful quilt across it. Moonlight sifted throughout the lacy curtains at the window, a warming breeze moving the filmy material now and then. As he laid her down on the bed, his large hands bracketing her head, she looked up, up into his dark, stormy eyes filled with desire—for her.

It was so easy to lift her hands, place her fingertips across his barrel chest and open his shirt, button by button. With each of her grazing touches, she saw him wince. But it wasn't a wince of pain; it was the raw pleasure of her touch he was absorbing. The moonlight carved shadows against Sam's hard, weathered face. Her lips parted as his hand moved slowly downward to caress and cup her breast beneath the soft material of her blouse, his own touch evocative, teasing. A small moan escaped her.

His smile was very male as she helped him off with his shirt. Her fingers trembled badly on the belt buckle, so he helped her with that. Instead of shedding his jeans, he turned his attention to her as they sat on the bed next to one another. His fingers burned a path of need as he outlined her collarbone beneath the lace.

"You're a wild and beautiful mustang, Kate," he rasped as his fingers trailed downward. "Let me taste your wildness, woman…" Then he leaned forward, capturing her parting lips. He took her hard and fast, pulling the breath from her. His callused hands caressed her breasts, and a cry of pleasure rippled through her, a cry of mounting, fiery need. He coaxed off her blouse and she saw him smile as he explored the silky quality of her white camisole. In moments he'd eased that from her, too. Her breath became ragged and her hands moved of their own accord across his massive chest. With each touch, she felt his muscles bunch and harden in response. She was barely aware of her skirt being pulled away from her ankles. His hands slid provocatively up the expanse of her thighs and she lay back, her lashes closing.

A hot weakness enveloped her as he followed the curve of her thighs. As her silky panties were eased away her skin burned with need of Sam's continued touch. She felt him shift and move, and she looked up appreciatively as he stood beside the bed and got rid of his Levi's and briefs. Her mouth went dry as she stared up at his strong male form. Sam was nothing but hard muscle shaped and formed by the unforgiving land and harsh weather. She saw many white scars over his body, reminders that ranching was tough and demanding and took more than a pound of flesh from those who rose to the challenge. As Sam eased back down beside her, she gloried in him, in his embrace.

She felt his insistent hardness pressing against her flank as he settled next to her, his arm beneath her head. Stretched out beside him, she turned toward him, a soft smile on her lips. Grazing his cheek with one hand, Kate could feel the brand-new stubble prickle her exploring fingertips. "I love you, Sam McGuire," she whispered, "with all my heart, my soul. I always did. I always will...." Then she sought and found his hot, hungry mouth, pressing herself against him. Her breasts met his chest, her hips grazed his and she felt his maleness meet the soft curve of her abdomen. Sliding her arms around his neck, she felt the ragged beat of his heart against hers, felt the iron bands of his arms encircling her, crushing her against him.

Taking, giving, his mouth slid wetly across her lips. The heat of his tongue thrust into her mouth and she moaned. Her thighs parted and she felt the delicious weight of him move on top of her. It was so right. So natural. She clung to his male mouth as she felt his hand slide beneath her hips, raising her just enough to welcome him into her awaiting depths. The ache in her lower body intensified almost to pain in those fleeting, heated seconds before she felt him move against her. Her nipples hardened against the wiriness of his chest hair. She moaned and flexed her hips upward to receive him fully. Unconditionally. No longer did she want to wait. She wanted him. All of him. Now. Forever.

The power and heat of his thrust made her arch her spine and throw back her head. Her cry shattered the silence, but it wasn't one of pain. It was one of glorious welcome. She felt the grip of his hands on her hips, guiding her, establishing the rhythm. In moments, they were melting into one another and she felt his body cover hers like a hot, hard blanket. She looked up as he framed her face with his hands, up into his stormy eyes glittering with love. She felt each thrust, moved with him, took him more deeply into her with each fluid movement. The ache turned to fire, and then to a burning longing. She saw a partial, triumphant smile tug at his mouth as the heat within her exploded violently, in a rush, like a volcano too long lain dormant.

Crying out his name, she gripped his damp, tense shoulders, her body pressing against his as the liquid heat flowed powerfully through her like lightning striking during a violent storm. Only the storm was one of raw need for Sam alone, the desire to feel his maleness mated with her femininity once again. She clung to him, gasping. He whispered her name, found her mouth and took it relentlessly as he thrust his hips more deeply, prolonging her pleasure. Moments became sparkling rainbows of color and light beneath her closed eyes as the heat peaked and then began to spread throughout her taunt, quivering form. Then she felt Sam turn rigid, a groan tearing from him, his hands capturing her face and holding her beneath him.

A few minutes later, he moved aside and then brought her up against him. They were breathing raggedly, and he could feel Kate's heart beating against his. He absorbed her soft, cool touches—on his face, shoulders and arms. How good she felt in his embrace! Opening his eyes, Sam stared into her blue ones, which danced with gold flecks of joy. He knew it had been good for her. He had made himself a promise that when it came time to love her, his needs would be secondary to hers. Kate was the one who had suffered all these years. She deserved the best from him now. No longer was he the selfish, egotistical football captain. No, he was a mature man who had made plenty of mistakes, and somehow he was going to make up for every one. One small gift was to make sure she enjoyed their lovemaking as much as he did.

Lifting his hand, Sam brushed several tangled strands of hair away from her damp, flushed cheek. His words came out low and husky. "I love you, Gal."

"I know that now," she whispered, touching his cheek. Kate felt her body tingling in the aftermath and she absorbed the pleasure of just being in Sam's arms, pressed against his hard, muscled form.

He ran his hand lovingly down her rib cage and across her hip. There wasn't an inch of fat anywhere on Kate. Ranching life guaranteed that. He saw the ring on her finger, the moonlight making the silver glint for a moment. Catching her hand in his, he brought it against his chest. "Just tell me that we have a chance, Kate. I don't want you to think that I'll bed you and that's it. Someday I want you for my wife. When you're ready."

Closing her eyes, Kate rested her brow against his chin.

"I never thought," she admitted hoarsely, "that you would ever be my husband, Sam. I've dreamed it over and over throughout the years, but I never thought..." She lifted her head and sighed softly. "This is all so new for me...."

"I know it is," he rasped. "Take your time, Gal. We've got it now.... You're home. You're where you belong. And you're with me...."

Epilogue

"Well, Jessica's got her greenhouse," Sam drawled with a smile as he placed the hammer back in his tool-box.

Kate smiled back and looked on admiringly at the small eight-by-ten-foot building of plate glass. "I think she'll love it, Sam." Much of a cowboy's work was repairing and building things around the ranch, and Sam had done a fine job making the little structure for her sister. Jessica had over fifty orchid varieties that she used in her natural essences, and was driving them down from Canada. In less than three days, her little sister would arrive at the Donovan Ranch to continue her successful business. In her spare moments, Jessica would help out with the demands of the ranch.

Sam grinned and wiped his sweaty brow with the back of his hand as he studied the building, which stood partly beneath the shade of an old cottonwood, near the rear of the red flagstone house that Jessica would live in. Jessica had sent him dimensions, details and the money to buy the necessary items to build a house for "her girls," as she called her orchids. Pleased with his work, he glanced toward Kate, who had helped him. His body held a warm glow and his heart became suffused with love for her. She stood so proudly and tall as she surveyed their mutual handiwork. It made him feel good that she thought so highly of his skills.

The June sun had risen at five-thirty, its golden rays starting to heat up the land. There were no clouds in the flawless turquoise sky. The scorching drought would continue for another unrelenting day. They would have to wait until July, when the monsoon rains arrived, driving thunderstorms and moisture out of Mexico sweeping northward into Arizona. Hopefully, plenty of rain would fall. Worried about the slowly lowering water table, a huge lake that lay beneath the Sedona-Verde valley, Sam picked up his toolbox.

"Breakfast about ready?" he teased, placing his arm around Kate's waist. They walked slowly toward the ranch house. What they needed was enough money to hire a full-time cook and housekeeper. Both of them ended up doing housekeeping chores, but haphazardly at best. Their fourteen-hour days were wearing on them after six months without help. Jessica would be a welcome addition, but Sam knew she would have to work hard to get her company set up, fill orders from around the world for her natural essences, and pay her own bills. Still, he felt Jessica's ebullient, bubbly presence would further heal Kate of her past wounds, because she was very close to her little sister.

Automatically, Kate fell into step with Sam. He always shortened his long, rolling stride when he was walking with her. He was always sensitive to her needs, she thought as she leaned against him, resting her head briefly against his shoulder. "We're so lucky…." she whispered, a catch in her voice as she looked up. Drowning in his tender gaze, Kate tightened her arm around his waist.

"The luckiest," he agreed huskily, leaning over and pressing a quick kiss to her flushed cheek. He saw her eyes dance with joy. So much of the old Kate was unfolding daily before his eyes. Sam knew it was because their love was allowed to take root once more and thrive. This time he was older and wiser. This time he wouldn't throw away the woman he loved.

They walked around the ranch house after he put his tools away. It was still early and he could hear the lowing of the cattle, the soft snorts of the Arabians nearby. Overhead, Sam heard the shrill call of a red-tailed hawk. Looking up, he saw two of them and pointed them out to Kate.

"Husband and wife," he said. Red-tails mated for life and this pair nested on the black lava cliffs above the ranch house.

Kate shielded her eyes with her hand as she watched the two hawks circling lazily five hundred feet above them. "They're catching the rising thermals."

Sam placed his arm around her shoulder and watched the birds gracefully flow on the unseen heat currents starting to rise from the earth as the sun grew warmer. "The Indians would say it's a good sign. They're in the East."

Kate nodded. "East is the direction of new beginnings. Creation."

"Jessica's coming," he said, grinning.

Kate nodded and relished his closeness, his protective arm around her shoulders. "Jessica is so close to Mother Earth."

"I think that of the three daughters, Jessica has your mother's close connection with the soil." He looked at Kate. "Not that you don't, but it's expressed in a different way."

She nodded. "I always used to worry about Jessica. She was so flighty and couldn't ever finish anything she started. Something would catch her eye and she'd take off in this direction or that. I often wondered what she'd grow up to be."

"She runs her own company," Sam murmured. "I'd say she's pretty steady and has a good head on her shoulders despite her wandering ways."

Laughing, Kate agreed. They walked toward the ranch house. She would make them a hefty breakfast and then they'd begin the daily chores of feeding the animals. Today the blacksmith was coming out to trim thirty of the Arabians' hooves. At six dollars apiece, the bill would run up quickly. In his spare time, Sam would do trimming, but he was spread thin as it was, with the weight of the ranch falling on his shoulders.

"Jessica's so excited about coming home," Kate said as they climbed the wooden steps to the porch. "When she called last night, she was worried her orchid girls wouldn't make the trip. I guess they need moisture in the air and the temperature can't be too hot or too cold."

Sam opened the screen door for her. "Coming to Arizona is going to be hard on them."

"Jessica thinks she can manage it with that greenhouse we just built."

"It sounds like she's going to need a full-time helper," Sam said, taking off his hat and placing it on a wooden peg behind the door.

Kate took her own hat off and hung it beside his. Both were dusty, beat-up and desperately needing a good cleaning. Money was tight. Hats weren't high on the list of priorities.

"She said that she's going to have to hire someone to help her, and we're to try and think of someone who might fill the bill." Kate went to the kitchen. While Sam went to the fridge to get the bacon and eggs, she retrieved the cast-iron skillet from a cabinet next to the stove. Their morning routine was wonderful and she loved working closely with him. He'd shred the cheese for their omelets, cut up red and green peppers, chop up some onion and broccoli while she got the eggs ready for the skillet.

"I've got an idea," Sam exclaimed, placing the eggs and slab of bacon on the counter next to Kate. He pulled the rest of the items from the refrigerator and shut the door. Washing his hands in the sink, he said, "There's a half-Navajo, half-Anglo by the name of Dan Black who *might* be the person Jessica's looking for. He's Indian, has close ties to the land, understands and accepts like Jessica does that plants have their own spirit and energy."

Kate nodded and broke a dozen eggs into a big blue ceramic bowl. "Dan Black—that name is sure familiar. Where have I heard it?"

"The Black family up on the Navajo Reservation," Sam told her, wiping off his hands with a towel. He

picked up the grater, unwrapped a block of sharp ched-
dar cheese and methodically began to shred it. "His
mother is a real famous Navajo rug weaver. She just received an award of recognition at the White House for
her artistry. And Dan is one hell of a wrangler. We can
use one. Besides, Gan needs to be gentled and trained.
Right now, he's dangerous to everyone."

She put the bacon in another skillet. "If I remember
right, they called Dan the 'stallion tamer'?"

"Yes, he's got a good reputation for taming wild mustangs, especially mean studs like Gan."

"So what're his bad points?" Sam was excellent at
assessing people.

His mouth quirked. "He's got a few problems."

Kate glanced at him and poured the beaten eggs from
the bowl into another skillet. "You're hedging, Sam."

Quickly cutting up the vegetables for their omelets,
Sam said, "He was in the Marine Corps for a long time.
He went through the Gulf War, Desert Storm. They
medically discharged him after that."

"Why?"

"Mental problems."

Kate rolled her eyes. "Mental problems? And you
want to hire him to work with Jessica and tame Gan?"

"Now, calm down," Sam murmured, placing the vegetables in a bowl so that Kate could add them to the
cooking eggs. "He's not crazy, Kate. Just a little introverted and a loner since coming back, that's all."

"That's nice to know. We have enough problems
keeping this ranch afloat without hiring someone who
has mental-health problems."

"I knew Dan over at the Maitland ranch in Flagstaff.
He worked as a wrangler for me before joining the Ma-

rine Corps. He was a hard worker, took orders well and took pride in his work," Sam said, watching her cook. Kate's black hair was brushing her shoulders now. It made a beautiful frame for her incredible sky blue eyes, which he regularly lost himself in when they made wild, unbridled love. "I haven't seen him of late, but I did see him right after his discharge. I think he's got PTSD."

"Post-traumatic-stress disorder?" Kate put the lid on the omelets to let them cook for a moment and turned her attention to the pan of bubbling, fragrant bacon.

"I think Dan's problems are controllable. He was a pretty outgoing young kid at Maitland's ranch. The war changed him."

"What war doesn't change a person?"

He nodded. "Let me do some snooping around about Dan. Fay Seward, the saddle maker, knows the family real well. I might stop in there and have a chat with her."

"If I had my way," Kate said, scooping up the finished omelets onto plates that Sam retrieved for her, "I'd hire people with Indian blood in them. They never lose their connection with Mother Earth. They have a harmony I want to reestablish here."

Sam put the plates on the table and poured coffee into some white mugs. "I don't have any," he teased.

Kate sat down and grinned. "You're Native American in your heart."

"*You* have my heart, Gal."

She loved this time of morning with Sam. They sat with their knees touching beneath the old wooden table. How many times had Kate looked at the ring she wore on her left hand? She wanted to marry Sam after all her sisters were home. Jessica would arrive in May, and Rachel would be home in late November, or early

December at the latest. Already the three of them were planning for Kate's coming wedding. It wouldn't be an expensive event, but a small, quiet one. Money was hard to find, and Kate certainly wasn't going to spend it on the wedding gown she'd dreamed of so many years ago. Sam agreed to the wait in order to meet the driving demands of the ranch.

"That's got hot peppers in it," she warned watching Sam as he spread salsa over his omelet.

"Makes it good."

Grinning, Kate said, "Mexican food is the way to *your* heart, cowboy."

Chuckling, Sam dug into the omelet. "Guilty as charged. I was raised on the stuff."

Who wasn't out in Arizona? Kate smiled and absorbed the taste of the omelet.

"So," Sam murmured, "your sisters got the details of our wedding worked out yet?"

Kate grinned. "Most of them. Rachel is so glad we're waiting until she can be here as the maid of honor. I don't know who is more excited, them, you or me."

He felt a bit of heat in his cheeks. Kate's eyes danced with merriment. Stilling the fork, he caught her gaze. "I probably am."

"No, I am." Kate laughed, thrilled with the thought that by the end of the year she would be Mrs. Sam McGuire. The idea always made her feel euphoric. She saw the happiness reflected in Sam's gray eyes, too. She picked up a piece of bacon and thoughtfully chewed on it.

Sam sipped his coffee, his gaze resting tenderly on Kate. "One time after we made love, early on, you told me that you had all these dreams about a big wedding.

You had the dress all picked out. You showed me that scrapbook you'd made up when we were going together in high school. You put it together, dreaming of marrying me someday. I know you and your sisters are pinching pennies and you're not going after the wedding you really wanted."

A rush of love flowed through her as she saw Sam's gray eyes grow tender. How much she loved him! Kate had always imagined what it might be like to be married to Sam, but never in her wildest dreams had she thought it would be possible—or this wonderful.

"It would cost too much to put on the wedding I'd originally planned, Sam. It's okay. Really, it is. Don't be giving me that look. I can do a lot on a shoestring, believe me."

She watched him shake his head. "No, I want to see you have the one I saw in your scrapbook. I've been giving this a lot of thought and I think I've come up with a way to have it happen. Let's sell one of your best broodmares. She should fetch at least five thousand dollars. That should be enough for that fancy dress you showed me from your scrapbook." He saw the tears gather in Kate's eyes. How soft and loving she'd become in the past months. The change was startling and wonderful.

Wiping her eyes with a look of embarrassment, she said, "I never thought of that angle." The fact that he wanted to give her a beautiful wedding dress instead of what she was planning on wearing—a cream-colored wool suit—made her love him even more fiercely.

"That's my job," Sam drawled, giving her a one-cornered smile meant to tell her he loved her.

Kate closed her eyes. "I've always dreamed of a beautiful white wedding dress like that…."

Sam nodded, feeling his heart expand with joy. Kate's voice reflected her sudden enthusiasm. Jessica coming home made Kate happy. She could hardly wait for her "Little Sis" to arrive. "Well, let's see what we can do then, about expanding plans for that big wedding you always dreamed of instead of the shoestring-budget one, shall we? We might be living hand-to-mouth right now, but things could change by the time your sisters get home. Besides, dreams need to be fulfilled." Especially Kate's dreams. Sam had stopped dreaming long ago and Kate had already given him back that gift. He could do no less in trying to fulfill her dreams, too.

Kate knew that with the ongoing drought, any bit of excess money they had saved was being eaten up in feed bills to keep the cattle from starving. "Okay," she whispered. "I'd love to wear a dress like that for our wedding day." How thrilled Jessica and Rachel would be about this news! She saw the love in Sam's eyes, his thoughtfulness toward her sending a wealth of emotion through her.

Slowly rising, Sam picked up their plates, took them to the sink and rinsed them off. "Good. Then it's settled. I've already got a buyer for that one black broodmare." He silently congratulated himself for giving Kate another gift she so richly deserved. He'd taken one look at the scrapbook that she'd pulled out and shared with him many months ago, and had realized the depth of her love for him was more than he thought possible. Kate had cut out photos of the dream house she'd wanted as their home, a lace-and-pearl adorned wedding dress, the white-and-purple orchids for the bouquet she'd wanted... They'd been the dreams of a young teenage girl, dreams that he aimed to fulfill because he loved her. She was giving him a second chance. He wasn't about to ruin it this time around. Now he had the capability of helping all her dreams come to life, and that made him feel good about himself for once.

Sam captured Kate's hand as she rose from the chair. In one smooth motion, he brought her into the haven of his arms. She felt good to him as she leaned against him, her hands resting on his arms as she smiled up at him.

"Miracles," he whispered, catching her mouth and kissing it softly, "happen every day of our lives when I'm with you." Her lips were pliant and sweet beneath his. He caressed her mouth and murmured against it, "And I want to stay in your life and show them to you every single day, Kate Donovan—for the rest of our lives...."

* * * * *

Delores Fossen, a *USA TODAY* bestselling author, has written over one hundred novels, with millions of copies of her books in print worldwide. She's received a Booksellers' Best Award and an RT Reviewers' Choice Best Book Award. She was also a finalist for a prestigious RITA® Award. You can contact the author through her website at deloresfossen.com.

Books by Delores Fossen

Harlequin Intrigue

The Law in Lubbock County

Sheriff in the Saddle
Maverick Justice
Lawman to the Core
Spurred to Justice

Mercy Ridge Lawmen

Her Child to Protect
Safeguarding the Surrogate
Targeting the Deputy
Pursued by the Sheriff

Visit the Author Profile page
at Harlequin.com for more titles.

TARGETING THE DEPUTY

Delores Fossen

Chapter 1

Deputy Leo Logan heard the movement behind him a split second too late. He whirled around, automatically reaching for his gun. But before he could draw it, he felt the pain slice over his arm.

He caught a glimpse of the knife. Another glimpse of the guy holding it. The man was wearing all black and had on a ski mask—also black. He was lunging with the knife to try to cut Leo again.

That gave Leo a major surge of adrenaline. And a hit of raw anger. He didn't know who the hell this idiot was, but Leo had no intention of just standing there while he stabbed him.

Leo ducked, avoiding the next slice, and in the same motion lowered his head and rammed right into the guy's gut. His attacker made a strangled sound, like a balloon dteflating. Leo had obviously knocked the breath out of him, but he took it one step further. He stood upright and plowed his fist into his attacker's face. The guy didn't fall but only staggered back, so Leo punched him again.

The man dropped to his knees on the ground, the knife clattering on the concrete next to him.

Leo heard another sound. Running footsteps behind him. He pivoted in that direction, this time managing to draw his gun. However, it wasn't the threat his body had geared up for. It was his brother.

Sheriff Barrett Logan.

It wasn't a surprise to see Barrett since this was the parking lot of the Mercy Ridge Sheriff's Office, but it was the last place Leo had expected to be attacked. It took a lot of guts, or stupidity, to come after a lawman on his own turf.

"What the hell happened?" Barrett snapped. He didn't wait for a response before he added, "Your arm's bleeding. Are you okay?"

Leo gathered his breath and tried to figure out the answer to his brother's question. He didn't think the wound was that deep, but it was already throbbing like a bad tooth. The knife had cut through his shirt, making a gash on his forearm. And there was blood. Thankfully, the wound wasn't gushing, but it was enough that he'd need it cleaned and bandaged.

"This moron attacked me," Leo growled.

As if he'd declared war on it, Leo kicked the knife away from the man, reached down and yanked off the ski mask. It was almost 6:00 p.m. but there was still plenty of light, so he had no trouble seeing the guy. Brown hair, brown eyes. Bulky build.

He was a stranger.

"Who are you?" Leo demanded, and that was just the first of many questions he had for this goon.

Barrett moved in to frisk him.

"I want a lawyer," the guy yelled.

Leo groaned. He didn't mind people exercising their civil rights, but this jerk hadn't minded violating Leo's rights by knifing him.

Barrett cuffed the man, dragging him to his feet. His brother took a wallet from the guy's pocket and handed it to Leo.

"Milton Hough," Leo relayed to Barrett. "He's got a San Antonio address."

Leo had known the guy wasn't local. Mercy Ridge was a small ranching town, and Leo had lived here his entire life. He knew every resident and vice versa, and he was certain he'd never laid eyes on Milton.

"I want a lawyer," Milton repeated, shouting now. "Call Olivia Nash, and she'll get one for me."

Despite his throbbing arm, that got Leo's full attention, and everything inside him went still. Unlike Milton Hough, that name was *very* familiar to Leo. In fact, Olivia was the mother of his one-year-old son, Cameron, and Leo and she were in the middle of a nasty custody battle.

One that Leo didn't want to believe had just gotten a whole lot nastier.

"Olivia?" Barrett questioned, his eyes meeting Leo's.

"Yeah," the thug verified. "Just get my phone out of my jacket pocket. The last call I got was from her, so her number's on top."

"Right," Leo snarled. "And I'm to believe some idiot who'd attack a cop."

"Check the phone for yourself," Milton offered.

Leo debated it for a few seconds before he reached into Milton's jacket pocket and took out his cell. It felt as if he'd been clubbed again when he saw Olivia's name and number there.

Hell.

"Told you she called me," Milton said, and while his tone wasn't exactly a gloat, it was close.

Barrett certainly wasn't gloating. He was cursing and looking at Leo with a mountain of concern. "I'll book this guy. Go to the hospital, get your arm checked and then you can go see Olivia. You sure you're okay to drive? I can have the ambulance pick you up."

"I'm fine," Leo snapped.

He ignored the pain in his arm, got in his truck and drove away once Barrett had Milton inside the police station. There was a deputy and a dispatcher working this shift, so Barrett would have help if he needed it. Maybe Barrett would be able to find some answers, too, but Leo hoped to get a jump-start on that by seeing Olivia.

Olivia didn't live far, only a couple of miles away in the nearby town of Culver Crossing, so it only took Leo a few minutes before he pulled into the driveway of the Craftsman-style house. It was small and modest, not exactly the kind of place most folks would believe an *heiress* should live, but Olivia had bought it so that Cameron would be closer to Leo. The For Sale sign in front of it reminded him, though, of the rift between them.

Had that rift caused Olivia to go off the deep end and hire someone to hurt him? Or even kill him?

Leo didn't want to believe it. After all, he and Olivia

had once been lovers. But they hadn't been in love. Not the kind of love that lasted anyway.

That was one of those "fine line" distinctions.

What they'd had was a short affair that had ended in her sudden breakup with him. When Leo had found out she was pregnant, Olivia hadn't denied it was his child, but she certainly hadn't done anything to remedy their breakup. And now she was challenging their agreement so she could move Cameron out of state.

Since his arm was still bleeding, Leo tore off his shirtsleeve and tied it around the gash like a makeshift bandage. That way, Cameron wouldn't see any blood. His little boy wasn't old enough to understand what'd happened, but he might be alarmed if he realized his dad had been injured.

Leo got out of his truck, went straight to Olivia's door and knocked. Impatience caused him to knock again just a few seconds later. He finally heard the locks being disengaged. The front door opened.

Olivia.

She clearly hadn't been expecting company because she was wearing jeans and a baggy T-shirt, and her dark brown hair was scooped up in a messy ponytail. Cameron wasn't with her. Under normal circumstances, Leo would have wanted to see his son, but he was thankful for some privacy. Privacy that he ensured by stepping inside and shutting the door behind him. Olivia didn't have any close neighbors on either side of her house, but there was one across the street.

"Oh my God, you're bleeding." Olivia's normally cool green eyes widened.

He ignored her and glanced around. "Where's Cameron? Is he with the nanny?"

She shook her head, her attention still on his arm. "He's asleep. He missed his afternoon nap and was so cranky that I went ahead and put him to bed early. I sent Izzie home."

Izzie Landon was the nanny, and while Leo liked the woman, he was glad she wasn't there, either.

"What happened?" Olivia asked.

"You tell me. Milton Hough." He threw the name out there and watched for any signs of recognition.

Leo didn't see any.

He wished he could say that he knew her well enough to know if she was hiding the truth, but he obviously wasn't a good judge when it came to Olivia. He definitely wouldn't have had an affair with her if he'd thought she was capable of sending a thug after him. And if she'd truly done that, there was no way in hell he was going to let his son stay another moment with her.

"Milton Hough?" she repeated, seeming genuinely confused. "Who is he?"

Leo continued to stare at her. "About ten minutes ago, he came after me in the parking lot of the sheriff's office. He had a knife and did this to me." He tipped his head to his injured arm.

Olivia opened her mouth. Closed it. Then she gasped. "This man tried to kill you?"

"Yeah." Leo dragged in a breath before he continued. "Then, as Barrett was arresting him, he cried for a lawyer and said I was to call you."

"Me?" she blurted out. "Why would he say that?"

"You tell me. I checked his phone, and you called him about a half hour ago."

"No." Olivia frantically shook her head. "I didn't."

"I saw your number in his phone," Leo argued, and

had to tamp down the anger. However, he didn't tamp down his own confusion and his cop's instincts. Now that he was thinking straight, he had to ask himself why Olivia would have left any record of her contact with Milton if she'd hired the man to do him harm.

And the answer was—she wouldn't have.

"Show me your phone," he insisted.

Some of the color drained from her face. "I can't. I lost it. I don't know where, but I was going to drive into San Antonio in the morning and get a new one."

"You lost it," he mumbled and then silently cursed. Before Cameron had been born, that was profanity Leo would have said aloud, but he'd learned to tamp that down, too.

"Yes." Her breath swooshed out, and Olivia looked as if she might stagger back. Or even collapse. She didn't. She steeled herself and met him eye to eye. "Someone must have used my phone to call that man."

Leo could see that happening. Of course, that led him to the next question. Or rather, to a comment.

"Your father," was all he said.

Samuel Nash. He was a rich cattle broker, and he hated Leo for getting involved with Olivia, his precious daughter.

She shook her head again, denial all over her face. "You can't think my father's responsible," Olivia insisted.

Samuel had never had a friendly word for Leo, had always treated Leo like dirt, but it was still a stretch to believe the man was capable of something like this.

"When and where is the last place you saw your phone?" Leo persisted.

More of that color left her face and she hesitated for a long time. "I was at work in my office…at my father's."

It didn't surprise Leo that's where she'd last used her phone. Olivia was often at her family's estate just outside San Antonio, and she did, indeed, have an office there where she ran her late mother's charity foundation.

"I didn't notice it was missing until I got home," she went on. "The pharmacy here had some of those no-contract phones and I bought one so I could call Bernice and have her look for mine."

Bernice Saylor, the household manager for the Nash estate, would have been a good person to contact. Well, good for Olivia anyway. Bernice had made it clear to Leo that she hated him as much as Samuel did. Apparently, Bernice didn't think her boss's daughter should have been slumming around with a small-town cop.

"Bernice couldn't find my phone," Olivia added. "But it's possible I dropped it somewhere. Maybe even here when I was getting out of my car."

Yeah, that was possible. But if that'd happened, it meant the person who'd found it had used it to set up Olivia, to make her look guilty of orchestrating the attack against him.

To the best of Leo's knowledge, there was no one in Mercy Ridge who had that kind of grudge against Olivia. But Milton might know for certain who'd hired him. Leo figured he was more likely to get a truthful answer from him than he would from Samuel or Bernice. Still, both of them would have to be questioned.

"You really need to have someone take a look at that arm," Olivia murmured.

When he glanced down at the makeshift bandage, Leo saw the fresh blood seeping through the cloth. Mercy. He might need stitches, after all. But there was an even bigger concern here.

"Look, I don't know what's going on," he admitted, "but if someone is setting you up, Cameron and you could be in danger."

That grabbed her attention. On a muffled gasp, Olivia pressed her hand to her throat. "You really believe that?"

"It's a possibility." He wouldn't sugarcoat this. "I don't want you two alone here tonight." Then he added what he knew Olivia wasn't going to like. "I'll stay with you."

He waited for her to object, and he could tell that's exactly what she wanted to do. Her father would give her all kinds of grief if he found out Leo had spent the night. But Leo didn't care a rat about that. He only needed to make sure his little boy stayed safe.

"You shouldn't be out driving anywhere tonight, either," Leo continued. That would nix any idea she got about going to her father's. "I also don't intend to get another deputy to do this. Cameron's my son, and I'm the one who should protect him."

Olivia finally nodded. "You can stay tonight."

Maybe it wouldn't take longer than that because Barrett would get the answers they needed from Milton. If someone had actually hired Milton to attack Leo, he might give them the name if he were offered some kind of plea deal. Then Barrett could make an arrest and there wouldn't be any sort of threat to Olivia or Cameron.

"You still need someone to check your arm," Olivia reminded him.

Leo huffed, knowing she was right. He took out his phone and called the Culver Crossing Hospital. He requested an EMT come to Olivia's house. That way, he wouldn't have to leave her alone.

"How good is your security system?" Leo asked, putting his phone away.

"It's very good. My father had it set up for me when I moved here."

Of course, he had. Samuel was overly protective of Olivia in every possible way. Not just her safety but her personal life, too. Leo supposed that might have had something to do with Samuel losing his wife in a car accident when Olivia had only been ten. But the man crossed too many lines as far as Leo was concerned.

"Your father's got to be upset about me challenging you for custody." Leo threw the words out there, already knowing the answer. Yeah, Samuel would be upset. Olivia was, too.

"He is," she admitted, dodging his gaze now. "He doesn't want me to move to Oklahoma."

That was probably the only thing that Leo and Samuel agreed on. Well, that and their love for Cameron. Even though Samuel could be a hardnosed SOB, Leo didn't doubt that the man loved his grandson.

"I'm not going to rehash all of this tonight," Olivia said, sounding a whole lot stronger than she had just seconds earlier. Leo could practically feel her digging in her heels.

They had indeed gone through all of this. Many times.

Olivia wanted to relocate to Tulsa to take over a nonprofit home and counseling center for troubled teens. She had an emotional connection to the center since it was something her mother had started twenty years ago, just months before her death. Leo couldn't dispute that it was a worthwhile cause, but he knew Olivia could run it from Culver Crossing, as she'd been doing for the past decade. Then, she wouldn't have to take Cameron out of state and to a place where Leo wouldn't be able to see him as often as he did now.

As much as Leo wanted to accommodate her on the no-rehashing, he had to know something. "Would Samuel do something to try to discredit you? Is he so pissed off at you over this move that he would try to take both of us out of the custody picture?"

There it was. All laid out for her.

"My father wouldn't do this," Olivia murmured, her voice shaky now.

Hell. There was enough doubt in her tone to confirm that her father was truly a suspect in this attack. He would need to pay Samuel a visit first thing in the morning.

Leo turned away from Olivia when he heard the vehicle come to stop outside her house. "It's probably the EMT. Stay back until I make sure."

That put a fresh round of alarm in her eyes, but Leo wasn't taking any chances. That's why he waited until Olivia had left the foyer and gone into the living room. He also put his hand over his weapon when he opened the door. The moment Leo did that, however, he heard a sound that he definitely didn't want to hear.

A gunshot.

Chapter 2

The terror shot through Olivia, causing her heart to jump straight to her throat as she ran back to the foyer. Because she knew what she'd just heard. Knew what it meant.

Someone had just fired a shot at Leo.

Oh mercy. Someone was trying to kill him.

She latched onto his arm, yanking him deeper inside the house, but Leo was already moving in that direction. He slammed the door, locked it and then raced to the window in the living room that faced the front yard. Obviously, he had already geared up for a fight.

"Cameron," Olivia said, her son's name gusting out with her breath.

Leo didn't try to stop her when she started running to the rear of the house. Even if he had, she would have fought him off. She had to get to her son. She had to make sure he was okay, protect him.

She heard another shot just as she reached the nursery, but she didn't look back. Olivia rushed to the crib and, thanks to the night-lights in the room, she saw her baby. Asleep. Unharmed.

Safe.

The relief came like a flood, and she scooped him into her arms, brushing kisses on his cheeks and head. Cameron woke and made a fussy sound of protest at being disturbed. Olivia ignored that, too, and raced into the bathroom with him. She stepped into the shower stall where she hoped the tiles would stop any bullets from reaching them.

But the shots could definitely reach Leo.

That brought on a fresh round of terror. It didn't matter that he despised her. Didn't matter that they were at odds over this custody issue and her intended move. He was still Cameron's father, and she didn't want him hurt.

However, she did want to know why this was happening.

First, the knife attack by a man who claimed she'd called him. Now this. Olivia prayed they'd find out soon what was going on so they could put a stop to it.

When her lungs began to ache, she released the breath she'd been holding and continued to listen. No more gunshots, thank goodness, but she did hear Leo talking to someone. Maybe to someone on the phone.

"Olivia, are you and Cameron all right?" Leo called out to her several moments later.

"Yes," she managed to say. "I have him in the bathroom."

The sound of her voice caused Cameron to start fussing again. Olivia tried to rock him so that he'd go back to sleep. If he was awake, he might pick up on her tense muscles and therefore her fears.

Olivia heard the footsteps and, even though she knew it was probably Leo, she turned Cameron away from the door, putting her body between him and anyone who might enter. But the person who came in was Leo.

He looked like a fierce warrior with his black hair and stone-gray eyes. Tall, rangy and ready for battle. The anger was coming off him in thick waves that she could practically see. But for once that particular emotion wasn't aimed at her.

"The shooter sped off. I couldn't go after him," he said, though she wasn't sure how he could speak with his jaw muscles set so hard.

"No," she quickly agreed. Because that would have meant leaving Cameron and her alone. Olivia didn't have a gun and wouldn't have wanted to face down an armed man when she had Cameron to protect. "Did you see who it was?"

He shook his head and moved closer, his attention on Cameron. Thankfully, the baby had gone back to sleep on Olivia's shoulder. Leo leaned in—so close that she caught his scent—and brushed a kiss on top of the boy's head.

Olivia looked away, unable to make herself resistant to Leo. She'd never managed to do that. But she had plenty of reasons why she couldn't give in to the flickers of heat he caused in her body.

"I locked the front door and then called the Culver Crossing PD," Leo said, gently brushing his fingers over Cameron's hair. Hair that was identical in color to Leo's. Ditto for her son's eyes. "Sheriff Jace Castillo will be here in a few minutes. It's his jurisdiction," he reminded her, not sounding very happy about that.

Olivia knew the reason for that unhappiness. There was bad blood between the Castillos and the Nashes because, several decades ago, Leo's mother had had an affair with Jace's father, and it had ripped both families apart. Olivia was well aware of how some events from the past could affect the present.

Not in a good way, either.

"I'm surprised you didn't call Della instead," she murmured. Since Della was a Culver Crossing deputy sheriff and also his soon-to-be sister-in-law, Leo would have no doubt found her easier to deal with.

"I heard my brother mention that Della had just finished a long shift. Besides, Jace would have had to come in on something like this anyway."

Yes, because what had happened was so serious— the attempted murder of a police officer. And not the first attempt tonight, either.

Sweet heaven, what was going on?

"We'll wait in here until Jace arrives." Leo moved in front of her then, taking up the stance to protect them both if someone made it into the house and came through the bathroom door.

"All the windows and the back door are locked," she told him.

Olivia was certain of that because it was something she did even in the daytime. Cameron was walking now, and he was fast. She hadn't wanted to risk him getting outside the house. But she'd never thought it was something she'd need to do to keep out a would-be killer.

"I locked the front door," he added. Leo paused, the muscles stirring in his jaw again. "The shooter fired at the house." There was fresh anger in his voice now and in his eyes. "I don't think the bullets got through the walls, but they could have. *They could have*," he repeated in a hoarse mumble.

Olivia also felt plenty of anger, but it was beneath the fear and the question. "Did that man, Milton Hough, escape and do this?"

"No. I called Barrett, too, and he still has Milton in custody."

Normally, she would have considered that a good thing, but in this case it meant there were two attackers. At least. It also meant whoever had done this had no regard for the safety of a child.

"Who would have done this?" Olivia came out and asked. When he didn't give her an immediate answer, she added. "And it wasn't me."

"I know it wasn't you. No way would you have put Cameron at risk."

That stung. Because while it was true about Cameron, she wouldn't have put Leo in harm's way, either. In fact...well, she didn't want to go there. Not when she had other questions and concerns.

"Is this maybe connected to one of your investigations?" she suggested.

He opened his mouth but didn't get a chance to say anything because there was a knock at the door.

"It's me, Sheriff Castillo," Jace called out.

"Wait here," Leo instructed her, his weapon drawn as he left the bathroom and closed the door behind him.

Olivia held her breath again. She didn't suspect Jace of being behind the shooting, but the gunman could still be outside somewhere, waiting for Leo to answer the door so he could fire more shots at him.

Thankfully, she didn't hear any gunfire. Just the murmurs of a conversation between Jace and Leo, followed by footsteps. Several moments later, Leo opened the bathroom door. He came in, but Jace stayed in the doorway.

Even though the men weren't saying anything to each other, Olivia could feel the tension. She hoped that wouldn't stop them from working together on this because she was going to need all the help she could get.

"Are you okay?" Jace asked her.

Olivia nodded, but it was a lie. She was far from being okay. "Did you see the man who shot into the house?"

"No," Jace answered. "But I'm going outside now to have a look around. I want Leo to stay in here with the baby and you, if that's all right."

Jace obviously knew about the custody battle. Heck, everyone in Mercy Ridge and Culver Crossing did. And Jace was clearly concerned that she wouldn't be comfortable with Leo being around her. She was uncomfortable, but that would skyrocket if she had to stay inside alone with Cameron.

"Leo should stay," she agreed.

Jace gave her a nod and shifted his attention to Leo. "You said the shooter's vehicle was a late-model pickup truck, either dark blue or black?"

"That's right. He was behind the wheel when he fired the shots, and he sped off after firing two rounds. I couldn't make out the license plate."

"And you're sure it was a man?" Jace pressed.

"Yeah. He had wide shoulders and beefy arms, and he was wearing a ski mask, just like the guy who attacked me earlier in Mercy Ridge."

That tightened Olivia's stomach even more. Someone had sent two men after Leo tonight, and both had used what could have been deadly force.

"After I've had a look around, I'll need to talk to both of you again," Jace said, sounding all cop. "I'll need statements. I'll also want you to tell me who you believe would do something like this, so be thinking about that while I'm gone."

Leo made a sound of agreement but, judging from his stony expression, it was a hard pill for him to swallow to be taking orders from a fellow cop. One he didn't especially like.

When Jace left, Leo stood in the bathroom doorway so he could look out into the hall. Keeping watch. Olivia tried to help by focusing on what Jace had told her to do—think about who had done this. She wished she could draw a blank, but she couldn't.

"Bernice." She hadn't intended to say that aloud, yet it was the first name that came to mind.

Leo looked back at her. "You think your father's household manager could have done this?"

"No. Not really." Flustered, she shook her head and wished she'd kept her mouth shut. "But she's upset about our custody fight. Upset with *you*," Olivia amended.

Leo certainly couldn't dismiss the possibility of Bernice's involvement. The woman could be overbearing, and she was fiercely loyal to Olivia's father. That meant Bernice was also upset with Olivia's move to Oklahoma.

"Bernice wouldn't have put Cameron in danger," Olivia stated. She would have added more to try to convince him about that, but his phone rang.

"It's Barrett," he relayed and, much to Olivia's surprise, put the call on speaker.

"How are things there?" Barrett immediately asked.

Leo took a deep breath before he answered. "No sign of the shooter. And Sheriff Castillo is on scene."

The sound that Barrett made conveyed both his sympathy and concern. Yes, there was definitely still bad blood between Jace and the Logan brothers.

"Milton clammed up," Barrett said a moment later. "He's waiting for a lawyer to drive over from San Antonio. Probably waiting for the DA to offer him some kind of plea deal, too."

"Hell," Leo muttered after he glanced at Cameron. No doubt to make sure he was still asleep. He was. "The shooter could have hurt my son." There was plenty of raw emotion in his voice.

"Cameron's okay?" Barrett asked.

"Yeah. It needs to stay that way. That's why I want to know if someone hired Milton and this other thug who fired into Olivia's house. I'll need the person's name, and if the two weren't hired, I have to know why they took it upon themselves to try to kill me."

"I want that, too," Barrett verified. "We might not need to deal with Milton, though. I'm getting a warrant to go over his financials to see if I can find a money trail. Then I might be able to figure out who paid him to do this. I'll also try to get his medical records."

That got Olivia's attention.

Obviously, it got Leo's, too. "Medical records?" he questioned.

Barrett paused again. "I found a bottle of prescription meds in Milton's pocket, and I looked it up. It's something that's given to patients with severe psychological disorders."

Olivia tried to process that. Maybe there'd been no

hired guns. Just a mentally ill man who'd attacked Leo. Of course, that didn't explain the person who'd fired the shots outside her house, but it was a start.

"Where's my daughter?" someone shouted. "I want to see Olivia now!"

She groaned because she easily recognized that voice. Her father. And his being here definitely wasn't going to make things better.

"I need to make sure Cameron and Olivia are all right," her father went on. "If somebody shot at her, I want to see for myself that they weren't hurt."

"I have to go," Leo said to Barrett. Obviously, he also knew her father was there, and he ended the call.

"I told you that Olivia and your grandson are fine," she heard Jace say. The sheriff sounded just as annoyed as Leo looked.

But Olivia was past the mere annoyed stage. Why had her father come? Better yet, how had he known about the shooting? Her neighbors didn't know her dad well enough to have his phone number.

Moments later, Samuel stepped into the doorway of the bathroom. He was tall, bulky and imposing, a bouncer's build. And somehow his iron-gray hair didn't make him look old, only more formidable.

As usual, her father was wearing a suit, a dark gray one this time, and he had a gold sycamore leaf pin on his classic red tie. The pin was the symbol of his estate, Sycamore Grove, and he didn't just wear the emblem, it was also on the iron gates that fronted the house, on the vehicles' license plates. Even on the front door.

Jace was right behind Samuel, and Leo didn't budge to let her father come any closer to her. However, Olivia stepped closer because she wanted to see her father's expression when she asked him the questions that were causing the anger to ripple through her.

"Were you having me watched?" Olivia demanded. Cameron stirred and she patted his back to try to soothe him. She definitely didn't want her son to hear any part of this conversation. "Is that how you found out about the shooting?"

Maybe it was her steely tone, but her father flinched as if she'd slapped him. Of course, he could have reacted that way to make her feel sorry for what she'd just said. But Olivia didn't feel sorry for him.

"No, I'm not having you watched." Her father's voice was tight now, and his eyes were slightly narrowed. "I got an anonymous text, saying that Cameron and you had been attacked. I tried to call you several times. When I didn't get an answer, I drove straight here."

Since Olivia's replacement phone was in the kitchen and set to vibrate, she wouldn't have heard the calls, but the other part of his explanation didn't make sense.

"An anonymous text?" She sounded skeptical because she was. Olivia huffed. "Look, if you had someone spying on me, then that person saw the shooter. You need to give your watchdog's name to Sheriff Castillo and Leo so he can help them find this gunman."

At the mention of Leo's name, her father slanted him a glare. Leo glared right back.

"Do you have a watchdog around here?" Leo demanded.

Her father's glower got significantly worse. "No. I got a text, like I said. And you have no right to question me."

"I have the right." Jace jumped in. "If you know anything about the shooting, I want to hear it."

Samuel ignored Jace and stared at her.

"Leo." Her father spat the name out like venom. "He's the one you should be doubting and questioning. Go ahead—ask him. Have him tell you what this is all about."

Everything inside Olivia went still. "What do you mean?"

Her father didn't actually smile, but it was close. "Leo's the reason Cameron and you could have been killed. This is all his fault."

Chapter 3

After dealing with Samuel for the past two years, Leo knew he shouldn't be surprised by the accusation. But there was something in Samuel's expression that had Leo wondering if there was any truth to it.

Olivia was already moving forward, but Leo motioned for her to stay back. It was somewhat of a miracle that Cameron was still asleep, and Leo didn't want him closer in case this *conversation* got loud. That was always a possibility when dealing with Samuel Nash.

"You actually believe these two attacks were my fault?" Leo questioned.

Samuel jabbed his index finger at Leo. "You bet they were. Because of your botched investigation, Randall Arnett is a free man and now he wants to get back at you."

Leo had wondered how long it was going to take for

Randall's name to come up. He'd already considered it. But what Samuel had just said was a mix of truth and lies. Randall wasn't behind bars, but Leo hadn't botched the investigation into the man's missing girlfriend. Simply put, there hadn't been enough evidence to charge Randall.

"Randall threatened you," Samuel reminded him.

"Yeah, over a year ago," Leo verified. What he wouldn't say was that he'd been keeping close tabs on Randall, looking for anything he could use to prove the man's wrongdoing. "It'd be stupid for Randall to come after me like this," Leo added.

Samuel shrugged. "That doesn't mean he didn't. The person who texted me said Randall was responsible for the shooting. I can show you. It's right here." He took out his phone, holding up the screen for Leo to see.

"'Get to your daughter's place now,'" Leo read aloud. "'There's been a shooting. Dig into Deputy Leo Logan's case files if you want to know who pulled the trigger.'"

So, the person who'd sent that text hadn't specifically mentioned Randall. Interesting. Interesting, too, that Samuel had jumped to that conclusion.

"How exactly did you know about Randall Arnett?" Leo asked.

Samuel blinked, maybe surprised by the question. But he shouldn't have been. He should have known that was something Leo would press, especially since the man didn't live in Mercy Ridge and wouldn't necessarily be privy to the town talk about Randall.

"I make it a point to know what you're doing because it affects my daughter and grandson," Samuel insisted.

Olivia huffed. "You've been digging into Leo's investigations. You're looking for something you can use against him in the custody case."

Bingo. Leo was glad Olivia had realized her father would do something like this. The man fought dirty. Maybe dirty enough to stir up Randall to get him to launch an attack?

Maybe.

It was definitely something Leo would look into.

Samuel shifted his attention to Olivia. "You know I only want what's best for Cameron and you. I have to keep you safe. That's why you'll need to come home with me. Look at Leo's arm, at his gunshot injury. Something worse could happen to Cameron and you if you stay around him."

And there was another *bingo*. Samuel would use this shooting and anything else he could come up with to get Olivia and Cameron under his roof.

Exactly where Samuel wanted them.

"No," Olivia said before Leo could tell her that he thought it was a bad idea. The shooter could follow Olivia there, and while her father likely knew how to use a gun, he wasn't trained in law enforcement.

Samuel sighed. "I know you're upset. And scared. But you can't stay here. The man who fired those shots could come back."

Now, Leo did manage to speak first. "Olivia and Cameron won't be staying here. But they'll be placed in protective custody until I can figure out what's going on."

Leo was surprised that lightning didn't bolt from Samuel's eyes. "Your protective custody?" he questioned as if that were a stupid idea.

"Either mine or Sheriff Castillo's." Leo hoped that, despite their differences, Jace would back him up.

He did. "Olivia and Cameron definitely won't be staying here," Jace agreed. "This is now a crime scene, and the grounds need to be processed. I've already called in a CSI team to look for tracks and spent shell casings. While that's going on, Olivia needs to be in a safe place, and Leo should be the one to decide where that safe place will be."

"Leo and Jace are right," Olivia said.

Her voice sounded strong but was edged with nerves. That was expected, Leo supposed, though he thought he detected something else beneath the surface. Maybe her father and she had had some kind of disagreement. If so, it probably had something to do with the move she wanted to make to Oklahoma. Samuel wouldn't want Olivia that far away from under his thumb.

"You'll go with Leo?" her father snarled.

She nodded, swallowed hard. "And before you tell me all the reasons why that shouldn't happen, remember this. Leo is Cameron's father and he'll do anything to protect his son."

"So will I," Samuel howled.

This time Cameron didn't just stir. The boy let out a loud wail, the sound tugging at Leo's heart. Samuel's shout had scared him.

Shooting a scowl at Samuel, Leo went to Olivia, who was trying her best to soothe the baby. However, the moment that Cameron spotted Leo, he reached out for him and babbled, "Dada." That tugged at Leo's heart, too, and he took Cameron into his arms.

"It's all right, buddy," Leo whispered to him and brushed a kiss on the top of his head.

Jace's phone buzzed. The sheriff gave each of them a long look, as if deciding whether or not he should leave them alone while he took the call. He must have decided a fight wouldn't break out because he stepped into the hall.

"You're a fool to trust him," Samuel immediately said to Olivia.

Leo didn't have to guess that Samuel was talking about him. Definitely no trust between them. But what did surprise Leo was his glimpse of a flicker of distrust in Olivia's eyes.

"I'd be a fool not to do what it takes to keep my son safe," Olivia countered.

Samuel huffed, and Leo decided if the man raised his voice this time, he would give him the boot. Cameron had been upset enough without adding more shouting to the mix.

"You can be safe with me," Samuel said, staring at Olivia. No shouting. In fact, his voice leveled and took on a pleading tone. "I need you home. I'll be sick with worry over Cameron and you."

Olivia's expression and posture stayed stiff as she moved closer to Leo and stroked her hand down Cameron's back. That put Leo arm to arm with Olivia. A sort of united front against her father.

Something that wouldn't last.

Olivia always caved to Samuel.

"You know this is already a tough time for me," Samuel added a moment later.

"Because of Mom," she muttered.

Leo knew it was a tough time for Olivia, too. The anniversary of her mother's death was in a couple of days, and it would no doubt stir up some bad memories. Olivia had been just ten when her mom, Simone, had been killed in a car accident. Olivia had been in the car with her, trapped inside, while she watched her mother die.

Yeah, it would be bad.

And now it'd be worse because of this attack tonight. No way to push aside the sounds of those shots that'd been fired into the house.

Leo wanted to put his arm around Olivia, to try to comfort her. That was his kneejerk reaction anyway. Not only wouldn't she welcome that, it also wasn't smart. After all, they weren't exactly friends right now.

"You shouldn't have been in the car with Simone that night," Samuel muttered, and it seemed as if he was lost in the grief. "You shouldn't have had to go through that."

Olivia cleared her throat, her gaze shifting to meet Leo's. She was certainly a puzzle tonight because he wasn't sure what he was seeing there. Maybe, though, it was just the start of an inevitable adrenaline crash.

"Come home with me," Samuel insisted. The plea was gone, probably because he didn't like all the eye and arm contact she was making with Leo.

"No," she said, and repeated it when she turned back to her father. "No. And I need you to leave now."

The muscles tightened in Samuel's jaw, and Leo didn't think he was mistaken that the look the man gave his daughter was a borderline glare. A glare that Samuel would have likely added some venomous words to if Jace hadn't come back into the room.

Jace stopped, eyeing them all again. "A problem?" Jace asked.

"No," Olivia quickly answered. She began to stuff some diapers, clothes and toys into a large diaper bag.

"I've already explained to my father that I'll be taking Cameron to Leo's."

Jace nodded, though he didn't seem convinced about Olivia's denial.

Neither was Leo. Something other than the obvious was wrong here.

"I need to go by the sheriff's office in Mercy Ridge," Jace told Leo. "I have to see Milton. But I'm in my cruiser, so I can take Olivia and you to your place first. I can go through it, too, just to make sure no one had tried to break in. Once you're there, the EMTs can have a look at that arm."

It was a generous offer, and it would free up Barrett from having to send out a deputy for backup duty.

"Cameron has a car seat in my truck," Leo explained. "I'll need to drive that, but I'd appreciate it if you'd make sure we get safely back to my ranch." He paused. "I'll want to question Milton, too, but I don't want to take Cameron there."

"I'll let your brother know what's going on," Jace assured him.

"Olivia," Samuel said, "reconsider this."

"No." She didn't hesitate, either. "Give me a minute to pack a bag," she added to no one in particular and hurried out of the room.

Samuel immediately turned to Leo. "You can convince her not to go to your house."

Leo gave him what he was certain was the flattest look in the history of flat looks. "Leave, Samuel," Leo insisted, making sure it sounded like an order from a cop. He'd had enough tonight and didn't want to deal another second with this man who'd tried to make his life a living hell.

Samuel shifted as if he might make that plea to Jace, but Jace managed a darn good flat look of his own. Leo didn't know how well the two men knew each other, but there didn't seem to be any tinge of friendliness.

"You're not going to take my daughter and grandson away from me," Samuel snarled to Leo, and with that, he finally headed out of the house.

"I'll lock the door behind him," Jace offered.

"Thanks," Leo muttered. He didn't want to take Cameron near an unlocked door until it was time to leave.

Leo fired off a quick text to his head ranch hand, Wally Myers, to alert him to be on the lookout for the shooter and to also patrol the grounds. Wally lived in the bunkhouse, along with two other hands, and Leo knew he could count on them to make sure the place was as safe as it could be.

Maybe that would be enough.

Olivia was true to her word about only taking a minute to pack a bag. She hurried back into the room, glanced around and seemed to take a breath of relief when she saw that her father wasn't there.

She hoisted her bag over one shoulder and put the filled diaper bag over the other. What she was also doing was avoiding eye contact with him. He would have called her on that, but Jace returned.

"There's no sign of the shooter," Jace said, "but I'd like to get Olivia and the baby inside the vehicle as fast as we can."

Olivia made a sound of agreement, and Leo handed Cameron back to Olivia. He also took her bag. As she'd done, he looped it over his shoulder to free up his shooting hand. He prayed it wouldn't be necessary, though, to do any firing. Not with his baby so close that he could be hurt.

"I want to see Milton, too," Olivia said as they made their way to the door. "I want to see if I recognize him."

There were safer ways for her to take that look. Leo fired off a quick text to Barrett to let him know they were leaving and to ask him to send a photo of Milton.

"Stay close to me," Leo instructed her, using his key fob to unlock his truck.

And he sucked in his breath, holding it.

Praying.

He fired glances all around but didn't see a gunman. Of course, the guy probably wouldn't just stand out in the open, not with two lawmen around. Still, the guy had been gutsy enough to launch an attack.

Jace moved when they did, and Leo and the sheriff kept Olivia and Cameron between them as they hurried outside and got into the truck. The moment Jace shut the passenger's-side door, he hurried over to his cruiser. Leo only waited long enough for Olivia to strap Cameron into his seat before he took off.

"Keep watch," Leo told her. He also wanted to tell her to get down on the seat so that she'd be out of harm's way, but he needed her eyes. If she could spot any signs of trouble, it could help him avoid being the target of more gunfire.

He hoped.

Right now, Leo was hoping a lot of things. He needed to catch the idiot who'd put Cameron and Olivia in danger, but he didn't want that to happen with his little boy around.

"Later," he said, giving her a heads-up, "I'll want to know what's going on between you and your father."

He'd figured Olivia would dole out a quick denial that anything was going on. But she stayed silent.

Hell.

Whatever this was, it had to be bad. Then again, things were rarely good when it came to Samuel. Leo wanted to know if her move to Oklahoma had anything to do with this father-daughter rift or whatever the heck it was.

His phone dinged. Rather than take his eyes off the road, he passed it to Olivia.

"It's from Barrett," she said. "It's a picture of Milton."

Thinking Barrett had gotten that photo rather fast, Leo made a quick glance at the screen. It was Milton's DMV photo.

"I don't recognize him," Olivia muttered. "I swear, I didn't hire him to kill you."

Leo had thought they'd already hashed this out. Apparently not. "Yeah, I got that."

And he left it at that. Because a conversation about a would-be killer could be a huge distraction, too.

Cameron made a fussy sound that caught Leo's attention. He never wanted to hear his boy cry, but such a sound now could drown out other things that he needed to be hearing. But the one fuss was it. While Leo drove on, the baby thankfully drifted back to sleep.

He heard Olivia make what he realized was a sigh of relief and, like him, she continued to keep watch as he drove. It wasn't a long trip, less than twenty minutes, but each mile felt as if it took an eternity. Leo didn't relax, however, when he pulled into his driveway. He did more glancing around, making sure there were no signs of an attacker. Nothing. And he hoped it stayed that way.

He spotted Wally at the side of the house. The ranch hand was carrying a rifle, but he gave Leo a welcoming nod, an assurance that all was well. Good. Leo pulled into his garage, but he didn't get out. He waited for Jace to join them and then shut the garage door to give them some extra cover.

"I can pause my security system with my phone," Leo explained as he pulled up the app.

No sensors had been triggered. That was the good news. The bad news was that no security system was foolproof.

"Wait here with Olivia," Leo instructed Jace once they were inside the mudroom. "I can go through the place faster than you can."

And *fast* would be key. Leo didn't want to be away from Olivia and Cameron any longer than necessary. That's why he drew his gun and started hurrying through the rooms—all twelve of them—checking each window, door and closet. He even looked under the beds and turned on all the lights as he went. That would help to illuminate the grounds, but it would also prevent a potential attacker from knowing which room they were in.

Leo had been raised in this house. The home that had once belonged to his parents before things had fallen apart. Before his mother had left them and his father had committed suicide. There were plenty of bad memories here. Plenty of really good ones, though, too. Right now, he needed to make sure nothing else bad happened to add to what had already taken place tonight.

While he made his way downstairs, he texted Wally again to instruct him to continue to keep watch. It'd be a long night for all of them, but any and all precautions were necessary.

"It's okay," Leo immediately told Jace and Olivia when he joined them in the mudroom. He looked at Jace. "Thanks."

Jace nodded. "I'll let you know if I find out anything about Milton."

Leo muttered another thanks and locked the front door when Jace left. He also reset the security system.

"We're staying in the nursery tonight," Leo insisted. "All three of us. You can take the sleep chair." It was an oversize recliner that Leo had used plenty of times himself when Cameron had stayed nights with him.

Olivia didn't object to them all sharing the nursery. She followed him upstairs to the room he'd set up for Cameron. Leo had purposely made it as identical as possible to the one at Olivia's so the boy would have some continuity.

Cameron didn't stir when Olivia put him in the crib, but neither Leo nor Olivia moved away despite the baby being sound asleep. They stood there several long moments, watching him, and Leo was pretty sure that, like him, Olivia was silently uttering some prayers of thanks that their little boy hadn't been hurt.

"We need to find out who's behind the attack," she whispered.

Yeah, they did, and Leo intended to get started on that tonight. First, though, there was another matter they had to discuss. He took Olivia by the hand and led her to the other side of the room. Far enough for them to keep an eye on the baby but not so close to the crib as to wake him.

"Okay..." Leo started, "want to tell me what's going on between you and your father?"

She dragged in a long breath, opened her mouth then

closed it as if she'd changed her mind about what she was going to say. A few seconds crawled by before she finally spoke.

"I think my father might be a killer."

Chapter 4

I think my father might be a killer.

The moment Olivia heard what she'd said, she wished she could take it back. This was definitely not something she should have brought up tonight, not when Leo and she were still recovering from the shock of the attack. In fact, she shouldn't have dropped the bombshell at all unless she had some proof to back it up.

She didn't.

But what she did have was a tightness in her chest and stomach. An unsettling feeling that what she'd said was the cold, hard truth.

Leo's eyes narrowed and he gave her a cop's stare. "You're going to need to explain that," he demanded.

Since there was no way Olivia would be able to dodge answering him, she gathered her breath and hoped this didn't blow up in her face. After all, Leo and she were in a custody battle, and he might be willing to use this against her.

"I got the police report of my mother's car accident," Olivia explained. "I read it, and I couldn't stop thinking about it."

Dreaming about it, too. The nightmares hadn't been as bad as actually witnessing her mother die. Nothing could have been that bad. But the nightmares had definitely shaken her.

"You hadn't read the report before?" Leo asked, no doubt hoping to spur her into continuing with her explanation.

"No. I didn't think reading it would help. It didn't," she added in a murmur. "There were drugs in my mom's tox screen. A combination of sleeping pills and amphetamines. I don't remember my mother ever taking either of those. Just the opposite. She was sort of a health nut and didn't even take over-the-counter pain meds when she had a headache."

Leo stayed quiet a moment, obviously processing that. "You think your father gave her those drugs?"

Olivia met his gaze. She wanted to shake her head again, wanted to erase all the doubts and worries about her dad having some part in this. But she couldn't.

"They were arguing a lot, and I heard my mom tell him that she wanted a divorce," she went on. "My dad might have drugged her out of anger. *Might*." She gave emphasis to the word, then groaned. "He wouldn't have done that, though, if he'd known I was going to be in the car."

"You sneaked into the car," Leo stated when she stopped. "Neither your mom nor your dad knew you were in the back seat. Isn't that right?"

Even though it was a question, Leo knew the answer. When they'd been lovers, she'd poured out her heart to him. No. Her parents hadn't known she'd been in the vehicle. After yet another argument, she'd heard her mother tell her father that she was packing her things and leaving. She hadn't heard her mom say anything about taking her along, though, so Olivia had hurried to the garage and gotten down on the floor behind the driver's seat. Her mother had only discovered her seconds before the crash.

"Right," she verified. "The drugs definitely affected my mother's driving. I remember her weaving on the road, and that's when I lifted my head and asked her if everything was okay."

It hadn't been okay at all and, within minutes, her mother was dead. The crash had injured Olivia, too, but in the grand scheme of things, a broken arm and bruises had been minor, especially considering she hadn't been wearing a seat belt.

"Where was your mom going that night?" he asked. "Did she say?"

"She didn't say specifically, only that she needed some fresh air and was going for a drive to try to clear her head. But I remember her telling my dad that she'd be filing for a divorce, that she'd had enough."

Leo continued to study her as if trying to pick apart every nuance of her expression. She didn't dare do the same to him. Best to avoid eye contact. Other kinds of contact, as well. Olivia didn't consider herself stupid; she'd felt the old attraction still simmering between them. An attraction that even an unplanned pregnancy and a custody battle couldn't cool. She couldn't play with that kind of fire again. It was too dangerous.

"You said your father could have drugged your mother out of anger," Leo said. "Had he done anything like that before?"

"Not that I know of. I don't remember him ever hitting her, either. They just argued a lot."

Leo touched his fingers to her chin, turning her head and forcing the very eye contact she was trying to avoid. And there it was. More than just a flutter of heat. The flash of it through her body. Leo had always been able to do that to her. Still could.

Olivia stepped back, away from his touch. But it didn't stop the need he'd stirred inside her. However, his expression helped with that. Obviously, he wasn't thinking about sex tonight. Nope. She was certain his expression was the same one he used when interrogating suspects.

"Why do you think your father might have had some part in the car accident?" he asked.

She seriously doubted the answer she'd give him would convince him that her father was guilty. Or that she was telling Leo the whole truth—which she wasn't. But she tried anyway.

"Because my father keeps bringing it up," she said. "For the past couple of weeks, he keeps telling me how sorry he was that I was in the car. Maybe it's just because of the anniversary of mom's death, but there seems to be more."

"*More?* You mean like guilt?" he pressed.

"Exactly like guilt," she confirmed. So, maybe Leo would understand her gut feeling, after all. "When I ask for more details of that night, he dodges the questions. Not hard questions, either. I asked him why they were arguing and wanted to know if Mom had threatened to leave him before."

Leo mumbled some profanity under his breath. "I'm betting he didn't like that."

"No." In fact, her father had stormed off during one of those conversations. The man definitely had a temper, and that hadn't been the first time she'd seen flashes of it. Many times, he'd aimed his temper at Leo.

"I also talked to Bernice," Olivia continued. "I asked her point-blank if my father could have had any part in that car accident, and she said absolutely not."

"Did she have an explanation for your mother's tox screen results?" Leo asked.

"None other than she was positive my father wasn't responsible. Of course, the woman idolizes him, so she probably wouldn't rat him out. The only reason I brought up the subject to her was that I thought I'd be able to read her expression if she thought there was any hint of wrongdoing on his part."

Again, Leo went quiet for several moments. "Is all of this why you want to move to Oklahoma?"

And here was the leverage this discussion could give him. Leo would use whatever info he could to keep her from taking Cameron out of state.

"It's part of it," she admitted.

But only part.

Leo wouldn't like to know that he was the main reason for her intended move.

He was obviously waiting for her to finish her explanation, but Olivia didn't get a chance to say anything else because his phone dinged. When he pulled it from his pocket, she saw Barrett's name on the screen.

"I need to take this call," Leo grumbled. "We'll finish our conversation when I'm done."

That last part sounded a little like a threat, and he hit the answer button while he went across the room and into the hall. No doubt so that he wouldn't wake Cameron. But Olivia followed him. This was likely an update about the investigation. Or more. It could be a warning that another attack was on the way. That possibility had her leaving the nursery door open in case she had to hurry in and scoop up the baby.

"Please give me good news," Leo said to his brother, and he surprised her by putting the call on speaker. Olivia had thought Leo would want to process any bad news before passing it along to her.

"Sorry, but I don't have any," Barrett quickly answered. "I just got a preliminary report on Milton. He's been in and out of mental health facilities for years. I can't get access to his medical records, but I've arranged for him to have a psychiatric eval. Unfortunately, that won't happen until morning when the doctor from San Antonio can get here."

"The doctor might be able to convince you that Milton is a liar," Olivia insisted.

There was silence, both from Barrett and Leo. Barrett might not have known she was listening, so perhaps he was rethinking the conversation he'd intended to have with his brother.

"Leo, are you okay with Olivia being there?" Barrett came out and asked after several long moments.

Leo paused again, just a heartbeat this time, but Olivia already knew the answer. No, he wasn't *okay* staying under the same roof with her. That wouldn't improve once they finished the talk they'd started before this phone call.

"I want to keep Cameron and Olivia safe," Leo finally said. "I stand a better chance of doing that with them here."

This time Barrett's response wasn't silence but a slight sound that could have meant anything. However, Olivia was pretty sure it was the concern that he hadn't been able to tamp down. Barrett was no doubt worried she'd hurt his little brother all over again.

And she could.

No matter what she did, Leo could end up getting hurt. Or worse. She needed to do whatever it took to make sure *or worse* didn't happen.

"Since Olivia can hear this, I just got an interesting call from Rena Oldham," Barrett threw out there.

Olivia pulled back her shoulders. Rena was her dad's girlfriend. Or rather his on-again, off-again girlfriend. Rena had held that particular status for years. Their pattern was for them to be together for a couple of months, break up and see other people, only to start up their relationship again.

"What'd Rena want?" Olivia asked.

"Info about Samuel and you. Info I didn't give her," Barrett quickly added. "Apparently, she'd heard about the attack and said she was worried, that Samuel hadn't answered his phone when she'd tried to call him."

"My dad often doesn't take her calls. And Rena can be…clingy," she settled for saying.

"She can apparently also be opinionated, and she doesn't appear to have a high opinion of you. She wanted to know if you had anything to do with the attack tonight."

Olivia groaned. "Even if Rena thought I was capable of something like that, she knows that I'd never put my child in danger."

"I mentioned that to her," Barrett assured her, "and then I ended the call because I had better things to do. She did say, though, that she was out looking for your dad, so she might try to get onto Leo's ranch. Just a heads-up."

The ranch hands wouldn't allow that. Well, hopefully they wouldn't because Olivia didn't want to deal with Rena and her drama tonight.

"What about the second attacker? Any sign of him?" Leo asked.

"No, but Milton said that Olivia hired him and a couple of other attackers to go after you."

"She didn't."

Barrett made a sound, as if reserving judgment about that.

"She didn't," Leo repeated, sounding much more adamant this time.

That helped with the tightness in Olivia's chest. Having Leo believe her was a start because she was going to need him on her side. She had to convince him to do some things that would keep him safe.

"If Milton was right about someone hiring other thugs," Barrett went on, "then I need to find them so I can question them. Maybe then, we can figure out what the heck is going on. What's your theory as to who's behind this?"

"Randall is my top pick," Leo answered without hesitation.

"I figured you'd say that, and that's why I called him. Or rather, I tried to call him. He didn't answer his cell, so I called his house. His sister, Kristin, answered. She said Randall was staying overnight with a friend in San Antonio. She didn't have the friend's name or contact info."

Leo groaned softly and rubbed his free hand over his face. "Kristin would lie for him."

"Oh yeah," Barrett agreed.

Olivia was right there with his agreement. She didn't actually know Randall's sister, but from what she'd heard, the siblings were very close. And both bitter that Leo was trying to put Randall behind bars for murder.

"I'm also trying to find out if Randall actually sent that text to Olivia's father," Barrett went on. "My guess is that he didn't. Randall wouldn't be that stupid."

"No," Leo quietly answered, glancing back at the crib when Cameron stirred a little.

Olivia did the same and moved a little closer to the baby but not so close that she wouldn't be able to hear the rest of Leo and Barrett's conversation.

"But maybe Randall did it using a burner cell," Leo continued. "One that couldn't be traced back to him. Then, it'd be sort of a reverse psychology. His lawyers could argue that he's innocent because he wouldn't implicate himself."

It sickened Olivia to consider that Randall's hatred of Leo was at the core of the attacks. A man who hated that much wouldn't care if an innocent child got hurt during his quest for revenge.

"I'll see what I can learn about Randall's whereabouts," Barrett assured his brother. "In the meantime, try to get some rest. If you get any kind of signal that something's wrong, just call me. I'll be working from home."

That was good because Barrett lived only a couple of minutes from Leo. The ranch hands were decent backup, but if there was another attempt on their lives, she wanted Barrett there.

Leo ended the call and stared at the phone a moment as if to process his thoughts. When he turned toward her, Olivia knew what he wanted. And it didn't have anything to do with this heat zinging back and forth between them.

"Cut to the chase," Leo said, his voice low but with an edge. "Tell me about your father and this move you want to make to Oklahoma."

Olivia mentally tried to go through her answer and decided there was no way she could sugarcoat this. No way to stop Leo from doing something—maybe something bad—about this gut feeling she had.

She gathered her breath before she spoke. "First of all, I don't have any actual proof, but this isn't something I can keep to myself." Olivia had to pause again. "I believe my father could have been the one who hired Milton to kill you."

Chapter 5

Olivia's words played through Leo's head for most of the night and had cost him some sleep. Of course, he probably wouldn't have actually gotten any sleep what with a would-be killer after him, but Olivia's accusation had only added more fuel to his mountain of worry. Not for himself but for Cameron.

And for Olivia, too, he reluctantly admitted.

Leo knew it had cost her to tell him about her fear that her father had possibly hired Milton. She'd always been protective of Samuel. Or so he'd thought. But in hindsight, he had to wonder if it was something else that'd kept her from straying too far from her father's side.

Fear.

That was something he'd pressed her about last night, but after dropping her bombshell, she'd dodged giving him any real answers to his questions and had insisted on going to bed. Her bottom line was that she didn't have any proof her father was guilty of hiring Milton or of killing her mother. Only the feeling in the pit of her stomach that something wasn't right.

He believed in those kinds of feelings. As a cop, trusting his gut had even saved his butt a time or two. That's why Leo had already started digging into not only her mother's car accident but also looking for a money trail that would lead from Milton right back to Samuel.

Leo poured himself another cup of coffee, already his fourth of the morning, and it was barely 7:00 a.m. He doubted it'd be his last because he'd need the caffeine to keep him alert and focused. He used some of that focus now to go through the reports and the latest emails on the investigation.

He turned when he heard the footsteps and spotted Olivia making her way into the kitchen. The diaper bag looped over her shoulder, she was carrying a squirming Cameron. She looked harried, and Leo immediately figured out why. Cameron's clothes were a little askew and, along with those wiggles and squirms, he was making fussing sounds. No doubt because he hadn't wanted to be dressed. The boy preferred stripping down to his diaper.

"You should have come and gotten me when he woke up," Leo said, setting his coffee aside so he could take the baby. Despite all the bad stuff going on, he gave Cameron a smile and a kiss. "I would have helped."

"I didn't want to pull you away from your work." Olivia's gaze drifted to his laptop open on the kitchen table. "Anything?"

He debated what to say and just went with the truth. "I've uncovered nothing that links your father to Milton. Not yet anyway." He would have continued, but Olivia interrupted him.

"How's your arm?" she asked.

Leo scowled when he glanced down at the bandage, one that an EMT had put on him after he'd cleaned the wound. It still throbbed, but he was hoping the over-the-counter pain meds would soon kick in and give him some relief.

"It's fine," he lied. "Are you ready to continue that discussion we started last night?"

However, the moment he asked it, he knew it'd have to wait a little longer. Cameron pointed to the high chair and kicked his legs to let Leo know he was ready for his breakfast. Olivia moved closer to help with that. As Leo strapped the baby into the chair, she took the makings for oatmeal from the diaper bag.

Olivia didn't look at Leo while she began to prepare the oatmeal, and she didn't object when he took the bag of cut-up fruit that he kept on hand for Cameron's visits. Leo put out some bits of peaches and pears that Cameron could manage to eat on his own. That kept him occupied while Leo turned to Olivia.

"'I believe my father could have been the one who hired Milton to kill you,'" Leo repeated to her to refresh her memory, though he was dead certain no refreshing was necessary.

She still didn't look at him, but Leo saw her hand tremble a little as she stirred the oatmeal. He finally took hold of her hand and turned her to face him. He saw it then. The fear. And he didn't think it was all related to the attack. It made Leo take a step back, but almost immediately Olivia stopped him by catching the sleeve of his shirt. It was the first time in ages that Leo remembered her actually touching him.

And he reacted.

Hell. His stupid body didn't seem to get it—that Olivia was off-limits. Not just because of the custody battle, either, but because it was obvious she was keeping things from him.

"Are you afraid of your father?" he came out and asked.

She opened her mouth, closed it and then squeezed her eyes shut a moment. "My father threatened you."

That was no big surprise. Samuel was always slinging barbs at him. But this seemed different. "Threatened me how?"

Olivia drew in a breath, moistened her lips. "He said if I stayed with you, that he'd figure out a way to ruin you. I was furious and told him to back off, but he said it'd be a shame if something happened to Cameron's father. Something that would take you out of the picture completely."

Okay, so her father had never actually made comments like that to Leo's face. With reason. Samuel probably hadn't wanted to risk arrest or to have Leo kick his butt. There was only so much he could take from the likes of Samuel Nash.

"You believed him?" Leo prodded.

He could tell the answer was yes even before Olivia nodded. And Leo didn't have any trouble filling in some very important blanks.

"Your father's threats are the reason you want to move to Oklahoma," he stated. It wasn't a question. "You want to put some distance between him and you."

She didn't nod. Didn't have to. He could see the confirmation in her eyes.

Leo felt the slam of anger that Samuel would try to manipulate Olivia this way. "Why the heck didn't you tell me?" But again, he knew the answer. "You knew I'd confront him."

"Yes," she admitted. "And I figured one of two things would happen. He'd hurt you, or you'd hurt him. Or kill him," Olivia added in a mumble. "That would have likely sent you to jail."

"Maybe, but it would have been worth it." Of course, that was the anger talking. Leo didn't want to go to jail and be separated from his son. Especially if Samuel would still be around to bully and threaten Olivia so he could try to bend her to his will. And that made him wonder something else.

Just how long had this bullying been going on?

Since it wouldn't necessarily be easy for her to answer, Leo checked on Cameron first. The boy was still chowing down on the fruit, but Leo added more to the tray to keep him occupied a couple of minutes longer.

He then turned back to Olivia. Leo had geared up to verbally blast her for not telling him all of this sooner, but she hadn't shut down her feelings fast enough. And he saw it.

The toll this had taken on her.

He wasn't immune to the emotion on her face. Leo didn't know everything about what she'd been through, but obviously it'd been plenty.

Before he could think, or stop himself, he reached out to pull her into his arms. He assured himself it was something he would do for plenty of people. But Olivia wasn't just anybody. She had been his lover, and this kind of contact was at best ill-advised and at worst, just plain stupid.

She made a small sound, a moan that sounded as if it was from both relief and pleasure. It confirmed the "just plain stupid" part. No way should they be playing with fire like this. Of course, if they gave in to the heat, it would fix some things. At least it would get them on the same side again.

Olivia didn't stay in his arms, though. She pulled back, moving several inches away, and he could practically feel her putting up barriers between them. "It was my decision," she blurted out.

Leo considered that a moment and bit off saying the profanity that nearly made its way to his mouth. "Exactly what decision are you talking about?" He was pretty sure he knew, but he wanted to hear it. And when he did, he figured he'd be doing plenty more mental cursing.

Olivia swallowed hard, but he had to hand it to her. She steeled herself, squaring her shoulders and looking him straight in the eyes. "To end things with you. If I hadn't," she quickly added in a whisper, "my father would have made our lives a living hell."

This time, the slam of anger was stronger. A hot smash of heat that hit him in the gut and spread. "You broke up with me to keep things smooth with Samuel." He'd had to speak through clenched teeth.

She didn't break eye contact with him. "Our relationship had run its course. I didn't see any reason to keep hanging on to it when it could have caused both of us so much trouble."

Our relationship had run its course. Well, that was news to him, but it explained why she'd given in to her father. If she'd loved Leo—hell, if she'd just cared enough about him—she would have stood with him so they could handle the *trouble* together.

"Besides," she went on a moment later, "this made things more peaceful for Cameron. I didn't want him to be around all the negativity."

He gave her a flat look to remind her that there was plenty of negativity over their custody fight and her plans to move to Oklahoma. He would have told her that verbally if Cameron hadn't started to fuss. Both Olivia and he turned toward the boy, but before Leo could go to him, his phone rang.

"It's Barrett," he relayed to Olivia after glancing at the screen. It was a call he had to take.

Leo went to the other side of the room, taking up position by the sink so he could keep watch out the back window. Olivia got started feeding Cameron his oatmeal, but Leo had no doubt she'd want to hear what his brother had to say. That's why he put the call on speaker.

"Olivia's listening," Leo told Barrett right off. "She and Cameron are in the kitchen with me." That would cue his brother to tone down whatever he had to say. "Is everything okay?"

"I was going to ask you that," Barrett countered. "Things are fine here. No signs of any other attackers."

"Same here. You got my email about Samuel? I'm running a financial check on your father," Leo added to Olivia when she looked at him.

"I got it, and I'll help you with that when I clear up some things."

"One of those things is Milton," Leo supplied.

Barrett made a sound of agreement. "The psychiatrist will be here any minute. I'll let you know as soon as she's done with her eval. In the meantime, I managed to get access to sealed juvie records for Milton."

It didn't surprise Leo that there was a juvie record since Milton had also been arrested as an adult for larceny, assault and public intoxication. He'd had no cage time though, only parole.

"Milton's pretty much been in trouble since he was old enough to sneak out of his house at night," Barrett continued. "And he has a history of violence. I'll send you the records to read for yourself, but Milton has a bad habit of being an accessory, situations where he was talked into doing something illegal or just plain stupid."

Leo would indeed read the reports, but he trusted Barrett's interpretation. It meant that Milton had possibly been coerced this time. Hell. More than possibly. Highly likely. Because, as Olivia had pointed out, her father could be behind this. Except that left Leo with one Texas-sized inconsistency. Even with all his faults, Samuel wouldn't have endangered Cameron.

"I'll need Olivia's official statement on the attack," Barrett went on. "And you can't be the one to take it."

No, because there were already enough conflicts of interest without adding that to the mix. "I'm keeping Cameron and Olivia in protective custody," Leo stated, though he was certain his brother already knew that.

"I've got no problem with that, but it means you'll either have to bring her here or else I'll need to go out to your place. I'm short-handed right now, but I should be able to get there by early afternoon."

Leo knew his brother was in a bind when it came to manpower, especially since Leo himself wouldn't be able to do his regular shift, but he wouldn't take Olivia outside unless he was certain it was safe.

"I'll let you know," he told Barrett. "Call me if you get any updates."

He'd just ended the call when he heard the sound of a car engine. Every muscle in his body went on alert, and in the same moment, a text flashed on his screen. It was from Wally.

Cameron's nanny just arrived, Wally had texted. Is it okay to let her in?

"What's wrong?" Olivia immediately asked. "Who's here?"

"Izzie," Leo quickly assured her, some of his own tension easing because Wally would have recognized the nanny on site. So, this wasn't a situation of someone trying to sneak onto the ranch.

Olivia released a breath that she'd obviously been holding. "I called Izzie last night and told her what was going on. I'm sorry I forgot to tell you that she'd insisted on coming in case we needed help."

Leo thought they might indeed need help with the baby, but he didn't like that Izzie was out and about and could therefore get caught up in another attack.

"Wait here," he told Olivia. "And stay away from the windows."

That last part was something he should have already warned Olivia about, but he'd let their conversation—and her—distract him. Not good. Right now a distraction could be fatal.

Leo went to the front of the house and disengaged the security system only long enough to open the front door and motion for the nanny to hurry inside. Izzie did. She raced across the yard and onto the porch.

As usual, the woman was wearing jeans and a plain cotton shirt, and she had her hair scooped up in a ponytail. Leo had run a background check on the nanny when Olivia had first hired her, and he knew Izzie was forty-nine and had a twenty-three-year-old son. She'd been a nanny for the past fifteen years. Plenty of experience and no smudges.

"Are all of you okay?" she immediately asked.

Izzie looked exactly as he'd expected. Worried.

Welcome to the club.

"We're okay for now. I want to keep it that way." He shut the door, locked it and rearmed the security system. Leo also glanced out the front windows to make sure no one had followed Izzie. He didn't see anyone and was certain that if Wally spotted an intruder, he'd call ASAP.

"Olivia and Cameron are in the kitchen," Leo told the woman.

He motioned for her to follow him even though Izzie knew the layout of his house. She'd been there several times since Olivia had had the nanny drop off Cameron for his visits when Olivia hadn't been able to do it herself.

Izzie greeted Olivia with a hug and murmured some reassurances that all would be well before she went to Cameron to greet him. Leo reached for his laptop, intending to take it into the living room so he could read Milton's juvie records, but he stopped when his phone rang again. He didn't recognize the number on the screen, and he got an immediate jolt of concern. It was too early for a telemarketer, but this could be connected to the investigation. Sometimes, would-be killers liked to taunt and gloat.

"Deputy Logan," he answered, ready to hit the record function on his phone. But it wasn't a stranger's voice he heard.

"It's me, Bernice Saylor," the caller said.

Since Bernice made a habit of giving him the cold shoulder whenever he ran into her, he couldn't imagine why she'd want to talk to him. Then he remembered that Olivia didn't have her phone and Bernice might not know the number of her prepaid cell.

"I'm sorry for calling at such an early hour," Bernice said.

"Did you want to speak to Olivia?" he asked.

"No. I need to talk to you. It's important. It's about the attack."

That got his attention. "What about it?"

"I need to talk to you in person," Bernice insisted. "I have information you need to hear. I believe I know who's trying to kill you."

Chapter 6

Olivia wasn't certain what Bernice had just told Leo, but whatever it was, he abruptly stepped out of the kitchen and motioned for her to join him. Olivia did, handing off the oatmeal to Izzie so that the nanny could finish feeding Cameron.

"Bernice, I need you to repeat what you just said," Leo instructed.

Even though he didn't put the call on speaker, Olivia moved close enough so she could listen. She figured this would be some kind of ploy to get her to mend fences with her father. Bernice was not objective when it came to Samuel. In fact, Olivia believed the woman was in love with him. Not that her father would return that love. No. Her dad relied on Bernice, but the woman fell very much into the close employee category.

"I told you that I believe I know who's trying to kill you," Bernice said.

Everything inside Olivia went still. She'd never known Bernice to say a negative thing about her father, but maybe the woman had seen or heard something to change her mind.

"Who?" Olivia blurted. "My father?"

She had no idea if Leo wanted her to make her presence known, but Olivia wanted to hear every word of this conversation. That included Bernice's answer to her question.

Bernice made a sharp sound of surprise. "No, not your father. Of course not him. Samuel would never do anything like that."

As far as Olivia was concerned, that was to be determined. Leo apparently felt the same way. "You're sure about that?" he fired back at Bernice.

"Positive. Samuel is a good man who loves his daughter and grandson. He wouldn't hurt you because it'd hurt them."

Again, that was to be determined. "Then who tried to kill Leo?" Olivia prompted, not waiting for the woman to respond before she added, "And you'd better not accuse me of it."

There was a long moment of silence before Bernice spoke. "Not you. But Samuel told me what happened with someone using your phone, and I think I know who's responsible. Rena Oldham."

"Samuel's girlfriend," Leo supplied.

"Ex-girlfriend," Bernice corrected. "Samuel broke things off with her a few days ago. She was pressuring him for marriage, again, and he got fed up with it."

Olivia didn't bother asking Bernice how she became

privy to such private information because it was possible she'd learned it from the source—Samuel. If not, Bernice would have made it her business to find out what'd happened. Olivia suspected there was very little that went on at the family estate that Bernice didn't know about.

Well, very little except for the real reason that Olivia had planned to move to Oklahoma. Bernice hadn't seemed to latch onto the fact that Olivia had been planning to protect Leo.

For all the good it'd done.

It certainly hadn't stopped someone from trying to kill him.

"Are you saying that you think Rena Oldham conspired to commit murder?" Leo bluntly challenged.

More silence. "Yes," Bernice finally answered. "And I have some things I think will convince you to arrest her."

"What things?" Leo snapped.

"I'm not getting into this over the phone. I'll meet you at the sheriff's office, but I want you to bring in Rena, too. I want you to question her after you see what I have."

Leo groaned. "You can take whatever you think you've got to my brother, Sheriff Barrett Logan. I'll call him to let him know to expect you."

"No." Bernice definitely didn't pause this time. "I'll only talk to you, so if you want to see what I have, you'll meet me at the sheriff's office. I'm sure Olivia will be very interested in what I have, too."

Olivia was close enough to Leo to see his eyes go cop flat. "If you're withholding evidence pertinent to an investigation, that's a crime. A felony. You want to be arrested Bernice?"

"No." Again, no pause, and there was a bitter edge to her voice. "If you won't meet me at the sheriff's office, then come here to Samuel's estate, or I can go to your place."

"You're not coming here," he snapped but then paused when he got an incoming call.

Olivia saw that it was from Barrett.

"I'll have to call you back," Leo told Bernice. Without waiting for her response, he switched over to his brother's call. "Is something wrong?" he asked Barrett.

"I'm not sure."

And just those three words put Olivia on full alert. Leo, too, and they both turned toward the kitchen to make sure Cameron was okay. He was. Izzie had moved him away from the window and was feeding him the rest of his breakfast. Thankfully, their son was oblivious to any bad news they were about to hear.

"Milton's psychiatrist isn't here yet, but he's insisting on talking to Olivia," Barrett explained. "In fact, he says he'll make a full confession to her."

"A confession," Leo repeated, and she heard the skepticism in Leo's tone. "Has he made any calls, ones where he could have arranged another attack?"

"No. But I think he's coming down from whatever high he was on. He's been pacing his cell and mumbling about this all being a mistake. I pressed him on exactly what mistake he meant, but he insisted he'd only talk to Olivia."

"It could still be a trap," Leo muttered moments later.

"Could be," Barrett agreed. "But if so, he would have had to set up an attack before his arrest. He was allowed one call, and he didn't use it, not even to contact a lawyer."

Interesting, but that didn't mean the man didn't have something up his sleeve. Still, Olivia would like to hear what Milton had to say.

"I wouldn't want to take Cameron to the sheriff's office," Olivia insisted. "But if you could arrange for a deputy to be here with him, maybe Leo and I can come in. My father's household manager, Bernice Saylor, wants Leo to meet her there, so we could kill two birds with one stone."

"Why does the household manager want to meet you?" Barrett immediately asked.

It was Leo who answered. "She claims that Samuel's ex-girlfriend is the person responsible for the attack and says she has proof. In fact, Bernice wants the ex brought in for questioning, which might not be a bad idea. Her name is Rena Oldham."

"She's Samuel's ex, you said?" Barrett questioned.

"According to Bernice, she is," Olivia explained. "She's been my father's longtime girlfriend, and they've broken up before. I didn't know about this particular breakup, though."

Barrett stayed silent a few long moments, obviously processing that. "You think Rena's capable of setting up a murder?"

Olivia hadn't had much time to consider the possibility, but she gave it some thought now. "Maybe. She's been on and off with my father for years, and she has a temper. She also claims she's in love with him, so I'm not sure how she'd react if he truly did end things with her for good."

"I'll bring her in for questioning," Barrett assured them. "Where does she live?"

"Culver Crossing." That wasn't far at all and was in the same town where Olivia lived. If Barrett could get in touch with Rena, he might have the woman in his office in under a half hour.

"What about Bernice?" Barrett asked. "Want me to bring her in, as well?"

"Sure. But I can text her," Leo said. "Can you spare a deputy to be with Cameron and his nanny?"

"I'll do better than that. I'm texting Daniel as we speak. He can be at your place in just a few minutes, and he can stay with Izzie and the baby."

Olivia released the breath she'd been holding. Along with being a deputy, Daniel was Leo's brother. He'd do everything within his power to protect Cameron.

"Keep your ranch hands on alert," Barrett advised. "And I'm sending Scottie out to your place for backup. He'll arrive in the cruiser, and Olivia and you can ride with him to town. He won't be able to stay once he's dropped you off because he's not on duty, but I'll get you back home after we're done here."

Again, Olivia was relieved. Scottie Bronson was yet another deputy, one that she knew Leo trusted. Plus, a police cruiser would be a lot safer than a regular vehicle. Still, it would mean leaving Cameron, and Olivia knew that wouldn't be easy, not even for a short time. But if they could get answers to help the investigation, it would ultimately make things safer for her little boy.

"I say we go ahead and bring in Randall," Barrett added. "And Samuel. That way I can ask about alibis and maybe rile at least one of them enough to spill something."

Her father would indeed be riled at being treated as a suspect, but Barrett was right. Sometimes, pushing the right buttons led to answers, and they very much needed answers right now.

Leo ended the call with his brother and immediately texted Bernice to let her know they would meet her at the sheriff's office. Bernice responded with I'm already on the way there.

Good. Olivia didn't exactly relish the idea of dealing with Bernice, but at least this way they wouldn't have to wait long for her to arrive. Besides, if Bernice actually had proof about Rena being involved in this, then maybe Barrett would be able to make an arrest today.

Olivia went back in the kitchen to tell Izzie their plans and to finish feeding Cameron, but only a couple of minutes had passed before she heard the sound of a car engine. Leo's phone also dinged with a text.

"It's Daniel," he relayed. "He's here." And he headed to the door to let his brother in.

Olivia filled in Izzie while Leo and Daniel made their way to the kitchen. Daniel's eyes met hers, and she felt the chill. No doubt because Daniel didn't care much for the custody fight she was giving Leo.

Correction—the fight she *had given* Leo.

Once the danger had passed, she really did need to figure out what to do. If her father was behind the attacks, then her leaving could end up only making things worse.

"Olivia," Daniel greeted, his voice as cool as his eyes. Ironic since they were a genetic copy of Leo's and Cameron's. Thankfully, though, there was no chill when Daniel went to Cameron and brushed a kiss on the top of his head.

Cameron babbled a greeting, grinned and offered Daniel a piece of peach. Obviously, her son was very comfortable around Leo's brother.

"I didn't see anything unusual on the drive over," Daniel explained. "But keep watch. I'll do the same."

Leo nodded in thanks. "I'll text Wally and explain to him what's happening." He shifted his attention to Izzie. "Daniel and some of my hands will be on guard while Olivia and I are out."

"We won't be gone long," Olivia assured the woman. She hoped that was true.

She could tell that Izzie was trying to put on a brave face. Olivia was doing the same thing, and she tried to keep up the pretense that this was just a normal breakfast while they waited for Scottie. However, the moment Leo got the text that the deputy was in front of the house, her nerves and fears returned. Not fear for herself but for Cameron.

"He'll be fine," Daniel said as if reading her mind. He ruffled Cameron's hair, grinned at him.

Olivia wanted to rattle off some instructions, repeating for them to stay away from the windows and reminding them to lock the doors. But Daniel would know to do those things. Once Scottie arrived, Olivia had to force herself out of the kitchen, but she didn't do that until she'd given Cameron several kisses.

When Leo led her out the front door, she saw that Scottie had parked the cruiser directly in front of the house. She also spotted the ranch hands that were standing guard.

As soon as Leo and she were in the back seat, Scottie took off. He didn't offer any greetings, instead keeping his attention on their surroundings. Leo and she did the same. She doubted a gunman would come after them in broad daylight, but she couldn't be sure since she didn't know who or what they were dealing with.

Soon, she hoped, that would change.

"I'm sorry," she muttered to Leo.

His gaze practically snapped toward her. He didn't ask "what for," but she could see the question in his eyes.

"I'm sorry for…everything," she settled for saying. "But especially for not telling you sooner about my father."

A muscle flickered in his jaw before he made a sound of agreement. Maybe he was accepting her apology, or it could be this was simply a discussion he didn't want to have in front of Scottie. Either way, it was her signal to table the subject. That was probably a good thing. It was best to have everything worked out in her mind before she had to hash things out with Leo.

Leo's phone rang, and he snatched it from his jeans' pocket. It was an understatement that they were both on edge, and Olivia immediately began to consider all the worst-cast scenarios.

"It's Randall," he told her.

That certainly didn't make her relax. After all, it was possible that Randall had been the one to hire Milton.

Leo hit the answer button and, like before, Olivia was close enough to hear when Randall snarled, "Deputy Logan, are you trying to get your butt sued?" The man didn't wait for an answer. "Because you and your sheriff brother are harassing me by dragging me in for an interrogation this morning, and that's grounds for a lawsuit."

"The sheriff and I want you in for questioning," Leo

stated. "You have means, motive and opportunity for attempted murder of a law enforcement officer. Me," Leo clarified just in case Randall had any doubts.

"I have an alibi," Randall wailed. "My sister told you where I was when you got knifed. I wasn't anywhere near Mercy Ridge or you."

Leo fired right back. "You know that doesn't get you off the hook. Someone hired the idiot who came after me, and you're a person of interest."

Randall spewed a string of raw profanity. "You're just pissed off because you couldn't pin murder on me, and you can't pin this one on me, either." He did more cursing. "I'll bring my lawyer for this witch hunt of an interrogation. Then I'll be filing that lawsuit right after. You'd better be prepared to pony up lots of cash because I'll sue you for every penny the Logans have." With that, Randall ended the call.

If Leo was concerned about the threat of a possible lawsuit, he didn't show it. He just dragged in a weary breath and continued to keep watch.

It took Scottie less than fifteen minutes to reach the sheriff's office, but every mile felt like an eternity to Olivia. So did the mere seconds it took to get out of the cruiser and inside. She immediately tried to steel herself up for Bernice, but the woman wasn't there. There was only a female deputy at the dispatch/reception desk and Barrett, who was making his way from his office toward them.

"The psychiatrist has been delayed, Bernice and Rena should be here any minute," Barrett told them. "Randall is due in an hour, and Samuel will be in this afternoon."

"Randall called me a couple of minutes ago," Leo

informed him. "He wanted to express his disapproval at being called in." He dragged his hand over his face. "This smacks of something Randall could have done, and he's at the top of my suspect list."

"Mine, too," Barrett agreed. "What better way to get back at you than to have you murdered and to set up the mother of your child to take the blame?"

That put a huge knot in Olivia's stomach. Because it could be true. All of this could be about revenge, and Randall probably wouldn't care if Cameron became collateral damage.

"I'll go ahead and move Milton to an interview room so he can get started with that confession he says he wants to give you," Barrett added to Olivia. "Leo and I will be in there with you, and I'll also be recording everything that's said."

She nodded and had fully expected the recording. What Olivia hadn't expected was to be in the same room with Milton. She had thought she'd be speaking to him while he was behind bars. In hindsight, she should have realized that Barrett would need to make this an official interrogation.

"Wait here, and I'll get Milton," Barrett said, heading in the direction of where Olivia figured the holding cells were.

"Want some coffee?" Leo asked, going to the small serving area on the far side of the room.

However, he stopped when a bell rang to indicate the front door had just opened. The adrenaline shot through her when she saw Leo place his hand over his weapon, and she whirled around to see what had caused that reaction.

Rena Oldham walked in.

She wasn't what anyone would call willowy. In fact, she had what Olivia thought of as an Amazon warrior's build on a sturdy five-foot, ten-inch frame. Rena obviously worked out a lot, too, because her arms and legs were well toned.

Despite the somewhat early hour, the woman looked well put together in her red summer pants, white top and sandals. There wasn't a strand of her shoulder-length honey-blond hair out of place. Ditto for her perfectly applied makeup, but then again Olivia had never seen her look any other way. Bernice had mentioned something about Rena being in her fifties, but she looked much younger than that.

"Where's Bernice?" Rena snarled, and her tone gave Olivia a taste of the temper that she'd mentioned to Leo. "I want to confront that busybody witch for lying about me."

Leo skipped getting any coffee and went to Olivia's side. "How'd you know Bernice is lying?"

"Because she called me and told me she was coming here, and that she had so-called proof that I'm the one responsible for you and Olivia nearly being killed." Rena turned her cool blue eyes on Olivia then. "I didn't have anything to do with that."

"So, why does Bernice think you did?" Leo challenged.

"Because she's a jealous, vindictive witch," Rena readily supplied. "She doesn't want anyone near her precious Samuel except her. Well, she can have him. I'm done with Samuel."

So, it was true that her father and Rena had broken up. Not really a surprise. Olivia had been down this path with them before.

"What exactly does Bernice have that she's calling proof of your guilt?" Leo asked.

Rena threw her hands in the air. "Your guess is as good as mine. But whatever it is, it doesn't point to me as a would-be killer because I'm not one. You put that on whatever official record you need."

Leo nodded. "Let's move this conversation to an interview room." He motioned for them to follow him, but they hadn't even reached the hall when Barrett came out with Milton.

Everyone froze.

Milton's gaze zoomed right to Olivia, and he smiled. She felt the flash of disgust followed by the rage. This SOB had tried to kill Leo and had tried to pin that on her. Olivia glared at him and had to rein in that rage to keep from going to him and slapping him. But Milton's attention was no longer on her. He looked at Rena.

And smiled again.

This was a different kind of smile, though. Not a taunt like the one he'd doled out to her. This one had a glimmer of recognition, and his eyes practically lit up. Rena, however, didn't have that reaction. She squared her shoulders and groaned softly.

"You two know each other?" Leo asked, clearly picking up on their body language.

"No," Rena said at the same moment that Milton answered. "Yeah, we do."

Leo aimed a scowl at Rena. "Do you know this man?" he pressed.

Rena huffed. "He knew my brother, Brett. They were drug users, so I distanced myself from both of them."

"Then, you do know Milton," Leo stated, his voice

flat. Obviously, he didn't care for the lie that Rena had told with her previous response.

Annoyance and anger sparked through Rena's eyes. "If you're trying to connect me to this piece of scum, then you'd better stop right there. I haven't seen or spoken to Milton in years, not since my brother died of an overdose from drugs that this snake gave him." She tipped her head at Milton to indicate *he* was that *snake*.

Milton tried to shrug despite the fact that he was cuffed and Barrett had his arm in a grip. "Brett supplied me with plenty of stuff, too. I just got lucky and he didn't."

Rena took a step toward him as if she might launch herself at him. Since Olivia had wanted to do the same thing just minutes earlier, she totally understood the woman's reaction. But Leo stepped in front of Rena to stop her. No way did he want a brawl when they hadn't even had a chance to deal with Milton.

"Wait here," Leo ordered Rena, and he glanced at the deputy at the desk. According to her name tag, she was Cybil Cassidy. "Stay with Miss Oldham while Olivia and I have a chat with Milton."

"I've changed my mind," Milton blurted when they started for the interview room. He smiled at Olivia again. "I've decided I don't want to make a confession, after all."

Olivia muttered some profanity before she could stop herself, and she got a second slam of anger. "Why not?" she demanded.

With a ghost of that sly smile still on his mouth, he shook his head. "I'm not feeling well. I should probably talk to the psychiatrist first. Then, if I'm feeling better, you and I can have a heart to heart."

Coming from Milton, that last part sounded like a threat. Felt like one, too.

"What kind of sick game are you playing?" Leo demanded, going closer to Milton.

Milton looked Leo straight in the eye. "I'm a sick man, didn't you know? And it's my right not to say anything that could incriminate me."

"Was this a ploy to get us off the ranch so someone else can try to kill us?" Olivia quickly asked.

Leo had already gone there, and he fired off a text to Daniel to make sure everything was okay. Daniel gave him an equally quick response to let him know that it was. Leo then warned his brother to be extra cautious, though he figured Daniel was already doing just that.

Leo shifted his attention back to Milton and didn't break the intense stare he had with the man until the door opened again. This time there were two visitors, both women. The first to walk in was a tall, slim woman with auburn hair that fell right at her chin. Leo didn't know her, but he figured she was the psychiatrist. Leo had no trouble recognizing the second one.

Bernice.

Like Rena, she was tall, but that's where the similarities ended. Bernice had a stocky build with wide shoulders, and her dark brown hair was threaded with gray. No makeup, and her clothes didn't look as if they'd have a designer label. She wore a fitted gray dress that wouldn't have looked out of place on a hotel maid.

Bernice and Rena started a glaring match of their own, but Barrett handed off Milton to Deputy Cassidy with instructions to take him to the interview room.

"Dr. Kirkpatrick?" Barrett asked, and the woman nodded. Once he'd checked her ID, he motioned for her to follow Deputy Cassidy and Milton. "I want a copy of your eval as soon as you have it."

"I'll give you any information that I can," the doctor countered.

That meant she likely wouldn't tell Barrett everything that went on in the eval. She followed Milton and the deputy, leaving Olivia with Barrett, Leo, Rena and Bernice. The air was practically crackling with tension, and most of it was coming from Rena.

"How dare you accuse me of trying to kill someone," Rena said through clenched teeth. "You're vindictive and jealous, and you have nothing connecting me to any of this mess."

Bernice's glare softened when she turned to Leo. She took a large manila envelope from her purse and handed it to him.

"I think once you read everything in there, you'll see what I mean about Rena being the one who hired Milton," Bernice calmly stated.

"I didn't hire him," Rena practically shouted, and she tried to snatch the envelope from Leo. He shot her a look that could have frozen the deepest level of hell.

"What's in here?" Leo asked Bernice.

The woman took a deep breath before she answered. "Copies of emails that Rena sent Samuel after he broke up with her this last time. She threatened to get back at him."

Rena rolled her eyes, obviously dismissing that, but the anger stayed on her face. "I was furious and hurt. Those emails meant nothing. And you had no right to read them," she added to Bernice. "Those were private emails I sent to Samuel."

"I run the estate," Bernice pointed out. "That includes going through correspondence and emails. You threatened to get back at Samuel, and you said it'd be awful if something bad happened to someone he loved."

"I was angry," Rena argued. "I didn't mean it. I didn't mean it," she repeated, aiming her plea at Olivia.

Olivia had no idea if Rena had meant it or not. Maybe her temper had just gotten the best of her. Maybe not. She could be looking into the face of the person who'd set up the attack.

"Rena broke into the estate just yesterday," Bernice added. "I found her trying to go through Samuel's office when he wasn't there."

"I didn't break in." Rena's voice held as much of a snarl as Bernice's. "Samuel gave me a key and the security codes—"

Bernice just talked right over Rena. "I had the locks and security system changed last night after I insisted she leave the premises. She wouldn't tell me what she was looking for in Samuel's office, but I suspect she was there to steal something."

Rena gave the woman a much cooler look, her mouth curved into a sly smile. "I was looking for my earring that fell off when Samuel and I had sex on his desk. Did you listen in on that, too, Bernice? Did you get an eyeful of your *employer* getting down and dirty with me?"

Olivia groaned. That was so not an image she wanted in her head. Apparently, neither did Bernice because she gave Rena a cold stare.

"Samuel's with so many women that I don't notice such things," Bernice said, her voice as icy as the look. "You are one of dozens. *Dozens*," she stressed. "And none of them, including you, lasted."

That clearly rattled Rena. She opened her mouth,

closed it and then narrowed her eyes. "Samuel still has feelings for me," Rena insisted. "You just wait and see. He'll come back to me. He always does."

"Keep thinking that," Bernice grumbled and turned to Leo. "I hired a PI to do a thorough background check on Rena, and I learned that she has criminal contacts. Your suspect, Milton Hough, for one. She knows him."

"So I just found out." Leo lifted the envelope and ignored the sound of outrage that Rena made. "I'll read what's in here, but I want to know if any of the emails mentioned Milton?"

"No. But there is something you might find interesting." Bernice tipped her head to the envelope. "Read the PI's report, and you'll see that Rena has another connection to you. Or rather, a connection to someone who wants you dead." She gave a satisfied nod. "Rena's been bedmates with none other than the man who'd do anything to ruin you."

"And who would that be?" Leo asked.

Bernice lifted her chin. "Randall Arnett."

Chapter 7

Randall Arnett.

Leo wasn't surprised to hear that particular name come up in this investigation, but he hadn't expected this kind of connection. He stared at Rena, waiting for an explanation. Olivia and Barrett were doing the same thing. However, it seemed to take Rena a couple of long moments just to compose herself.

Rena made a throaty sound and whipped out her phone. "I'm calling my lawyer."

"Good," Barrett advised her. "Because you're going to need one." He glanced at Leo. "You want to take her in for questioning, or should I do it?"

Leo stared at the envelope a moment. "I want to go through this envelope first. That'll give her lawyer a chance to get here."

Rena was already speaking to someone on the phone,

presumably her attorney, and it made Leo wonder just how often the woman required legal services that she would be able to make contact this quickly. But that was a question for another time, another place. For now, he wanted to get a look at what Bernice had put in the envelope.

"You can have a seat out here," Barrett told Bernice. "I'll need to take your statement, too, but you'll have to wait your turn."

"Oh, I'll wait," Bernice assured him. "I'll do whatever it takes to get that piece of temperamental fluff out of Samuel's life."

Beside him, Leo saw Olivia go a little stiff. "You do this sort of thing often for my father?" she asked.

Bernice's chin came up. "I take care of him. Which is more than you do," she snapped. "He's worried sick about Cameron and you."

There it was again. The territorial attitude that Bernice had always had for Samuel. Normally, Leo didn't see anything especially sinister about it, but this felt… well, different.

Bernice had obviously gone to some expense and trouble to dig up dirt on Rena, but he knew from experience that a person doing the digging could be selective about what they found. In other words, Bernice could have looked solely for info to discredit a woman she saw as competition for Samuel's attention. Or a woman Bernice wanted to punish because she had not gone quietly after this latest breakup with Samuel.

Since he wanted to get Olivia away from Bernice—and away from the windows—he motioned for her to follow him. He didn't have an office of his own, none of the deputies did, so they went into Barrett's and he shut the door. He'd still be able to hear if anyone came in because the bell on the door would alert him, but this way he and Olivia would have some privacy to go through the envelope. Plus, there was no worry about Bernice not staying put. It was crystal-clear that the woman intended to put the screws to Rena.

Leo took a moment once they were alone to try to absorb all the information he'd just gotten from Rena and Bernice. Apparently, Olivia was doing the same because she didn't say anything, and he heard her draw in a long, deep breath and then slowly expel it.

"If there's anything in the emails, can you actually use it to arrest Rena?" she finally asked as she sank into the chair next to the desk.

Leo shrugged and sat, too. Opening the envelope, he took out the papers. "Maybe. There could be a chain of custody issue, though. Bernice could have altered the emails she's printed out, so we'd have to see the originals and verify that Rena did, indeed, send them."

Of course, Rena hadn't denied the sending part, only the intent. And intent in an email was hard to prove. Even if she'd threatened Samuel to hell and back, it didn't mean the woman had actually gone through on the threats. Then again, she did have those criminal contacts.

Including Randall.

Leo pondered that a moment while he glanced through the first email. Yeah, it was a threat, all right. One peppered with a lot of profanity, capital letters and exclamation marks. What he didn't see were any details of how Rena would carry through with getting back at her lover for dumping her. There were no specifics, no time and place references, just the "something awful" that might happen to someone Samuel loved.

But it wasn't as black and white as Bernice had painted it.

I was in love with you, Rena had written. Just imagine something awful happening to someone you love, and that's how I feel right now. You've crushed my heart, Samuel, and I hope that one day you'll hurt as much as I'm hurting now.

Definitely no "I'm going to kill someone you love" as Bernice had made it seem. Still, there was a lot of emotion in that handful of sentences, and sometimes emotion could cause people to do all sorts of bad things.

He handed the email to Olivia so she could read it for herself and then went onto the next one. There were five total, all where Rena had vented and spewed some venom. He passed those to Olivia, as well, and studied the next page. It was an account of what Bernice had overheard when Rena and Samuel had argued about the breakup. It was clearly hearsay, but if Samuel verified it, then it could be used to show that Rena had had motive to set up the attack.

"Did your father say anything to you about his breakup with Rena?" Leo asked Olivia.

"Nothing specific, but they've broken up so many times that it's not something he'd talk to me about." She looked up from the paper and their gazes met. "It doesn't feel as if Rena would try to get back at my father through you. With her hot temper, it seems as if she'd just go directly after him."

"That'd be what everyone would expect. But maybe Rena reined in her temper long enough to figure that out. After all, if someone tried to kill Samuel, she'd be a prime suspect. This way, he's still punished because you were set up to take the blame for the attack."

She nodded, took another of those long breaths. "So, Rena could have hired her late brother's friend." Olivia paused. "Or hired Randall."

"Yeah," Leo agreed as he put aside the rest of Bernice's account of the breakup so he could look through the PI's report.

It was thorough. That was Leo's first impression. The PI had basically provided details of the last twenty years of Rena's life. He'd used social media posts and info that he'd garnered from her friends to detail a pattern of being with Samuel, followed by a breakup, followed by short romantic relationships with other men. Short career ventures, too. Rena came from money and had a trust fund, one that she'd practically drained to set up one failed business after the other.

"If this report is accurate," Leo remarked to Olivia, "then Rena is hurting financially. In fact, she's flat broke and financing her lifestyle off credit cards. Maybe that's one of the reasons she was pressing your father for marriage."

"Maybe," Olivia agreed. "But if she's broke, then she wouldn't have been able to pay Milton for the attack."

"No, but it could be she didn't need cash for that. Perhaps she just stirred him up enough. Or he could have done this as a favor since he knew her brother."

"Maybe," Olivia repeated, not sounding convinced.

Leo was on the same page with her. He wasn't convinced, either.

Olivia stood so she could read the report from over his shoulder. Of course, that meant her face ended up very close to his.

He caught her scent.

When she'd showered that morning, she'd obviously used the same brand of soap that he had. That's what would have been in the guest bath. It was pretty basic soap, but it managed to smell damn special on her since it mingled with her own unique scent. One that he remembered all too well. And one that stirred him in the wrong places.

"Rena was with Randall for about two and a half months," Olivia said, going through the report. She was totally unaware of the effect she was having on him. "Do I have the timing right? Rena was with Randall shortly after he was with the girlfriend who went missing?"

"Jessa McCade," Leo provided. Yes, the timing was right for that. "I'll want to question Rena to find out if Randall said anything to her about Jessa. Or if Randall was ever violent with her—as I suspect he had been with Jessa."

In fact, Leo figured the violence had maybe started as an argument and had escalated when Randall had killed Jessa in a fit of temper. Then Randall had disposed of the body and it hadn't been found. It was the only thing that made sense to Leo since he wasn't buying that Jessa had just run off, leaving her family and five-year-old son. No. All the indications were that Jessa loved her little boy and had just gotten mixed up with the wrong man—Randall.

He felt Olivia brush her hand over his shoulder, but it took him a moment to realize she'd done that as a gesture of comfort. Apparently, she'd picked up on the vibes he was giving off. Regret over not being able to bring Randall to justice.

"Randall killed Jessa," Leo stated. "There's plenty of circumstantial evidence, but I wasn't able to do what I needed to do to find something more concrete." Maybe Rena could provide that missing piece.

He glanced over to where Olivia still had her hand on his shoulder. But it was bad timing on his part. Because he did that at the exact moment she looked down. His mouth grazed her cheek. And he felt that slight touch in every inch of his body.

Every inch.

Hell. He still wanted her. Bad.

She didn't pull away from him. Instead, Olivia shifted her gaze so they were staring directly into each other's eyes. Leo could have sworn that the temperature in the room heated up a full twenty degrees, and he fought not to latch onto her and kiss her. It was a battle that he thought he was winning.

When Olivia kissed him.

She made a small sound, a mix of surprise and pleasure. Not good. Because that pleasure kicked his need for her into overdrive. Now, he did latch onto her, turning in the chair so that he could take her mouth the way he wanted. He made the kiss long and deep, more than enough to qualify as foreplay. Foreplay that shouldn't be happening. No way should he be muddying the waters like this with her.

Olivia seemed to agree with him on that last part because she pulled away. Her breathing was way too heavy. Her face flushed. She took several steps back to put some distance between them.

"We should be talking about Randall," Olivia muttered, still fighting to level her breathing. "And about Milton. We shouldn't be kissing."

Leo couldn't argue with any of that. Of course, at the moment, he couldn't speak to argue about anything. It took him several moments to shake off the heat and gather some common sense. The investigation. That should be their focus because the only way to stop the danger was to find the person responsible.

Olivia cleared her throat and sat back down. "Did Randall's alibi check out for the attack?" she asked.

Since she'd managed to get past the kiss, Leo made sure he did, as well. "On the surface." He'd gone through Barrett's report first thing this morning. "His current girlfriend said he was with her, but that doesn't mean he's innocent."

It also didn't mean the girlfriend was telling the truth. Lovers lied for each other all the time. Heck, Olivia had lied to him when she'd ended their relationship. Lied because she hadn't wanted him to incur her father's wrath. Later, it was a discussion that Olivia and he needed to have, but for now he went back to the PI's report on Rena. He'd barely finished the next page before the landline phone rang on Barrett's desk.

"Deputy Logan," Leo answered.

"Deputy Logan," the caller repeated. "Good. I would have called you next. I'm Deputy Chief Trey Mercer from the Culver Crossing Fire Department. I'm trying to reach Olivia Nash."

Leo immediately felt the punch of dread. "She's here. What's wrong?" he demanded, and he put the call on speaker.

"I've got a crew on the way out to her place now," Trey said. "A call came in from an anonymous source about twenty minutes ago, and the person said he'd set fire to her house."

Olivia practically leaped to her feet. "You've verified there really is a fire?" she asked. And Leo knew what she was thinking—that it could be a lure to draw them out.

"Not yet. But the caller said there was a second fire. This one is out of my jurisdiction, though. He claims it's in Mercy Ridge, so I've alerted the fire chief there."

Leo got to his feet, too, just as his own phone rang. "Where in Mercy Ridge?" he snapped.

"According to the call," the deputy chief answered, "there's an incendiary device on a timer, and it's set to go off at your house in ten minutes."

Chapter 8

The fear cut through Olivia like a switchblade and, for a second, the air vanished from her lungs. She couldn't catch her breath, but she turned and started out of the office. Leo, right behind her, took hold of her arm before she could bolt out the front door.

"Wait," Leo insisted over the sound of his still ringing phone. "This could be a trap."

Olivia hadn't even thought of that and didn't want to think of it now. She only wanted to get to Cameron and to make sure he was okay.

"What's wrong?" Bernice asked. "Is there trouble?"

Leo didn't respond to the woman, but he did answer his phone. Olivia saw Mercy Ridge Fire Department on his screen. "Are you on your way out to my place?" Leo demanded the moment he had someone on the line.

"Yes," the caller assured him. "Our ETA is about ten minutes."

That felt like an eternity. Way too long to make sure Cameron was safe.

"Get there as fast as you can," Leo insisted.

He ended the call and immediately made another one. This time to Daniel. And he did all that while hanging on to Olivia's hand, probably to ensure that she didn't run outside.

"Daniel," he said when his brother answered. "Culver Crossing PD got an anonymous tip that there could be a device rigged to set a fire at my house. Any signs of trouble?"

"None," Daniel said without hesitation. "We've all been keeping watch, and no one has gotten near the house."

That didn't cause Olivia to breathe any easier because, if there truly was a device, it might not have gone off yet.

"Go get Barrett," Leo told Olivia.

She wanted to leave, to get into the cruiser and head straight to Leo's, but she did as Leo asked and hurried to the hall where there were two interview rooms. Deputy Cassidy was standing guard outside one of them, no doubt where Milton was having his eval with the psychiatrist.

"What's wrong?" the deputy asked.

"There's a problem!" Olivia exclaimed as she threw open the second door where Barrett was questioning Rena.

Barrett clearly saw the alarm on Olivia's face because he was already on his feet. "Wait here," he told Rena before rushing out into the hall with Olivia. "Keep an eye on both Milton and Miss Oldham," he directed the deputy.

Olivia didn't waste any time running back toward Leo. He was still on the phone, but he tossed Barrett a set of keys that he took from the dispatcher's desk. "Let's go," Leo demanded. "I'll fill you in on the way."

Barrett didn't question his brother. He snatched the keys out of the air, and the three of them raced to the cruiser that was still parked directly in front of the station. As they'd done on the drive to the sheriff's office, Leo and she jumped in the back, but this time it was Barrett who got in behind the wheel.

Olivia's pulse was thick and throbbing, making it hard for her to hear, but she caught bits and pieces of the instructions that Leo rattled off to Daniel. *Truck. Car seat. Road.*

"Someone might have put a firebomb at Leo's house," she explained to Barrett when his eyes met hers in the rearview mirror.

That was all the info Barrett needed to hit the siren and the accelerator. They sped away from the sheriff's office. Judging from the way Barrett started firing glances all around them, he must have thought this could be some kind of ruse, as well. If so, it had worked because it'd gotten her and Leo out of the building and on the road where they'd be easier targets.

"Daniel and the hands haven't seen anything suspicious," Leo relayed to them the moment he'd finished his call. "But we're taking precautions anyway since it's possible that someone planted a device days or even weeks ago before we were on watch."

Oh mercy. She hadn't even considered that, but Olivia certainly considered it now. "Cameron," was all she managed to say.

"He'll be fine," Leo quickly told her, but she saw that

the assurance didn't make it to his eyes. He was just as terrified for their baby as she was. "Daniel's moving my truck into the garage, and Izzie will get Cameron into his car seat before they drive out. They won't go far, just about twenty yards from the house, and the hands will guard the truck to make sure no one tries to sneak up on them."

Those were good security measures, and it would prevent Cameron from being in the house in case it did catch fire. But Olivia wasn't sure those measures would be enough.

"Someone could fire shots into the truck," she reminded him.

"No. Because no one will get close enough to do that. The hands are armed with rifles, and they're all good shots. No one will get in position to try to hurt Cameron."

Olivia wanted to latch onto that. Wanted it to be the gospel truth. But there were thick trees along Leo's property line, and a sniper could climb one of those and start firing. Of course, if that happened, Daniel would almost certainly protect Cameron with his life, but it might not be enough.

It might not be enough.

She had to choke back the sob that tried to make its way out of her throat, and she forced herself to keep it together. If she gave in to the fear and panic now, it wouldn't help and in fact could hurt. After all, they needed to be focused on any possible threats waiting for them between here and Leo's place.

Leo's phone rang again, the sound shooting through the cruiser. Shooting through her, as well. Olivia's gaze automatically flew to the cell's screen where she expected to see Daniel's name. But it wasn't. It was the Culver Crossing Fire Department again. Leo answered the call right away and put it on speaker.

"It's Deputy Chief Trey Mercer," the caller said. "I've got some bad news."

Olivia could have sworn her heart stopped. Just stopped. A thousand thoughts went through her head, none good.

"We're out at Olivia Nash's place," the fireman continued, "and we're not going to be able to save it. The roof's already collapsed, and the fire's spread into the yard. My men are working to contain it now."

Under most circumstances, Olivia would have found that new devasting, but it was a relief because the *bad news* didn't involve Cameron. She was finally able to release the breath that was now burning in her chest.

"Are you on your way out here?" the fireman asked.

It was Leo who answered. "No. I'm not sure when Olivia will be able to get there. Days, maybe. She's in protective custody."

"Oh." Judging from his surprised tone, the deputy chief hadn't expected that. "All right, then. I'll send you my preliminary report when I can get it done. It'll take a while, though, because this is definitely an arson investigation. There's a strong smell of accelerant."

She hadn't doubted that the fire had been intentionally set. But why? Was it just another distraction, or had their attackers thought she was there? Obviously, someone had wanted to set her up to take the blame for Leo's murder, but maybe she was now the primary target. Or else someone wanted them to believe that.

Leo's phone dinged again with a text message. "It's from Daniel," he said to Barrett and her. "The fire department is at the house, and there are still no signs of a device. The bomb squad's on the way."

Olivia grasped the part about there being *no signs of a device*. The seconds ticked by slowly, and she moved to the edge of her seat as Barrett took the turn to Leo's ranch. It wouldn't be long now before she could see Cameron and, better yet, get him in the cruiser so he'd be better protected. However, the house was still out of view when Barrett slammed on his brakes, sending the tires screeching on the asphalt.

Olivia immediately saw why Barrett had done that. There was a man in the middle of the road, and he was waving his hands around as if trying to flag them down. There was a truck behind him, from which he'd likely made a quick exit because the driver's door was still open.

"Randall," Leo snarled. "What the hell does he want?"

That revved her heartbeat up again. Olivia hadn't recognized the man, though she'd seen his photo in the news during the investigation of his missing girlfriend. Unlike the picture that'd been taken at a party where he'd been dressed in a suit, today he was in jeans and had an unbuttoned denim shirt over a white tee.

Randall was also armed with a rifle.

Barrett didn't lower the window but instead spoke to Randall through the microphone that he unclipped from the siren. "Stop where you are and put down your weapon," he ordered when Randall came closer.

Randall didn't stop. Just the opposite. With both hands gripped on the rifle, he began to run toward the cruiser.

"Get down," Leo told her. He drew his gun. Barrett did the same.

Olivia didn't want to get down. She wanted to hurry to the ranch to check on Cameron, especially since Randall could be there to set off the timer on any firebomb he might have planted. But there was no way they could ignore this threat that was coming right at them.

Barrett got out and, using the cruiser door for cover, took aim. Leo did the same on the other side of the vehicle.

"Stop," Barrett shouted out again.

However, the moment Barrett gave that command, the blast tore through the air. Not a gunshot. No. This was an explosion, and Randall's truck became a fireball.

The blast caused the cruiser doors to slam into Leo and Barrett. Leo cursed and nearly dropped from the pain when the door caught his injured arm. But he forced himself to stay on his feet. to focus. And to assess what the hell was going on.

Barrett was cursing in pain, too, because his door had rammed into his shoulder. Randall was on the ground where he'd landed face-first. His rifle was no longer in his hands, probably because it'd been thrown clear from him in the fall. That was the good news, that Randall was no longer armed. Good, too, that Olivia wasn't hurt—Leo glanced at her to see that she was shaken up, but she hadn't been injured.

The bad news was that pieces of Randall's truck were raining down around them. Fiery bits of metal and rubber that could be just as deadly as bullets.

"Get back in the cruiser," Leo told his brother, and

he did the same. He got another jolt of pain from his arm when he had to use his hand to slam the door shut.

In the front, Barrett did the same, and he grabbed the microphone again. "Randall, if you can move, take cover under the cruiser. There could be a secondary explosion from the gas tank."

Randall lifted his head, shook it as if to clear it and, with plenty of effort, got to a crouching position. He was bleeding. Leo couldn't tell how badly he was hurt because the black smoke billowing off what was left of his truck immediately engulfed him.

"You tried to kill me!" Randall shouted. "So help you, you Logans will pay for this."

Obviously, Randall thought they were responsible for whatever had caused his truck to explode. It was possible, though, that this was some kind of sick plan to make himself look innocent. If so, the ploy had clearly gotten out of hand. He could have been killed.

Randall came out of the smoke, walking now. Or rather, stumbling and limping. But he didn't move toward the cruiser. Instead, he made his way to the side of the road, dropped down into the ditch and headed for a cluster of trees. What he hadn't done was pick up his rifle. It was still on the ground.

"I'll call for assistance," Barrett said, using the phone on the dash as he put the cruiser in Reverse. "I can't get past the fire, so I'll have to use the ranch trail."

The trail would indeed get them to the house, but it would take longer than the road. Plus, there was the huge concern that someone might be lying in wait along the route since his ranch hands weren't patrolling that particular area of his property.

Leo took out his phone to call Daniel, but it rang in his hand and he saw his brother's name on the screen.

"We heard a blast," Daniel said the moment Leo answered. "Are you all okay?"

"Yeah. What about Cameron, Izzie and you?" Leo countered.

"Fine. What blew up?"

"Randall's truck. He wasn't in it at the time, so he's still alive," Leo added, and he glanced in the direction where he'd last seen the man. He was no longer in sight. "The road isn't passable right now, so we'll use the west trail. Our ETA is about ten minutes. Eight," he amended when Barrett hit the accelerator and got them speeding out of there.

"Any idea who blew up Randall's truck?" Daniel asked.

"Not yet. Maybe Randall himself. Possibly the person who hired Milton. Just keep Cameron safe," Leo stressed.

"Will do. See you in a few."

Leo ended the call and turned to Olivia to do another check on her. She was way paler than usual, but she looked a lot steadier than he'd thought she would be.

"You're hurt," she muttered, reaching for his sleeve that now had some blood on it. The impact of the cruiser door had obviously reopened the wound.

"I'll clean it when I get home," he assured her, hoping there'd be a home for him to go back to.

Until he'd seen Randall's truck get blown to bits, Leo hadn't been sure there truly was a device rigged with an explosive. Obviously, there had been, and now he could only pray there wasn't a second device. Especially one anywhere near Cameron that someone else could set off.

Olivia didn't listen to his comment about taking care of the wound when he got home. She eased up his sleeve and had a look for herself. Leo didn't glance down when she started to dab away the blood. He kept his attention on the turn that Barrett made onto the trail.

Unlike the main road, the west trail was narrow, only wide enough for one vehicle. Along with plenty of potholes in the gravel surface, it was lined on both sides with trees and thick underbrush. Plenty of places for someone to hide, though Leo didn't think they had to worry about Randall. Even if the man had managed to run at full speed, he wouldn't have been able to get here and set up position for an attack.

Going as fast as he safely could, Barrett sped down the trail, hitting his breaks to take a deep curve. The moment he did, Leo heard a sound he definitely didn't want to hear.

A gunshot.

Hell. This was exactly what Leo had feared would happen. And what he'd hoped they could avoid.

The first bullet didn't hit the cruiser, but the second one did. It slammed into the front of the vehicle, and Leo immediately pushed Olivia down onto the seat. He also glanced around, looking for the shooter.

And he soon found him.

There was a man just ahead, leaning out from a spindly tree. He wasn't wearing a mask, so Leo saw his face but didn't recognize him. A stranger. That meant this was likely a hired gun.

"Hold on," Barrett warned a split second before he aimed the cruiser in the direction of the shooter.

Obviously, the guy hadn't been expecting that because he scrambled out of the way before he could get off another shot. Barrett slammed on his brakes, the side of the cruiser scraping against the tree.

Leo already had his weapon ready. So did Barrett. They fired glances around, looking to see if this idiot was alone or if he'd brought backup. Leo didn't see anyone else.

The moment the cruiser stopped, Leo and Barrett threw open their doors, both taking aim at the gunman who was still trying to get his balance.

"I'm Sheriff Logan," Barrett called out. "Drop your weapon and put up your hands or I'll shoot."

The man whirled around and in the same motion, brought up his gun. Definitely not a move to drop the weapon as Barrett had ordered. And Leo got confirmation of that when the man fired a shot at them. Leo had no doubts that this idiot would kill all of them if he got the chance. And that's why Leo pulled the trigger. He aimed for the guy's chest and sent two rounds into him.

That stopped him.

The man froze, the look of shock washing over his face. He dropped his gun so he could clasp his hands to his chest. Not that it would do any good. No. Leo could see that the guy was bleeding out fast.

"Call an ambulance," Leo told Olivia, tossing her his phone.

Maybe, just maybe, they could keep this SOB alive so he could tell them what the hell was going on.

Chapter 9

Olivia made the call for the EMTs to come to the ranch trail to try to save the man who'd just tried to kill them. Maybe the same man who'd also blown up Randall's truck. If they got lucky, he'd be able to tell them for himself.

"Take the cruiser and get Olivia out of here so you can check on Cameron," Barrett instructed Leo. "I'll wait here until the ambulance arrives."

Leo shook his head and glanced around. "I don't want to leave you alone because this guy could have a partner or two."

Barrett made a sound of agreement. "And if he does, he'll be going after Olivia and you. Take her to your house, and move Cameron and the nanny into the cruiser where they'll be safer. Then, all of you can go back to the sheriff's office until we get the all-clear on your place."

Olivia also had worries about leaving Barrett, but she was desperate to see her son and to make sure he was okay.

"All of you can bunk in the breakroom until we figure out a better place," Barrett added and then motioned for Leo to move. "Go ahead. Get Olivia away from this."

Leo nodded, but there was a lot of hesitancy in his expression. However, he finally got behind the wheel and took off. He also called Daniel and gave him a brief explanation as to what was going on and asked that Daniel come to assist Barrett as soon as Olivia and he were back at the ranch. It wasn't a great plan because any or all of them could be in danger from a sniper, but at the moment he had no great plan other than to make things as safe for Cameron as he could.

Olivia dug her fingers into the seat as Leo maneuvered the cruiser through the snaking trail. She also kept watch, praying that there wasn't a second gunman. Thankfully, she didn't see anyone until they reached the edge of the ranch, and she recognized the man as one of Leo's hands. He gave Leo a nod of greeting and continued to stand guard.

"Don't get out until I'm right next to the truck," Leo told her, figuring that she would indeed scramble to see Cameron.

Olivia obeyed, but she put her hand on the door, ready to open it, and waited for Leo to park side by side with his truck. Daniel must have been ready, too, because Leo and he moved as if they'd rehearsed it. Within seconds, both Izzie and Cameron were in the back seat of the cruiser with Olivia.

She immediately took her son from his seat and into her arms.

Cameron was smiling and babbled some happy sounds, so he obviously wasn't aware of what was going on. Good. She wanted to shelter him as much as she could. For now, Olivia showered him with kisses and lifted him when Leo looked back at the boy. Cameron had a big smile for him, too, and reached out for his dad to take him, but Leo just gave him a kiss and ruffled his hair.

"He needs to go back in his seat," Leo instructed. "I don't want to stay here in case the place explodes."

Izzie didn't gasp, but Olivia saw the nanny's bottom lip trembling. "Daniel told you what's going on?" Olivia asked and got a nod. "We'll be okay," Olivia tried to reassure her.

While Olivia strapped Cameron back in, Daniel hurried over to the truck, no doubt to go to Barrett. Leo also made a call and, within just a couple of minutes, two of his hands drove up in a dark blue truck.

"They'll follow us back to the sheriff's office," Leo advised, driving away the moment she and Izzie had on their seat belts. "We can't go out the main road because of Randall's truck, and we can't use the west trail since Daniel and the ambulance will have that way blocked. We'll have to go through the trail that leads off the back pasture."

Olivia was grateful for the backup and hoped it would be enough. She didn't want the reassurance she'd just given Izzie to be lip service.

Leo's gaze met hers in the mirror for a split second. Maybe he was trying to dole out some encouragement, too, but Olivia also took it as a signal to keep watch. After all, there could also be another sniper on this trail.

And that caused her to consider something.

Even if the person behind these attacks hadn't actually paid Milton, he or she would have likely had to pay the wounded man on the trail. Perhaps had to pay others, as well. She doubted payments like that would be cheap.

That brought her back to Randall and her father.

They had the kind of money to order a hit and to create this kind of chaos. Rena did not. Olivia didn't know if Bernice did, either, but if money was a factor here, it'd rule out Rena. Then again, money could be borrowed or stolen, and services could be bartered or coerced. In other words, any one of their suspects could have pulled this off.

Olivia pushed all of that aside and continued to keep watch. Every few seconds, she also checked on Cameron. It was still too early for his morning nap, but his eyelids were getting droopy. so it was possible he'd sleep through the rest of this horrible ordeal.

It took nearly twenty minutes for Leo to thread his way through the rough trail and back to the road, and he did so by using his hands-free set on the cruiser to make some calls. One was to the dispatcher to report that Randall had been injured and had run from the scene. He asked that an APB be put out on the man.

When they passed by what was left of Randall's truck, she spotted the fire department and the bomb squad. Good. Once they finished with the burned-out vehicle, then they could check Leo's place.

"Daniel said your house burned," she heard Izzie say. "I'm so sorry."

Olivia wasn't surprised she'd actually forgotten about that. It was a loss, not the house itself, but the things she had in it. Her photos, Cameron's favorite toys, and the

cedar chest filled with things that had once belonged
to her mother—jewelry, photos and even her journals.
She was certain that later she'd feel the sting of losing
those things, but it was hard to feel loss when her son's
safety was her priority. Thankfully, it was Leo's priority, as well.

"Thank you," Olivia murmured to Izzie just as Leo
pulled to a stop in front of the sheriff's office.

Deputy Cassidy was in the doorway, clearly waiting
for them, which meant Barrett had likely alerted her.
"This way," she said once Olivia had Cameron out of
the cruiser. She kept him in his car seat since he was
not only sound asleep now but because the seat would
also better protect him if someone fired shots at them.

But no shots came.

Olivia said a quick prayer of thanks for that and was
also relieved that neither Rena nor Bernice was in the
large front office space. It was empty except for another deputy, a lanky built man, who was now at the
dispatch desk.

"Where are Milton, Rena and Bernice?" Leo asked,
glancing around but aiming his question at Deputy Cassidy.

"Milton's back in his cell. The psychiatrist finished
with him and left about twenty minutes ago. Barrett
told Rena and Bernice to leave after the trouble at your
place. He said he'd reschedule their interviews."

Olivia wasn't sure when Barrett would find time
to squeeze that in since he now had a new facet of the
investigation. One that involved a firebomb that'd destroyed Randall's truck. That reminder that her wondering where the man was.

Even though it was maybe too early for the APB to

have gone into effect, Olivia turned to the deputy. "Any sign of Randall?"

Deputy Cassidy shook her head. "Nothing yet. And call me Cybil. I've tried to call Randall twice, but it goes straight to voice mail. Could be he's just trying to avoid being brought in for questioning."

True, but the man had been hurt. "I'm guessing you checked the hospital?"

Cybil nodded. "The one here and the one in Culver Crossing. He hasn't gone to either." She led them through the hall and toward the back of the building. "Barrett asked me to fix up the breakroom as best I could."

Even though she'd visited Leo several times at work when they'd still been together, Olivia had never been to this part of the sheriff's office, and it wasn't as bad as she'd expected. It was actually two spacious rooms, one with bunkbeds, probably for anyone who got stuck pulling long shifts. The main room had a well-worn brown-leather sofa, a TV, some lockers and even a small kitchenette. It smelled like coffee and the cinnamon bagels that were in a plastic bag on the counter.

The place looked safe enough what with the wired-glass window, but it gave Olivia an uneasy feeling to know that they were now under the same roof as Milton.

"I changed the sheets on the beds," the deputy told Leo, and he muttered a thanks. "Wasn't sure how long you'd have to be here, but I thought you'd need a place to sleep," she added, shifting her attention to Olivia. "The sheriff said you might need someone to get baby supplies."

Olivia had no idea and had to look at Izzie for the answer. The nanny had brought the diaper bag, but Olivia didn't know what she'd managed to stuff in there before they'd had to evacuate the house.

"We're okay for now," Izzie replied. "But if we're still here tomorrow, we'll need extra diapers, wipes and some baby food."

"Just give me a list and I'll get whatever you need," the deputy assured her. She pointed to the door on the left side of the sofa. "That's a small bathroom with a shower. Maybe you'll want to get that blood off you. You, too," she added to Leo.

Olivia glanced down at her top and saw there was indeed blood. She'd probably gotten it when she'd examined the wound on Leo's arm. There was blood on his shirt, as well.

"You need an EMT to take a look at that?" Cybil asked him.

"No." He answered fast while taking the infant seat with Cameron from Olivia. "I've got a first-aid kit and a change of clothes in my locker. There's also an extra shirt in there for Olivia."

Olivia nearly asked if someone could go by her place to pick up some of her own clothes, but then she remembered that the only clothing she owned was what she was wearing.

"Why don't I take Cameron into the bunkroom so he can finish his nap?" Izzie suggested when Cybil left. "That'll give you two a chance to change and redress that wound."

Neither Leo nor Olivia objected. If Cameron woke up, she didn't want him to see the bloody clothes. Plus, Olivia needed some time to steady herself. She wasn't sure that was actually possible, not with the adrenaline still pumping through her, but she had to try.

Once Izzie and Cameron were in the bunkroom, the nanny eased the door shut. Leo must have taken that as his cue to get started with their "chores" because he went to his locker and took out a small first-aid kit along with two shirts, one a black tee and the other a pale blue button-up. He tossed the blue one to her and shucked off his bloody shirt.

He also winced.

Leo had probably hoped to cover that up, but Olivia saw it, all right. On a heavy sigh, she went to him. "Let me clean that wound before you put on the T-shirt."

That would make it easier to deal with the gash, but of course, it also meant she'd have her hands on a bare-chested Leo. Considering their earlier kiss and the steamy attraction that was always there between them, that probably wasn't a bright idea, but his injury needed some tending.

"I need to text Barrett first to make sure he's okay," Leo muttered.

She waited for him to do that, waited some more for a response from Barrett, who confirmed all was well and that the signs were that the gunman had been working alone. Barrett added that he'd call as soon as he had more info.

With that weight off Leo's mind, Olivia had him sit on the sofa as she looked through the kit to find some fresh bandages, antiseptic cream and gauze pads. She wet a couple of the pads in the sink in the bathroom so she could wash away some of the blood. The wound had, indeed, reopened, and it was red. It had to be hurting him.

"You really should see an EMT again," she said, frowning when she saw him grimace in pain.

"It'll be fine. It's not that deep of a cut."

It really wasn't, and it would almost certainly heal on its own if he kept it clean and didn't flex the muscles beneath it. She could make sure the first happened but not the second. If they came under attack again, she knew that Leo would definitely do some *flexing* to protect Cameron and her.

She sank next to him on the sofa to apply the fresh bandage and felt him shudder when the back of her hand brushed against his chest. Olivia lifted her gaze to apologize for hurting him, but then she realized Leo's wince wasn't from pain.

No.

There was some heat in his eyes. Heat spurred by her touch. Maybe other things were playing into this, too. After all, they'd just survived nearly being killed, which had almost certainly left them as raw as the cut on his arm.

"You keep saving me," she said, her voice thick.

She hadn't intended for it to sound like a whispery come-on, but it did. No doubt because she had been affected by that touch, as well. And just by being this close to Leo. His scent was like foreplay to her. Ditto for his incredible face. It didn't help when the corner of his equally incredible mouth lifted into a near smile.

"At least this gets your mind off the fire and the attack," he drawled. That voice was like foreplay, as well.

"It gets your mind off things, too," she countered, figuring that would jar him back into remembering that the last thing they should be doing was looking at each other like this.

Olivia had no trouble remembering that. Still, she stayed put and didn't take her eyes off him. She didn't move, either, when he leaned in and brushed his mouth over hers. It seemed to be some kind of test to see how she'd react. Or maybe how *he* would react. Apparently, not good, because he squeezed his eyes shut a moment and ground out some profanity.

That's why she was shocked when his mouth came back to hers.

This time, it wasn't just a touch. It was a scalding kiss that sent a wave of fiery need straight to the center of her body. That was the problem with kissing a former lover, one she was still seriously attracted to—the heat instantly skyrocketed and made her want to do a whole lot more than just kiss him.

Leo accommodated her on the *more*. He hooked his uninjured arm around her and pulled her to him. Olivia landed against his bare chest. That definitely didn't help cool things down any.

Her pulse kicked up a notch, and she couldn't stop herself from sliding deeper into the kiss. Or stop herself from touching him. She slid her hands around his back and gave herself the thrill of feeling all those taut, toned muscles respond to her touch. Then again, Leo had always responded to her.

And was responding now.

The sound he made was one of pure need. An ache so strong that it seemed to come off him in thick, hot waves and wash over her. She fought to get closer to him, adjusting her position so that her breasts moved over his chest. Another thrill. More fuel for this blistering heat that'd make her crazy if it didn't stop.

Leo must have remembered where they were and that anyone could come walking in at any second because he broke the kiss. He didn't move back, though.

He sat there, his breath gusting, his forehead pressed against hers.

The air was so still, it felt as if everything was on hold, waiting. Olivia was certainly waiting for his reaction, to see if he would be disgusted with himself. However, it wasn't disgust on his face when he finally pulled back and locked eyes with her. The heat and need were still there, still eating away at him as it did her.

"Well, at least you have a foolproof way of making me forget about the fires and danger for a couple of seconds," she murmured.

He smiled. And, mercy, it was good to see it. It'd been so long since she'd seen Leo happy. Even though she doubted he was actually happy right now. He'd just grabbed on to something to anchor himself and create a distraction. She understood that because the kiss had shaken her to the core.

"When I kiss you like that," he said, his voice husky, "I have a hard time remembering that we're not together. And an equally hard time remembering why we broke up."

She had the same problem. But she didn't get a chance to tell him that because his phone rang and she saw Barrett's name on the screen. That got Leo moving away from her. He hit the button to put the call on speaker and set down his phone long enough to slip on the black T-shirt.

"Everything okay there?" Barrett asked.

"Yeah," Leo answered and then quickly followed with a question of his own. "Did they find a firebomb at my house?"

"No. Not yet anyway. That's the good news. The bad news is that the shooter died before the EMTs arrived.

He never regained consciousness, so I couldn't question him. His wallet was in his pocket, though, so I got his driver's license. His name was Lowell Jensen."

Leo's forehead bunched. "That sounds familiar."

It rang a bell for Olivia, too, but it took her a moment to figure out where she'd heard it. Or rather, had seen it. "I'm pretty sure a Lowell Jansen was in the PI report that Bernice gave us. Lowell was one of Rena's ex-lovers and he has—*had*—" she amended, "a police record."

"That report is in your office," Leo interjected. "I'll go get it."

"That can wait a couple of minutes. What I'll need you to do is arrange to have Rena brought back in. I'd let her go when all hell broke loose out at your place, but I want to ask her about this."

"I'll also look for any money trail," Leo noted. "But if he's her ex, then maybe she didn't pay him with money. It could be she used sex, or maybe he was just doing a favor for her."

The anger rolled over Olivia again and she hoped that this time when they questioned Rena, the woman broke down and confessed. If she were guilty, that was. Since someone had used her own phone to set her up, Olivia knew that things weren't often as they seemed on the surface.

"There's more," Barrett went on. "We found Lowell's Jeep just off the trail, and there were some things in it that might have been taken from Olivia's house. It was a bag with her mother's journals."

Olivia drew in a sharp breath. "Yes, they were at my house." But she had to mentally shake her head. "Why'd he take those?"

"I was hoping you'd have the answer to that. And,

no, I'm not accusing you of anything," Barrett quickly added. "I just wondered if you had any ideas as to why someone would want to steal them and only them. There was nothing else of yours in the Jeep."

Olivia forced away the fog from the spent adrenaline and the kiss, and tried to make sense of it. She couldn't. "The journals, all thirteen of them, were right next to some of my mother's jewelry. Some of the pieces were worth a lot of money and looked it, too. By that I mean anyone who saw them would know they were valuable."

Barrett didn't ask her why such pieces weren't in a safe or a safe-deposit box, and Olivia was thankful for it. She didn't want to explain that she'd needed to keep close what few things she had of her mother's. It was a way of remembering her and not just the car wreck that'd claimed her life. However, there was something about the journals she thought he should know.

"I made digital copies of the journals," she told him. "Just in case something happened and they were damaged or destroyed. I knew that wouldn't be the same thing as having the originals in her own handwriting, but it was a way to preserve her memories."

Especially since those journals were something Simone had devoted plenty of time to keeping up. Her mother hadn't written in them daily, not even weekly, but there were at least a couple of entries every month.

"Any chance there's something in the journals that could connect to what's going on now with the attacks?" Barrett prompted.

She opened her mouth to say an automatic no but then rethought that. "I don't think so. I mean… I've read every entry multiple times." Some, like the ones her mother had written days following Olivia's birth, she'd read hundreds of times. "They have great sentimental value to me, of course, but my mother didn't say anything in them that would hint of a crime or such."

At least, she didn't think Simone had, but once she got her hands on them again, Olivia wouldn't mind taking another look. It'd been years since she'd actually looked through any of the entries.

"All right," Barrett said a moment later. "I'll have to take the journals into custody as evidence for a while, but I'll see that you get them back."

She muttered a heartfelt thanks just as an incoming call flashed on Leo's screen. It was from her father.

Olivia could see the hesitation pass through Leo's eyes. He was likely considering if he should just let the call go to voice mail. However, he must have decided against that.

"Samuel's calling," Leo explained to his brother. "Let me see what he wants and I'll get back to you."

Leo switched over to her father, but he took a deep breath before he said anything. "I'm busy," Leo snapped. "Make it quick."

"Where are Cameron and Olivia?" Samuel fired back.

"They're safe," Leo assured him while also dodging the question. "And if that's why you called, this conversation is over—"

"It's not the only reason I called." Her father was talking quickly, his words running together, probably because he thought Leo might just hang up on him. "I'm at Olivia's house now, and it's been burned to the ground. I heard the firemen talking, and they said it was arson. What they wouldn't tell me was if Olivia and Cameron were inside when the place caught fire."

Leo sighed. "They weren't in the house. They're okay."

"I need to see them," he insisted. "I need to see you."

"Me?" Leo snarled. "Why?"

"I take it you haven't gotten a call about it yet?"

Her father's question had Leo glancing at her to see if she knew what he was talking about. She didn't.

"Explain that," Leo ordered. "And just know, if this is some kind of scheme so you can try to see Olivia and Cameron, then I'll arrest you for impeding an investigation."

"It's not a scheme," her father insisted. He muttered a curse. "Someone just called me from an unknown number. I didn't recognize the voice, but the person said I was to go to Olivia's house and look for…something."

"Something?" Leo questioned.

"A body," Samuel said after a long pause. "The caller said that someone had been murdered."

Chapter 10

"A body," Olivia murmured.

Even though her voice was barely audible, Leo could hear the fresh worry. And the fear.

Hell. Would this never end?

Leo was about to tell Samuel—and maybe reassure Olivia in the process—that the anonymous call to report a murder could be bogus. A foolish prank by someone who'd heard the news reports of the attack and just wanted to stir up trouble. But his phone dinged with another incoming call and his gut tightened when he saw the name on the screen.

Sheriff Jace Castillo.

Without saying anything else to Samuel, Jace hung up on him and switched over to Jace. He also slid his arm around Olivia. Coming on the heels of that kiss, touching her probably wasn't a good thing, but he hated the look this had put back in her eyes. She was having too much dumped on her too fast, and he didn't want her caving into the fear.

"Let me guess," Leo greeted when Jace was on the line. "You got a report about a body being out at Olivia's?"

"I did," Jace verified. "I'm on my way there now. Do you have ESP or did you get a call, too?"

"Not me, but Samuel did. Any chance the caller told you specifically where to look for this body?" Leo prompted.

"No. I guess he or she didn't want to make it too easy for me. And I didn't have any luck tracing the call, either. The person was using a burner cell."

That didn't surprise Leo. But the first part of what Jace had said did catch his attention. *"He or she?"*

Jace made a sound of agreement. "The caller's voice was muffled. Not like through a scrambler. It was much more low-tech than that. Probably a cloth or hand held over the mouthpiece."

"Samuel didn't say anything about that, but if he's still at Olivia's place when you get there, you'll want to ask him about it."

"Oh, believe me, I will. If I miss him, I'll bring him in for questioning. And won't that be fun?" Jace added in a grumble.

Leo nearly smiled. Nearly. Jace and he didn't have much in common, but apparently they both had an extreme dislike for Olivia's father.

There was a sound from the bunkroom—one that Leo quickly recognized. Cameron was fussing about something. Olivia untangled herself from his arms and hurried in that direction. Leo looked in, as well, but

Cameron was just having a finicky spell after waking from his short nap.

"Any chance this caller mentioned to Samuel the identity of this DB I'm supposed to be looking for?" Jace asked.

"He didn't say, but it could be someone connected to the arsonist." Since Leo didn't want Cameron to hear any part of this, he stepped back into the breakroom. "Or maybe he was the arsonist." This could all be tied together with the other attacks. "You've heard about the dead gunman near my place?"

"I did," Jace confirmed. "Also heard that someone rigged it so that your house would go up in flames, too."

"Nothing so far," Leo assured him, and hoped it stayed that way. Not just because the ranch was his and Cameron's home but also because it'd been in his family for several generations. Still, the house was something he could rebuild if it came down to it. The important thing was to keep Cameron safe.

And Olivia.

Somehow, she had become as important as Cameron in that "keep safe" equation. It was because of the kisses and the damn heat that just wouldn't go away. But it was more than that, too. It wasn't just his body that was revving up for her again. No. The rest of him had gotten in on it, as well, and he knew without a doubt that he was falling hard for her again.

That meant Olivia would have a second chance to crush his heart.

It was really bad timing for that thought to pop into his head, so he forced it aside. Not just for the moment, either, but he told his body to knock it off, to stop thinking about anything but the investigation that would hopefully lead to them all being safe. Because right now, the danger wasn't just limited to Olivia, Cameron and him. Anyone caught in the crosshairs of these attacks could be hurt or worse.

"I'll let you know if I find anything at Olivia's," he heard Jace say, and that helped snap Leo the rest of the way back.

Leo thanked him, ended the call and just stared at his phone for several more seconds. His "knock it off" lecture to himself had apparently paid up because he started mentally ticking off things he should be doing. And none of those things involved kissing Olivia or thinking about kissing her.

"Are you okay?" Olivia asked, touching his arm to get his attention. He'd been so lost in thought that he hadn't heard her come back into the room.

Leo nodded and put his phone away. "How's Cameron?"

"Cranky. Izzie's taking out the toys from the diaper bag. That should distract him."

Maybe, but Leo couldn't imagine there were a lot of things for the boy to play with in that bag. If he couldn't take Cameron home to his place soon, then he'd need to have some brought here.

"I'm going to Barrett's office to get the envelope Bernice gave us, a laptop and any other files that I think will help me start sorting out some details of this case," Leo explained, tipping his head to the table where many of the deputies often ate lunch. "I can work there."

She glanced in at Cameron, who was indeed occupied, for the moment anyway, with a book. "I'll go with you and help you bring back the stuff." She relayed that to Izzie and followed Leo down the hall to Barrett's office.

Cybil was back at the dispatch desk, and she looked up when they came in. "Everything okay?" It was obvious she was on full alert because she shifted as if she might have to spring to action.

Leo shook his head. "Just need some things." He went into the office, handed the envelope and some other files to Olivia, and grabbed two laptops. One he took from Barrett's desk and the other from his own. "You can read through some reports," he said to Olivia. "It wouldn't hurt to have a fresh eye on them. Plus, there'll be reports coming in from Culver Crossing."

Reports on the fire that had destroyed her house. Maybe even one on the "body" that Jace was looking for. She welcomed the task because it would make her feel as if she were actually doing something to help. However, they hadn't even started back to the breakroom when the front door opened and Barrett walked in.

The brothers' gazes met and held for a few seconds, and she thought that maybe they were assessing to make sure each was okay. Barrett frowned when he saw the fresh bandage on Leo's arm.

"Olivia couldn't talk you into having an EMT check that out?" Barrett asked.

"No," she answered on a sigh just as Leo said, "It's fine."

Leo tipped his head to the evidence bags in Barrett's hand. "Is that what you got from the dead gunman?"

Barrett nodded, but he sighed, too, probably because he knew that Leo had just shut him down on the possibility of getting medical treatment. "I have his phone. A burner," Barrett added, "so I don't expect we'll get much." He shifted to show the other bag, a much larger one with a form attached to it. Since it was clear plastic, Olivia could see what was inside.

Her mother's journals.

No mistaking those distinct Tiffany-blue covers or the size. Not large notebook journals but rather more the dimensions of slim diaries. Each of the thirteen had only fifty pages, and her mother had filled those pages front and back.

She automatically moved to take them but then remembered they were now evidence. Evidence that might somehow help them unravel this case. Well, it would if they got lucky and figured out why a now-dead arsonist/would-be killer would have taken them in the first place. Olivia was giving that more thought when she saw someone approaching the sheriff's office. And she groaned.

"My dad's here," she warned Leo and Barrett. Obviously, he'd driven straight over from her place after he'd called Leo.

Both Leo and Barrett adjusted their positions, stepping so that they were like a shield in front of her. Leo took it one step further. He put the laptops on the nearest desk to free up his hands. One of those hands he slid over the weapon in his holster.

Olivia wanted to think that wasn't necessary, that her father wouldn't harm her, but with the memories of the latest attack still right at the front of her mind, she didn't have a lot of trust for him right now.

"I figured you'd be here," Samuel said and, as usual, he threw a glare at Leo. One at Barrett, too.

Maybe Leo was also feeling distrustful of her father because he slipped his free arm around her, easing her behind him. It wasn't a gesture that her father missed. She hadn't thought it possible for him to narrow his eyes even more, but that did it.

"Olivia, please tell me you're not thinking about getting back together with him," her father snarled, adding some extra venom when he said the word *him*.

She thought of the kisses. The heat. The intimacy that was now between them because they were working to solve this case and to keep Cameron safe.

But it was more than just the investigation.

Her feelings for Leo were as strong as ever, and she wasn't sure there was a reason to continue putting up barriers to keep them apart. Her father had created those barriers by threatening to ruin Leo, and maybe he would follow through with those threats. Or perhaps he'd try to do worse if he was the one behind the attacks. But she still couldn't see that as a reason to shut Leo out. It was past time that she dealt with her father head-on.

"It's none of your business whether I'm with Leo or not," she said. Olivia made sure it sounded like the warning it was. "In fact, nothing I do is any concern of yours."

He flinched, as if she'd actually slapped him. Her father stayed quiet a moment, but she could see the anger simmering. Anger that he might have intended to aim at Leo. However, his attention landed on Barrett. Specifically, on the large evidence bag that Barrett was still holding. He flinched again, but this seemed different than his reaction to what she'd said.

"Those are your mother's diaries," Samuel murmured, glancing at her before turning back to Barrett. "What are you doing with those?" he demanded.

"They're potential evidence," Barrett said. His voice

was calm, but after one glance, Olivia could see that he was studying her father. Leo was, too. "The man who tried to kill Olivia, Leo and me apparently stole them from Olivia's house. Would you happen to know anything about that?"

Her father's shoulders went back, and it seemed to her that he changed his mind as to what he'd been about to say. "You kept them?" he demanded from her.

Of all the questions she'd thought he might ask, that wasn't one of them. She nodded. "After she died, I went into her office and got them. She used to let me read some of the entries she'd made when she was pregnant with me, so I knew where she kept them."

They'd been in a small wooden storage box on her bookshelf. It had looked like part of the rest of the decor in her office except this particular box had a false bottom. Her mom had called it her private place to keep her secrets. Others had known about the journals, of course, since they'd seen her mom writing in them from time to time. Obviously, her father had known for him to have instantly recognized them.

"Why would someone steal them?" Samuel asked, and his confusion seemed genuine.

Seemed.

"You shouldn't have kept them," he continued without waiting for an answer. "All they can do is stir up old, bad memories."

Well, that seemed to be what they were doing for him. And that brought Olivia right back to the doubts and suspicions she'd been having about him.

"Did you drug my mother the night of her car accident?" Olivia came out and asked. "Are you the reason she's dead?"

Clearly, she'd shocked Barrett because he glanced at her and then, obviously wanting to hear the answer, turned his cop's stare on Samuel. But her father was well beyond being stunned. His jaw went slack, and she didn't think it was her imagination that he lost some color. Or stopped breathing. Her breath had even seemed to have stalled in her chest.

"You think I killed Simone?" he finally managed to say. There was no anger in his voice. Hurt maybe. But oh, the anger came. Olivia saw it flare in his eyes. "You think I risked your life by drugging her?"

"I don't believe you thought I'd be in the car," she countered and then repeated a variation of her question. "Did you drug Mom because you wanted to get her out of your life?"

The anger in his eyes went up a huge notch. "No," he answered despite his jaw being set as hard as stone. "I've never killed anyone, and I never gave your mother any drugs."

"Her tox screen proved she had drugs in her blood," Leo quickly pointed out.

Samuel shifted that stony look to Leo. "Well, she didn't get them from me. Is this some kind of witch hunt?" Samuel volleyed glances at all of them before he settled on staring at her.

Leo shook his head. "No. We're just after the truth, and that's the reason I'm planning to ask the Texas Rangers to reopen the investigation into Simone's death. Who knows—maybe there's something in those journals that'll help them find out what really happened that night."

The anger was a raging storm inside her father now, practically coming off him in thick, hot waves. This was a man who could kill, she realized. This was a man who could have drugged his wife and gotten away with murder.

"If there's anything in Simone's journals that points to me, then she had it wrong," Samuel decreed.

"She wanted a divorce," Olivia said. She'd heard enough of their argument that night to know that.

Her father certainly didn't jump to deny it. In fact, he lifted his shoulder in what he probably thought was a casual dismissal, but his muscles were too tense to dismiss anything.

"There's no reason to hash all of this out now," Samuel concluded.

Leo disagreed. "Yeah, there is. There's no statute of limitations on murder, and if you drugged your wife, then it's murder."

Samuel froze. For a moment anyway. And he turned for the door. "If you have anything else to say to me, go through my lawyer."

"You're not leaving," Barrett warned him, stopping her father in his tracks. He glanced at Cybil. "Deputy Cassidy, why don't you wait here with Mr. Nash until his lawyer arrives? Then I'll start an interview."

Since Barrett had planned to interrogate him anyway, it didn't surprise Olivia that he'd want to go ahead and do that. But it clearly didn't please her father. Neither did the rest of what Barrett said.

"Leo, go ahead and contact the Texas Rangers about reopening the investigation into Simone's death. I'd like for them to get started on that ASAP in case it connects to what's going on now."

Her father stayed quiet for several moments, but he conveyed a lot with his glare, which had intensified.

"You'll be sorry you ever started this," he said like a warning. A warning that he aimed at Olivia.

She didn't respond. Didn't have to. Leo saw to that. He picked up the laptops and motioned for her to follow him. She did. Not only because she wanted to put some distance between her father and herself but also because they were heading for the breakroom where she could check on Cameron. Olivia didn't even cast a glance at her dad, though she could practically feel him staring holes in her back.

"You okay?" Leo asked her.

No, she wasn't. She was shaken up by what'd just happened, but she wasn't going to dump that on him, too. He was already dealing with enough. Besides, he knew how hard that had been for her to face down a man who'd made an art form of bullying her.

And maybe an art form of murder, as well.

After all, it'd been years since her mother had died, and if he'd been responsible, then he'd been a free man all this time. Unpunished. But that could change. If that happened, if he did end up in jail for it, then she was just going to have to cope with the fact that she hadn't tried sooner to get justice for her mother.

Leo and she had just made it to the breakroom door when his phone rang again. He shifted the laptops in his arms so he could take it from his pocket. He hit the answer button and put the call on speaker.

"Well, I wish it'd been a hoax," Jace started the moment he was on the line, "but it wasn't. I found the body just up the road from Olivia's house. And yeah, the guy is definitely dead."

Chapter 11

Leo had hoped that Jace was calling to tell them that all was well, but that hope vanished when he heard Jace's words.

A dead body.

Two in one day, and Leo figured it wasn't a coincidence that Jace had found it so close to Olivia's house. No. This was connected to the attacks and the fires. Maybe even connected to her mother's death. Hell. It could be all one tangled mess with her father at the center.

"Who's dead?" Leo asked Jace.

"Not sure yet. That's because he's been shot in the face, and there's not much left of it."

Leo saw Olivia flinch, and he figured that had turned her stomach. It wasn't an easy image to have in your head.

"I've got my CSIs on the way out here," Jace went on, "and once they arrive and the scene is secured, I'll have a look around. There's no vehicle, no sign of a struggle in the immediate area. It looks like a body dump to me."

A body dump that was probably meant to be some kind of message to Olivia. A warning maybe or perhaps just a tool to torment her. But who was he and why had he been used as that warning/torment? Had he been a hired gun who'd screwed up enough that it'd cost him his life? If so, then Leo sure as hell wouldn't feel any sympathy for him. His only regret was that he wasn't alive so they could possibly get answers from him.

"I'll let you know when I've got an ID on the body," Jace said and ended the call.

Leo took a moment to gather his thoughts, looked at Olivia and figured she was going to need more than moment. He carried the laptops into the breakroom and put them on the table. Did the same to the files she was carrying. Then he turned to her.

Yeah, she needed some time.

She certainly wouldn't want to go check on Cameron while her nerves were this frayed. Of course, there wasn't much he could do to help with that, but Leo still pulled her to him. Olivia came into his arms as if she belonged there. Leo didn't miss that, and apparently neither did she because the sound she made was part relief, part moan.

"I'm sorry," he told her because he didn't know what else to say.

It'd been a helluva morning what with being shot at, her house burned down, confronting her father and now this. Her life as she'd known it had vanished in a matter of a few hours. Added to that, they were about to take a step that could end up with Samuel being charged with murdering her mother. That would also mean he'd come darn close to getting Olivia killed, too.

"I'm trying to make sense of it," she said, her voice barely a whisper.

He was doing the same thing, but it wasn't adding up the way Leo wanted. He preferred it when all the pieces fit, and that wasn't happening.

Unless…

If Samuel had truly felt he was losing Olivia, he could have maybe set up her to take the fall for hiring Milton to kill Leo. Then Samuel could have petitioned for custody of Cameron, which Leo and Olivia had already considered. Considered, too, that everything after that could have been part of a plan that had just gotten away from him. Because, as much of a bullying snake as Samuel could be, Leo just couldn't see him endangering Cameron. It could be that this latest DB was a way of wrapping up a scheme that Samuel was trying to ditch.

"The danger could be over," Leo said, which had Olivia easing her head back to meet his eyes.

He saw her latch onto that hope, and it was a hope that he wished he could give her. Give *them*, he mentally corrected. But it was just a theory and they'd have to wait to see how it played out.

"Milton's in custody," he explained. "The second gunman's dead, and since he had your mother's journals, it points to him being the one who set fire to your house. Maybe to Randall's truck, too."

Yet that was one of the puzzle pieces that didn't fit. Why Randall? Unless the person behind the attacks wanted to make Randall riled enough to come after Leo and kill him. Considering that possibility, Leo made a mental note to check on the man since Randall was scheduled to come in for an interview.

"You're thinking our attacker might just give up?" she asked.

"Might," he said emphatically. "I still want us to take precautions, and I want this investigation to play out." He started to launch into some questions, but that could wait a couple more minutes. "Let's check on Cameron. If he's settled, then we can do some work."

She nodded but didn't move away. Leo didn't loosen his grip, either. They just stood there, both wearing their emotions on their sleeves. Not just the emotions of the dangers and threats but also the personal stuff.

He cursed. Groaned. "I don't know what the hell I'm going to do with you," he grumbled.

The corner of her mouth lifted into a half smile. "I feel the same way about you. We've been on opposites sides for so long that this feels wrong." She tipped her head into his arm that was around her. "And it feels right, too."

Leo totally got them. They couldn't just go back and erase the nasty breakup or the way she'd shut him out of her life. But apparently the breakup and fallout afterward hadn't soured him on the notion that—yeah, it did feel right.

"Check on Cameron," he reminded her. Reminded himself, as well. And even then it still took several seconds for them to peel themselves away from each other and head to the bunkroom.

Izzie had put a quilt on the floor where both Cameron and she were sitting, his toys scattered around him. He was eating a snack, but he didn't seem especially happy about it.

"He's still so tired that I'm going to try to get him to finish out his nap after he eats," Izzie explained.

"You need me to help?" Olivia asked.

Izzie shook her head. "I can manage." She paused. "How's everything going?"

Leo didn't want to fill her in on the dead bodies with Cameron around so he settled for saying, "There have been some new developments in the case. As soon as the bomb squad's done at my house, though, we should be able to go back."

The nanny seemed to understand that "going back" might not happen for a while. "All right. Then, let me get this boy to sleep."

Olivia and Leo gave Cameron a quick kiss and left them to go back to the breakroom. The first thing Leo did was point to the fridge. "There'll be Cokes, water and maybe even some snacks in there. Help yourself."

Leo settled for a cup of coffee. While he was pouring it, he called a friend, Texas Ranger Griff Morris. The call went to voice mail so Leo left him a message, explaining that some new concerns and questions had resurfaced in the fatal car accident of Simone Nash and that he wanted Griff to use some leverage to have the case reopened. Leo had no doubts that Griff would make it happen.

When he turned back around, he saw that Olivia was staring at him. "A problem?" he asked.

She quickly shook her head. "I, uh, it's hard to explain." She paused and eased into the chair as if her legs had given way. "It's just…if my father is guilty, then it'll be hard. In some way, it'll be like losing her all over again."

He understood that and hated this was something

Olivia would have to go through. "Do you still have nightmares about the accident?" Because he recalled her having a bad one when they'd been lovers and she'd stay the night at his place.

"Sometimes." She shook her head again, but this time he thought she was trying to push aside the images. Ones that didn't wait until nightmares to surface. "That's why the reopened investigation will be hard. The Rangers will have to question me, and I'll have to go through it in detail."

Leo frowned. "You'd rather keep this as is?"

"No," Olivia quickly answered. "No," she repeated on a heavy sigh. "If my father killed her, then he needs to answer for that. And my reliving it will be just a price I have to pay for making sure he doesn't get away with it."

Reliving it wouldn't be easy, and Leo wasn't sure he could help her with that. He'd try, though. Especially since it was his attack that had brought all of this back to the surface.

He slid his hand over hers and cursed himself because he was going to have to bring even more to the surface. "I know Barrett asked you if there was anything in the journals that connect to the attacks…" he reminded her. "You said no, but is there a chance there's really something in your mother's journals to incriminate your father?"

Olivia drew in a long breath and then released it before she spoke. "Nothing that I can think of. I've read every entry multiple times," she added.

"What about your father?" Leo asked. "Has he read them?"

"I'm not positive, but I don't think he did. My mother

didn't keep them in plain sight, and I'd never heard my father mention them before today."

Leo gave that some thought. "She didn't keep them in plain sight, but Bernice could have snooped around, found them and showed them to your father. Any reason she'd do something like that?"

"Oh, Bernice would do it. She's always been fiercely loyal to my dad. I knew that even when I was ten years old. So, yes, Bernice could have found them and showed them to him if she thought my dad would *appreciate* her doing it."

"'Appreciate'?" Leo repeated. "Nothing sexual between them, though?"

"No. I'm sure of that. There's a different vibe when he's with Bernice than there is when he brings his other women around. Like with Rena, for instance."

Leo paused again. "Could Rena have known about the journals? How soon did she start seeing your dad after your mom's death."

Her mouth tightened. "Rena's been around a long time, and yes, maybe he was with her while my mom was still alive. Rena and he used to do charity fundraiser stuff together. As for the journals, maybe Rena would know, but if she did, she wouldn't have learned about it from my mother."

"Your mom didn't like Rena?" he asked, obviously considering that.

"I don't think so. I remember Rena's name coming up in a couple of their arguments."

Interesting. So, maybe Rena could have egged Samuel on to kill his wife. Then again, Rena could have done it.

"Do you remember if Rena was around the estate about the time of your mother's car accident?" he asked.

"No." She stopped, her eyes widening. "Oh, I see. You believe Rena could have given my mom those drugs?"

"Do you believe it?" he countered.

She took another of those deep breaths, but this one had a weariness to it. And Leo knew why. Her mother's case hadn't even been officially reopened, and here Olivia was having to pull all these memories back to the surface. To the surface where they could take little bites out of her all over again.

"I don't know if Rena could have done it," she finally answered. "Sometimes, I think she's as obsessed with my father as Bernice, just in a different kind of way."

Yeah, Leo was coming to the same conclusion. Both women had their own way of being toxic. Then again, Samuel was a toxic kind of guy himself, so he deserved them both.

He hated to keep digging at Olivia, but Leo couldn't get past the look on Samuel's face when he'd seen the journals in the evidence bag. "Your father didn't know you'd kept the journals. I'm guessing that means you didn't show them to him over the years?"

"No," she readily answered. "My mom always said they were secrets that she shared only with me. So, a couple of weeks after her death, after I got out of the hospital, I went into her office and got them because I heard Bernice say they were going to clean out the room. I didn't want them getting tossed. Or read," she added. "I wanted to keep her secrets."

"So you hid them," Leo concluded, and he waited for

her to confirm that with a nod. "But your father did recognize them, so he must have seen them at one point?"

Again, she gave him a confirming nod. "I can't say, though, when that happened. My mother wrote in them for years, so there would have been countless opportunities for him to see them."

Definitely. And countless opportunities for Samuel to object to what his wife had put in those entries. "Your mother wrote about the arguments and such that she had with your dad?"

"She did a couple of times. You can read the entries for yourself," Olivia offered. "When I was in high school, I scanned the pages and put them in an online storage cloud. That way, if anything happened to the journals, I'd still have what my mother had written."

Though Leo figured it'd take more time than he had to go through years of her mom's journal entries, he knew it was something that had to be done. He'd need to read them with an objective eye, a cop's eye, to see if there was anything that Olivia had missed. Of course, that likely meant Olivia would be rereading them, which wouldn't help her tamp down those memories that still gave her nightmares.

"Download them," he instructed and gave her hand a gentle squeeze. He knew it was a lame gesture considering what this would end up costing her. But apparently Olivia didn't consider it so lame because she smiled at him.

Oh man.

A smile wasn't good. Not now anyway. It made him want to taste that smile. Taste the rest of her, too. Thankfully, he didn't have to dig up enough willpower to resist her because his phone rang and he saw a familiar name on the screen. Morgan Strait, the head of the bomb squad unit that'd been at his place.

"Morgan," Leo greeted when he answered the call. "You have good news for me?"

"I do," the man assured him. "We've gone through every inch of your house and the grounds surrounding it, and we haven't found a thing."

Leo felt some of the tightness in his chest ease up a little.

"I still have men working their way through your barns and outbuildings," Morgan went on, "but none of those are close enough to your house to do any damage if there happened to be an incendiary device in any of them. I've instructed your hands to stay away from them just in case."

"That is good news," Leo told him.

"The bad news is that I don't have the manpower to go through every acre of your ranch, so someone could have rigged something on the trails or the pastures. Heck, even in the shrubs or trees. My advice would be to have your hands be on the lookout for anything suspicious."

"Thanks. I will."

"No problem," Morgan said. "We'll be wrapping up here in about an hour if you want to come back."

Leo very much wanted to do that. The sheriff's office was safe, but Cameron, Izzie and Olivia would be much more comfortable at his place than here. Of course, that'd mean not having the hands check the pastures since Leo would want them close to the house.

"What about Randall's truck?" Leo asked. "Have you had a chance to look at it?"

"I did, and there was definitely something used to

trigger the explosion. Not sure what yet. The lab will need to look at it, but they should be able to tell us something. In the meantime, I'm having what's left of the truck towed to a large evidence holding facility in San Antonio. Have the owner contact me if he has any questions about when and if he can get back his property."

"I will." Though so far Leo hadn't had any luck getting in touch with Randall. Still, when the man surfaced, he'd probably want answers, not only about the truck but maybe about everything else, as well.

Leo thanked Morgan again and turned back to relay what he'd just learned to Olivia.

"You can go home," she said, letting him know that she'd gotten the gist of the conversation.

He nodded, would have added more, but he heard a loud voice coming from the front of the building. Leo couldn't make out the exact words, but the tone was definitely one of anger. And that anger was coming from none other than Samuel.

Olivia sighed, got to her feet. "I can see what he's yelling about," she offered.

But Leo had no intention of sending her out. Not when Samuel was at the top of their suspect list. With Olivia right on his heels, he hurried from the breakroom to see if Barrett or Cybil needed any assistance.

"I didn't try to kill anyone," Samuel was shouting. "Not my wife. Not your brother." He'd added his usual venom to the *your brother*, and Leo knew that part was for him.

Rena was there, as well. She was behind Samuel, had hold of both of his arms and was a doing a fairly decent job of keeping him from charging at Barrett and Cybil. That would have been a Texas-sized mistake because not only were Barrett and the deputy armed, Barrett could have taken down the man with a single punch.

Samuel immediately shifted his attention to Leo and Olivia, and Leo hadn't thought it possible, but the man's scowl was even worse than what it had been earlier.

"The sheriff just read me my rights," Samuel roared. He stopped struggling, but Rena kept her arms wrapped tightly around him.

"Because he wouldn't shut up," Barrett explained. "I figured if he kept yakking, he might blurt something out, something I couldn't use against him if I didn't Mirandize him first."

So, apparently Samuel hadn't waited for his attorney, and it was also obvious that he wasn't going to heed his right to remain silent.

"I won't be treated like this," Samuel snarled. "I won't let my daughter taint my name with nonsense allegations that I killed her mother. Those journals mean nothing. Nothing! And they shouldn't have any part in this."

He hadn't said *my daughter* with any affection whatsoever. Just the opposite. Olivia was his enemy now, too. Apparently, so were those journals.

"Calm down, Samuel," Rena insisted, her voice a lot calmer and softer than his. The woman was practically cooing to him. "Your blood pressure's probably through the roof right now. Come with me and let's talk. I can get you some water."

Samuel put up some resistance. At first. But after a couple of seconds where he glared at Olivia, the man allowed Rena to lead him to the other side of the room where there was a water cooler. She did, indeed, get him a drink and then practically sandwiched him against the wall while she continued to talk to him in a murmur.

Cybil waited for the nod from Barrett. When she got it, the deputy went back to the dispatch desk. Barrett stayed next to Olivia and Leo, not exactly in a huddle but close, and all three of them cast wary glances at Samuel.

"Olivia's downloading the pages of her mother's journal." Leo kept his voice low when he spoke to his brother. "After hearing Samuel's latest outburst, I'm even more interested in reading them."

Barrett made a sound of agreement. "Samuel's definitely worried about them."

As if to prove that, Leo saw Samuel's eyes drift into Barrett's office. He was pretty sure the man was looking at the evidence bag of journals on Barrett's desk. Rena followed his gaze and then saw, too, that Barrett, Olivia and Leo were watching them. She caught Samuel's chin, turning him back to face her. Leo couldn't hear what the woman said to him, but Samuel seemed to be listening.

Leo thought about Rena's claim that Samuel and she would get back together. It certainly seemed as if that was exactly what was happening.

Olivia sighed, causing Leo to turn to her. He was pretty sure they were on the same page of thought when it came to Rena and Samuel. The easy intimacy between them had Leo considering if maybe they had worked together to stage the attacks and set up Simone's car accident. But that didn't feel right because, if that's what had indeed happened, then Leo couldn't see Rena keeping that to herself when Samuel and she were on the outs. A woman capable of writing those threatening emails didn't stay silent about much.

"I told Leo that I thought my father was more agitated than usual about my mother because the anniversary of her death is coming up," Olivia explained. She stopped and shook her head. "But maybe it's more than that. Maybe it's guilt."

Neither Barrett nor Leo disputed that, and Leo watched again as Samuel glanced over at the journals.

"He thinks Simone wrote something incriminating," Leo concluded. "He's worried about what we'll find when we read them."

Barrett made a sound of agreement.

"I wish there was something incriminating to find," Olivia said, punctuated with another of those sighs. "I wish there was something in them that would make him come clean about what happened, because I believe there could be more to it than what he's admitted."

Leo thought that, as well. That's why he considered something. It was a long shot. More of a weak bluff. But sometimes all it took was a nudge, and maybe this would be the right one.

"What if you tell your father that there is something?" Leo suggested, still whispering. "What if you lie and say that your mother wrote that someone was trying to kill her?"

Leo figured it would take Olivia a couple of minutes to mull that over. She didn't. She nodded and immediately moved away from Barrett and him. Walking closer to her father, she pointed to the journals.

"You're worried about what's in those," Olivia said, her voice surprisingly strong. "Well, you should be."

It wasn't anger now that flashed in Samuel's eyes but rather concern. Maybe even fear. Rena didn't have as extreme of a reaction, but she definitely quit cooing and soothing.

"What do you mean?" Rena asked. "Did Simone say something...bad?"

"Yes," Olivia said, adding to the lie. "She said some-one was trying to kill her." And with that, she stared directly at her father.

Leo steeled himself for the burst of outrage he figured they were about to get from Samuel. But no outburst. The man just wearily shook his head and squeezed his eyes shut. Then he said a single word that Leo definitely hadn't been expecting.

"Bernice," Samuel muttered, still shaking his head. "Bernice wanted Simone dead."

Chapter 12

When Olivia had decided to go with the impromptu ruse to get her father to say something incriminating, she hadn't actually expected it to work. Nor had she thought that name would come out of his mouth.

"Bernice?" Olivia repeated.

Both Barrett and Leo moved closer, flanking her, while the three of them faced down her father. Their stares were definitely demands for him to explain why he'd just blurted out Bernice's name.

Samuel cursed, pushed the cup of water away that Rena was offering him, and he began to pace. "I shouldn't have said that," he grumbled. "I don't have any proof that Bernice did anything wrong."

He was backpedaling, which wouldn't help them get to the truth.

"But you must suspect her," Olivia quickly pointed out. "Did Bernice give my mother those drugs the night of the car wreck? Did she?" Olivia pressed when her father didn't answer. She finally stepped in front of him, stopping him and facing him down. "Did she?"

Her father looked at the spot just above her shoulder. Definitely avoiding eye contact. "Maybe," he finally said.

"She's certainly capable of that," Rena insisted. "The woman is a control freak. She probably wanted your mother out of the way so she'd have a better shot at getting more of Samuel's attention."

Samuel sniped Rena a scowl. "If Bernice did it, it wasn't because she wanted Simone out of the way," he snapped.

"Then why?" Olivia demanded.

Her father groaned and tried to pace again, but Olivia did another block, pinning him between Rena on one side and Barrett and Leo on the other.

"Bernice thought Simone was no longer thinking clearly," her father said, and it sounded to Olivia as if he were carefully choosing his words. "Bernice believed, wrongfully so, that Simone would leave—disappear," he amended, "and that Simone would take you with her so I'd never be able to see you again. Bernice knew that'd crush me."

Olivia tried to pick through that to see if she could tell if he was lying. She just didn't know. But it didn't surprise her that Bernice would have such a strong opinion of her mother or that her father's household manager would be privy to her parents' marital problems. The truth was Simone had spoken of a divorce, so it wouldn't be much of a stretch for Bernice to believe that Simone would take her daughter with her when she left the estate.

"I want you to go through every detail of what happened that night," Barrett told her father as he took out his phone. "I'll call Bernice and get her back in here. I'll need to hear what she has to say about all this."

Her father cursed again, and Olivia could see that he regretted opening the subject. But it could lead to something. A confession, maybe. Then again, even if Bernice had had something to do with her mother's death, it wouldn't clear up the recent attacks and fires.

Barrett stepped into his office to make the call, and Olivia continued to stare at her father. "Why didn't you say anything about Bernice before now?" she demanded when he didn't continue.

"Because I don't know if my suspicions are right." He dragged his hand over his face. "What I do know is your mother didn't use drugs, period. So, either she dosed herself up that night for the first time, or someone else did it. I didn't do it, so that leaves Bernice."

Maybe, but Olivia shifted her attention to the woman who was now patting her father's arm. "Were you at the estate that night?" Olivia asked her.

Rena's eyes widened and her mouth dropped open. "You're accusing me now?" she shrieked.

"*Asking* you," Leo clarified. "But I'm going to insist that you answer the question."

Rena's indignance meshed with the anger. "No, I wasn't there. If I remember correctly, your father and I had some business a week or so before that, but I wasn't in the house when Simone died."

Both Leo and Olivia looked to her father to confirm what Rena had just said, but he only shrugged. "I don't remember a lot about that night," he admitted. "Simone and I argued, and she stormed out. She said she was going out for a drive. After she left, I had a few drinks. Maybe more than a few," he added in a mumble.

"Was Simone acting as if she'd been drugged while you two were arguing?" Leo pressed.

Her father stayed quiet a moment and his forehead bunched up as if he were trying hard to pull out the memories. Or else that's what he wanted them to think. But it could be an act. All of this could be an act.

"No," her father finally said. "Not drunk or high. She was just pissed off." He paused again. "But she didn't leave right away after she stormed out. I think it was at least a half hour before she left."

"At least a half hour," Olivia agreed.

And here it came. Her own flood of memories. She didn't know how they could manage to stay so fresh, so raw, after all this time. Her father's recollections didn't include the wreck itself. Nor had he heard the sound of her mother's dying breath.

Leo turned to her. "Are you okay?" he whispered.

Olivia nodded and, even though the nod was a lie, she pushed the images and the sounds aside so she could explain her version of the timing of that night.

"I heard the argument between my parents," she said. "I heard my mom say she was going to leave, so I sneaked into the garage and got into her car. I didn't have a watch, but I know she didn't come out in only a few minutes. It was much longer than that. In fact, I'd fallen asleep."

Olivia had no idea how long it'd been before the drugs in her mother's system had taken effect, but that was something she intended to find out.

"Bernice will be here in a couple of minutes," Barrett announced when he returned from making his call. "She's at the diner just up the street."

It surprised Olivia that Bernice hadn't gone back to the estate. Then again, the woman might not have wanted to make that trip since Barrett had made it clear earlier that he wanted to interview her. Now, he'd have something else to question her about.

Her possible involvement in Simone's death.

Olivia didn't have to guess how Bernice would react to that. She would be many steps past being enraged, and the woman was likely to aim that rage at Samuel. After all, he'd been the one to throw Bernice's name into the mix of suspects.

Leo's phone rang, and he showed her the screen after he checked it. Jace. That meant this could be important.

"We can take this in Barrett's office," Leo told her, and Olivia headed there with him.

Obviously, Leo hadn't wanted to have this conversation in front of her father and Rena, and he shut the door before he put the call on speaker.

"I got an ID on the body," Jace said, not starting with a greeting. "And it's someone you know. Randall Arnett."

Leo jerked back his head. No doubt in surprise. Olivia was having a similar reaction and because her legs suddenly felt a little unsteady, she caught onto the edge of Barrett's desk.

"You're sure it's Randall?" Leo asked, taking the question right out of her mouth. After all, the body that Jace had found had been shot in the face, which would make it hard to ID him. Olivia couldn't help but wonder if Randall had set up his own death.

"Yeah," Jace verified. "I did a quick fingerprint check and I got a hit. It's Randall, all right."

So, not a faked death. Probably not suicide, either, because she remembered Jace saying it'd looked like a body dump.

"He can't have been dead for long," Leo said. "His

truck blew up at my place just a couple of hours ago. He was injured, but he was still able to run off."

"Why'd he run?" Jace wanted to know.

"He said something about me trying to kill him. I guess he thought I'd put the firebomb in his truck." Leo stopped. "But I don't know why he drove to my place to tell me that. And I sure as hell don't know how he got from my ranch to Olivia's."

She was trying to figure out the same thing. Her house wasn't far from Leo's, but it would have taken Randall hours and hours had he been traveling on foot. Plus, on foot wouldn't mesh with Jace's body dump theory.

"So someone gave Randall a ride," Olivia concluded.

"Or else he went back to his ranch and got another vehicle," Leo suggested.

True. A trip like that wouldn't have taken nearly as long as getting to her place. "Did you find another vehicle near Randall's body?" she asked.

"No. But I did find a phone, and I'm taking it into evidence. Maybe it belongs to the killer. Or if it's Randall's, he could have called the person who ended up killing him." Jace muttered some profanity that had a frustrated edge to it. "Or the phone could belong to one of the responders to the fire. I'll let you know when I figure it out."

Leo thanked him, ended the call and glanced back toward the squad room where they'd left her father and Rena. He dragged in a deep breath as if steeling himself for another round, but he didn't move. Neither did she because she, too, needed a moment to compose herself.

"Since I believe Randall got away with murdering his girlfriend," she said, "it's hard for me to feel sympathy for him. Still…" She left it at that.

Leo's nod let her know that his feelings were leaning the same way. Randall's murder now made him a victim. A victim almost certainly connected to the attacks on Leo and her. Why else would his body have been left so close to her house? Even if the reason was just to muddy the investigation, it was still another body to add to the death toll.

A toll that the killer would no doubt like to add to by murdering both Leo and Olivia.

"This takes Randall off the suspect list," she muttered, talking more to herself than to Leo.

But Leo made a sound of agreement. "That doesn't mean, though, that he didn't set up the attacks."

Her mind took a mental stutter and she shook her head. Olivia was about to say that didn't seem possible, but then she considered it from a different angle.

"You think Randall's own hired gun could have killed him?" she asked.

"It's possible. Maybe the hired gun got spooked when his comrade, Lowell, was killed. Or Randall could have reneged on payment or done something else to make this guy off him. Killers aren't known for playing by the rules."

No, they weren't, and this could certainly have been a plan that'd backfired on Randall.

"Milton," Leo added a moment later. "He might be willing to talk now when we tell him about Lowell's and Randall's murders. It could make him scared enough to finally rat on who hired him."

Yes, Olivia could see that happening and, if so, Leo might have been right about the danger finally being over.

Leo ran his hand down her arm. "I have to go out

there and help Barrett deal with this mess. You can go back to the breakroom if you want."

It was tempting. Mercy, was it. She was drained and shaky, and Olivia doubted being around her father and Rena would improve that. Still, she couldn't just put her head in the sand, especially since one of them might say something that would help shed some light on her mother's fatal car wreck and the current investigation.

The sound of a bell ringing had them both moving. Because it was the bell on the front door and it meant someone had come in. Olivia didn't have to guess who that someone was because she immediately heard Rena say Bernice's name.

Leo and Olivia entered the squad room, but before they dealt with Bernice, Leo pulled his brother aside and whispered, "The DB at Olivia's is Randall's."

Barrett got the same shocked expression that Leo and she had had. "I'll want details about that later," he said on a sigh just as Rena blurted something to Bernice.

"Samuel thinks you killed Simone."

Olivia turned in time to catch Bernice's reaction. If looks could kill, Bernice would have certainly accomplished it with the stony glare she aimed at Rena.

"What are you blathering about now?" Bernice asked.

"Rena," her father warned, taking hold of her arm.

But Rena just shook off his grip and went closer to Bernice. "Samuel thinks you might have killed Simone," Rena repeated. There was a smugness to her tone and expression, probably because she'd waited for years to have Samuel put Bernice in her place.

But this was more than "her place." This was an accusation that could land Bernice in jail for the rest of her life.

Bernice shifted her attention to Samuel. "What's she talking about?"

His head dropped down for a moment and then, on a heavy sigh, he stepped closer to Bernice. "I know you didn't like Simone," he said.

That was it. Apparently, the full explanation he intended to give her. But it was enough. Olivia saw the verbal blow land on Bernice as effectively as a heavyweight's fist. The woman flinched, and there was no longer anger in her eyes. Just the unbearable hurt of betrayal by someone she almost certainly loved.

The shock didn't last long, though. She pressed her lips together for a moment, cleared her throat and turned to Olivia.

"You told your father that I might have killed your mother?" Bernice asked. There was a coldness now; a thick layer of ice far more formidable than anger.

Olivia ignored the question and went with one of her own. "Did you kill her?"

Bernice looked her straight in the eyes. "No. It's true that I didn't like her, but I didn't have anything to do with her death." She turned, aiming that cold at Samuel now. "But you believe I did?"

He didn't break eye contact with Bernice, either. "I believe it's possible that you could have been trying to protect me by getting Simone out of the way."

Again, that was a blow, and this time Bernice's icy facade shattered a little. The sound she made was a hollow laugh. This time, it took several more moments for her to compose herself. And just like that, the anger was back. Anger she aimed not at Samuel but at Rena.

"I don't have to guess that you put all of this nonsense into Samuel's head," Bernice said, not waiting for the woman to respond. "Did you also remind him that you had a much stronger motive than I did for *getting Simone out of the way*?" She added some extra bite to those last words.

In contrast, Rena looked completely unruffled. "I had no motive. Simone and Samuel's marriage was falling apart. It was only a matter of time before they got a divorce. There was no reason for me to hurry that along."

"No reason other than the biggest one of all," Bernice argued. "You could have killed her so you could get your claws into Samuel sooner. No waiting for a divorce. But that didn't work, did it? Here it is, all these years later, and you still don't have Samuel."

That caused Rena's *unruffled* to shatter and she hooked her arm possessively through Samuel's. "You jealous witch. You're the one who's tried to get her claws into him—"

"Stop!" Barrett snapped, issuing his cop's glare at Rena, Bernice and her father before looking at his deputy. "Go ahead, Deputy Cassidy, and take Bernice to an interview room so we can get her statement on record. I'll need the same from both of you," he added to Samuel and Rena.

That didn't please any of the three. They turned their displeasured looks to Barrett, which he ignored. He motioned for Cybil to go ahead and take Bernice out of there.

But Bernice held her ground. "Did Rena tell you that she was at the estate a lot in those days before Simone's death?"

"I wasn't," Rena insisted. "It'd been at least a week."

"I keep very good records," Bernice said, and it sounded like a threat. "You were there nearly every day the week she died. And I suspect you're the one who drugged her."

"What!" Rena howled in outrage.

"I think you put the drugs in Simone's tea or maybe that energy juice she was always drinking. Maybe you got lucky with the timing of her getting behind the wheel, or maybe you just thought she'd die of a drug overdose. Either way, I'm sure the sheriff will take a hard look at you."

"Oh, I will," Barrett assured her and gestured again for Cybil to take Bernice away. This time, Bernice cooperated but not before she shot Samuel one final glare.

Her father muttered some curse words that seemed to be aimed at himself. Perhaps because he hadn't wanted things to play out like this.

That seemed to be Rena's take on things anyway.

"Don't you dare feel sorry for that woman," Rena snapped. "You should have fired her years ago. She's done nothing but run your life, and she's done that by trying to shut me out."

That put some strength in her father's spine and he pulled back his shoulders while staring at Rena. "Don't you dare try to make this about you." He turned to Barrett. "I'd like to wait in an interview room, too, while I call my lawyer."

Barrett nodded and motioned to the hall. "Just go that way and take the room that isn't occupied by Bernice."

"It is about me," Rena called out to him. "It's about Bernice turning you against me any chance she gets."

Apparently, Rena couldn't see that she was trying to do the same thing to Bernice. Olivia found the two exhausting and wasn't surprised when her father walked away, turning his back on Rena.

Tears filled Rena's eyes, but that didn't stop her from giving one of the desk chairs an angry kick.

"You wait there," Barrett warned her and motioned toward the chairs in front of the dispatch desk. "If you leave, I'll charge you with obstruction."

That didn't improve Rena's mood, and she whipped out her phone, saying she was calling her lawyer. Barrett left her to that and tipped his head for Leo and Olivia to follow him into his office.

"Tell me what happened to Randall," Barrett said the moment he had his office door closed.

"Jace and I both got a call about an hour ago to tell us about a body near Olivia's," Leo explained. "Jace checked it out and found Randall. He'd been shot in the face, but Jace ID'd him through fingerprints."

Obviously processing the information, Barrett sat on the edge of his desk. "About an hour ago," he repeated. "Shortly after the time Olivia and you got back here to the sheriff's office."

"Yeah," Leo said, and it seemed to Olivia as if he was also agreeing with something else his brother hadn't spelled out. "It means Rena, Samuel or Bernice could have gotten to Randall, killed him and dumped the body."

"The question is—why?" Barrett continued. "Other than to distract us or to throw a wrench in the investigation, I can't see why. Unless—"

"Randall's connected to the attacks or the hired thugs used in the attacks," Leo finished for him.

Barrett nodded and took out his phone. "I'll text Cybil and have her ask Samuel about an alibi. He probably won't want to say anything without his lawyer, but he might slip up. I also need to call the diner. I want to see how long Bernice was there before I had her come back here."

Olivia considered herself a step behind the two lawmen when it came to following the threads of this investigation, but she latched onto this angle right away. The person who'd killed Randall had called both Leo and Jace. Had maybe even personally done the body dump. Bernice couldn't have managed that if she'd been sitting in the town's diner for the past couple of hours.

While Barrett made the call, Olivia glanced out at Rena, to make sure she was still there. She was. And the woman was still on the phone, maybe griping to her lawyer.

Or plotting another attack.

"Don't worry," Leo said. "We'll check her alibi, too."

Rena would probably claim she wasn't capable of killing Randall and shoving him out of a vehicle. And maybe she wasn't. But Rena worked out a lot. In fact, of their three remaining suspects—Rena, Bernice and Olivia's father—Olivia thought Rena might be the strongest of them physically. Of course, it wouldn't have taken strength had the person responsible hired some muscle to do their dirty work.

"Bernice had only been at the diner for about ten minutes when I called her," Barrett relayed when he got off the phone.

So, no alibi. Well, not one in the diner anyway. That didn't mean the woman couldn't account for where she was and what she was doing. Barrett would certainly try to get the info out of her.

"I have another possible angle," Leo said, making his own call. He held up a finger in a wait-a-second gesture when Barrett questioned him. The person he'd called had obviously answered. "Jace," Leo greeted, putting the call on speaker. "Anything on that phone you found near Randall's body?"

"No. I haven't gotten into it yet. It's got a passcode, so I'll have to see if the lab can do anything with it."

Leo groaned. "That could take days," he mumbled to her. "Weeks even."

Olivia wanted to groan, too. They didn't have that kind of time. Heck, they might not even have hours before someone tried to attack them again.

"But I was about to call you about something else," Jace continued a moment later. "I've got an eyewitness in Olivia's neighborhood who saw a black SUV around the time the body would have been dumped. It's a woman who lives across the street, and she said she's seen that vehicle or one like it many times before. She said she couldn't see inside because the windows are tinted."

That got Olivia's attention. "What vehicle?" she asked.

"One with a logo on the driver's-side door."

And suddenly Olivia knew exactly what logo Jace meant. "A sycamore leaf?" she managed to ask.

"Yeah," Jace verified. "I was just checking, and the only vehicles anyone around here has seen like that all belong to your father."

Chapter 13

What he was doing was a risk, but Leo knew anything he did at this point would be. Still, it'd bring some normalcy back to Cameron's life. Or at least it would if Leo could get his son, Olivia and Izzie safely back to the ranch.

The fire department and bomb squad had given Leo the all-clear to return, so at least he didn't have to worry about the specific threat of the place going up in flames. And he'd added even more security, bringing over some ranch hands from Barrett's place to patrol the grounds and prevent someone from sneaking onto the property and putting some sniper skills to bad use.

Still…

Yeah, that *still* was going to haunt him until he had everyone tucked safely inside the house.

Izzie was treating the ride in the cruiser as a fun adventure for Cameron by reading to him from a book that made animal sounds whenever Cameron touched one of the pages. His son was giggling, definitely not showing any signs of worry or fear. Unlike Olivia and Leo.

Olivia was keeping watch as he drove to the ranch. Leo was, as well, and so were Cybil and Daniel, who were in the cruiser behind them. Unfortunately, his fellow deputy and brother wouldn't be able to stay at the ranch. There was just too much going on at the sheriff's office, and that's where Leo needed them to be. Their best chance at ending the danger was to get answers from their now three suspects and to follow the new lead they'd gotten from Jace.

Someone had used one of the vehicles from the Sycamore Grove estate, and Leo wanted to know which who. If Barrett couldn't pull that info out of Rena, Bernice and Samuel, then maybe he'd be able to hold them for at least a couple of hours.

Until Leo could make this drive and get off the roads.

As long as they were out in the open, the risks skyrocketed. It would have been worse, though, to make the trip at night. That's why Leo had timed it so that it was still a while before sunset.

He held his breath when he took the turn to his ranch and then released that breath when he realized someone had already removed Randall's truck from the road. Good. That was one of the reasons Leo hadn't left the sheriff's office any sooner and had in fact stayed nearly eight hours after getting the call from Jace.

Along with setting up those extra security measures, Leo had wanted to give the bomb squad time to deal with the truck. If not, he would have had to use the trails to get to his house, and he hadn't wanted to risk driving them since they would be prime areas for another sniper to lay in wait.

He drove past the burned-out area left by Randall's truck and spotted the first of the hands. There were others, all armed and clearly on guard, just as Leo had instructed. Another was on the porch where he would stay until Leo had Olivia, Izzie and Cameron inside. Then he would join the other hands to patrol the ranch. If a gunman managed to get past the ranch hands, then Leo would have the security system turned on to alert them if anyone tried to break in.

Leo parked the cruiser in the garage and quickly got Cameron into the house. Olivia and Izzie were right on his heels, and the moment he'd reset the security system, he fired off a quick text to Daniel and Cybil to let them know it was okay for them to go back to town.

"I can take Cameron to the nursery," Izzie volunteered, easing Cameron into her arms and looping the diaper bag over her shoulder. "I'm sure he needs to be changed. Then I'll bathe him and get him ready for bed. I'll let you know before I put him down so you can say good-night to him."

Leo was thankful the nanny was there to keep Cameron on schedule. Doing that was huge, and it freed him up to try to make some headway on the investigation.

"I can sleep in the nursery with Cameron, if that's okay," Izzie offered.

Leo thought that staying with his son was something he'd like to do. The trouble was, he wasn't sure when Olivia and he would be turning in for the night, and Izzie probably didn't want to stay in limbo, waiting for them to decide. He nodded, thanked her, but knew that he'd be sleeping very close to his boy. No way did he want to be too far away from Cameron in case something went wrong.

When Izzie left with Cameron, Leo turned to Olivia to see how she was holding up. As if she knew he was checking for that, she lifted her chin and put on what he thought was a decent attempt at a strong expression. But he knew beneath the surface that she was just as rattled as he was. Heck, they were all rattled, including his brothers, which was a reminder for him to get in touch with Barrett to let him know that they'd arrived safely.

He took out his phone and pressed Barrett's number. He answered on the first ring. "We're home," Leo told him. "We're okay."

"Good. I didn't want to call you while you were on the road. Didn't figure you'd want the distraction."

"If it's good news, it's not a distraction," Leo quickly assured him.

"Sorry. It's not good. Bernice, Rena and Samuel have all lawyered up. The three of them did insist, though, that they're innocent, but since none of them is spouting proof of an alibi, I'm guessing they don't have any."

So, they wouldn't be able to eliminate any one of them. Not yet. But now that Bernice wasn't so chummy with Samuel, the woman might be willing to spill some secrets about him. Samuel might be willing to do the same.

Leo ended the call with Barrett and turned back to Olivia. Even though he hadn't put the call on speaker, she'd obviously heard, and she sighed.

"Hiding behind their lawyers," she muttered. "I guess it was too much to expect for one of them to confess."

Yes, it was. A confession now would result in charges

for first-degree murder, attempted murder, assault with a deadly weapon, and conspiracy. If convicted, the death penalty would be on the table. Plus, Leo doubted that any of the three had their consciences troubling them enough to come clean.

"I'm sure you didn't get much sleep last night," he said after she made another weary sigh. She looked exhausted and no doubt felt it, too. "You should probably try to rest at least for a little while. There's a bed in the guest room or you could go into my room."

Olivia lifted an eyebrow, and he realized that his suggestion had sounded a little like a come-on. Probably because they'd had sex in his room and it'd been damn amazing.

"You're too tired for sex," he added.

He'd tried to go for light, but he'd failed big-time. Her eyebrow quirked again, and she stepped into his arms, sliding her hands around him until they were body to body. Until breath met breath.

Suddenly, he didn't feel too tired or too busy for sex. But it couldn't happen. Not when their little boy could still be in danger.

Leo settled for brushing his mouth over her cheek. It was the kind of kiss meant to soothe. And maybe it had. But the rest of his stupid body reminded him that it was only a short distance from her cheek to her mouth. Of course, a real kiss would break some rules and only make him want more. *More* couldn't happen. Not right now anyway. But it would be night soon, and eventually they'd have to go to bed.

Maybe even go to bed together.

Sex did seem inevitable between them. It didn't seem

to matter how much they fought it, how much they knew it shouldn't happen.

And that's why Leo broke one of those rules and kissed her.

Since the kiss was a huge mistake and couldn't last long, he made it count. He deepened it, letting the taste of Olivia slide right through him. The heat was right behind the taste. Then the need. Of course, the need had never been far from the surface when it came to the two of them.

As the heat urged him to kick things up even more, Leo pulled away from her. Her breath was gusting. Her face flushed. And her mouth looked as if it'd just been thoroughly kissed.

"I'm glad you weren't too tired for that," she murmured in a voice that was as effective as a siren's lure.

So was he. But now he had to do something to get rid of the cloud the kiss had put in his mind. It took some doing to focus on something other than Olivia.

"I need to go through your mother's journals," he said, and he watched as that shifted her back to reality.

No gusting breath or flushed face for her now. Just a resigned nod. "Barrett copied everything that was in the envelope Bernice gave him," she said. "I can look through that while you're on the journals."

It seemed like a good way to divide the work. Then, if neither of them hit on anything new, they could trade stashes. Leo also needed to make time to get warrants to go through the financials for all of their suspects. With the eyewitness account of the vehicle that'd been at Olivia's, that might be enough to convince a judge to let him take a look at bank accounts to see if anyone had recently paid for a hitman or two.

Leo picked up the bag with the laptops and files he'd brought from the sheriff's office. "We can set up in the room next to the nursery," he suggested. "That way, we can keep an eye on Cameron."

Olivia readily agreed and didn't say a word about a bed being in there. That made her a wise woman since there was no need to add any more sexual fuel to this attraction.

Leo took the bag upstairs to the smaller of his two guestrooms just as his phone rang. It was Barrett again, and Leo nearly groaned. He'd spoken to his brother only about ten minutes ago, so something must have come up.

"This time I have good news," Barrett said the moment Leo answered.

"I'm definitely ready to hear some." Since Olivia was, too, Leo put the call on speaker.

"The psychiatrist is going to certify Milton competent to stand trial," his brother explained.

Leo certainly hadn't been expecting that. Everything they'd learned about Milton had pegged him as having mental issues. Apparently though, Milton did understand the judicial process and the charges that'd be levered against him.

"You're charging him with attempted murder of a police officer?" Leo asked.

"I am. I just told him this, and after he got past the shock, Milton said he wants to talk. He wants to tell us all about the person who's trying to kill you."

Olivia didn't bother to groan or huff. Yes, it was good news that Milton finally realized he was in scalding hot water and would likely spend the rest of his miserable life in jail.

But she felt another ploy coming on.

Another attempt to get Leo and her out into the open, maybe so one of Milton's cohorts could try to murder them.

Apparently, Leo felt the same way because he huffed and muttered something profane. "I'm not taking Olivia back to the sheriff's office," he insisted. "It's getting dark, and I don't want her outside."

"I agree," Barrett said as fast as Leo had objected. "No need for it. When Milton insisted on talking to the two of you, I told him he'd have to do that with a video call. I can have that set up in just a couple of minutes if you want to hear what he has to say."

"Oh, we want to hear," Leo assured him. "And who knows, this time Milton might stop playing games long enough to give us some real info. Has he asked for a plea deal?" he added.

"Of course. That was one of the first things out of his mouth. I told him that I'd consider a deal if he actually gave us anything we could use to convict the person who hired him."

Good. Because Olivia didn't want Milton to walk unless they had his boss in custody. It twisted at her to think that the boss might be her father. Still, if he'd done these horrible things, then she wouldn't want him anywhere but behind bars.

"I'll call you after I have everything set up," Barrett said right before he clicked off.

Leo put aside his phone so he could set up one of the laptops that he apparently intended to use for the video call. While he was doing that, Olivia took a moment to go check on Cameron. He was splashing in the tub in the nursery bathroom, and she gave him a quick kiss.

"Is everything okay?" Izzie asked her.

Olivia nodded. "There might be a break in the case."

And Olivia hoped that wasn't all wishful thinking. Still, she held on to the hope that they'd soon have the name of the person responsible for terrorizing them. Then they could all deal with the fallout. Even if it wasn't her father who'd done this, it was someone she knew. Someone he'd trusted.

When Olivia made it back to the guest room, Leo already had the laptop booted up and she could see the camera feed of the interview room on the screen. The room was empty, but that changed almost immediately as Barrett ushered in Milton. Barrett had kept the man cuffed. A good thing, as far as Olivia was concerned. She didn't want Milton using this as a chance to try to escape.

"This is being recorded," Barrett told Milton. "And I've already read you your rights. I need you to say on record that you understand those rights and that you're waiving your right to an attorney."

"Yeah, I understand all that stuff. Are Leo and Olivia listening?" Milton immediately asked.

"We are," Leo said. "You'd better not be wasting our time."

"I'm not. I swear I'm not." Milton looked straight into the camera. "But I need a deal. I need immunity."

"You're not getting a free ride," Barrett assured him. "I've already told you the only deal you're getting is that I'll put in a good word for you with the DA if you give us your boss. That's it, Milton. That's the best you'll get from me."

Milton shook his head, muttered something Olivia didn't catch. *Great.* He was going to clam up again, or so Olivia thought. But the man's gaze zoomed to Barrett.

"You've got to swear to me that you'll work your butt off to get me a lighter sentence. Swear it," Milton repeated.

Barrett gave him a flat look. "You tried to kill my brother, and because you withheld information, it resulted in another attack, one where Olivia and my nephew could have been hurt. Added to that, there are two people dead. Working my butt off for you isn't high on my priority list. But," Barrett quickly added, "help me arrest the person behind the attacks, and I'll spell out to the DA that you're just a lackey."

Olivia thought that maybe Milton would be insulted with the term "lackey," but it seemed to make him relax a bit. Maybe because he thought being a hired gun would give him a lighter sentence than the person who'd hired him. She didn't think it would, though, and was pretty sure that accessory to murder, even after the fact, would carry the same penalty as murder itself.

"Okay," Milton said, gathering his breath. "I don't actually know the name of the person who hired me, but I can give you a description. He's in his thirties, is tall and has dark brown hair."

Well, that ruled out Bernice, Rena and her father, but it must have triggered something for Barrett because he paused the interview. He then searched through something on his phone. When he obviously found what he was looking for, he turned the screen in Milton's direction.

"That's him," Milton said right off. "That's the guy who hired me."

Barrett shifted the phone screen so that Olivia and Leo could see, as well. It was Lowell, the dead gunman.

"What?" Milton asked when he noted the frustrated expression on Barrett's face. "That's the guy, I swear."

"He's dead," Barrett provided. "Now, I'm wondering if that's a nice coincidence for you so you can make us think that all of this is tied up in a neat little bow."

"No." Milton seemed adamant and repeated his denial when he looked at the laptop screen where he knew Leo and she were watching him. "He's dead? Who killed him?"

Olivia didn't think it was her imagination that the news had alarmed Milton. Maybe because he'd known Lowell. Or perhaps because he thought he might next in line to die.

"I had to shoot him," Leo answered. "To stop him from murdering Olivia and me. So, tell me why Lowell had it in for us and would hire you to come at me with a knife?"

"The only thing he said was that I could make a lot of money if I took you out. I swear," Milton repeated, probably because Barrett was looking plenty skeptical.

Olivia was skeptical, as well. Milton would probably tell them anything to save his hide, and he'd withhold info, too, for that very same reason.

"Money?" Leo questioned. "That's why you agreed to kill me?"

Milton groaned and generally looked about as uncomfortable as a man could look. "I'm in trouble. I owe money to the wrong people, and I had to come up with some quick cash."

Leo jumped right on that. "How did you know Lowell? How'd he know you'd be willing to become a killer for hire?"

Milton shrugged. "I figured he worked for the men I owed the money. He just came up to me and asked if I wanted to get out of the hot water I was in. Not many people knew about my debts, so I just assumed he worked for the guys who'd lent me the funds."

"But you didn't find out for yourself?" Leo demanded.

"No. I was desperate. Those guys were going to kill me if I didn't pony up, so I saw the job Lowell offered as sort of self-defense."

That made Olivia sick to her stomach with disgust. This snake had been willing to end a good man's life to save his own one. And all because of money.

"How much did Lowell pay you?" she snapped. She wanted to add more, to blister him with some backlash from her temper, but that wouldn't help. It might even hurt if it caused Milton to realize how much trouble he was in and clam up.

Milton hesitated, and she could see the battle he was having with himself as to how much to tell them. He maybe thought he should paint himself in the best light possible, but he was well beyond that. There was no "light" that would make him appear to be a decent human being.

"Ten grand," Milton finally said.

Oh, that didn't help with her bubbling temper and disgust. For ten thousand dollars, Milton had been willing to kill Leo, and for her father, that would have been chump change. Maybe for Bernice, too. Olivia didn't know her financial situation but suspected that the woman had saved most of her high salary. Bernice had certainly never taken a vacation, and to the best of Olivia's knowledge, she didn't have any expensive jewelry. Didn't even have her own car. Whenever Bernice needed to leave the estate, she used one of the vehicles.

Like the one that'd been spotted around the same time as Randall's body dump.

Bernice could have been in that vehicle. Then again, her father used the same type of SUV. And if Rena had access to the estate, she could have been behind the wheel of one, too. The keys for the vehicles were kept in the ignitions while they were in the garage.

"And FYI," Milton added a moment later, "I didn't get the full payment. Lowell only gave me three thousand up front and said I'd get the rest when I finished the job. Then he made me do a confession of sorts so that I wouldn't renege on the deal and run with the cash that I had."

"A confession?" Barrett asked, jumping right on that.

Again, Milton hesitated before he explained. "Lowell used a phone to record it. He had me say my name and that I was going to kill Deputy Leo Logan."

Olivia exchanged a glance with Leo. He was probably wondering the same thing she was—whether Lowell had planned to set up Milton to take the fall for Leo and any other attacks. Milton certainly made a perfect fall guy, and as he'd admitted himself, he was desperate.

"From everything we've gathered so far, Lowell was a hired thug, too," Barrett pointed out. "So, who hired him?"

That put some fresh alarm on Milton's face. "I don't know. That's the truth," he added in protest over their groans.

Leo huffed. "If you don't know that, then you're wasting our time," he snapped. "No information, no good word for you with the DA." His tone made it sound as if he was about to end the video session.

"Wait!" Milton pleaded. "I've got something. Something that should be worth more than just a good word with the DA."

"What?" Leo and Barrett asked at the same time, and both had plenty of skepticism in their expression. Olivia was right there with them.

"Lowell gave me a burner cell that he used to call me," Milton went on. "He told me to toss it right before I went after Leo, and I did."

"And how the heck is a burner going to help us?" Barrett fired back. "Lowell's dead, and what does it matter if he called you on it? He was probably using a burner himself."

"Probably," Milton admitted and then flashed an oily smile. "Lowell wasn't the only one who called me on it, though. I got another call, right before I went after Leo."

Suddenly, Olivia was very interested in what the man was saying. Leo, too, and they automatically moved closer to the laptop screen.

"Who called you?" Barrett urged.

The smile stayed on Milton's mouth. "The person didn't say who he or she was. The voice was all muffled-like. But the caller said Lowell was having trouble with his phone reception, but that I should go ahead and finish off Leo Logan."

There were indeed plenty of areas with bad reception near her place where the second attacker—Lowell—had likely gone. Someone had fired shots into her house shortly after Leo had arrived.

"I'm betting that caller was Lowell's boss," Milton insisted.

Barrett stared at him. "Let me guess. You have no idea where you tossed this burner phone."

"Oh, I know, all right. And this really oughta be worth more than just a word with the DA."

Obviously, Milton wanted to use this as a further bargaining tool, but Barrett just shook his head. "So far, you've given us little to nothing. Give me something now, or you're going back to your cell."

"All right," Milton said after what was obviously a mental debate with himself. "I figured if I could finish off Leo all quiet-like, then I could go back and get the burner and my own phone, which Lowell said I wasn't to have on me during the attack. So, I hid my cell and the burner in the bushes in the back of the parking lot and covered them with some leaves."

With his restraints rattling, he motioned toward the side of the building where there was indeed a parking lot. One with a row of hedges at the back.

"Go ahead and look," Milton insisted. "You'll see the number of the person who called me on the burner. Then you can listen to the conversation on my phone."

"You recorded it?" Leo asked before Olivia could jump right on that.

Milton's smile widened. "I did with my own phone. Listen to it, and you'll hear the voice of the person who wants you dead."

Chapter 14

Leo wished he could be in two places at once. He wanted to be at the sheriff's office, helping Barrett look for those two phones Milton had claimed he'd tossed. But Leo couldn't do that at the possible expense of Cameron and Olivia. Just because Lowell was dead and Milton was in restraints, it didn't mean the person who'd hired them hadn't sent another killer after them.

Olivia was pacing across the guest room, so obviously she was on edge, too, while they waited for word from Barrett. They had used some of their waiting time to go into the nursery to say good-night to Cameron. Leo had also brought in some covers for Izzie who'd insisted on using the sleep chair next to Cameron's crib. That was good because Cameron wouldn't be alone, but Leo figured when he and Olivia finally went to bed, they'd be bunking in the nursery, as well.

Leo checked the time and cursed when he realized it

was only two minutes later than when he'd last checked. It hadn't been long—less that fifteen minutes—since Milton had told them about the phones, so it wasn't as if Barrett was dragging his feet on this. Plus, it was possible that the phones weren't where Milton had said they were.

Or they might not even exist.

The sigh he heard from Olivia told Leo that she was probably stressing over the same thing.

"Milton would be stupid to lie about this," Leo told her, though it probably wasn't much assurance because Milton clearly wasn't a smart man. Still, Leo could see how a stall tactic would help him.

"He or she," Olivia muttered. She stopped pacing and turned toward him. "That's what Jace said about the person who'd called him with the anonymous tip about Randall's body."

Leo nodded. Yeah, he'd remembered that, and if an indistinguishable muffled voice was all they had, then this wouldn't be much of a lead. Then again, he or Olivia might recognize something. Maybe even some background noise.

"Even if these phones end up ID'ing the killer," Olivia said, "I want Milton in jail. I want him to pay for what he did to you."

Yeah, but more than that, Leo wanted the person who was pulling the strings. Or rather, pulling the trigger. Because that's what this person was—a killer.

Because she looked as if her nerves were worse than his, Leo went to her and pulled her into his arms. He'd stopped trying to talk himself out of doing stuff like this. Plain and simple, he didn't even want to try to keep resisting Olivia.

He could hear the whirl of the AC, feel the cool air

spilling on them. Feel the heat of her body, too. And her warm breath hitting against his neck.

Leo gave her another of those cheek kisses, but she didn't exactly melt against him. She was definitely wired, not only by the wait but from the stress of the constant threat of danger. The tension went up a significant notch when his phone rang.

Even though Leo had been anticipating the call, he still bobbled his phone when he yanked it from his jeans. Barrett's name was on the screen, so Leo answered it as fast as he could.

"I found the cells," Barrett said, his voice pouring through the room as Leo put the call on speaker. "They were right where Milton told us they'd be."

Leo released a long breath. "That's a good start. Please tell me he actually recorded his boss giving the order to kill me."

"He did. I've only listened to it once, so all I can tell you is that the voice is indeed muffled. Barely audible, in fact. But I'll send it to you so you can hear it for yourself."

Leo was certain both Barrett and he would be listening to it multiple times. So would the crime lab.

"I expected the caller to be using a burner, too," Barrett continued a moment later. "He or she didn't."

Olivia made a small gasping sound. "You know who made the call?" she blurted.

"No, but I know where the call originated," Barrett corrected. "It came from a landline at your father's estate."

It took Leo a moment to wrap his mind around that, and he didn't like the conclusions he reached. "Lowell gave Milton a burner, but the person who hired them didn't take that simple step to cover his tracks?"

"Yes," Barrett agreed.

It was obvious they thought that maybe this was some kind of stupid scheme meant to make Samuel look guilty.

"It's just like the vehicle," Olivia said. Her forehead was furrowed, the worry plentiful in her eyes. "Any of the three could have used a landline phone in the house."

Bingo. That could have been intentional or an oversight. After all, maybe the culprit hadn't thought Milton would record the call or ditch the phone so it could so easily be found.

"I'll get a warrant to access the phone lines at the estate," Barrett advised. "After I have the info I need on the calls, I'll question Samuel, Rena and Bernice again in the morning. In the meantime, listen to the call and let me know if you hear anything that I've missed."

A moment later, Leo's phone dinged with the recording Barrett had just sent him. Leo ended the call with his brother so that he and Olivia could listen to it.

"Lowell's got bad phone reception," the caller said. Either Milton hadn't managed to record the "greeting" or there hadn't been one. "Do the job on Leo Logan, and when we have proof it's done, you'll get the rest of your money."

That was it. No flashing neon light of information, and Barrett and Milton had been right about the voice. It was muffled and, to Leo's ear, indistinguishable. Apparently, it was the same for Olivia because she cursed, as well.

Leo hit Replay, listened, and then hit Replay again. On the fourth listen, Olivia sank onto the foot of the bed and shook her head.

"I hear some background noise," she said, "but it only sounds like wind blowing or maybe a ceiling fan."

"Same here," Leo agreed. And if it was indeed wind, it could have been coming from the parking lot of the sheriff's office. In other words, no help whatsoever.

He sank beside her, took her hand and tried to put at least some positive spin on things. "Once Barrett gets the warrant and the phone records from the estate, we might be able to pinpoint which landline was used."

Though he figured there were many extensions off a single line, he thought it best not to remind Olivia of that since she already looked as if she was about to crash and burn. He knew how she felt. He'd clung to the hope that the phones would give them a solid clue. And *that* they had. The call had come from the estate, which meant the killer had been there. That wasn't a surprise, but maybe they could use the phone records and compare them to the alibis or statements of their suspects.

Or they could bluff.

"Barrett's allowed to lie in interview," Leo explained. "He could bring in Rena, Bernice and Samuel, tell them that Milton recorded the order for the hit on me, and the person responsible might break."

"Might," she repeated in a mumble.

Even though it hadn't helped with the stress the other times he'd done it, Leo pulled her into his arms again.

"I wish Barrett could arrest them all," she added.

Yeah, too bad he couldn't do it. But even that might not end the danger because there could already be other hired guns out there, waiting for their shot. When Olivia pulled back and met his gaze, he knew that she was well aware of that scenario, too.

"We should listen to the recording again," she said, not breaking eye contact with him. "We also need to go over my mother's journals. And brainstorm as to why Bernice, Rena or my father wants us dead."

They did indeed need to do all those things. But Leo went for something totally different.

He kissed her.

Again, there was no *melting*. In fact, Olivia went stiff, and he figured she would put a quick stop to this. After all, kissing wasn't one of the options she'd just spelled out for what they should be doing.

The weariness was still in her eyes. Actually, on every part of her face, and because he had his arms around her, Leo could feel the knotted muscles in her back.

"Bad timing," he said and started to move away from her.

Olivia stopped him by catching the front of his T-shirt. "The timing is awful," she agreed. "Plenty of things are awful. You're not. This isn't."

And this time, she kissed him.

Leo didn't stop her. He wasn't an idiot. This was exactly what he wanted. He could even try to make himself believe that it'd be a great stress reliever. A way for them to forget the hell they'd been going through. Well, forget it for a short time anyway. But this wasn't about stress or forgetting. This kiss was about giving in to the heat that they'd both been fighting for way too long.

She was the one who deepened the kiss, threading her fingers into his hair, bringing him closer to her. Not that Leo needed any such adjustments to get him closer. He had already headed in that direction and made some adjustments of his own so that her breasts landed against his chest.

The kiss continued, but he added some touching to this make-out session. He slipped his hand between them, cupped her breasts and swiped his thumb over her nipple. The silky sound of pleasure Olivia made nearly brought him to his knees. Thankfully, though, it didn't rid him of common sense. He stood, leading her with him to the door so he could lock it. No way did he want Izzie walking in on them.

Even with all the moving around, Olivia didn't miss a beat, and she didn't haul him back to the bed. Instead, she pushed him so that his back landed against the wall and she went in for a kiss that was well past the make-out stage. This was a carnal invitation to sex.

And Leo's body responded.

He went hard as stone, and every part of him urged him to strip off her clothes and take her now, now, now. Leo wanted *now* more than he wanted air in his lungs, but he didn't want to take Olivia in some frantic coupling. It would leave them both sated, that was for sure. However, it would be over way too fast. He didn't want fast. He wanted—no, he *needed*—to hang on to this even if just for the night.

"Your arm," she said out of the blue. "You're hurt."

"I'm not hurting," he told her. That was the truth. He wasn't sure he could feel a mountain of pain right now.

"You're sure?" she pressed.

He took her hand and put it over his erection. "I'm sure."

She smiled. A sly, wicked smile, and kept her hand in place. "I haven't had you in over a year and a half."

She looked at him. Her eyes hot now. The need had replaced the weariness and fatigue. He thought for a second that she was going to tell him they needed to rethink this, that there were reasons why they'd been apart for over a year and a half. That there were reasons, like the investigation, why they should table this and go back to it when Barrett had made an arrest.

"A year and a half is too long," she said.

Her voice was a throaty whisper. Like the rest of her, it tugged and pulled at him until Leo felt the snap. The one that told him he wouldn't be able to draw this out, after all. The *now* was going to win.

So, he took her now. He kissed her, the hunger and need clawing through him. Through her, too. Because she kicked off her shoes and began to tug at his shirt. Leo helped her with that and did the same to hers. Their tops landed on the floor. He unhooked the front clasp of her bra and tossed it down with the other items of clothing. This wouldn't be pretty, but they'd get it done.

Suddenly her hands were on him. On his bare chest. His back. Touching him. Making him crazy. The craziness climbed when she went after the zipper of his jeans. *Now* was winning for her, too, but through all of that, she made sure she didn't touch his wounded arm.

He backed her toward the bed. Kissing her. With skin sliding against skin. Her nipples were too much to resist, so he dipped his head and took one into his mouth. His reward was that she made that silky moan of pleasure again and bucked against him.

They fell onto the bed together.

Leo kept tugging at her nipple and then he kissed his way down her stomach. To her jeans, which he shimmied off her. Her panties came next, and he did even more kissing. Pleasing her. Pleasing himself.

"Don't mention the stretch marks," she muttered.

Because his pulse was throbbing in his ears, it took him a moment to realize what she'd said. Since his mouth was still right there, he kissed the marks, as well.

"If you think they're a turn-off, you're wrong," he

told her. Just the opposite. She'd had his child, their son, and the marks were a reminder of that.

Olivia made a sound that let him know that she wasn't quite convinced. Leo would have *convinced* her, too, but she rolled on top of him. Again, she was mindful of his arm.

"I don't want you reopening the cut," she said, levering to straddle him and go after his zipper.

Leo was about to insist that he wasn't concerned about the damn cut, but then she got off his jeans. Got off his boxers. And nearly got him off when her hands skimmed over him.

He gritted his teeth and let her do what she wanted. Apparently some kisses and touching as he'd done. Or maybe she was just trying to drive him insane. She nearly managed it, too, before she finally made her way back up his body and, sliding her hips against his, took him inside her.

Now he had to grit his teeth from the sheer pleasure of the sensations firing through him. Mercy, the woman was good at this.

Olivia stilled, giving them both a moment to catch their breath. She waited until their eyes were locked before she braced her hands on his chest and started to move. She was good at this, too, but there was no way Leo could just lie there and not get involved. He caught her hips, adding some pressure to those thrusts that would soon push them both right over the edge.

His body begged for release while he also tried to hold on. To make this last as long as possible. He was doing a decent job of it when he felt the orgasm ripple through Olivia. She fisted around him, giving him no choice but to give in to the need.

Leo pulled her down to him and followed her.

Chapter 15

Olivia lay on top of Leo and tried to level her breathing. Tried to shut out the thoughts, too. She succeeded in doing the first but failed big-time with the second. The thoughts came. Both good and bad.

Making love with Leo had been something starved for. It'd been like coming home, Christmas and her birthday all rolled into one.

And that was the problem.

Great sex only made her want him more, and while he certainly seemed able to put their past troubles behind him, they had a very rough road ahead of them. One that might involve her own father's arrest for attempting to murder them. Even if it wasn't Samuel, she and Leo wouldn't have an easy time putting aside everything that'd happen and just move on with their lives.

Besides, Leo might not want to "move on" with her.

He'd certainly not said anything about an ever-after or even a commitment. Of course, they had a commitment because of Cameron, but being with Leo like this made Olivia realize that she wanted more. She wanted the whole package. Leo. Their son. A life together.

Even though the timing was lousy for it, Olivia worked up enough steel to open that "life together" conversation with him. Best not to do that, however, while he was still inside her, so she eased off him, mindful not to touch his arm, and dropped onto the bed so they were side to side. She pulled the edge of the quilt over her and looked at him.

Just as he cursed.

It wasn't a mild oath, either, and she figured it had to be aimed at her. Or rather, their situation. Mercy. Here she was fantasizing about a life with him, and he probably thought this had been a huge mistake.

"No condom," he groaned.

Olivia blinked. Then her eyes went wide when his words sank in. She practically snapped to a sitting position and stared down at him.

"Yeah," Leo said, obviously noting the extreme shock that had to be on her face. He straightened, as well, groaned and cursed some more. "I'm so sorry."

She opened her mouth but wasn't sure what to say. This wasn't something she could just blow off and tell him not to worry about. Still, she could give him a little reassurance about one possible pitfall to not practicing safe sex.

"I'm okay," she said. "I mean I've been tested, and I haven't been with anyone since you."

He turned his head, slowly, his gaze snaring hers. "No one in nearly two years?"

Olivia realized that it sounded as if she was stuck on him and unable to move on to anyone else.

And that was the truth.

However, since it was the truth, she didn't intend to admit it to him, not now when declaring her feelings for him would be the last thing he'd want to hear.

"No one," she verified. "I stay really busy with Cameron. I don't have time for a relationship."

He just continued to stare at her with those stone-gray eyes. Eyes that seemed to see right through her to suss out the lie she'd just told. Yes, she was busy, but she hadn't wanted another man. Hadn't wanted to be with anyone other than Leo and maybe would have been had it not been for her father.

"I haven't been with anyone since you, either," he said.

Olivia was certain her look of shock returned, intensified. She nearly laughed because it seemed a joke that someone who was at hot as Leo would go that long without having a woman. But he was serious.

Cursing again, he rubbed his hand over his face and then groaned. "No condom," he repeated as if to get them back on track with the conversation. Apparently, he didn't want to launch into a discussion of why they'd been living celibate lives. "Any chance you can tell me it's the wrong time of the month?"

No chance whatsoever, and that's why Olivia settled for a shrug. Her cycle hadn't been regular since she'd had Cameron so, as far as she knew, there was no such thing as the wrong time of the month.

"It'll be okay," she insisted though she had absolutely nothing to back it up. Well, nothing except what would certainly sound like lame logic. "We used protection before, and I still got pregnant with Cameron, so maybe that means the odds are in our favor that I won't get pregnant now."

He turned to stare at her again. A flat stare that told her he'd had no trouble figuring out the "lame" part. But the turning and staring put his face very close to hers and, despite this serious concern, Olivia felt a little weak in the knees just looking at him. Here, only minutes had passed since she'd had him and she wanted him all over again.

Olivia leaned in and saw the surprise flash in his eyes before she kissed him. She'd thought he'd resist. After all, they had work to do, and there was that whole part about them literally having had sex just minutes earlier. But he didn't resist. Leo muttered something she didn't catch, slid his hand around the back of her neck and hauled her to him. She laughed, kept kissing him and slid back onto his lap.

The kiss turned instantly hot. Then again, it wasn't possible to kiss Leo and not feel the heat. But this time they didn't get to push it any further. That's because Leo stopped.

"I think I hear something," Leo said, causing her laughter, and the heat, to vanish. "I need to talk to the ranch hand."

He swore when he reached for his phone and it wasn't there. That's because it was in jeans' pocket and all their clothes were scattered on the floor. As soon as they got off the bed and located it in his jeans by the nightstand, Leo made the call.

"Wally," Leo greeted. "Is something wrong?"

Alarmed at Leo's tone, Olivia moved closer to hear,

but Leo fixed that by putting the call on speaker so that it'd free up his hands to pull on his jeans.

"Maybe," Wally answered. "There's someone walking up the road toward the house. Or rather, staggering. I can't tell who it is, but it is a woman."

Olivia certainly hadn't been expecting Wally to say that. Her worst fear was that he had been about to tell them he'd spotted a gunman. That's why Olivia had practically been throwing on her clothes so she could hurry to Cameron. But this didn't seem like an immediate threat.

Well, maybe it wasn't.

It quickly occurred to her that it could be some kind of ruse. Something set up so an attacker could get closer to the house.

"Is the woman armed?" Leo asked the hand.

"I don't think so. She's not carrying a purse or anything…hell, she just fell down. Should I go out and check on her?"

Olivia saw the sleek muscle tighten in Leo's jaw and knew he was debating how to handle this. His ranch was miles from town, so he didn't normally get foot traffic out here. However, it could be someone who'd been in a car accident and was looking for help.

"Wait," Wally said a moment later. "She's getting up and looking up at the house. She's coming this way, boss."

"Don't go check on her yourself," Leo instructed. "Send two of the other hands and make sure to tell them to be careful. We have two women who are suspects, so whoever it is, she could be armed and dangerous. Report back to me as soon as you know who she is."

"Will do," Wally assured him.

The moment Leo ended the call, he finished getting dressed and motioned for Olivia to follow him. "Tell Izzie to take Cameron and get in the tub with him. I'm going to the front windows to see if I can spot our visitor."

Olivia hated to alarm Cameron or Izzie, but when she hurried into the nursery, she could see that Cameron was asleep. She relayed Leo's orders and then tried to reassure Izzie that it was simply a precaution.

She prayed that's exactly what it was—a precaution.

Once she'd helped Izzie move Cameron into the bathroom, Olivia rushed back out to find Leo. He was in his office, a room on the second floor at the front of the house. He had a pair of binoculars pressed to his eyes and was looking out the window. She hurried to him, but he motioned for her to stay to the side. That, of course, was so that she wouldn't be in the line of fire. Unlike Leo. He was standing there, his weapon drawn and ready for whatever was about to happen.

"I can't tell if it's Bernice or Rena," he told her. "But two hands are in a truck and heading her way."

Olivia stayed to the side of the window, but peered around the frame, hoping to get a glimpse of what was happening. She did. She saw the headlights of the truck making its way down the road. Several moments later, the truck stopped, and the headlights shone right on the woman.

"It's Bernice," Leo muttered. "She's got blood on her face."

So, maybe the car accident theory was right. Except that wouldn't explain what Bernice was doing out here in the first place.

Olivia continued to watch as both men got out of the

truck and walked toward the woman. Bernice fell forward, practically collapsing, before one of them caught her. The second man took out his phone and, seconds later, Leo's phone rang. He put the call on speaker and it didn't take long for the ranch hand's voice to pour through the room.

"The woman says her name is Bernice Saylor," the hand explained. "And she says she needs to see you. She claims that that somebody ran her off the road and then tried to kill her."

Leo had already cursed way too much tonight, so he didn't add more. Though this was definitely a situation that called for profanity.

And caution.

His first instinct was to dismiss this as some kind of dangerous ploy for Bernice to get to him, but then Leo thought of Randall. He, too, had said someone had tried to kill him.

That someone had succeeded, too.

Leo didn't want to take the risk that the same thing would happen with Bernice. Especially if the woman was innocent. But he would need to add some layers of security to the help he gave her.

"I'm calling Barrett," Leo told the hand, Carter Johnson. "Stay put until I do that."

He hadn't even had time to end the call with Carter when there was a loud blast and a fireball shot up from the pasture just to the right of where his ranch hands were standing with Bernice. The two men dropped to the ground, pulling Bernice down with them.

"What the hell?" he heard Carter grumble just as Bernice shouted, "She's trying to kill me."

At least that's what Leo thought they'd said before their voices were drowned out by another blast. Then another. All three flare-ups had been in the pastures, too far from the house to do any damage, but his two hands and Bernice could be in immediate danger.

"Check to make sure Bernice isn't armed," Leo instructed Carter when he came back on the line. "If she's not, put her in the truck and drive her to the house, but don't bring her in. Get out of there fast," he added when there was a fourth blast.

"The flames aren't big enough to burn through the pasture grass," Leo tried to assure Olivia. "But I'll call the fire department anyway."

"I'll do that," Olivia volunteered, taking his phone. "You keep watch."

He didn't turn down her offer because keeping watch was critical right now. Leo doubted that the person who'd set those fires had actually been close enough to light them. No, the fireballs were probably on some kind of timer or device, the way the one in Randall's truck had been. There hadn't been time for Leo to send the hands into the pastures to look for any devices, but clearly there'd been some.

"Tell the fire department to approach with caution, that there could be a sniper in the area," Leo rattled off to her. "And then call Barrett to let him know what's going on. Same rules apply to him," he insisted. "I don't want him caught in the crosshairs of a gunman."

Olivia gave him a nod, a very shaky one, and her hands were trembling a little, but she made the calls. Leo half listened to her relay what he'd told her to say, but he kept his focus on his ranch hands and Bernice. She didn't protest when Carter frisked her. He must not have found any weapons because, seconds after, he all but carried Bernice to the truck and put her inside.

Another fireball shot up. This one was at the end of the drive, and it was different from the others. Those first ones had been blasts, but this was more of a line of fire that created a wall to prevent someone from getting to or from the house. It was as if someone had poured gasoline onto the asphalt and then lit it. Of course, that could have been done with a timer, as well.

And that was also why he had no intention of trusting Bernice.

Olivia was still on the phone with Barrett when the truck started toward the house. The lights slashed through the darkness, and Leo used that light to try to glimpse anyone who might have managed to sneak onto the grounds. He didn't see anyone, but that didn't mean someone wasn't out there. That's why he wanted Izzie to stay put with Cameron until he was certain the place was secure.

"Oh God," he heard Olivia say.

Leo whipped toward her. "What's wrong?" he demanded.

"Barrett was leaving his house and a firebomb went off at the end of his driveway."

Hell. Leo knew that wasn't a coincidence. "Is Della there with him?"

"Yes," Olivia verified, her voice now shaking as much as the rest of her.

"Then tell Barrett to stay put," Leo insisted.

Barrett's fiancée, Della, was pregnant, and Leo didn't want to put her or their baby at risk by Barrett leaving her alone. Della was a deputy sheriff and could likely take care of herself, but the person behind these attacks could try to take Della hostage and use her as leverage. Leo couldn't do that to Della or Barrett.

"See if Daniel can come," Leo told her. "But let him know what he could be up against and tell him that he'll have to use the trails to get here."

Olivia finished her call with Barrett and made the one to Daniel just as Leo watched Carter pull the truck to a stop in front of the house. Not too close, though. And there was a lot of open yard between the vehicle and the house. If Bernice got out and tried to run toward them, there'd be plenty of ranch hands to stop her.

He heard the soft ding on his phone to indicate an incoming call. A moment later Olivia said, "It's Carter." Handing him his phone, she added, "Daniel's coming ASAP."

Leo had no doubts that Daniel would indeed try to get here fast, but he had to wonder if there'd be another fire. Another distraction. Something that would stop backup from getting to the ranch.

"Carter," Leo said when he took the incoming call. "What's going on?"

"The woman wasn't armed," the ranch hand answered. "That's about all I know right now. That, and what she's saying about somebody trying to kill her. But I don't know who set those fires. I didn't see anybody, boss, and I've been keeping watch for hours."

"The fires could have been rigged days ago," Leo explained. In fact, they could have been set even before the one that'd taken out Randall's truck. The bomb squad hadn't gone out into the pastures to look for more devices because they'd concentrated on the house and the outbuildings.

"Put Bernice on the phone," Leo instructed Carter.

It didn't take long for Carter to do that and Leo soon heard Bernice. "Thank you for saving me," the woman blustered, her words running together. "She nearly killed me."

Leo had plenty of questions, but he started with the big one. "Who tried to kill you?"

"Rena." Bernice didn't hesitate, either. "She ran me off the road and then tried to shoot me. I got away from her."

"Rena," he repeated, both skeptical and curious. He didn't doubt that Rena was capable of doing something like this, but he also had no doubt that Bernice could be lying. "Where did all of this happen?"

"Just up the main road, not far from your ranch. I was coming here because of Samuel. He's distraught, and I thought I could talk Olivia into calling him. I guess Rena followed me."

Leo didn't press the point that it was a stupid idea for Bernice to try to convince Olivia to call her father. There were too many other things he needed to know. Obviously, things that Olivia should know, as well, because she was leaning closer to listen to the conversation. Leo didn't want her in front of the window so he switched the call to speaker.

"You're sure it was Rena who ran you off the road?" Leo pressed. "You saw her?"

Now, Bernice paused. "Not exactly. But I saw the logo on the door of the SUV. Rena was at the estate, and she must have taken it."

Maybe. Or it could have been Samuel in the vehicle. The man might have had motive to off his estate manager after what'd gone on between them in the sheriff's office. Then again, maybe Bernice and Samuel had mended fences if she was telling the truth about trying to convince Olivia to speak to him.

But that was a big *if.*

"Stay put in the truck with my ranch hands," Leo told Bernice. "And I mean stay put. I'm going to call Rena to see if I can get her side of this."

"She'll just lie," Bernice insisted. "She'll say I made it all up."

Yeah, she might, but Leo ended the call with Bernice. Since he didn't have Rena's number handy, he worked his way through the dispatcher to have the deputy place the call. During that wait, he also looked at Olivia to make sure she was okay.

She wasn't.

All of this was giving her another slam of fear, and he hated to see it in her eyes. Hated that he wouldn't be able to stop it until he'd worked out this situation with Bernice and now Rena.

"You could wait in the nursery," he suggested. "You could be with Cameron."

She glanced at the doorway. Then back at him. And Olivia shook her head. "No one can get into the nursery without us knowing. The security alarm would go off if someone tried to get into the house."

He nodded and would have tried to give her some kind of assurance that everything would be okay, but the call to Rena finally went through. The phone rang and rang, and just when Leo figured a voice mail recording would kick in, she answered. Or rather, someone did.

"I'm hurt."

It was a woman, and it was possible it was Rena. It was hard to tell, however, because the voice was muffled—a reminder of the other calls that had been mentioned in this investigation.

"Rena?" he asked.

"Yes, it's me. I'm hurt," she repeated.

A muffled voice as well as injuries could be faked, and Leo had no idea if that was the case. "Where are you? What happened?"

"I'm hurt," she repeated. "Help me."

Leo frowned because she hadn't answered either of his questions. He tried again. "I'll help you as soon as you tell me where you are."

Of course, he could try to have the call traced and her location pinpointed by using the cell towers, but all of that would take time.

There was a long silence before Rena muttered, "I'm in one of your pastures, I think. I think I can see the lights from your house."

Hell. He didn't want her that close, and it really didn't help him pinpoint her location since he had hundreds of acres of pastures. Plus, it was possible that the lights she was seeing weren't from his house but rather one of the outbuildings.

"How'd you get in my pasture?" he snapped.

"Um, I was looking for Samuel." Her breath was pitched and labored.

Well, that seemed to be tonight's trend for the women in Samuel's life. Leo didn't bother to ask her why she thought Samuel would be at his place.

"Use the landline," he instructed Olivia, tipping his head to the phone on his desk. "Call an ambulance and tell the EMTs what Rena just said. But they need to approach with caution."

"Because this could be a trap," Olivia supplied with a nod.

"Not a trap." Rena's voice was even more slurred now than when she'd first answered. In fact, if this was an act, she was doing a damn good job of it.

"The ambulance is on the way," Olivia relayed several moments later.

"You hear that?" Leo asked Rena as he kept watch out the window. Because this entire conversation could be a distraction so that someone could sneak onto the ranch. "An ambulance will be here soon. What are your injuries?"

There were some moans, and it sounded as if she was moving around. "My head. Everything's spinning around. And I'm bleeding. God, I'm bleeding."

"Tell me what happened," Leo persisted.

"I'm not sure. I was driving and everything started spinning. My head's bleeding. I'm hurt, so I must have wrecked. I wrecked and then I got out and started walking to get help."

"You could have used your phone to call 9-1-1," he pointed out.

"Not thinking straight. So dizzy." There was a thud. It sounded as if Rena had fallen.

Leo wasn't ready to give up. Besides, he needed to keep Rena on the phone until the EMTs arrived and managed to find her. If she was talking, they might be able to hear the sound of her voice. However, he did have to wonder if she'd been drugged—just as Simone had been. But that was something he'd need to figure out later.

"Did you just try to kill Bernice?" Leo demanded. "She said you did."

"Bernice?" she mumbled.

"That's right. Bernice. Did you try to kill her?" he asked.

"No." She muttered some things he couldn't make out. "But I know who tried to kill you."

"Who?" Leo snapped.

Nothing. No moans, no more sounds of Rena moving around.

"Rena?" Leo said. "Say something. Keep talking to me."

Still nothing, and that started a war within him. If Rena was indeed hurt, he needed to get to her to try to save her life. But he couldn't leave Olivia, Cameron and Izzie. He certainly couldn't leave them long enough to go wandering around his pastures, looking for Rena.

"I need to talk to Bernice," he declared. "Not on the phone. I need to get in her face to see for myself if she knows what's going on."

Olivia touched her fingers to her lips for a moment. Obviously, she was having the same internal battle as he was. Except she had the added concern of not wanting him to get hurt.

"I'll get Carter to move the truck closer to the house so I won't have to cross the yard," Leo explained. "And I'll have him wait inside with you until I'm done with Bernice. You can stay up here but keep away from the windows." He paused, hating to add this last part since he knew it was only going to put more alarm on her face. "There's a gun on the top shelf of the closet." He tipped his head to the door just a few feet away from his desk.

Olivia nodded, and because he figured they both could use it, he gave her a quick kiss. Leo pulled back, looked at her. And then gave her another kiss that wasn't so quick.

"I won't be long," he said and hoped that was true.

Keeping his gun ready, he called Carter while he went downstairs. Leo waited at the front door until the hand had moved the truck right up to the porch. Even then Leo waited until Carter was out and at the door before he disarmed the security system to let the hand in.

"No matter what happens," Leo told him, "protect Olivia, Cameron and Izzie."

"I will, boss," Carter assured him.

Leo dragged in a long breath and, hoping this wasn't a huge mistake, stepped outside and hurried to the truck. He got in behind the wheel and immediately turned to face Bernice who was in the center with the other hand, Edwin Dade, on the passenger's side.

Bernice did have blood on her face, along with some cuts and scrapes. None looked serious. Being the skeptical cop that he was, Leo decided they could have been self-inflicted.

"Start talking," Leo told Bernice. "You said Rena tried to kill you, and I want details."

"Of course." Bernice took her own deep breath.

But before she could say a word, all hell broke loose and the front end of the truck exploded.

Olivia's heart went to her knees when she heard the blast. This one was much louder than the others, and when she glanced out the window of Leo's office, she saw smoke and flames shoot out from the truck.

Oh God.

Someone had used a firebomb on the truck, and Leo was inside it.

She hurried out of the office, made it halfway down the stairs before she saw the thick black smoke. Not only in the truck now. It was billowing in through the front door where Carter stood. "Go help Leo," she insisted.

Carter had already started in that direction, and Olivia went down the rest of the stairs to look out to see if she could spot Leo. She couldn't. She couldn't even tell how much of the truck was still intact. It could be blown to bits.

Leo could be dead.

The hoarse sob left her throat. Tears stung her eyes. But then so did the smoke and it wasn't long before she started to cough. She had no choice but to close the door because she couldn't breathe. She also couldn't risk the smoke and fire getting to Cameron.

As much as she wanted to see Leo, Olivia knew she had to protect their son. She raced back up the stairs, going straight to the nursery. The fist around her heart loosened a little when she saw that her baby was asleep in Izzie's arms.

"What happened?" Izzie asked.

Olivia couldn't speak. Her throat had clamped shut and her fear for Leo was skyrocketing.

"Just stay put," she managed to tell Izzie. She ran back out, racing into Leo's office so she could get a better look at the truck.

She cursed the smoke that had blanketed the entire front yard and the front of the house, but she could see someone moving around. Carter, she realized when, a moment later, he pulled someone from the truck.

Leo.

Mercy, Leo looked unconscious, or worse, and the hand had to drag him away from the burning truck. She reached for the landline to call an ambulance, only to remember that one was already on the way. So was the fire department. Maybe they would both get here soon. And while she was hoping, she added a plea that the EMTs would be able to get past that fire on the road. It was still blazing, as were the ones in the pasture. But those fires didn't have the thick smoke like the one in the truck.

Olivia continued to keep watch, knowing that she was breaking Leo's order for her to stay away from the windows. She couldn't. She had to see if he was all right; it crushed her to think that she could lose him.

She was in love with him and had been since they'd first become lovers. Olivia knew that now—for all the good it'd do because she might not get a chance to ever tell him.

There was more movement in the smoke, but she lost sight of where Carter had taken Leo. She lost sight of pretty much anything when the smoke billowed up, blocking any view she had from the window.

But Olivia could still hear.

And she heard something that put her body on full alert.

She hadn't seen anyone come into the house, but she was pretty sure she heard footsteps in the foyer. Then the front door closing. She nearly rushed back downstairs to see if it was Leo, but everything inside her warned her that it wasn't.

Someone was in the house.

Someone who could try to kill her and get to Cameron.

Everything froze for a moment. Her feet. Her breath.

Maybe even her heart. But nothing stopped the fear that shot like icy fingers up her spine.

She forced herself to stay quiet. To think. And she remembered Leo telling her about the gun. Stepping as softly as she could, she went to his office closet and, moving to her tiptoes, felt around until she found it. She'd had some firearms training—*some*—and prayed that she remembered it. Maybe, just maybe, it wouldn't even be necessary.

With the gun gripped in her hands, Olivia made her way to the office door and looked out. The smoke was still there, thick in the foyer and drifting up the stairs. There were just enough breaks in the drifts for her to see someone walking up the steps toward her.

"Leo?" she blurted.

"No," someone answered. The voice was muffled, but Olivia had no trouble hearing what was said. "Move, and I start shooting. And I won't be careful about keeping the shots away from your little boy."

Chapter 16

Leo's lungs were on fire, and he couldn't catch his breath. Worse, he couldn't see squat, but he forced himself to try to clear his head. To think. To remember what the hell had happened to him.

He felt around and realized he was lying on the grass. Maybe his yard. There was smoke everywhere, along with the stench of burning rubber and gasoline. He was coughing, but so was someone else. He soon realized that someone else was Carter. The ranch hand was on his knees next to Leo, and he was trying to bat away the smoke.

Groaning, Leo tried to sit, but he failed on the first try. His head was throbbing, and he was dizzy, but he'd thankfully managed to hang on to his gun.

"The truck blew up," Carter mumbled in between coughs.

It wasn't easy, but Leo picked through the memories

in his spinning head and tried to piece things together. Yeah, there had been some kind of explosion. Maybe one of the firebombs. And it'd indeed ripped through the front end of the truck. The airbags had deployed. But that wasn't the reason his head was throbbing.

No.

Leo remembered someone clubbing him.

Who had done that? Bernice maybe? Maybe someone who'd come up from outside the truck? He just didn't know, but he sure as hell was about to figure that out.

Cameron. Olivia. Those two names made it through the blistering pain and the dizziness. Olivia and Cameron were inside his house, a house that could be on fire, and he had to get them out.

He cursed, getting to his hands and knees so he could try to lever himself up and stand. Leo finally managed it, with Carter's help, but he wasn't sure he could make it even a step without falling.

"I think Edwin's still in the truck," Carter said, still coughing. "Wally and some of the other hands went running over there, I think. I think," he repeated to let Leo he wasn't sure of that at all. "I need to get Edwin away from the fire."

Damn. Leo hadn't worked his thoughts around to the ranch hand who'd been in the truck with him, but now he looked back at the truck. Or rather, what was left of it. It was about thirty feet away from him, and the front end was definitely on fire. It was those flames that were causing the smothering black smoke.

"Go to Edwin," Leo told Carter. "And if Bernice is still in the truck, get her out, too."

Leo wanted to help, but he had no intention of doing that at Olivia's and Cameron's expense. He needed to get to them, to take them to safety. Heaven knew, though, where that would be right now, but the cruiser was still in the yard. He could get them inside and drive away from the burning truck, away from the house. Maybe then they'd be safe.

Carter hurried in the direction of the truck and disappeared into the curtain of smoke. Leo got moving, too, though each step was an effort. The seconds were just ticking by, and each second was time he needed to rescue Izzie, Olivia and his son.

Leo hadn't even made it to the porch when he heard the footsteps behind him. With his gun aimed as best he could manage, he whirled in that direction. He'd expected to see one of his hands since they'd no doubt be coming to help, but it wasn't.

It was Samuel.

"Don't shoot," the man said, lifting his hands in the air. His breath was gusting and his face was covered with sweat.

"What the hell are you doing here?" Leo snarled, but figured he knew the answer. Samuel was there to try to kill him.

Maybe.

Leo shook his head because that didn't make sense. If Samuel had wanted him dead, he could have shot him in the back. Leo knew with his head injury, he probably wouldn't have even seen it coming.

"I got an anonymous call," Samuel answered. He was coughing, too, and trying to bat the smoke away from his face. "And the caller said Olivia had been taken hostage, that I was to get here as fast as I could. I had to leave my SUV at the end of the road because of the fire, and I ran the rest of the way here."

Leo wished his head would stop throbbing for just a second so he could figure out if that was the truth. Then, he decided it didn't matter. The only thing that mattered right now was Olivia and Cameron, and he didn't have time to interrogate her father. Or to arrest him.

"Wait here," Leo told him. "I'll deal with you when I get back."

Samuel didn't listen. He was right on Leo's heels as he made his way up the porch steps. "Is Olivia inside? Has she really been taken?" Samuel's two questions ran together, and his panic and fear sure sounded genuine.

Sounded.

But Leo wasn't about to take that reaction at face value. Too bad he didn't have any cuffs on him that he could use to restrain Samuel, but he did do a quick frisk of the man. Samuel didn't stop him and voluntarily handed Leo the handgun he'd been wearing in a shoulder holster.

"I need to make sure Olivia and Cameron are okay," Samuel said between his coughs. His breathing sounded more labored than Leo's.

Leo didn't waste time arguing with the man. He bolted into the foyer and glanced around. Olivia wasn't there, but someone had tracked dirt onto the floor. Maybe Carter when Leo had sent the hand in to stay with Olivia.

But the feeling in his gut told him it hadn't been Carter, that it'd been someone with bad intentions.

That got Leo moving faster as he headed for the stairs. Again, Samuel was right behind him.

"I didn't know," Samuel said. "I swear I didn't."

While Leo very much wanted to know what the man meant by that, he didn't respond. "Olivia?" he called out.

He listened for her to answer while he drowned out the other noises. The ranch hands in the yard who were apparently trying to put out the truck fire. He could hear water running, so they were likely using the hose. In the distance, he also heard the wail of sirens. Maybe the ambulance and fire department. Maybe Daniel. But what Leo didn't hear was Olivia.

Leo called out her name again and, despite his blurred vision, he hurried up the stairs. There was some smoke here, too, and the lights were off. But Leo could still see the gun on the floor. The gun that Olivia had no doubt taken from his office closet.

And he could see Olivia.

His heart stopped.

There was Olivia in the dark hall. Not alone. Someone was behind her. And that someone had a gun aimed at her head.

Dragging Samuel with him, Leo automatically ducked for cover behind the wall at the top of the stairs, but he glanced out to see if he had a shot to take out Olivia's captor.

He didn't.

The person was using Olivia as a shield. Hell. Olivia could be killed.

"The caller was right," Samuel declared, and he would have darted from cover if Leo hadn't held him back.

Yeah, the caller was right, and later, Leo would figure out if Olivia's captor had made that call and if Samuel was in on this plan. He didn't appear to be. He seemed to be just as shaken as Leo, but Leo didn't trust the man one bit.

"If you do anything stupid," Leo warned Samuel, "I'll kill you. Understand? You're not going to do anything that'll put Olivia or Cameron in any more danger than they already are."

Samuel must have seen that Leo wasn't bluffing, that he would indeed kill him, because the man quit struggling. Groaning, he sank onto the stairs.

"Help her," Samuel said like a plea. "Help her."

That was the plan. Well, as soon as he had a plan, that would be Leo's top priority. For now he had to figure out what was going on. Since Olivia was obviously a hostage, he had to find out what her captor wanted.

"I'm Deputy Leo Logan," he said, identifying himself. And while he was a thousand percent sure it wouldn't work, he added, "Throw down your weapon."

He couldn't be sure, but he thought the person laughed.

"I'm sorry, Leo," Olivia called out, her voice trembling. "I didn't have a choice."

Hearing her caused so many things to hit Leo at once. Fear—yeah, it was there big-time—and a sickening dread that he'd made a huge mistake by going outside to question Bernice. If he hadn't done that, if he'd stayed put, he would have been inside and stopped this.

Leo glanced out just as Olivia opened her mouth as if to say more, but her captor jammed the gun harder against her head. Leo wanted to rip the person apart when he saw the trickle of blood slide down Olivia's cheek.

"I told her if she didn't throw down the gun," the captor said, "that I'd start shooting."

The rage came like a low, dangerous simmer, and Leo had no doubts that it would soon go full-boil. This SOB had just threatened not only Olivia but also Cameron. The nursery was just two doors down from where Olivia was standing.

Leo pushed everything out of his mind—or rather, tried to do that—to focus on the voice. Not a normal speaking voice. This was a mix of gravel and hoarse whisper. Obviously a ploy to disguise who was speaking. And it was working. Leo didn't know if this was a hired thug or one of their two remaining suspects, Rena and Bernice.

"I was afraid one of the bullets would hit Cameron," Olivia said in a mutter. "So I yelled for Izzie to stay put with him."

Yeah, he was right there with her on this. Like Olivia, he would have done whatever it took to stop someone from firing a gun this close to Cameron. Still would. That meant this couldn't come down to a shooting match even if Olivia could get clear enough for Leo to have a shot.

"Who are you?" Leo asked. "What do you want?"

"I'm leaving with Olivia, and you're going to make sure that happens," her captor readily answered. "I need a vehicle."

"That's your plan?" Leo taunted. "To go driving out of here with Olivia?"

"That's my plan that'll work," the person countered. This time the voice was louder, not so much of a whisper, and Leo was almost certain that it was a woman's voice.

"Is that Bernice or Rena talking?" Leo murmured to Samuel.

The man's head snapped up, the shock in his eyes, which meant he hadn't considered it to be either of them. And maybe it wasn't. After all, it could be a female hired gun.

To give Samuel another chance to listen to the captor's voice, Leo went with another question. "I'll get you the vehicle," he said, "but tell me what you want. Is it money?"

However, before Leo got an answer, someone called out from the bottom floor. "Boss? You okay?"

Wally.

Leo had to make a snap decision. He didn't want to put another person in danger, and that's exactly what would happen if Wally came upstairs. Added to that, it might spook the captor and cause her to start firing.

"Wally, I need a truck brought around to the back of the house," Leo instructed. "Park close to the porch and leave the keys in the ignition."

"Uh, sure. Are you okay?" Wally repeated. Since Wally wasn't an idiot, he knew something was wrong, but hopefully he wouldn't do something to escalate this standoff.

"Tell him to hurry," the captor snapped.

"Hurry," Leo added to Wally and looked back at Olivia. He wished he could do something to ease that terror in her eyes, but the only thing that would make that go away was to get her out of this situation.

"How much money to do you want?" Leo asked the person holding her. "Or are you after some kind of leverage. I'm guessing this is a whole lot more than you wanting me to fix a parking ticket."

"I'll pay whatever you want," Samuel added. "Just name your price."

The person made a strange sound. A snarl dripping with outrage.

"Enough of this!" Olivia's captor spat the words out and before Leo could even react, bashed Olivia on the head.

"Stop!" Leo shouted, trying to take aim. But he didn't have a shot because the captor dragged Olivia back up and put her in a choke hold.

And that's when he saw the face.

Bernice.

* * *

The pain shot through Olivia, so fast, so strong, that she wouldn't have been able to stay on her feet had her captor not latched onto her. And was now choking her.

Bernice.

She was trying to kill her.

Olivia didn't know why—not yet—but it had to have something to do with her father. Was that why he was there? Olivia had only caught a glimpse of him, but she'd seen him with Leo.

And Leo had been hurt.

There'd been blood on his head and, while he'd looked formidable, he'd also looked a little dazed. Like her. Mercy. Had her father done that to him?

Olivia somehow managed to catch her breath and jab her elbow into Bernice's stomach. The woman grunted in pain but only dug the barrel of the gun in harder on Olivia's head.

She didn't know where Bernice had gotten the weapon since she knew the ranch hands had frisked her before they'd put her in the truck. But, obviously, she'd managed to get her hands on one.

And would without hesitation use it to kill.

Olivia only hoped she found out why this was happening. She didn't want to die without knowing that, and not without knowing that Leo and Cameron would be safe. If necessary, she'd sacrifice herself for them.

But so would Leo.

In fact, he was no doubt trying to figure out how to get her out of this.

Olivia heard Leo's phone ring. It was in his jeans' pocket, but he didn't answer it. Seconds later, it rang again.

"Let's move," Bernice ordered and practically shoved

her forward. Something that Bernice didn't need to do. Olivia desperately wanted to put as much distance as she could between Cameron and Bernice's gun. "If the truck's not there waiting for us, then I start putting bullets in you. Is that what you want, Leo? You want your lover to bleed out in front of you?"

"No." Leo stepped out, much too far, and gave Olivia a quick glance before he fastened his gaze on Bernice. "I'd make a better hostage than Olivia," he proclaimed, attempting to bargain. "Nobody will fire at you if you have me."

"I don't want you." There was so much anger and venom in Bernice's voice.

"But you tried to have me killed," Leo fired back. "That's why you hired Milton. You called him from the estate to tell him to go ahead with the attack."

Bernice certainly didn't deny that, and with her grip still tight on Olivia's neck, they moved forward a few more steps. "I wanted Olivia arrested," Bernice spelled out. "I wanted her in jail."

"For Samuel," Leo stated. Unlike Bernice's, his voice was nearly calm now, but there was a dangerous cop's edge to it. Like a rattler ready to strike. "You did all of this for him, didn't you?"

"Did you?" her father asked. He moved out from cover, too. "God, Bernice. Did you do this for me?"

Bernice wasn't so quick to answer this time. "Yes, and you repaid me by getting back together with Rena. I would have done anything for you. *Anything.*" She emphasized the word, sounding more than a little frantic. "And you kept throwing that gold-digging bimbo in my face."

Olivia thought of Rena and wondered if the woman was still alive. Maybe Bernice had taken care of her before she'd come here. Clearly, this was a last-ditch mission to finish what she'd started. A mission that had left two dead. Possibly even more.

"I'll go with you, Bernice," Samuel offered. He stepped even farther out, too far now to dive back to cover if Bernice fired at him. "Leave Olivia, and I'll go with you. We can get out of the country, some place that doesn't have extradition."

Olivia sucked in a breath. Held it. She knew there was no way her father would actually do that. This was a ploy to try to free her, and she welcomed it. Not because she thought it would work, but because he might be able to at least distract Bernice while Leo and she did something.

"Move down the stairs now," Bernice ordered Leo and Samuel. "No stupid tricks, either, or I'll start firing. I know where the nursery is. I heard when the nanny answered Olivia, and that's where I'll aim the shots."

Olivia was close enough now to see the look in Leo's eyes. The rage. She felt the same. How could this witch threaten their son like that? And all because she had wrongly believed that Samuel owed her something. Maybe owed her love. Well, Olivia wasn't going to let Bernice take away the people she loved.

Leo and her father walked backward down the stairs, each of them watching every move that Bernice and she were making. Olivia tried to calculate the best place for her to make a stand—whatever that stand would be, though, she didn't know. Not yet. But if she could just get Bernice out of the house, then it might lessen the risk for Cameron.

It would increase her own risk, though. Because there was no way Bernice would keep her alive once she'd finished using her as a shield.

"Bernice," Samuel tried again. "Please stop this."

"Shut up," she snapped. "Leo, you'd better tell your ranch hands to back off once we're outside."

"Hear that, Wally?" Leo said, and from the corner of her eye, Olivia saw the man in the foyer. He was still armed, but like Leo, he didn't have a safe shot. "Let the other hands know to back off."

With his eyes wide, Wally nodded and took out his phone. "Daniel's at the end of the road," he relayed. "He's walking up now. Said he tried to call you but that you didn't answer your phone."

So that's who had been trying to get in touch with Leo. Good. Daniel was a smart lawman. He might be able to lie in wait and do something to stop Bernice.

The moment Bernice had Olivia on the bottom floor, the woman started moving her through the open living room and into the kitchen. Olivia kept her attention focused on Leo, looking for any signs of what they could do. He seemed steady. Determined. And he was watching every step that Bernice took.

Olivia wished the woman would trip but then rethought that. Bernice's first instinct might be to pull the trigger, and they were literally right below the nursery.

Bernice's hold finally loosened as Olivia felt the woman reach behind her. She heard the rattle of the doorknob as Bernice unlocked the door and used her elbow to push it open.

Olivia immediately felt the rush of the still hot summer air. Air tainted with the stench of smoke. She prayed that the hands had been able to put out the fire so that it couldn't spread to the house.

"The truck's waiting for you," Leo said.

Because Bernice quickly regained her choke hold,

Olivia couldn't see the truck, but she could hear the engine running. Could also hear some muffled conversation, no doubt from the hands.

Bernice's arms were already tense, the muscles knotted to the point where it had to be painful. Olivia hoped she was in pain anyway. Hoped that her pain would get a whole lot worse before this was over. Olivia wanted the woman to pay for all the misery she'd caused.

Muttering obscenities, Bernice stepped onto the porch and immediately shifted Olivia to the side. No doubt so that she could check out the truck while keeping an eye on Leo and Samuel.

"Bernice, if you do this, I'll kill you," her father said. He was practically shoulder to shoulder with Leo as they slowly made their way to the porch. Leo still had hold of his gun, and her father's hands were balled into fists.

Olivia felt Bernice's muscles tighten even more. "No, you won't kill me," Bernice snapped like a challenge. "Because I'll kill you first."

Bernice shifted the gun, obviously trying to aim it at her father. Leo brought up his weapon, too, and in that split second, Olivia knew she had to do something to stop Bernice from killing them both.

With the adrenaline slamming through her, Olivia threw her weight against Bernice, ramming her body into the woman's. It worked. Bernice started to fall backward.

But she took Olivia with her.

Olivia's head bashed against the porch floor and the two of them tumbled down the steps together.

Just as Bernice pulled the trigger.

Chapter 17

Leo shouted for Bernice to stop, but he knew it wouldn't do any good. Nor could he get to Olivia in time. He was running toward the women as they fell.

And as the shot blasted through the air.

He refused to think that the shot had hit Olivia. Refused to believe that she could be hurt or dead.

Bernice was definitely alive, though. Despite the fall, the woman tried to aim her gun at him. Leo did something about that. He kicked it out of her hand. The gun went flying and he didn't bother to look where it landed. He gave Bernice a kick, too, right in her face, and the woman wailed, falling back into the yard.

Leo kept his eye on Bernice, but he took hold of Olivia's arm and pulled her back onto the porch. That was a risk, since moving her could aggravate her injuries, but he needed to get her away from Bernice.

He cursed when he saw the blood on Olivia's face. Blood on her shirt, too, and she was moaning in pain. Maybe from a gunshot wound, or maybe just from the wounds she'd gotten in the fall.

"Check on Cameron," Leo called out to no one in particular, but he knew one of his hands would do that. After all, the shot Bernice had fired could have gone into the nursery.

"Help Olivia," Leo added to Samuel as he readied himself to ease her out of his arms so he could jump down in the yard and deal with Bernice.

But Samuel beat him to it.

Samuel rushed past him, barreling down the steps and snatching up Bernice's gun. He dropped to his knees and in the same motion grabbed on to the woman's hair, dragging her head off the ground.

He put the gun to the center of Bernice's forehead.

"Any last words before I kill you?" Samuel asked. Of course, there was emotion in his voice.

The wrong kind of emotion.

Not anger or fear from what had just happened. This was an icy-cold hatred that Leo knew could cause the man to commit murder. And that's exactly what it would be if he pulled the trigger now and shot an unarmed woman. Leo couldn't let her life end like this.

"Samuel," Leo said, keeping his tone as calm as he could manage. "We need to help Olivia. We have to make sure Cameron is okay."

"Any last words before I kill you?" Samuel repeated, shouting the words at Bernice.

The woman's face was covered with blood, and her nose was likely broken, but she still managed to look defiant. "I loved you," Bernice told him. "And you betrayed me. Go ahead. Kill me. Then, you'll have to live with that for the rest of your life."

A life Samuel might spend behind bars if he actually pulled the trigger. Leo didn't care much for the man, but he didn't want things to end like this.

"Dad…" Olivia murmured, her soft voice carrying over the sound of the truck engine and Samuel's ragged breaths. "Let Leo arrest her. Bernice will spend every day she's got left in a cage."

A hoarse sob broke from Samuel's throat, but he kept the gun in place. "I believe Bernice killed your mother. I think she gave Simone those drugs that made her wreck the car. She could have killed you."

Bernice certainly didn't deny any of that. Just the opposite. "I did what I needed to do."

And there it was. The confession that Olivia had no doubt waited years to hear.

Keeping watch on Bernice and Samuel, Leo slipped his arm around Olivia and helped her get to her feet. She practically sagged against him, but considering everything that'd happened, she was a lot steadier than he'd thought she would be.

"I stopped Simone from divorcing you and taking your daughter," Bernice told Samuel. There was the same cold rage in her voice now that had been in Samuel's. "I would have done the same to stop Olivia from taking Cameron from you."

So, that was her motive. It turned Leo's blood to ice to think that Bernice had nearly gotten away with it.

Leo spotted Daniel peering around corner of the house, but motioned for his brother to stay back. With Samuel still armed, Leo didn't want him getting spooked and shooting Bernice.

"Dad, you need to put down your gun," Olivia tried again. "We don't want any more shots fired. It could scare Cameron."

Leo finally saw something he wanted to see. Samuel pulled back the gun. It was still aimed at Bernice, but was no longer pressed to her forehead.

"I want her dead," Samuel said, his shoulders shaking with his sobs. "I want her to pay."

"And she will," Leo assured him. Since he wasn't sure Olivia could stay standing without his support, he motioned for Daniel to move in. "My brother will take Bernice into custody. She'll be charged with murder, murder for hire and a whole bunch of other charges. Olivia was right about her spending the rest of her life in a cage."

"As if I care," Bernice snarled, still challenging Samuel with her fierce stare. "Go ahead and kill me." She smiled, a sick smile given the blood trickling out of her mouth.

"Bernice wants to die by your hand," Olivia told her father. "That way, she can keep on punishing you because you'll have to come to terms with what's gone on here. She wants you to suffer. Make her suffer instead."

That finally seemed to get through to Samuel. He leaned away from Bernice and sat back on the ground. Daniel moved in closer, reached down and took the gun from Samuel's hand.

"You were supposed to kill me!" Bernice shouted, darting glances around the yard. "It wasn't supposed to end like this."

Daniel ignored her shouts, hauled Bernice up and slapped a pair of plastic cuffs on her wrists.

Leo didn't want to give the woman another moment

of his attention, nor did he want to keep Olivia outside. He turned to lead Olivia back inside so they could check on Cameron. And so he could see how bad her injuries were. However, before he could do that, Wally came hurrying out.

"Cameron and the nanny are fine," Wally said. "Not a scratch on them."

This time Leo thought Olivia sagged from relief as she went into his arms and buried her face against Leo's neck. "He's okay. Our baby's okay."

Yeah, and Leo felt a mountain of relief of his own. Bernice hadn't done her worst. She hadn't managed to hurt their son.

"I would have killed her had she hurt Cameron," Samuel said, looking up at them. He moved closer and sank onto the bottom porch step. He looked exhausted and beaten down. Like a man who'd lost way too much and might not recover from those losses.

Considering their past, Leo was surprised that he felt any sympathy for Samuel. But he did. It had to be hard coming to terms with the fact that he'd been living under the same roof with his wife's killer.

"I told Izzie to stay put until you got up there," Wally said, breaking the silence. "Didn't figure you'd want Cameron out here. Also didn't figure you'd want him to see Olivia and you like this, all covered with blood."

They were, indeed, covered with blood, and Wally was right. Leo didn't want Cameron anywhere near Bernice.

Leo pulled back and took a moment to examine Olivia. There was a gash on her head that needed tending, and from what he could tell, that's where most of the blood had come from. Still, she'd need to go the hospital.

"The truck fire's out," Wally told them a moment later, giving Leo yet more good news. Wally tipped his head to Bernice. "You want me to help Daniel get her out of here?"

Leo definitely wanted that. "Yeah. Bring the cruiser to the backyard and see if Carter or one of the other hands can go through every inch of the house to make sure it's secure. And call for an ambulance," Leo added.

"It's already here," Daniel supplied. "Well, it's nearby anyway. The fire department's putting out the flames on the road, and the ambulance can get up here then. We might need two ambulances, though. Edwin's hurt. So is Rena. I found her trying to crawl through the pasture to get to the road."

Leo certainly hadn't forgotten about Rena, but she wasn't a high priority for him now. Obviously, though, she was for Samuel.

"How bad is she hurt?" he asked.

Daniel shrugged and kept his hand clamped around Bernice's arm. "Not sure. But I don't think she has a lot of injuries. She seemed drugged to me."

"That bimbo was supposed to die in a car crash like Simone," Bernice snarled.

So that's what had happened to Rena. It would add another count of attempted murder to the charges that would be filed against Bernice.

"The idiot I hired to steal the journals from Olivia's house was going to doctor them," Bernice added, "to make it look as if Simone was afraid Rena would kill her."

It wouldn't have worked since Olivia had made copies of the journal pages, but Bernice obviously hadn't known that. That also meant burning down Olivia's house had been all for nothing.

Bernice glanced around the yard again, putting Leo on alert. He eased Olivia behind him and readied his gun in case there was about to be another attack.

"I think she's looking for her hired thug," Daniel said, his voice as calm as a lake. "When I was walking up the road, and before I spotted Rena, I caught some guy hiding in a ditch. According to his driver's license, his name is Frank Sutton. I cuffed him, and a couple of the hands are guarding him until I can get back down there."

Bernice made a sound of outrage and tried to ram her body into Daniel's. Daniel just slung her around and yanked back her arms.

"Guess Bernice isn't too happy about losing the last of her lackeys," Daniel commented.

"You're sure he's the last one?" Olivia asked.

"Yeah," Daniel confirmed. "Sutton was pretty chatty and got even chattier when I mentioned that the first to make a full confession would be the one to get a lighter sentence. I didn't bother to tell him that the lighter sentence would just be taking the death penalty off the table, so the guy prattled on. He claims that Bernice hired him to attach a firebomb to underside of the truck when the hands drove down to check on her."

Leo hadn't spotted anyone doing that, but it would have been possible. The guy could have used the ditch for cover and sneaked out of it when the hands had been talking to Bernice.

In the distance, Leo finally heard the ambulance sirens coming closer. It wouldn't be long before they arrived and he could get Olivia the medical help she needed.

Carter and another ranch hand came out from the side of the house, heading straight to Daniel in case he needed help with Bernice, but Leo thought his brother had it under control. Better yet, Leo no longer had that feeling in his gut that something was wrong. For the first time since this all began, he thought the danger might finally be over.

"You took a risk putting a firebomb in the truck and having it go off while you were in it," Leo pointed out to Bernice just as Wally pulled the cruiser into the backyard.

Bernice clammed up. Probably because she didn't want to fill in any blanks for them. But apparently her lackey had already done that.

"According to our chatty *friend*, Frank Sutton, the firebomb didn't have much juice," Daniel explained. "Just enough to mess up the front of the truck and create a distraction."

A distraction that Bernice had used to her advantage. It'd helped, too, that she'd known it was coming and had been ready to bash Edwin and Leo.

"How'd Bernice get in the house?" Olivia asked.

Again, it wasn't Bernice who answered but Carter, just as Daniel and the ranch hand stuffed Bernice into the back seat of the cruiser.

"Edwin told me that Bernice grabbed his gun," Carter explained, "and she bashed both him and you on the head when the airbags deployed."

Leo hadn't needed to be told about the head bashing part. He had a knot on his temple, and it was throbbing badly. Still, he'd been lucky that his injuries hadn't been a whole lot worse.

"How's Edwin?" Leo asked Carter.

"Fine. He might need a couple of stitches. You might need some, too," Carter added, giving Leo the once-over. "You want me to ride with your brother to the sheriff's office?"

"Sure." Though Leo figured with Bernice cuffed, she wasn't much of a threat. Still, it wouldn't hurt to have a little overkill, considering the woman was a murderer.

"One more thing," Leo said before Daniel could get behind the wheel of the cruiser. "Did Sutton mention who killed Randall?"

Daniel huffed. "He volunteered that it was Bernice, that she'd tried to rile up Randall to get him to kill you, but then he figured out what she'd done. He says Bernice killed Randall and got him to dispose of the body. He claims it was Bernice's idea to use a Sycamore Grove SUV because she intended to set up Rena."

Leo gave that some thought. "You think Sutton is the one who killed him?" he proposed.

"That'd be my guess," Daniel answered.

Leo nearly added for Daniel to push getting that info during interrogations, but knew his brother would do that without the reminder. Besides, even if Bernice hadn't been the one to pull the trigger that'd killed Randall, she'd still go down for his murder.

"Come on," Leo said, slipping his arm around Olivia again. "Let me take you to the front to the ambulance."

She stopped, held her ground and stared up at him. "I don't want to go to the hospital. *Please*. I don't want to leave Cameron."

It wasn't the *please* that got to him. It was the look

on her face. Not pain or panic. Just a mountain of concern for her child.

"All right," he agreed. "We'll have the EMTs check you, but if they say you should be in the hospital, then you will be." He kissed her to try to soften the order he'd given her. "I'm not going to risk losing you."

"You shouldn't risk losing her," he heard someone say. "Olivia loves you."

Leo was surprised those words had come from Samuel. Sighing, her father got to his feet, walked closer to them and gave Leo a pat on the arm. It felt awkward coming from Samuel, but it was a helluva lot better than the verbal jabs he'd given Leo in the past.

"I'm sorry," Samuel said, his gaze moving to Olivia. "I swear, before tonight, I didn't know it was Bernice who'd killed your mother."

She hesitated as if, Leo presumed, trying to gauge if that were true. She must have decided it was because she nodded.

"If I could fix things between us, I would," Samuel added and then turned to walk away.

"Wait," Olivia said, causing him to stop in his tracks. "Why do you think I'm in love with Leo?"

Leo tensed because he sure as hell didn't want to hear Olivia say that her father had it all wrong, that it wasn't true.

"Because you are," Samuel simply said. "And he's in love with you."

Obviously, that stunned both Olivia and him into silence because neither confirmed nor denied it. They just stood there, waiting for Samuel to leave. He did. Not through the house, though. Instead, he went in the direction of the front yard. Hopefully, one of the EMTs would check him out, as well.

"I want to hate him," Olivia muttered. There were tears shimmering in her eyes when she turned back to him. "But right now, I'm just so tired of the hate. I'm ready for that being-in-love part."

That sounded…well, hopeful, and despite his throbbing head, Leo found himself smiling. And kissing her. He'd intended it to be a quick reassurance, but it turned into something longer. Deeper. And hotter. The kind of kiss that could land them in bed—if they hadn't been so banged up, that is.

"You're in love with me," he said when they finally broke for air. "And if you're not, then—"

"I'm in love with you," Olivia verified.

Smiling, and then wincing because the smile must have caused her face to hurt, she kissed him. And, yeah, it was one of those long, deep hot ones that made Leo forget all about such things as pain and injuries.

"If you're not in love with me," she said after she'd just rocked his world with a third kiss, "then—"

He stopped her with a fourth kiss. "I'm in love with you," he assured her.

Leo used the fifth kiss to show her just how much.

* * * * *

Get 3 FREE REWARDS!

We'll send you 2 FREE Books plus a FREE Mystery Gift.

FREE
Value Over
$20

Both the **Harlequin® Desire** and **Harlequin Presents®** series feature compelling novels filled with passion, sensuality and intriguing scandals.

YES! Please send me 2 FREE novels from the Harlequin Desire or Harlequin Presents series and my FREE gift (gift is worth about $10 retail). After receiving them, if I don't wish to receive any more books, I can return the shipping statement marked "cancel." If I don't cancel, I will receive 6 brand-new Harlequin Presents Larger-Print books every month and be billed just $6.30 each in the U.S. or $6.49 each in Canada, a savings of at least 10% off the cover price, or 3 Harlequin Desire books (2-in-1 story editions) every month and be billed just $7.83 each in the U.S. or $8.43 each in Canada, a savings of at least 12% off the cover price. It's quite a bargain! Shipping and handling is just 50¢ per book in the U.S. and $1.25 per book in Canada.* I understand that accepting the 2 free books and gift places me under no obligation to buy anything. I can always return a shipment and cancel at any time by calling the number below. The free books and gift are mine to keep no matter what I decide.

Choose one: ☐ **Harlequin Desire**
(225/326 BPA GRNA)

☐ **Harlequin Presents Larger-Print**
(176/376 BPA GRNA)

☐ **Or Try Both!**
(225/326 & 176/376 BPA GRQP)

Name (please print)

Address   Apt. #

City   State/Province   Zip/Postal Code

Email: Please check this box ☐ if you would like to receive newsletters and promotional emails from Harlequin Enterprises ULC and its affiliates. You can unsubscribe anytime.

Mail to the Harlequin Reader Service:
IN U.S.A.: P.O. Box 1341, Buffalo, NY 14240-8531
IN CANADA: P.O. Box 603, Fort Erie, Ontario L2A 5X3

Want to try 2 free books from another series? Call 1-800-873-8635 or visit www.ReaderService.com.

*Terms and prices subject to change without notice. Prices do not include sales taxes, which will be charged (if applicable) based on your state or country of residence. Canadian residents will be charged applicable taxes. Offer not valid in Quebec. This offer is limited to one order per household. Books received may not be as shown. Not valid for current subscribers to the Harlequin Presents or Harlequin Desire series. All orders subject to approval. Credit or debit balances in a customer's account(s) may be offset by any other outstanding balance owed by or to the customer. Please allow 4 to 6 weeks for delivery. Offer available while quantities last.

Your Privacy—Your information is being collected by Harlequin Enterprises ULC, operating as Harlequin Reader Service. For a complete summary of the information we collect, how we use this information and to whom it is disclosed, please visit our privacy notice located at corporate.harlequin.com/privacy-notice. From time to time we may also exchange your personal information with reputable third parties. If you wish to opt out of this sharing of your personal information, please visit readerservice.com/consumerchoice or call 1-800-873-8635. **Notice to California Residents**—Under California law, you have specific rights to control and access your data. For more information on these rights and how to exercise them, visit corporate.harlequin.com/california-privacy.

HDHP23

Get 3 FREE REWARDS!

We'll send you 2 FREE Books plus a FREE Mystery Gift.

FREE Value Over **$20**

Both the **Romance** and **Suspense** collections feature compelling novels written by many of today's bestselling authors.

YES! Please send me 2 FREE novels from the Essential Romance or Essential Suspense Collection and my FREE gift (gift is worth about $10 retail). After receiving them, if I don't wish to receive any more books, I can return the shipping statement marked "cancel." If I don't cancel, I will receive 4 brand-new novels every month and be billed just $7.49 each in the U.S. or $7.74 each in Canada. That's a savings of at least 17% off the cover price. It's quite a bargain! Shipping and handling is just 50¢ per book in the U.S. and $1.25 per book in Canada.* I understand that accepting the 2 free books and gift places me under no obligation to buy anything. I can always return a shipment and cancel at any time by calling the number below. The free books and gift are mine to keep no matter what I decide.

Choose one: ☐ **Essential Romance** (194/394 BPA GRNM)   ☐ **Essential Suspense** (191/391 BPA GRNM)   ☐ **Or Try Both!** (194/394 & 191/391 BPA GRQZ)

Name (please print)

Address   Apt. #

City   State/Province   Zip/Postal Code

Email: Please check this box ☐ if you would like to receive newsletters and promotional emails from Harlequin Enterprises ULC and its affiliates. You can unsubscribe anytime.

Mail to the Harlequin Reader Service:
IN U.S.A.: P.O. Box 1341, Buffalo, NY 14240-8531
IN CANADA: P.O. Box 603, Fort Erie, Ontario L2A 5X3

Want to try 2 free books from another series? Call 1-800-873-8635 or visit www.ReaderService.com.

*Terms and prices subject to change without notice. Prices do not include sales taxes, which will be charged (if applicable) based on your state or country of residence. Canadian residents will be charged applicable taxes. Offer not valid in Quebec. This offer is limited to one order per household. Books received may not be as shown. Not valid for current subscribers to the Essential Romance or Essential Suspense Collection. All orders subject to approval. Credit or debit balances in a customer's account(s) may be offset by any other outstanding balance owed by or to the customer. Please allow 4 to 6 weeks for delivery. Offer available while quantities last.

Your Privacy—Your information is being collected by Harlequin Enterprises ULC, operating as Harlequin Reader Service. For a complete summary of the information we collect, how we use this information and to whom it is disclosed, please visit our privacy notice located at corporate.harlequin.com/privacy-notice. From time to time we may also exchange your personal information with reputable third parties. If you wish to opt out of this sharing of your personal information, please visit readerservice.com/consumerschoice or call 1-800-873-8635. **Notice to California Residents**—Under California law, you have specific rights to control and access your data. For more information on these rights and how to exercise them, visit corporate.harlequin.com/california-privacy.

STRS23